Chalkhill Blue

Richard Masefield is himself a working farmer in the Sussex downland country he describes so vividly in *Chalkhill Blue*.

Born in 1943, a cousin of John Masefield the poet and son of the transport and aviation executive Sir Peter Masefield, he was educated in Sussex at Eastbourne College. After leaving school he worked variously as an agricultural labourer, a repertory actor, a journalist, a salesman and for some years as an executive in a London advertising agency – before finally realizing his earliest and most constant ambition to run his own farm.

He first seriously set pen to paper twenty years ago in the Middle East, after inadvertently becoming embroiled in the Shah of Iran's so-called 'White Revolution', and has been writing in his spare time ever since. He and his Australian wife, Lee, have three children, two of them now in their teens.

Chalkhill Blue

Richard Masefield

Pan Books
in association with **Heinemann**

First published 1983 by William Heinemann Ltd
This edition published 1984 by Pan Books Ltd,
Cavaye Place, London SW10 9PG
in association with William Heinemann Ltd
9 8 7 6 5 4 3 2 1
© Richard Masefield 1983
ISBN 0 330 28397 9
Printed and bound in Great Britain by
Hazell Watson & Viney Limited,
Member of the BPCC Group,
Aylesbury, Bucks

*In very loving memory of my grandparents,
Gordon and Marian Masefield, who were in
many ways the inspiration for this novel*

Acknowledgements

I am very much indebted to Rose E. B. Coombs M.B.E. and to Susan Burgess of the Imperial War Museum for their indispensable help with my First World War researches. Also to Rear Admiral J. W. D. Cook C.B.E., Mary Batchelor and Major Graham Barnett for additional advice and guidance on the subject of the war and its aftermath. I am furthermore extremely grateful to Mr J. W. Coleman, Mr Clement H. Fowler and to Mr Mortimer G. Lee for their memories of and insights into agricultural methods of the past; and no less to Dr Noël Carr, Gertrude Smith O.B.E. and Dr David Rice for much helpful advice on psychiatric and medical phenomena.

Additionally my thanks are due to the following for the unfailingly generous help they have given me in my search for authentic background material for this novel: Mrs Irene Benjamin, Mrs Lucy Brecht, the Hon. C. A. Colville, Mr C. J. Davies-Gilbert, Mrs V. E. Hogg, Mrs Henrietta Kessler, Virginia Lloyd-Owen, the late Mrs E. R. Lodge, the Librarian and staff of The London Library, Fiona Masefield, Sir Peter and Lady Masefield, Sybil Oldfield, Mr Hugh Stewart-Roberts, Mr A. Wesencraft and Christine Wilson.

I am also grateful to Frederick Warne P.L.C. for their permission to quote from *The Tale of Two Bad Mice* by Beatrix Potter.

The verse in Chapter Twenty-One comes from *Sussex at War and Poems of Peace* by Arthur Beckett, published by Sussex County Herald Offices in 1916.

Book 1
(1903–1907)

Chapter One

"Meriel!"

The woman's voice was penetrating and unmistakably English – a voice to be obliged, obeyed even. Yet no one hurried forward to do so. The big colonial house slumbered on in the sun. The cockatoos fed uninterrupted amongst the cumquats. Mulvany continued to rake the gravel of the carriage drive, and Meriel herself remained conspicuously absent. Her mother frowned and tightened her grip on the verandah rail. She was a woman of generous frontage – a shade too generous possibly for the straining silk net of her afternoon dress – and the lace on her bosom rose impressively like a great cresting wave as she filled her lungs for a second assault on the peace of her own garden.

"Meriel! Me-ri—el! Where *is* the graceless child?" She hadn't been addressing the wiry little man on the drive, not especially. But the sight of him scratching away at the gravel with such an irritating show of indifference was more than she could countenance.

"Mulvany – I'm talking to you, Mulvany!" she added sharply, "so will you kindly stop that this minute and tell me where on earth Miss Meriel has got to?" For a terrifying moment she thought that he was actually going to ignore her. But eventually, and to her immense relief, he'd spoken.

"Dunno," he said economically, without looking up or in any way interrupting the steady rhythm of his work. And Lord in heaven, what could one do with him? What could one do with any of them in this damnable godforsaken country! Harriet Llewellen had never enjoyed any degree of success with her

Australian servants, she hadn't the nerve for it. To Mulvany's own disappointment she concluded the interview then and there without any kind of a fight, blundering back into the house and slamming the screen door behind her.

As it happened, her younger daughter Meriel was sitting under the verandah more or less directly beneath her all the time, in the open latticed area that cooled the house and protected it from white ants, snakes and carriage dust. It had always been a favourite haunt of Meriel's, this sandy no-man's-land beneath the house. As a child she'd regularly crept in amongst the old sunblinds and cluttered garden equipment to escape the frequent domestic crises of her mother's household, or to collect the coloured parrot feathers the cats left behind. More recently it had come in handy for illegal open air smoking concerts, or for eavesdropping on her brother's verandah spooning sessions with his fiancée. And of course it had always been one of the best places for glooms and fantasies and generally being alone.

In December 1903 Meriel Llewellen had just turned seventeen, and if she could have seen herself then as Mulvany had seen her when he came in for the rake, with her strong little arms clasped around slim, black-stockinged knees, she'd certainly have been surprised at the quality of her own appeal. Her sister Vicky was the pretty one, everybody said so; and for her own part Meriel had never totally forgiven providence for failing to make her a boy.

She was too short ever to make a beauty. Her brown hair was too thick and straight – straight as pump water Vicky said – and she'd acquired an inadvertently glowing complexion that would have driven any aspiring Gibson Girl to the brink of suicide. Worse, the features that she'd exposed so recklessly to sunlight were strong rather than delicate, with a horrifying tendency to grimace. Worse still, her eyes were quite incapable of reproducing the demure expression that was so widely held to be the essence of good breeding. They were a deep, unfashionable sherry colour. And even now, in the face of the direst possible developments – through scowls and angry tears, they still shone with a raw vitality that nothing could quench.

It wasn't so much the beastly boredom of a drawing room

tea that had driven Meriel to earth beneath the verandah that afternoon; nor even the attendant horrors of hairpins and collar stiffeners and all that they implied. It was the *reason* for the tea party that she objected to – the necessity of entertaining some ridiculous shipping agent person from Brisbane, and at the root of it all her father's cruel instruction to up sticks and follow him across the Pacific to Chile. To leave Australia, for heaven's sake, without so much as a backward glance!

If it had been the Mater who was asking, Meriel would assuredly have refused point blank. She'd have locked herself in her room – taken off into the bush – dived overboard from the moving ship – anything to remain behind here in Queensland. But it was her father, it was Da, who was asking her to abandon her freedom, her lovely horses, everything she treasured. And Meriel was incapable of refusing Da anything.

Robert Llewellen had always been an Olympian in Meriel's eyes. As a consultant mining engineer with the North Borneo Trading Company, he had first set eyes on Queensland in 1891. Having instantly grasped the financial possibilities of the expanding Ipswich coalfields, he sat down in his hotel room to dash off an amazing and now famous telegram to his family back home in England. Meriel still had it, proudly pasted into the front of her scrapbook:

'HAVE FOUND GODS OWN COUNTRY STOP SELL UP AND JOIN ME STOP LETTER FOLLOWING RL'

By the time the family reached Queensland, Da had not only established himself as Senior Engineering Manager to the important Swanbank and Dinmore collieries, but had also purchased a substantial property two miles outside Ipswich – with stables and horses and twelve acres of grazing. Everything, in Meriel's opinion, that anyone could possibly want. The mines produced bituminous and cannel coal in highly satisfactory quantities, the four Llewellen children had been put through the Ipswich Grammar schools as day boarders, and for some years life had revolved happily around the dynamic personality of Da himself.

For Meriel the years before Australia had been full of shadowy comings and goings – mostly Da's. But looking back on her childhood, it seemed to her that her father had always contrived to be at the centre of everything that was exciting and fun to do. She could see his tanned face laughing at her, demanding her approval through so many sunlit adventures; winning, always winning at polo, swimming clear across the Brisbane river in shirt and breeches, driving the wagonette himself faster by far than Mulvany would have dared; riding fast, talking fast, giving orders and commanding love. He was so mature, she thought, so confident – everything that the Mater wasn't. He held his daughter's world in the palm of his hand, and she adored him.

Then one day a cable had arrived from England to announce the death of Da's own mother, their old French Grandmère, and to summon him to London to wind up her estate. He'd be away, he said, for at least a year; and Meriel quite believed that her heart would break.

The night before Da was due to leave the Mater had almost begged her to turn her hair up and to wear her white Indian muslin down to dinner – "Just to show how grown-up and normally feminine you can be when you try, dear". But Meriel refused. She didn't care to be fussed and finicked into normal femininity, and anyway she wanted Da to remember her as she liked to be – with her hair loose about her shoulders and a short skirt, and a back that was straighter by far than Vicky's for all her starch and stiffening.

Da had been in high good humour over that last dinner – full of travel plans and business opportunities – oblivious, it seemed, of his wife's reproachful gaze or his younger daughter's unusual silence at the far end of the table. Just as soon as the meal was over, and despite the others' objections, Meriel had boldly taken his hand and dragged him outside to smoke his after-dinner cigarette with her on the front steps.

She'd rehearsed this private conversation with him a dozen times since the appearance of the fateful cable. But somehow there'd always been good reasons for delaying, for putting the thing off for one more day. And now that she'd finally got him to herself – now that it was almost too late – Meriel felt unaccountably lost for words. For a little while they sat in the silence together, listening to the cicadas and breathing in the heavy atmosphere of the garden. The scents of baked earth, eucalypts and peppercorns mingled and blended most beautifully with the stronger aroma of Da's expensive Egyptian cigarette. Every now and again an exotic whiff of frangipani drifted across to them from the shrub border, and high above them the stars sparkled seductively. Some people confessed to feeling humbled by the constellations and the vastnesses of time and space that they represented. But not Meriel. Glancing up at the Southern Cross, she saw a pretty diamond circlet on a black velvet cushion – nothing more. All very well in its place, but of no practical use to her in the problem of what to say to her father and how to prevent him from leaving.

"Incredibly beautiful, isn't it?" Da sighed, blowing a thin stream of smoke into the air.

"Then how can you be so beastly mean as to leave it?" she burst out. "Why do you have to go to England at all, when Harry says that Uncle Vincent could easily manage things over there by himself."

Da smiled the slow, teasing smile that always so disarmed her. "Which only goes to show how much young Harry still has to learn," he said lightly. "As an executor it really is my business to be on hand to sign things and see about Grandmère's property – and to whisper words of wisdom in your Uncle Vincent's shell-like ear."

"Oh, do be serious, can't you?" Meriel cried, covering her own smile with a hasty scowl. "Just tell me why you have to stay away so jolly long then, Da, if that's all there is to do."

"But it isn't all, my seraph. Your grandmother's affairs are a deal more complicated than you kids seem to imagine. Besides, I have other business to attend to and other people to see while I'm over there."

He shifted his long legs on the verandah steps, staring out beyond her into the starshine. Meriel could see the glowing tip of his cigarette reflected like a tiny flame in the depths of his dark eyes. For an instant a hideous, disloyal suspicion flashed into her mind – a suspicion concerning Da and other women – before she stamped on it, quick as a thought, and tossed it into a remote corner of her subconscious.

"Like who?" she demanded recklessly, "who do you need to see in London, then?"

"Well if you must know, Meriel," Da said in an altered tone, "I'm thinking of sounding out one or two people on the subject of a new overseas appointment. It's high time we made another move."

"A move? You don't mean away from Australia – you can't?" Everything in her rushed forward to reject the idea. But this time it wasn't so easy, Da wouldn't let her.

"Possibly, very possibly," he continued smoothly. "You see, if I'm any judge, there'll be more labour problems and less profit in coal during the next few years under this grand new Commonwealth of ours. And if something interesting turns up elsewhere I'd be a fool to refuse it. Don't worry Meriellie," he added, seeing the desolation in her face, "we won't make you live in sooty old London. I'll be back before you're very much older with some splendid new plans for us all, and the prettiest London party frocks that you girls have yet clapped eyes on!" And he leant forward to give her a moustachy kiss.

The party frocks hadn't materialized. Meriel never thought for a moment that they would. And the first news they received of Da on his arrival in London had been in the form of a cable announcing his imminent appointment as Administrator of the Schneider Mining Company, south of Valparaiso in central Chile.

'SELL UP AND JOIN ME THERE . . .' The message had been curiously familiar. So had Harriet's reaction.

"Too cruel!" she wailed, "too cruel to be borne!" And once again the Llewellen household was plunged into chaos and confusion.

From her position beneath the verandah Meriel could hear her mother now, plaintively calling the maid to fetch her the Dovers Powders for her latest nervous headache. Outside on the drive Mulvany's rake swished victoriously on through the gravel, to be followed by another sound that she recognized – the uneven crunching rhythm of horses' hooves. Peering out through the latticework Meriel could distinguish the figure of her elder brother Harry riding up to the front door, with a fine looking man on a chestnut thoroughbred at his side. In a flash she scrambled to her feet – all thoughts of leaving Australia abandoned, forgotten, swamped in a deluge of excited admiration. Meriel had always believed implicitly in love at first sight – and now she achieved it, on the instant.

"Prime –" it was a new word of hers – and he was undoubtedly the primest thing ever. She simply had to see him close to! A gravelled tributary of the drive passed close by the door of her hiding place *en route* to the stables. She had only to duck out beneath the legs of the rainwater tank to intercept Mully leading the horses round. And as she'd waited there for him, half-hidden between the dusty oleanders, the object of her admiration passed directly in front of her. He walked with a loose graceful stride, his muscles rippling visibly in the sunlight.

"Prime – oh prime!" Meriel would willingly have given a year of her life then and there for a ride on the shipping agent's prime chestnut stallion. She'd always adored horses – dead nuts on them Harry said. When they'd first arrived in Australia Da had made her a present of a tubby little Shetland, and she had been riding ever since. At ten she graduated to Harry's polo pony; and after Da left for England she had even been permitted to exercise his Irish hack, Kildare. But she'd never come within ten yards of an animal as fine as this one – never!

Meriel perched on the top of the stable yard gate to watch the stallion submit to the rigours of Mulvany's grooming. Hoof pick, curry comb and both brushes – the ritual never varied. The little man worked steadily away at the horse until he was satisfied that the polish on his silken flanks could not be improved.

"Flamin' beauty ain't 'e, Miss?" he said with a covert glance at the girl, as he made the final adjustments to the bridle and prepared to lead the animal in.

"I should jolly well think he is, Mully! And I'll put him into the box if you don't mind," she said, jumping down from the gate and almost snatching the reins from his hands. "You get on with Pinto."

The big horse stepped out so lightly across the yard behind

13

her – it was next thing to impossible, she told herself, not to wonder how he'd ride. Anyone would! She was still with him in the loose box in fact, still wondering, when Mulvany brought Pinto in. As soon as she heard the yard gate click behind him, Meriel was up on the chestnut's back. 'After all, it can't possibly do any harm,' she thought, 'simply to see how it feels!' And it did feel too good for words. She sat astride like a man in the abbreviated English saddle, and thought with satisfaction of how scandalized the Mater would·be to see her in such a shamelessly *outré* posture. The horse lifted his head to consider this unfamiliar lightweight, looking round at her with earnest luminous eyes.

"He's bored, he wants to go!" Meriel dismounted to shorten the stirrups. The stallion walked-on like a dream, so smooth and easy and beautifully contained. But as she nudged him up to a trot she could feel him pulling against her, testing her strength, and Meriel's spirit rose to the challenge. The paddock was too blessedly small to allow a decent horse to show his paces, of course it was. "And it really isn't fair to hold you back, is it my beauty?" she said aloud. "I bet anything that you're just dying to put on some pace. You are, aren't you?"

Beyond the cane fields and ultimate straggling homesteads of the town the land was still uncultivated – a dusty bushland scrub of gums and wattle and brigalow acacias – undulating, hard-baked and first class for riding. As she rode the horse towards it Meriel's only concern was of whether she was strong enough to keep the bit back from his teeth. He knew what he was about all right, he'd known all along. At the first tentative kick of her heel he'd responded like a bullet from a rifle, leaping forward from a sitting trot to a thundering full gallop.

Thrown back in the saddle, she clung like a jockey. The hot wind rushed to meet her, flinging her long hair back from her face, and feeling the strength of the great straining animal between her thighs she was filled with a wild elation. They were no longer separate, she and the horse. They responded together – powerfully, joyfully – leaping fallen logs, brushing the last fragile blooms from the wattle along the trail, shaking the earth with their passing as they flew onwards towards the beckoning purple hills. And when at last they slowed to a canter, Meriel experienced a sense of conquest and completion such as she'd never known.

Dismounting, she led the horse to a patch of dappled shade at the edge of a broad drove trail and sat on a stump to watch him forage for red grass, lifting the heavy hair from her own neck and fanning her face with it. Above them the sky was a vivid uncompromising blue, and the midsummer sun beat down through the leaf canopy, intensifying the marvellous pungent odours of the gum trees and the sweating horse. Too late she remembered her battered straw hat, still lying in the dust beneath the house. But she didn't care. Tomorrow she'd look like a boiled lobster and the next day her nose would peel. But what did it matter – what did anything matter beside the confirmation of courage and capability that she'd discovered in herself on that madcap ride?

"I managed you didn't I?" she said to the horse, "I should just about think I did! And if I can manage you, my fine fellow, I can manage anything – even Chile if I have to!"

A pale diamond-shaped leaf fluttered down to her from the gums, and she caught it effortlessly in one hand. She was invincible, queen of the world – and the world was good. She felt so proud of the tall pillared strength of the eucalypts and the flute-like calls of the magpies as they swooped between them – proud of the distant sounds of cattle and stockwhips moving down the long trail from the Darling Downs – and proudest of all just now of herself.

She waited to see the cattle pass by, mounted and ready at the side of the trail. If the poor beasts themselves were unlovely, the sight of their passing procession had been worth the wait. They were bony, pike-horned individuals, depleted in numbers by years of drought. But as a herd they still made a fine spectacle, surging down the trail in a great dust cloud of their own making. Bellowing, swishing at flies, pulling at bushes along the way they were constantly urged forward by yapping cattle dogs and the pistol cracks of stockwhips on either flank.

"Steady down the lead there!" a drover bawled hoarsely from Meriel's side of the track, and she watched him with frank curiosity as he rode towards her through the dust.

'Never look at a strange man as he approaches you,' that's

what the Mater had always cautioned. 'Look preoccupied, dear, and keep your eyes averted – a lady generally only has herself to blame if she's spoken to.'

Not that Meriel had ever especially wanted to look. 'Men are lucky dogs who get away with forty thousand exciting things that we girls are forbidden.' That's what she thought – and that's what she'd written on the subject in her sister's Confession Book (and afterwards the soppy thing had gone and torn the page out!) But now, fresh from her conquest of the shipping agent's horse, she was beginning to see things differently. She saw the male of the species in the light of a physical challenge, and for the first time in her life she began to wonder what it would actually be like to have one of her own.

As with other girls of her age, Meriel had long ago constructed a mental effigy of the man she'd one day marry – a glamorous, predestined mate with whom she was certain to be happy. In her own case the character had been largely drawn from her mother's novelettes and periodicals and the *Girls' Realm* annuals that her Aunt Alice sent out from England – and had little to do with her father or brothers or the ordinary masculine inhabitants of the Ipswich colony. He would be tall and splendidly strong, brave but gentle, fresh-faced with a fine open countenance, calm blue eyes, a square determined jaw and crisp, wavy golden hair – quite perfect in every way. He'd wear a Norfolk suit or a swagger Guard's mess uniform with scarlet tunic and tight red-striped breeches. His name would be Vincey, Travers, Carstairs, or something of the sort – and naturally enough he'd be English.

Up until now there had been nothing beneath Carstairs' close-fitting uniform but a tailor's dummy of calico and sawdust. But as Meriel registered the expression in the drover's eyes, squinting at her through the glare, the image of her prospective husband began to twitch into life.

'He's out there somewhere at this moment, sleeping and waking and moving about like this man is!' And with the thought came a cold little stab of pleasure to the solar plexus.

"G'day, Miss," the drover said, swiping at the flies as he spoke. "You Miss Llewellen?"

"Well what if I am?" Meriel had just realized that in this

posture her bloomers must be clearly visible beneath the starched hem of Vicky's old reach-me-down pinny, and she wasn't inclined to be gracious.

"Only that yer kid brother's back there doin' 'is block,'" the drover replied, pointing behind him down the drove and grinning all over his bearded face. "Says you've done a bunk with some bloke's 'orse, and yer Ma's gone off 'er top."

She found Gareth within a matter of minutes, whistling loudly and brandishing her missing straw hat. "You'll really catch it this time," he called out cheerily, and on reflection Meriel was inclined to agree.

Mully met them at the end of the drive with his own hat pushed well to the back of his head – a sure sign of trouble. On the verandah Harriet stood with folded arms and a face like thunder, the shipping agent at her side and Vicky behind her – whaleboned up to the ears and smiling her prettiest smile.

'Oh well, it's been worth it!' Meriel thought grimly, dismounting and walking the chestnut forward to the foot of the steps. And in the wake of her defiant sand-shoes a series of long, angry scuff marks scarred the smooth surface of Mulvany's gravel.

Chapter Two

At very much the time that Meriel was first giving serious thought to the paragon of masculine beauty she'd one day marry, a young Englishman who just about answered to the specification was opening his eyes on a new day.

Ned Ashby lay in the drowsy darkness of his own bedroom, listening to the sounds of an English winter morning and struggling to rid himself of the soft golden flesh of his dream. He had to get up. The clock on the front stairs had just struck six, its familiar chimes cutting through the gurgle of the water pipes and the gusty sighs of the wind outside. Down in the farmyard a couple of Maran cocks were crowing with monotonous persistence. And in the eaves above his window the sparrows were irritably rehearsing their first arguments of the day – 'chavishing' his grandmother called it.

To Ned's ears it was all as much a part of The Bury and home as the musty smell of his bedroom rug or the smooth texture of the linen pillow case beneath his head, and it scarcely impinged on the tumescent images of his sleeping hours. 'Worth her weight in gold,' that's how the man had described her, and in his persistent dreams Ned had unconsciously transferred the gold to the intimate curves and shadows of a woman's body. He was young and fit and better looking than most, he knew that. He was ready for love in every sense. The need for some physical experience of it was humming through him now like a hot current. And although he'd yet to meet his golden woman, he'd seen the man who loved her – and that was more than enough to set the wheels of his imagination in motion.

He had come upon the man one foggy evening the previous November, in the bar of the Lord John Russell in London. He and a number of other university freshers were in the habit of eating there on Saturdays while their landladies made the most of their weekly night out at the Music Hall. But on that particular evening Ned was alone, consuming a one and sixpenny dinner from a high stool at the counter, and doing his best not to attract attention.

From the moment the man arrived, Ned had been aware of him. He was one of those people who made you aware of them simply by being there – a gentleman in an elegant tailcoat and striped cashmere trousers, and at the same time a predator with a glittering black eye. Beside him Ned felt dull and pedestrian, like a hedge dunnock contemplating a glossy great crow. And yet he was curiously drawn to the man, watching him furtively between mouthfuls of boiled beef.

> 'There was a crow sat on a tree
> And he was black as black could be . . .'

The crow was leaning back against the wall at the end of the bar, with his high silk hat on the tin counter beside him and a glass of whisky cradled against his watchchain. As Ned glanced across at him a third or a fourth time, he raised his glass.

"Wondering what I'm doin' here, young feller-me-lad?" he enquired in an embarrassingly familiar manner. "Feeling envious of my fine feathers?"

It was precisely what Ned was feeling, of course, and he choked on a small potato to prove it. For one so obviously inebriated the man acted surprisingly swiftly, leaning over to strike him hard between the shoulder blades and then forcing him to take a man-sized gulp of his own neat scotch. The spirit scalded Ned's already bruised throat, bringing the tears to his eyes; and in his pain and confusion he allowed the stranger to order two more whiskies.

"Shall I tell you something, young 'un?" the man continued as if nothing had happened. "I feel envious of you – I'd give my back teeth for your youth and your damned innocence, d'ye know that? How old are you – eighteen?"

"I'm twenty." And why the devil did everyone go thinking he was younger?

"Twenty – you amaze me! Why when I was your age I already had a son of my own. Not entirely by choice, mind," he added with a reminiscent smile. "We sometimes had 'em a bit quicker than intended in those days y'know!" The man swayed forward until their faces were almost touching and Ned could smell the whisky on his breath. His eyes were quite unusually dark, fringed with thick black lashes and deeply lined beneath. And like all dark eyes, there was something very sad about them as soon as they stopped smiling.

"Canada, Peru, year in Borneo, ten in Queensland – kudos, capital, women . . . " the man intoned, producing an engraved silver card case from his inside pocket and fumbling a calling card out onto the counter. "But what's it all brought me, eh?"

The card said, 'Robert Llewellen, B.Sc., Consultant: Mining and Civil Engineering,' and it provided two addresses – one in New Broad Street, London and the other in Queensland, Australia.

"I'll tell you, I'll tell you what it's brought me, boy – it's brought me the devotion of a woman I despise and the contempt of another that I care for." He smiled again wryly at his own lack of originality. Then to Ned's alarm he placed a large, unselfconscious hand square on the striped cashmere crotch of

19

his own trousers – and proceeded to pat it affectionately. "Oh yes, it makes fools of us all in the end, this gentleman's gentleman of ours," he said in ringing tones, "you'll find out, boy! Like it or not this is the sceptre that commands our emotions. They understand that in the East all right – by George they do! Women and eunuchs have the advantage over us d'ye see, that's the devil of it all."

Very clearly the time had come to leave. But as Ned pushed his stool back from the counter, the man's hand left its awkward resting place and shot out to restrain him. "I went to see her today y'know," he said irrelevantly, "in the fog . . . Stood on her doorstep like some giddy swain, but couldn't go in – funked it . . . "

It wouldn't have been hard for Ned to shake him off then, to spare himself the image of that teasing golden woman. But something held him, something of the quality that had first attracted him to the man. Llewellen had more to say, that was obvious, a confession of some kind that he needed to make. Perhaps it was an instinct for his own future that told Ned to wait, and to listen – or then again it may simply have been the whisky.

"The woman you care for?" he asked, settling back onto his stool to toy with the congealing remains of his dinner, "is that who you went to see?"

But Llewellen's mood had changed. As he looked at Ned the expression of self-contempt disappeared from his face and he actually began to laugh. "'Pon my word, I've caught your interest haven't I?" he chuckled. "You want to hear all about it, don't you – what she looks like and how she feels, and what kind of a female she can be to bring down a man like me?"

"If you want to tell me," Ned muttered miserably, feeling the blood rising to his hairline and wondering if every man-Jack in the pub was listening.

"Damnably fine woman – that's all I have to say! Worth her weight in gold, that woman!" And disappointingly it was very nearly all he did have to say. Although at the same time he reached across to where his calling card still lay face up on the counter, turned it over and scrawled something on the back with an expensive fountain pen.

"Find out for yourself, Sonny-Jim," he concluded grandly, tucking the card into a pocket of Ned's Norfolk jacket. "Oblige me by paying a call on the lady – give her the benefit of that pretty face and unstained character of yours – and make her forget, if you can, about bounders like me."

Ned had the card still, with its impressive engraving on one side – and on the other the name and address that had haunted him ever since.

But that was all very well. For the present he still had forty wether lambs to move before breakfast, and he really did have to get up. So with a truly manful effort he heaved himself free of bedclothes and golden dream women, to light a candle and struggle into some warm togs.

He dressed quickly, shivering and cursing over his collar stud and necktie and the innumerable buttons of his waistcoat, and altogether ignoring the sandy tangles of his hair. The light from his candle stirred the shadows of the old Sussex farmhouse as he crept out onto the landing. A clock ticked with hollow persistence and the uncarpeted back stairs creaked beneath his weight. He took care to brace himself in advance for the big cupboard at the bottom, and barely jumped at all when it sprang out at him from the darkness. The maids used it as a hidey-hole for their brooms and mops and pails, and the whole place reeked of carbolic and turpentine even with the door closed. There was really nothing sinister about it, nothing at all. But as a little boy Ned had made the great mistake of identifying it with the rather similar cupboard that Bluebeard had used as a hidey-hole for decapitated wives, and even now he could never feel entirely happy about the back stairs.

The passage from the foot of the stairs ran along the pantry wall to the closed door of the big kitchen. A thin strip of yellow lamplight showed clearly beneath it, and from the murmuring drone on the far side he gathered that its occupants must by now be well into their first pot of tea. As he opened the door, the brilliant warmth of the kitchen engulfed Ned in an atmosphere that spoke louder to him of his childhood than anything in the world. It smelt of soup stock, tea leaves and dripping pans, lamp oil, tile polish and burning coke. And in that first delicious whiff he felt the years roll backwards in a succession of jammy treats and supervised tummy-glides through the hatchway, from Nanny to Father and back again – black beetle races, hucklebones and cod's-eye marbles on the flags, vast Christmas teas for the village children, daring raids on the pantry with his sister Helen, and Cook's celebrated homily – "No pickin' an' stealin', Master Edwin, an' this time I *means* it!"

Cook herself sat at the big pine table, with Bridget and the new tweeny, one on either side of her and the brown teapot handy. Her name was Betsy Ann Tinsley and she was really a cook-housekeeper, but nobody for as long as Ned could remember had called her anything but 'Cook'. She'd been at The Bury forever, and must have been quite young when he'd first known her. But in his memory she'd always been exactly as she was now – stout and well-upholstered in lilac print and an old plaid cross-over, with smoothly plaited hair and a complexion as clean scrubbed as her own back kitchen drainer.

"Marnin' Master 'Assock-'Ead!" she sang out as soon as he appeared in the doorway. "Cuppa tay than is et?"

Twenty minutes later he was still there at her table, dividing his attention between an unco-operative gaiter strap and Cook's own confident pronouncements. "Oh glory yes," she was saying, "Nanny'll be back fer thad ol' job of 'ers surelye, soonasever you git crackin' an' start a brood of yer own, Master Edwin."

"I bet she won't," Ned retorted, busy with his gaiter and wondering why the deuce he had to blush so easily, "you know she always said Helen and I were more than flesh and blood could stand."

"Blow thad, kiddy – 'course she'll be back! Just about said as much in 'er last letter didn't she? 'Course she will. An' ef you'll 'scuse us the liberty of sayin' so," Cook was settling down to a favourite theme, "I know as 'ow poor dear Missus Walter 'ud want ter see you settled afore long, Gor bless 'er."

Ned made a face. Everyone always called his mother 'poor Mrs Walter' or 'poor dear Lillian' because she'd died before her thirtieth birthday. In fact 'poor' had become so much a part of her character that he pictured her with a permanently sorrowful expression – an image that the two poker-faced photographs of her in his grandmother's sitting room had done nothing to contradict.

"An' ef ye'r a-thinkin' as ye'r too green fer sech things," Cook continued relentlessly, "I'll tell yer, boy, my ol' Alf wus no more 'n nineteen when we wus wed – an' the'r some as say 'e wus past 'is best deeds then!" And as he jumped up for a rapid exit, Ned had intercepted the broad wink she gave Bridget across the table.

"Hang it, Cook – I won't marry, not for years!" he said. "So you and Nanny and everyone else will just have to jolly well wait, won't you?" And he took care to slam the back kitchen door behind him as he left.

It was no longer dark outside. There was a sharp earthy tang in the air without a touch of frost. Somewhere in the wood above the house the rusty-ratchet call of a cock pheasant was competing with the farmyard roosters. But the wind had dropped and the topmost branches of the beeches barely stirred. Bess was ready and waiting for him in her run behind the old brew-house, and she circled joyfully around Ned as he released her – tail pluming, eyes intent on her master's face.

The male wether lambs were grazing the Brooks Laine away below the furthermost farm buildings; and as they walked down to them through the rutted yards Ned automatically glanced back at the house. The main body of the existing Bury farmhouse had been plainly built of brick and pitcher-flint by Ned's ancestor Charlie Ashby in the reign of Queen Anne; and it wasn't until Ned himself was almost seven that his grandmother persuaded the estate trustees to modernize and extend the place to a plan of her own. Inside she divided some rooms and enlarged others. She'd installed an elaborate plumbing system that included a proper bathroom, two inside lavatories, hot water pipes and a monstrous clothes drying cabinet. There'd also been a splendidly gloomy new mock-Elizabethan entrance hall with Doulton tiles, stained glass and a sweeping staircase of Sussex oak that Amy Robsart might have felt privileged to fall down. Outside, she'd added a heated conservatory, a porch and a studded oak front door – and above it all a soaring, wildly unlikely medieval façade – gabled, oversailing and as lavishly half-timbered as anything in a Grimm's fairy tale.

It was a bit of a sham now, like Grannie herself. No amount of corsetting or London education could disguise Margaret Ashby's stubborn Sussex breeding. And looking back at that ostentatious, timbered gable amongst the trees, Ned felt much the same thing about his home. For all its romantic pretension the essential agricultural spirit of The Bury could not be altered. It was there for all to see in its proud stance above the great body of farm buildings that crowded the valley beneath it. The struggles and triumphs of generations of Ashby farmers were clearly visible to Ned in that single reassuring glance; and when he walked on down through the yards, his own commitment to the farm came up to meet him. It was his, all of it, by right and by inclination – and he rejoiced in the feeling.

In the centre of the farm, like the keep of an old castle, stood the great aisled-barn – flint-built like the house, with crop-eared gables and grey slates. In bygone days it had opened its doors to hundreds – no thousands – of laden waggons, to horses and oxen teams and red-faced men of Sussex, to long processions of carts bearing corn sheaves and pockets of woollen fleeces, fertilizer, mangles and potatoes. Its old beams had echoed to the infernal roar of the steam thresher, to the rattle and thump of hand flails before that and to the shouted exchanges of men long dead. It had witnessed bacchanalian harvest suppers in the great old days when almost the entire village of Sellington had been employed at The Bury, one way or another. And its cobwebbed rafters had sheltered generation upon generation of sparrows and starlings – and swallows from Africa who'd faithfully returned to it every season for more than two centuries.

On either side of the barn to north and to south, the valley cradled a rambling complex of flint buildings and barton-yards, each with its allotted purpose. The shearing yard was closest to the village at the northern end. Then came the main stable yard, with its raised granary and rows of blue and red waggons and tip-carts in the cartlodge beneath. And beyond the stables, on a level with the path up to the house, were the cowshed and dairy – with lights in their windows and Danny Goodworth's soulful young voice softly serenading the shorthorns:

"Now that lit'le tin soldier 'e sobbed an' 'e sighed,
Soo I padded 'is lit'le tin 'ead,
'What vexes yer lit'le tin soul?' sez I,
An' this is what 'e said . . . "

The morning milking was in progress.

There were other buildings and enterprises ranged behind the great barn. A second shed and fattening pens housed Grannie's pedigree Red Sussex cattle. There were rickyards and steaming maxon-heaps, pigscots, fowlhouses and a duckpond. There was a slaughterhouse and a bullpen, a workshop with a grindstone – and any number of unoccupied sheds where hand implements and sacks, oil cans and hurdles were stored. At the far southern end of it all a smaller ramshackled barn presided over the dig-yard where the ewes would come in for lambing. Beyond that the southerly cultivations of the Sellington Valley ran unrestricted to the sea.

As Ned climbed the final dig-yard gate and Bess wriggled beneath it, they had a clear view down the valley to the rising cliffs and the shining silver wedge of water at Sellington Gap. In the foreground there was a half eaten field of kale, smelling powerfully of cabbages – and in the middle of the field a solid woolly mass of five hundred or more ewes and young ewe tegs.

The ewe flock was held tightly together by two circling dogs, while the shepherd and his boy dismantled the wattle fold from around them and re-pitched it alongside the tegs on a fresh patch of kale. It was an ancient process that was still repeated daily throughout the year, summer and winter. Every day the sheep were released from the fold and taken up to graze the downland on either side of the Sellington Valley. And every night they were returned to a new fold on kale, mustard or rape – on rye, trefoil, tares or hay stubble, depending on the season. The folds gave the sheep the additional nourishment they needed after a day on the close downland turf. And in return they contributed the traditional 'fold-tare' – they fertilized the spare chalky soil – an essential element in the farm's four-course-shift rotation, with the plough and the seed drill to follow on behind.

"Morning Bat – morning Jemmy!" Ned called out to the two shepherds, jumping down from the gate and crossing the kale stalks towards them. They both looked up to nod at him gravely in the way that Sussex men have of greeting one another, and to chorus "Marnin' Mus Ned!" in unison.

"Not a bad sort of morning is it?" Ned ventured as he lifted another oak wattle and held it against its neighbour, shackles aligned and ready for the pitch-bar. And he was treated to the briefest glance from beneath the wavy brim of the shepherd's weather-painted felt hat. Bartholomew Vine seldom looked you in the eye more than once in a conversation, any more than his dogs did. It made him feel uneasy and it wasted time.

"Onnat'ral muggy an' mild ef y'asks me, Mus Ned," he said to the pitch-bar as he drove it home. "Now than, better watch that dry flock o'yourn fer pewmony, lad, soonasever et turns round ter rain."

And Ned was struck yet again with the absurdity of a situation in which The Bury workers conspired to train him to be good enough, eventually, to give them orders. Of course it wasn't his dry flock. He was only expected to look after the wethers temporarily while he was down from university. Bat Vine would fatten them off, grade them, trim them and mark them up. Bat would drive them into Lewes market and see them sold well. But they'd be known as 'Mus Ned's lambs' all the same, and it would be he and not Bat who'd be congratulated for the good price they'd undoubtedly make.

"Lookin' good, them wathers," the shepherd added with an encouraging nod in their direction. "Reg'lar credit ter you, Mus Ned, I rackon."

They were looking good, that at least was true. They were all of them deep chested and level-backed in the best traditions of the Southdown breed Ned's great-grandfather had done so much to improve. And in spite of himself, he couldn't help feeling just a little proud as he counted them. Bess pressed herself close against his legs when he unlatched and swung back the gate into the Brooks Laine, trembling with the effort of her self-control. The lambs watched her fixedly with slowly rotating jaws. Then as soon as she moved, they were off, bounding stiff-legged like woolly rocking horses. But Bess knew her business, and she had them flanked, wheeling back into the gateway before Ned was halfway across the field. At the entrance of the old wapple-way up through the wood the sheep stood uncertainly, facing outwards. As Ned walked up and Bess crept in, belly to the earth, the flock circled and eddied, coughing nervously and riding up on each other's backs. One or two of the bolder wethers even turned to stamp their forelegs at the dog.

'Slow an' steady,' that's what Bat always said; and that's how it worked. With some gentle hissing and shushing from Ned and two or three darting little side runs from Bess, the sheer pressure of bodies eventually forced the first lamb through into the wood. Then suddenly it was as if a dam had burst, and the little flock tore harum-scarum away up the wapple – leaving nothing for Ned to do but to follow on and shut the gate into the Wood Croft field behind them.

Afterwards, on an impulse, he decided to walk Bess on up through the beechwood to the top of the hill. From the higher field gate a flight of slippery plank-faced steps joined the main path that wound up through the trees and laurel shrubberies behind the house. And at the end of it, on a strange little mound of its own just beneath the brow of the hill, stood the Bury-house.

No one knew how the Bury-house mound had come into being, or why, although it was clearly shown on a seventeenth century plan of the estate in The Bury library. Its later function was well attested, though. For generations it had been indispensable for love trysts and Ashby family proposals – to which object Ned's grandmother had replaced the delapidated wooden arbour that had stood there with her own concept of a classical temple. Inside this romantic structure were a genuinely ancient stone bench and table, which Margaret Ashby confidently declared to be prehistoric; and the view from its steps had been described as the loveliest in all Sussex.

Every winter when the leaves were off the trees, an interested party of family and farm workers met in the wood to decide which of the beeches should be lopped to preserve the marvellous view. And when Ned adopted the approved viewing position on the Bury-house steps, he could smell the nutty sawdust scent of their most recent adjustments. Below him the wood fell sharply to the angled roofs and chimneys of the house, with the farm buildings beyond. Up the valley to the north the old village of Sellington sprouted from the chalk as if it had literally grown there. And to the south the land slipped away between the bastions of the downs to the flat surface of the English Channel.

It was Ned's world and the world of all the Ashbys. In effect they owned the valley, the chalk hills on either side of it and most of the houses in the village; for Ned's grandfather had entailed the entire property on his lineal descendants, with trustees in Lewes to administer its future succession from Ashby to Ashby.

The sun was just visible now above the further ridge. It shimmered and sparkled on the water, illuminating the rusty sails of half a dozen small fishing smacks. It seeped down over the sage haunches of the chalk hills, giving these too the illusion of movement. As Ned watched, it crept into the combe between them, burnishing the thorn hedges and picking out the yellow lichen-covered slates of the farm roofs. It also revealed Bat Vine and his dogs moving the Southdowns up through the lower fields, and ahead of them a great flock of plovers mewing up from the turf. From above, the arching patterns of their wings looked like a child's drawing of birds. Then they wheeled and a hundred white breasts reflected the sunlight, like aspen leaves turning in the wind.

And improbably, in the midst of it all, Ned Ashby thought of Robert Llewellen. What would old Bat make of a fellow like that, as he plodded up the hillside behind his beloved ewes?

"Now than, Mus Ned, doan' you go worryn' yer 'ead over furriners an' sech! 'Cos you know as wull as I do thad a Sheere man an' a Hill man be as bleedy differen' as an 'orse an' a coo!"

As far as someone like Bat was concerned, 'furriners' and the 'sheeres' started the other side of Brighton. And if they weren't directly involved with farming or with the downland flocks, then they weren't reckoned one little bit in this part of Sussex. It was all so simple for people like Bat and Cook – even for Grannie. To them the continuity of their pleasant ordered life in the Sellington Valley was all that really mattered.

'Poor breeders,' that had been Gran's verdict on recent generations of Ashby males. She'd never forgiven her own husband for dying so inconveniently soon after the birth of his heir, nor her son for refusing to remarry after poor dear Lillian's demise. And Ned knew that she and the farm trustees were looking to him now to field them a regular cricket team of heirs. He was to find a suitable girl of the right class, who'd provide for his physical needs and bear his children and eventually become mistress of The Bury household. It was all so simple and fundamental, a plain duty that he owed to his ancestors and to his own love of the chalk hills. He was bred for an agricultural destiny just as Bat and Danny Goodworth were – as much a part of the unchanging scheme of things as Bess was, lying at his feet, or the Southdowns, or the heavy horses in The Bury stables.

Yet there was something just too fundamental and dutiful about it that Ned's youth and imagination rejected. Life was all tied up for them, but he was still a loose end. He wasn't like Bat and Dan and the others, not entirely. There was something missing in this ordered world of his, something beyond the compass of his experience or expectations – a stimulant, an adventure, a question mark that had somehow become associated in his mind with Robert Llewellen, and with the name of the woman on his calling card.

Chapter Three

"People who can't adapt to change should be shot!" Meriel was hanging head downwards above the poop deck from the lower topsail clue-line, her blue serge skirts lashed firmly to her ankles. "The Mater first and foremost," she added provocatively.

She and Gareth had been making their usual daily attempts to impress each other with their gymnastic feats in the rigging of the *Catriona*, now six days out from Newcastle on its voyage to Valparaiso. The Mater, on the other hand, was impressing no one very much at all just now, prostrate on her bunk – a martyr to seasickness and nervous headaches.

Harriet Llewellen's unwillingness or inability to adapt to her changing circumstances was a cross that they'd all had to bear over the past few weeks. Before she'd even finished repacking her Davenport china a fourth time her daughter Vicky had suffered a little 'crise' of temperament, and the Ipswich maid had left abruptly without notice. Harriet had gone on to be train-sick for the entire five hundred mile journey from Brisbane to the port of Newcastle – to pass out cold at her first glimpse of the vessel in which they were to sail – and to voice her terrors of the new life that awaited them in Spanish America at every possible opportunity since.

"I'm not sure that Da would be all that gone on the idea of having the Mater shot," Gareth said mildly, with one eye on the gyrating form of his sister in the running rigging.

"Rot!" It was Meriel's new word. "You know perfectly well that he'd consider it a favour, Garry. Why she can't even open his letters without going into palpitations!" Meriel had always taken a positive pleasure in out-facing and out-doing her younger brother in any way that she could. And the admiring, slightly shocked expression that she now perceived on his freckled face brought joy to her heart – even upside down.

Now that Da had finally forced her to put Australia and her childhood behind her for once and for all, she was gratified to discover that life had become even more interesting and exciting than before. The Darling Downs and the mountains of New South Wales had been a visual revelation, rolling so splendidly past the train window. And the reality of a voyage across the Pacific in a dashing square-rigged clipper thrilled her to the very soles of her boots. She'd often thought that she might like to run away to sea, if only it were permitted for girls – and even the prospect of having to leave Harry behind to become a dull married accountant had failed to dampen her.

The *Catriona* was a cargo vessel with a hold-full of high grade coal for Valparaiso. Her sails had been furled when they boarded her, and every part of her superstructure filmed with black coal dust. But Meriel was enchanted nonetheless. From the quay the ship had looked like a great grey swan, majestically dipping her prow to the swell. And from her grimy decks one could so easily imagine oneself embroiled in all manner of perilous enterprises with buccaneers and blockade-runners, and people like that. Better still, the Llewellens were to be her only paying passengers; and Meriel's newfound awareness of the male sex had singled out their Canadian captain for special attention on the voyage.

The man was rather serious and briefly spoken, to be sure, and not exactly young. The eyes were perhaps a little pale-lashed and pink-rimmed for preference, but they were certainly half way to blue. His jaw was squarish too, and his hair fair rather than otherwise. And there'd been a certain equine quality about Captain McIntyre's thick neck and muscular rump that greatly endeared him to his youngest female passenger.

Meriel was new, admittedly, to the business of romance. But from what she'd read and observed it seemed clear enough to her that men, like horses, were there to be broken. She'd get this one to propose to her. And why ever not? It would be the greatest possible lark, and sixty days at sea should be ample time to pull it off, even for a novice – just so long as Vicky remained below decks.

Harriet and Vicky had surrendered to *mal de mer* almost as soon as the Newcastle steam-tug left them. And although Vicky was now showing some feeble signs of recovery, Mother continued to subsist on nothing more nourishing than an occasional sip of the captain's vintage champagne, fortified with iron pills, rhubarb, Black Draft and sal volatile.

"And be honest," Meriel remarked from the clue-line, hauling herself back into an upright position and signalling for her brother to let her down, "don't you suppose Da's heart must sink into his boots every time he sees the Mater heaving over the horizon?"

"Af'noon Mister Gareth – Miss Meriel, Mam." Neither of them had heard the captain's plimsolled feet on the poopsteps, and Meriel instantly plummeted to the deck, landing with a healthy thud beside him.

"Guess you young folks are mekkin' good use of the rat-lines then?" His eyes did protrude a little, particularly when he was making an effort to be polite. But as the unfortunate image of a white rabbit formed itself in Meriel's mind, she swiftly obliterated it with something more heroic – and hastened to her captain's aid with what she imagined to be a gently encouraging smile.

"Well they do say that a little moderate exercise is beneficial to the health," she said sweetly, entirely unaware of the expression of frank appraisal in her own brown eyes.

For the two weeks that it took the *Catriona* to round the North Island of New Zealand and to reach Pitcairn Island in the mid-Pacific, the weather was predominantly fine, although scarcely calm, and more than somewhat chilly. To Meriel's vexation Vicky had made a number of appearances above deck, nonetheless, in her new Art cape. Even Harriet recovered sufficiently to accept the little delicacies with which the ship's cook plied her – soda biscuits, waffles, turtle soup and clam chowder. Although, curiously, she never seemed quite well enough for the boiled pork and Boston beans that formed everyone else's staple diet.

After such an optimistic start, Meriel was soon bored beyond belief, bored with the pervasive odours of canvas and Stockholm tar and with the trivial monotony of their days. Having once set her sights on the captain, she was impatient for results. She took pains to be discovered by him in a variety of elegant attitudes at the rail. But maddeningly, the object of her attention remained as formal and as courteous as ever. The trick was going to be harder than she'd thought!

In the meantime, alternative sources of entertainment were strictly limited. A book or a journal or a game of cards were pretty poor sport in Meriel's opinion, and never succeeded in holding her attention for long. She loathed needlework and it loathed her. Porpoises, black-fish and even whales appeared from time to time, but scarcely ever when you felt like them. And there was something horribly samish about an empty sea. You could visit Percy the pig in his funny little sty amidships, or hob-nob with the helmsman at the wheel. On calm days you could fish for mollyhawk albatrosses from the stern, hooking them in by their great curved beaks with baited rings on the end of wire lines. But although Meriel had originally laughed louder than anyone to see these foolish-looking creatures actually becoming seasick on the pitching deck, even that amusement palled with repetition.

Only Sundays were different. Sundays were days to look forward to, when the captain got down his wind and current charts for their inspection, and measured their progress for them across the Pacific. No work was done of a Sunday, beyond what was totally necessary. Captain McIntyre and his crew became different men – barbered and laundered, sweetly smelling of shaving soap and coconut oil. And after their session with the charts, the captain could sometimes be persuaded to stay on and take his coffee with the young Llewellens amongst the varnished wood and polished brass of the chart room.

On the second Sunday out, Meriel personally invited the captain to join the family for their evening service in the little saloon beneath the poop deck, and her presumption was fully justified. She herself played the piano – with more enthusiasm than accuracy to be sure, but she played. And the captain sang in a confident baritone that proved splendidly unlike his quiet speaking voice. The others sang too, of course – Vicky faintly, fighting nausea, Gareth with his voice on the change – and Harriet's quavering contralto, joining in a beat late from her cabin across the companionway. But Meriel heard only her own voice, and the assertive masculine sound that over-rode it:

> "Bring me my bow – of burning gold,
> Bring me my arrows of desire . . . "

On their third Sunday out from Newcastle there was a freshening southerly blowing. The fiddles were on in the dining saloon, and at dinner Meriel experienced some little difficulty in successfully transferring her soup to her mouth rather than her lap. She also noticed something strange about the sea. It was quite dark outside, without a moon – and yet there were lights visible through the porthole, dancing in the waves nearest to the ship.

"Phosphorescence," the captain explained in answer to her first exclamation, "an' I reckon that means we kin count on some foul weather by an' by."

From the deck the sea presented an amazing spectacle of shifting, sliding luminescence – a silvery-bluish light that moved with the waves in all directions around the ship. Even Harriet was inspired to stagger up to view the phenomenon, before the sight of so much moving water overcame her once again. From Meriel's point of view, it was a heaven-sent opportunity, of course, and one that was not to be missed. She shut the lid of the piano with such finality after the last of their hymns that evening, that Gareth and the captain both started quite violently. And when she turned to speak, her eyes seemed to have caught the extraordinary luminous quality of the sea itself.

"Oh Captain," she said eagerly, "won't you take me up to the fo'c'sle to see the phosphorescence from there? The helmsman says it's always ever so much better from the bows." And she treated him to her best, most fascinating smile.

"Oh yes, rather!" Gareth chipped in – only to recall that he'd promised to read to the Mater from Scott's Poetical Works immediately after prayers. "But you go," he said generously, smarting from a second sharp kick beneath the piano stool.

"Good, that's settled then." Meriel was up and half way to the door before the captain had time to object. "I'll just run and fetch my cape. But I won't be a jiff, Captain, so don't you go away now, will you?"

In the tiny cabin that she shared with Vicky she splashed herself recklessly with her sister's eau de cologne. Vicky herself had slipped in next door to commiserate with the Mater. 'And she's hardly in a fit state to worry about clothes and things,' Meriel thought cheerfully, as she helped herself to the cape that she'd always admired so much on her sister, with its stand-up Medici collar and appliquéd art nouveau trim. 'My necessity is greater than hers, in any case.'

Captain McIntyre was still obediently sitting where she'd left him in the saloon, and together they strolled and rolled the length of the main deck to the steep little ladder that led up to the top-gallant forecastle. The proper thing would have been to allow the gentleman to lead the way, and then to take his hand for her own ascent. But Meriel never thought of it – or not at least until she had already reached the top in a scramble of rubber soles and flounced petticoats.

There was a first-watch lookout on duty on this steep, triangular little deck high in the bows of the ship. The captain nodded to him curtly as he joined his young charge at the head of the ladder. "I'll take over for a spell, Gregory," he said, and Meriel felt a distinct thrill of excitement as the sailor slipped past them and away. Things really were going on very nicely.

They stood together at the rail then, she and her captain, near the point where the great bowsprit jutted out over the sea. Above them the jib-sheets cracked and billowed under the force of the southerly. Ahead of them, as at the stern, the waves broke in a continuously moving pattern of light. Away down below the carved profile of the *Catriona* figurehead, the water foamed and sprayed up from the bows with a pale and unearthly radiance. Fish darted from the slicing prow leaving brilliant silvery trails in their wake, and fountains of sparkling droplets glittered like gems against the dark swell of the ocean.

"No end of a sight, isn't it?" Meriel said, and at the same time she placed a small naked hand square on the rail, close beside the captain's. She had left her gloves behind deliberately.

The captain's silence was almost oppressively intimate. 'In a moment he'll cover my hand with his own calloused palm, and break into an incoherent declaration of love,' she thought hopefully. 'By jove, Miss Llewellen, I do think you're splendid . . .', that's how it would begin. She'd read about it heaps and heaps of times. In the right circumstances, it seemed, men could be fairly counted on to act romantically, particularly in the silent watches of the night. They were the slaves of their own emotions – everybody said so.

"I've heard tell, you know," the captain said at length, "that phosphorescence in sea water comes from the disturbance of marine animalculae by the movements of ships an' sech . . . "

'Great heavens, the man's a perfect fool!' Meriel thought, snatching her hand back from the rail. If she'd wanted a scientific explanation for sea-shine she'd have asked for it, wouldn't she? And so much for Vicky's niminy-piminy roundabout way of doing things!

"Yes I daresay" she cut in impatiently, "but tell me, Captain, don't you ever feel lonely at sea?" And she replaced the hand in such a way that it accidentally brushed against his.

"Sure," he conceded after another little pause, "I guess we all of us get lonesome from time to time, Miss Llewellen." He removed his hand to rub his nose thoughtfully, setting it down again a little beyond her reach.

Really, men could be incredibly dense when they chose! "I mean don't you ever get lonely for female company?"

"Well now Missy, I don't reckon there's too much chance of that, do you – so long as I have charming young ladies like you to hold my hand for me."

For a moment she was baffled, nonplussed. She simply couldn't think what had come over him. Then it dawned on her that he was laughing, he was actually laughing at her! And as she turned to stare at him in amazement, she saw the captain's kindly smile as a beastly, mocking grin.

'Impertinent clever-dick white rabbit!' she thought, 'what a sell!', and turned back on her heel without another word.

Chapter Four

There were days when Ned Ashby positively hated London, and this was one of them. It was a still grey day in October 1904. Everything seemed devoid of colour. The buildings closed in around him as he walked, in long depressing corridors of sooty brick. The leaves, curling on the trees, were caked with grime – even the air he breathed felt dirty. Beyond the pavement the traffic progressed in a constant stream of turning spokes and thin, bored-looking horses – carts and cabs and carriages, donkey-shays, bumping bicycle wheels, and costers' barrows propelled by urchins with dangling cigarettes and caps two sizes too big for them. More horses, more traffic wheel-to-wheel, more noise and dirt with every day that passed – the modern Babylon.

Despite the warmth of the summer past, almost every face that Ned encountered on his way looked pallid and unhealthy. It was one of those days for Ned when the entire urban population was ugly, with compressed mouths and mean little eyes. He hated the affected way that the swells walked, with their sticks and their gamps and their pouter-pigeon chests. They were all shoeshine and blinkers, these London Johnnies – half a world away from the sunburnt folk of the Sussex chalk hills with their watchful eyes and unhurried pace.

As the traffic rattled and jingled past him, Ned recalled something that Bat had said that summer, up amongst the harebells on the long grey-green ridge of the downs. They'd watched the sun chase cloud shadows across the valleys that afternoon, with the music of the sheep bells and the clear song of the skylarks all around them. And as they walked together, the little bell flowers had danced in the fescue grass with the butterflies that matched them so perfectly, blue for blue.

"There y'are, Mus Ned, reg'lar picturesome I calls it," Bat had said, flinging an arm wide to embrace it all. "Search England through, an' yer'll not find ets match. An' only you an' me ter see et, lad – whiles all them cliver, bettermost folkses is fer everlastin' a-rooshin' about tarrifyin' theirselves, an' niver stoppin' ter enjoy things or racken 'em up – 'til one fine marnin' they wakes up deader'n a cold potater."

Ned smiled to himself at the thought – and of course Bat was right. On the days when he himself had felt bored and frustrated in Sussex, on the farm or away at school in Lancing, he'd imagined that simply to be in the metropolis would be exciting. But now that he was here, he saw all too clearly that life in this capital of the greatest empire the world had known was inferior in almost every way to life in the country. Not that Ned was permanently unhappy in the city. He'd just embarked on his second year at University College, reading zoology. And on the whole he rather enjoyed dissecting dogfish and white rats, for all their obvious irrelevance to his future as a farmer. Left to his own devices he'd undoubtedly have preferred one of the new farming schools – at Uckfield or Wye in Kent. But his grandmother wouldn't hear of it.

"If you want to rub shoulders with a bunch of rustic hobbledehoys, you'd do better to stay home," she declared. "No – what you need now, boy, is some proper society, and the chance of meeting one or two suitable young gels from good County families."

In Margaret Ashby's eyes London was a necessary adjunct indeed, to civilized country living – handy by rail for dressmakers, accountants, educators and suitable gels from County families. She knew of a number of wealthy Sussex landowners' daughters who'd be doing the London Season while Ned was at university. And with her contacts in town, she could see that he met all of them at least once before returning to Sellington to settle down. Nor had she envisaged or received any opposition to this idea from Ned's father, who had long since relinquished his family responsibilities to his own mother, in much the same way that he'd delegated the practical running of his farm to a competent foreman.

Thus it was that Ned had been enrolled at University College the previous year, and lodged in small but convenient rooms in Tavistock Place – in preparation for some doubtful education and three years of concentrated socializing. Although as it turned out, the education had been more doubtful and the socializing less concentrated than even Ned had anticipated – with laboratory sessions five afternoons a week leaving mercifully little time for 'At Homes' or teatime functions of any kind. The evening invitations he could accept were also, happily, few – and the whole wretched business of calling and leaving cards was of necessity confined to weekends.

On this particular grey October Saturday, however, Ned's first call was not to be one of those on his grandmother's priority list. And although he'd set out bravely enough from Tavistock Place in a well cut morning suit and high silk hat, a miserable worm of dread had been squirming away in his bowels to jaundice his view of the city and its inhabitants with every step he took. As he turned out of Lamb's Conduit and into Dombey Street, he watched the black polished surface of his shoes marching like automatons across the paving stones. They seemed to have a will of their own to carry him forward, when everything else inside him wanted to make a bolt for it full tilt in the opposite direction. But the shoes knew and the feet inside them knew, that when Ned really made up his mind to do a thing he did it, whatever the cost. And Ned had finally made up his mind to pay a call on Robert Llewellen's woman.

During the previous term he'd passed her house in Harpur Street more than once. He'd peered at it through the railings, even on one occasion mounting the steps to the door. But he never quite had the audacity to ring the bell. Not until now. This time, this time though, he wasn't going to allow himself to stop and think. He actually stepped right up to the door and rang, just like that, with the nervous perspiration trickling down his back. '*Stood on her doorstep like some giddy swain – and couldn't go in...*' But Ned Ashby *was* going in, that was the difference!

There was no glass in the door and no sound from behind it. And in spite of himself, Ned jumped convulsively when it swung open.

"Yeas, wattcher want?" He was confronted by a boot-faced maid with a jaw like a man trap and an expression of intense disdain on her craggy features.

"You ain't sellin' nuffink I 'ope" she added tartly while he plunged for a card in his inside breast pocket. "Cos if you are, you kin tike yerself orf son, an' that precious sharp!"

"No, no indeed!" He found himself praying, basely, that the lady of the house might be out for the moment. But there was no going back now. "I just wondered if I might see – er, Simmie – if she's in to callers?"

He was backing down a step and fiddling with his tie – anything to distract from the familiar crimson blush he could feel creeping up above his collar. He knew he was out of order to use a pet name like that to a servant. But what else was he to call her? Apart from the address, it was all there'd been on the Llewellen fellow's card.

"Well, I like your sauce!" the maid exclaimed, pouncing on his own card and holding it at arm's length as if it might explode. "And 'oo might we be when we're at 'ome, pray, to call 'er such a fing? The Hemperor of 'Olloway is it?"

"You can tell her that I'm an acquaintance of Mister Robert Llewellen's," Ned rejoined with as much dignity as he could muster. "And if it's at all inconvenient, I'll be pleased to wait on her another day."

"Not in those trousers yer won't!" The maid jerked her heavy jaw at him and slammed the door in his face.

Whether or not he'd actually been dismissed wasn't at all clear. But Ned had just decided that he had, and stepped back onto the pavement, when the door was flung open once more.

"Miss Sims sez she'll see you," the maid announced beligerently, "This way, yer Lordship!" And Ned had no choice but to follow her white apron ribbons into the house, still red as a peony, with his fragile confidence all in tatters.

She pitched him into an impossibly cluttered little parlour on the first floor, and abandoned him there amongst the hassocks and occasional tables and a faint odour of potpourri. There was altogether too much mahogany and chintz in the room, and every flat surface was smothered in plush-framed photographs and gewgaws, half-finished mending, periodicals and potted plants. Ned weaved his way through and stood awkwardly beside the fireplace. The carpet was threadbare, he noticed. But the mantel was lavishly draped with maroon velvet, scalloped and bobbled and crowded with *objets d'art* – bronzes, Staffordshire dogs, Japanese fans and Wedgwood china, a porcelain shepherdess in a glass bell jar, a pot of coloured spills and a large black marble clock.

It really wasn't at all what he'd expected, and suddenly the complicated introduction that Ned had prepared fled from his mind. It had gone a total blank. He was about to meet Llewellen's golden woman, and hadn't the faintest idea what to say to her. '*It makes fools of us all in the end, this gentleman's gentleman of ours.*' He began to feel cold all over. He couldn't seem to swallow properly; and when the door slowly began to open of its own accord, he took an involuntary step backwards.

A very fat black Chinese pug waddled into the room, sniffing loudly and glaring at him with wet, bulging eyes. Ned shouldn't have spoken to it, he realized that afterwards. But he liked dogs, and the relief made him incautious. The next moment all hell was let loose. At the very first word the thing charged him like a miniature hippo, yapping insanely – and Ned in retreat had stumbled on the brass fender. He put out a hand to save himself, clutching at the mantelboard – and to his utter horror he felt it give – slowly descending with its velvet and its bobbles and all its precious adornments, to crash down into the hearth.

Beatrice Sims heard it from the corridor – a loud splintering smash, intermingled with hysterical barking from Gussie and a short, somewhat surprising, Anglo Saxon oath. From the doorway she was faced with the truly pitiful picture of a sweating, beet-red young man in a constricting starched collar, kneeling amongst the debris of her ornaments. And her very first thought was of how she could release the poor boy from his agony of embarrassment.

"Oh dear," she said with deliberate understatement, smiling at him ruefully as he leapt to his feet. He really was a singularly solid and personable young man, with corn coloured hair and a pair of the bluest blue eyes imaginable. Her heart bled for him in his nervous terror, as he struggled to apologise, and to explain.

"Sorry – most fearfully sorry," he stammered. "It was an accident . . . the dog barked – I stepped back you see . . . "

At which point Gladys came thundering up the kitchen stairs and burst into the room behind her demanding, "Nar ven! What the blue Moses 'as 'e bin an' done now, fer gawd's sake?" in her most strident Billingsgate.

"All right, Gladys, it's just a little accident," Simmie said mildly, "and certainly nothing that this young gentleman and I can't clear up between us, if you'll just run and fetch the dustpan."

"Dustpan? Dustcart, more like!" Gladys jerked her chin pugnaciously. "I'd best bring the cinder-box." Leaving Simmie to calm and reassure the young man all over again. He'd been tossing his forelock and shuffling about amongst the broken china and scattered spills like a great restive colt. And if she didn't look lively, she could see that the one surviving ivory fan would soon be crushed beneath his large, heavily dispersed hooves.

"Don't mind Gladys, my dear, she's not nearly as bad as she looks," she whispered as the affronted maid had stalked forth into the hall, bearing with her an equally indignant Chinese pug dog. Furthermore, she'd successfully retrieved the fan – only to go and make things worse by laughing aloud as the poor wretched boy stepped back onto his top hat.

"Dear me, oh dear I am sorry. But you do rather seem to be in the wars this afternoon, don't you?" And then he smiled too, a painful shamefaced kind of grin, and she began to like him in earnest.

"Really I collect so many odds and ends, that I scarcely know what I had on there anyway," she lied bravely as Gladys returned with the cinder-box and the three of them solemnly committed the more hopeless remains to its interior. The little shepherdess was one of the only things she'd brought with her from Richmond, and she'd miss that most dreadfully. But the Wedgwood jug might be rivetted perhaps, and miraculously the clock was still ticking. She was relieved too, to see that the blush had now drained back as far as the young man's neat, magenta-coloured ears.

"Thank you, Gladys; and now I think we'll have some tea, shall we?"

Over an impromptu tea, Simmie was able to establish that young Mr Ashby had actually made Robert's acquaintance the previous autumn. He had apparently undertaken to visit her as a favour – a duty call, on discovering how conveniently close she lived to the university. The question of why he'd left it quite so long to do so had at first puzzled her – until the reticent young man happened to mention how cramped and disagreeable his lodgings were in Tavistock Place. Then of course she understood perfectly. He was hoping that she might be offering rooms herself in Harpur Street, but was too wretchedly bashful to say so.

It was an intriguing idea, though, most intriguing; and during the remainder of their rather stilted conversation, Simmie gratefully applied her mind to the pros and cons of boarding university students. Because whatever else she thought of, she was determined that she wouldn't think of Robert – not now. And questions of finance and of empty rooms proved a most effective distraction.

As soon as the young man left, Simmie ran upstairs to do something about her hair. The hair ritual was an invaluable aid to concentration, she found, whenever she wanted to think seriously. And of course she knew that it was bound to need attention. It was so mousy and wispy and unsatisfactory in every way, her hair; and they'd yet to invent the pin or the net that could hold it at the back. 'Sugar floss', was how Robert had described it when she'd finally brushed it out for him in that

Richmond hotel room. But *no!* She was *not* going to think of Robert.

Simmie sat herself resolutely down at her dressing table, groping for the hair-tie beneath her bun and trying desperately hard to concentrate on the problem in hand. But Simmie's concentration had always been an uncertain thing, particularly where administration was concerned; and after a few minutes' consideration of annuities and rentals and available bed linen, she abandoned the subject of university boarders for a frank consideration of her own features in the triple mirrors of her dressing table.

She was thirty-eight, and naturally there were lines to prove it – a fine tracery of them around the eyes and some faint little ripples of surprise across the forehead. Nothing to boast of, certainly, but then nothing to be ashamed of either – no bags or double chins or frowning creases. It was a pale oval face – delicate, decidedly town-bred. The nose was perhaps a little more prominent than it had been, despite the fact that she'd put on weight – and the mouth was definitely wider. But the carriage of the head was good, and the eyes were still candid – a pretty, flecked hazel-green. And yes, she could honestly say that she was still attractive.

So why hadn't he come? Simmie had caught the familiar gleam in his eye – still there after almost thirteen years abroad – that day in the solicitor's office in Boswell Street, when they met to reassign his mother's house. And although she dared not acknowledge that look, she'd hoped – oh how she'd hoped that he'd come to her later at Harpur Street! Each morning, every morning she dressed for him. For weeks she'd raced Gladys to the doorbell – until one day she heard from his brother that Robert had sailed for South America – and the hope had died a swift and mortifying death. Life could really be rather cruel sometimes, particularly when it sent handsome young messengers blundering in to destroy one's shepherdesses and re-open old wounds.

"And bother it all!" she cried to herself in the mirror. Robert was like Rome, every confounded road led back to him! And then, because none of her resolutions had ever been very strong

43

where that gentleman was concerned, Simmie shamelessly began to re-examine her first treasured recollection of him – as if she'd just discovered it amongst the tortoiseshell and Venetian glass of her dressing table.

It had been autumn, the best time of all the year for Richmond, when the leaves lay in golden drifts beneath the chestnut trees and the river looked like a Chinese painting through the mist. Simmie had always felt uncomfortably romantic and emotional in the autumn. Something to do with the evidences of change and passing time that she saw around her, she supposed – the death of a summer one could never recapture. And that autumn in particular, the feeling had reflected a real sadness within herself.

A few months before, she had been so happy and excited at the prospect of her father's remarriage to a young widow with a little girl of her own. Isobel had been less than ten years older than she was – and little Francie was a treasure, with bouncing curls and fat, dimpled little legs. They could have had such fun together! Beatrice had so much to tell them and show them, so much of herself to offer. But somehow it hadn't happened. Isobel hadn't wanted to walk by the river or in the park, and refused to allow her to take her little stepsister anywhere on her own. Isobel enjoyed sewing circles and whist drives and afternoon calling. Isobel insisted that the house should be kept in perfect apple-pie order for every living minute of the day. Isobel considered her stepdaughter to be untidy, undisciplined and unhealthily fond of her father. In short, within six months Isobel had reduced Beatrice Sims' happy home to a claustrophobic hen-house from which she escaped at every possible opportunity.

Her little fox terrier, Kit, had naturally been forbidden the house very early in the piece. But after a rare intervention from Papa, Beatrice was permitted to keep the dog in an old beer barrel kennel behind the coalshed. And together they'd walked the green and the river towpath, and explored the glorious wilderness of the park. For her part, Isobel had found herself torn between a natural desire to get the girl out from under her feet, and the obvious impropriety of allowing a young lady of twenty-three to walk abroad so freely on her own. But in the end she'd settled for the compromise of letting her go, every time, with a token warning.

"If I've warned you once, Beatrice, I've warned you a hundred times that no possible good can come of parading around the town like this without an escort. Mark my words, one of these fine days some man is going to take you for an abandoned woman! And what will you do then?" (Or something very much along those lines.) "So just make certain you're back before your father," she'd add – often as not in the same breath.

Yes, it had been a peculiarly emotional time for Simmie, that lovely lonely autumn of 1889. And she could see now that she was as ripe for her encounter with Robert as if she'd actually been waiting for him. Perhaps in a sense she had. Looking back on the afternoon that she and Kit climbed the long hill to the park, she could certainly remember a feeling of expectancy in the air, as if something was almost bound to happen. It had rained that morning. The air was like crystal, and everything looked bright and clean-washed, ready for some new beginning. The leaves in the gutter smelt of conker forays and Guy Fawkes' night; and columns of blue smoke wafted over garden walls along the way.

In the park itself the carriage folk were out in force, eager to admire the hues of threadbare chestnuts and gilded oaks – and themselves to be admired. The ladies were proud as peacocks behind their high-stepping horses – resplendent in velvet mantles and feathered bonnets, and the sable tippets and muffs that were *de rigueur* that season. The gentlemen raised their hats, and often their voices, as they passed – dispensing orange peel from the sides of their carriages and compliments that were extavagant in their flattery. For it was well known that a number of the women inside the fine clothes were to be had for little more than a lavish blandishment.

Watching them pass by, these outrageous creatures, it amused Simmie to picture herself as one of them – as everything that she really wasn't – titled and deplorably rich, modishly dressed and scandalously fast. This afternoon she'd take a new lover, why not? The silver-haired patrician in the little landau perhaps? Or the swarthy, dangerous-looking character in the victoria with the little girl on his knee?

The child from that particular carriage had pointed at Kit and shouted something at her as it passed by; and at the same time the mud from its wheels had spattered Simmie's bottle green tailor-made from bodice to hem. So much for flights of fancy! It was such a pretty dress too, with frogging and a scooped apron and an absurd little tournure bustle at the back.

'And murder to get clean!' Simmie thought with dismay, entirely failing to notice that the victoria had stopped, or that the gentleman had alighted. He was very nearly upon her, in fact, before she heard his footsteps and looked up.

"Dear me," he said, "it would seem that we owe you an apology." And he'd removed his hat to compensate for the mischief in his eyes. His hair was very dark, almost black, and Simmie was secretly rather tickled to see that he'd had to recover it exceedingly smartly to prevent the little girl in his arms from mauling his hat. She was a lively little handful certainly – dressed to the nines in tartan outers and a floppy tam-o'-shanter with a red pom-pom on the top. A tiny auburn haired tintype of her father – without the moustache!

"The dress won't stain I hope?"

"No, no it's nothing – not of the least importance. Please don't trouble yourself – I'm sure it will all brush out when it's dry." The narrow dark eyes flustered her slightly. So she hurried to offer the required assurance and continue on her way. But now that the conversation had begun, the little girl was determined to have her say too, it seemed.

"It's by birfday today!" she announced importantly, "I'm free!" And then of course Simmie had been duty-bound to say the right kind of things – and to linger.

"Three! Gracious, you *are* getting a big girl, aren't you!"

"Yes I am," the little poppet agreed downrightly. "An' we've been to the past'ycook's – an' now my Da's brought me to see the deers!"

"Has he now? Well that is a nice treat. And have you seen any yet, I wonder?"

"'Course we have! Lots an' lots an' lots – but I like your doggie best," the child confided, delighted with this grown-up exchange of views and anxious to prolong it. "What's its name?"

"Nosey Parker, that's what it's called!" Her father laughed – but rather nicely, Simmie thought.

"And now, if Meriel will allow me to get a quick word in – perhaps you would permit us to drive you home – before you come to any further harm from reckless drivers?"

He wasn't handsome exactly. But he was tall and beautifully slim, and he carried the child with a nonchalance that showed he was no weakling. Then suddenly Simmie realized that she hadn't answered.

"No, no thank you," she said quickly. "I mean – it's very kind of you, but really I should prefer to walk." And this time she couldn't meet his eyes.

Of course she longed to go with them – who wouldn't? But imagine Isobel's face if she'd sailed up to the door in a victoria with a man like that, child or no child!

"Well then, perhaps we'll have the pleasure of seeing you in the park on some other occasion? I think it might be a capital idea to drive back this way every week at about this time. Don't you agree?"

It had been an invitation, she was almost sure of it. And he was a philanderer! Although naturally, she told herself, there was no way on earth that she could meet him. Why goodness knows where such a thing might not lead! When it had rained, though, the following week and prevented her from going out, she had sat despondently for hours with her cheek pressed against the cold window pane. And the next week she and Kit were ready and waiting beside the carriage drive a good half hour before he was due to pass.

What if he didn't come? Worse still, what if he *did*?! It was *comme il faut* that he should simply raise his hat and bow. Then she would smile politely and turn away – and that would be that. Then all of a sudden there he was, bowling up the hill from Ham alone in the victoria behind his coachman – waving to her bold as brass as if he'd known her for years.

"Beg pardon." A loud knocking sound recalled Simmie abruptly to the present – to be followed a moment later by the sight of Gladys' gaunt visage thrust around the bedroom door.

"Beg pardon, Mum, but that young gent's bin an' left 'is gloves be'ind."

"Has he, Gladys, how tiresome! Well I suppose that we'll just have to invite him back to reclaim them then, won't we?"

"If you say so, Mum."

"And I'm glad that you looked in just now, Gladys, because there's something I rather wanted to ask you. What would you say I wonder if I told you that I was thinking of taking in university students as lodgers?"

Gladys was a past master of the old-fashioned look, always had been. "I'd say you'd be best advised ter lock away what's left of yer good china, Mum," she said bleakly.

Chapter Five

"I say come on, Ashby! Come on in and have a soak!" The invitation came from somewhere amongst the steam and hearty laughter of the baths in the Acton changing rooms; and the speaker was the captain of Ned's victorious rugby team.

"Come on old man! It's ever so – ever so nice when you're in, as the Duchess said to the Curate!"

Ned was a popular fellow today because he'd scored two of their five tries. He climbed in, grinning self-consciously, to celebrate with the rest of them in hot water and ribald bonhomie. You sat on a kind of shelf in the Acton baths with the water up to your armpits; and the heat closed in around you like a womb, soaking mud and sweat and stiffness and pain out of you with a marvellous sensuality. Ned could have survived though, he had to admit, without the catcalls and rumbustious bellows of laughter, and the excess of pink nudity that surrounded him. He wasn't gregarious, not awfully. He'd joined the University College Hospital team partly because they needed players and partly to avoid the dreaded At Homes – but mostly because he actually enjoyed the game. In the lecture halls and laboratories of the university his body had been reduced to a series of limited faculties – a brain, an eye, an ear, with hands only to serve them and legs only to move them from room to room. And it was only on the rugby or the cricket field that he could regain the sense of genuine physical usefulness that he experienced daily on the farm. That was the real celebration for Ned, not this.

There was beer afterwards, oceans of it, and more overt celebrations of masculinity in the clubhouse. Eventually, in an hour or two, a private omnibus would bear the victors back to Holborn in soggy triumph. But Ned couldn't wait that long. It was a goodish hike to Shepherds Bush, and he wasn't likely to find a crawler outside the two bob limit, but he wanted to walk. The alcohol had combined with the effects of the exercise and the bath and the cool evening air to give him an especial sense of physical wellbeing. As he swung his arms he could feel the breadth of his shoulders, the weight of the blood in his hands. He gloried in the loose-moving power of his hips and his buttocks and the quivering, heavy rhythm of his boots on the road. It was fine to be alive – absolutely!

"Where to, Guv?" the cabbie called down through a little window in the roof of the hansom. It smelt of horse-leather and old newspapers inside, and the headlamps winked companionably on either side of the glass windshield.

"Theobald's Road please, Harpur Street."

"Right-o!" the cabbie sang out; and as the hansom jerked into motion Ned settled back contentedly in his seat to watch the yellow gaslamps flickering past and listen to the soothing jingle of the cab bells.

He had rather changed his mind about London since he started boarding with Simmie. The stroll down from the College to Harpur Street, once so drab and depressing, was now he discovered positively brimming with the stuff of life. Everyone seemed so much more cheerful and good natured than they'd been before. The horses were somehow glossier and better-fed than he thought. The yards and gardens and stables along the way were full of unexpected interest. And in Harpur Street itself there was a house waiting and a woman in it who made him feel at home.

Tonight after supper there'd be cocoa by the fire – with Simmie sitting in the pool of light under the gas chandelier, sewing and chatting away in the wonderful chaotic cocoon of her parlour. And when she looked up at him and smiled, as she would often, he'd see in her face the girl she'd once been. When she leant forward to poke at the fire, he'd catch the scent of lavender water – and he'd be irreverently aware of the curve of her back and the tautness of her dress against her thigh – and the movements of her breasts within their soft cage of cotton and lace. In the morning when he woke, it would be Sunday. There'd be no whistling or scraping of shovels from the mews beneath his window. The other chaps would be home for the weekend, and it would be quiet in the house. He'd breakfast alone and scan the newspaper, waiting for Simmie to emerge in her Sunday finery, all dressed up for church. And then he'd settle down again to read it properly from cover to cover, while he waited for her to return and unpin her hat and sit down with him to Sunday roast.

It seemed to Ned now, cabbing it to Harpur Street, that he'd known Simmie all his life. Sometimes he even succeeded in forgetting Robert Llewellen and his calling card altogether. In one of her more forthcoming moments Gladys had let it slip that her mistress had inherited the house in Harpur Street from Mr Llewellen's mother, an old Frenchwoman to whom she'd acted as Lady Companion. And Ned had entertained a brief unpleasant vision of the philandering married son creaking up the back stairs to Simmie's bedroom – before deciding that it was really all too long ago to be worth worrying about. He knew for a fact that Llewellen had deliberately avoided Simmie on his last trip to London – and now he was safely out of the way in South America, in any case.

'And best left well alone – best forgotten,' Ned thought, nodding solemnly in time with the high swinging motion of the cab, and burping up an evocative aftertaste of Acton Pale Ale.

"I'll be orf then, Mum," said Gladys, hovering in the parlour doorway. "I've laid aht a cold supper for yer in the dinin' room - an' fer 'is nibs, if 'e should be so good as to show 'is nose. So's I'll be back first thing ter git yer breakfast, if that suits?"

"Oh yes, thank you so much, Gladys, that'll do splendidly. I do hope you enjoy yourself."

Gladys had special bookings to see George Robey at the Oxford. And as the niece she was going with lived only a few steps from the theatre across the Tottenham Court Road, she'd been given special leave to stop over for the night with her.

"Thank yer, Mum. I'll be sayin' goodnight then." But Gladys wavered. "You'll be all right alone wiv 'im I 'spose?" she added casually, jerking her bonnet towards the empty armchair.

"Of course I shall! Why Gladys, what on earth do you think could happen?"

"Well if you don't know, Mum, I'm sure it ain't fer me to tell yer. All I will say is they're all tarred wiv the same brush, men – even if they do look like bloomin' angels! I won't say no more, but I've seen the way that one gawps at yer, Mum, don't think I 'aven't!"

"Oh come, Gladys! You're being absurd, you know you are! In the first place I'm quite old enough to be his mother. And in the second – well honestly, can you see our Mr Ashby hurling himself impetuously at my feet?!"

"It ain't yer feet I'm worried abaht!" Gladys said darkly – then took herself off sharpish. Because if there was one thing she couldn't abide in this life, it was being laughed at.

And Simmie was still laughing to herself, helplessly, when the front door closed behind her. 'Really!' she thought, 'what would I do without Gladys and her street philosophies to brighten my lonely days?'

She prodded unconsciously and quite ineffectually at some loose wisps of hair that had escaped from her bun, and took up another piece of mending from the basket beside her chair. It was a shirt of Ned's, with two of the buttons smashed by the laundry mangle. As she removed the casualties and searched for a good match in her button-box. Simmie awarded the garment a look of quiet satisfaction. The old lady's death had left such a vacuum in her life, more than she sometimes realized, and it was so pleasant to be needed again. She wasn't bound to sew for her boarders, but she liked to see their clothes in her mending; and she cherished the feeling that these hulking young men were dependent on her in some way – for their appearance as well as their board and their lodging. It made her feel almost as if they were her own, her own sons.

It had been simple, far simpler than she expected, to have her name added to the official Register of Boarding Residences for college students. And what a joy they were to have! They were all of them such sweet things in their different ways – Ned Ashby in particular. There was always something very touching about the transition from youth to manhood; and Ned's especial vulnerability was written all over his handsome face. He was without a mother, as she had been at his age, and he needed someone like her to boost him and to give him confidence.

On an impulse Simmie lifted Ned's shirt to her face and buried her nose in the clean whiteness of it. But it smelt only of starch and linen – and as she acknowledged her own disappointment, she smiled wryly.

'Which is what comes of letting Gladys put ridiculous ideas into your head,' she admonished herself, returning the shirt to her lap and smoothing it out flat again. 'You're far too old for that kind of nonsense, Simmie, and you know it!'

But of course it had been too late. It always was by the time she caught herself at it. The thing she'd unconsciously sought was the faint tang of male sweat. And she realized with a pang that the image that suggested it had been that of another white shirt, Robert's, lying in a bar of sunlight on the floor of a hotel bedroom. She'd be unwise, so unwise to go over all that again now. But then wasn't it rather nice to be unwise sometimes, she thought, suddenly reckless, when one was all alone, with nobody to witness one's foolishness.

"You are wicked!" she said aloud, mechanically threading the first button into place as the hidden spring of memories within her rose and overflowed.

It was so easy to remember, even now, how young and carefree she'd felt that afternoon as she watched Robert striding up towards her through the park, large as life and twice as natural in a pale grey summer suit and panama hat.

"Mamma has taken the carriage out on the razzle," he called to her, "and I've been left with poor old shanks' mare!"

It was midsummer and hot. The sky was a vast blue playground for the swifts – rising high, sweeping low, swooping and turning with sheer joy. There'd been enough breeze for someone to fly a kite, and as Simmie and Robert strolled down towards the Pen Ponds, the grass swirled around them in a great sea of pink seedheads and sorrel plumes, and nodding dog daisies. Kit had been in his glory, bouncing and bounding through the grass to retrieve the sticks that she'd thrown for him; and Robert stooped to gather a bunch of daisies for her along the way. She held his cane for him and his hat, and in the other hand a discarded silk parasol of Isobel's. And as she watched him, bareheaded in the sunlight, she had known that at last she was in love.

In the months since Robert first stopped his carriage to apologise for splashing her dress, they had met often in the park – and there had been no bowing or smiling and turning away. So long as he was in town he visited his mother in Ham regularly each week; and whenever the weather permitted, Simmie and Kit were there to intercept him on his return journey. At first she had gone to elaborate lengths to pretend that they met by chance, stationing herself in a different position each time along the carriage drive. But their meetings brought such colour into her life that she soon abandoned the pretence to welcome him as a friend.

She could tell him little of her own life, there was so little to tell. But he had spoken to her openly of his wife and his children. His profession had taken him to so many different parts of the world. And he enthralled her with the tales of his adventures abroad – in France and in Portugal, quarrying lime in Canada and exploring ancient Inca silver mines in Peru. Then, as the park traffic lessened with the winter months, she had consented to ride with him in his mother's victoria. He had twice taken her to tea with him in a discreet Kingston teashop, pointing out Mamma's grand house on Ham Common as they passed by. And time after time he stepped down from the carriage to walk with her through the wet leaves of the park, while the old coachman brought the horses on behind. All week, every week, she walked Kit to allay Isobel's suspicions. But she counted the days to the only day that counted – the day when she'd see Robert.

For all of the short time that she was with him, she was aware of his dark eyes on her face and on her body – of the current of unexpressed excitement that passed between them; and the fact that she could never quite tell what he was thinking only added to his attraction. Already she had broken the rules of her upbringing and her society, simply by being with him alone. There was more to come too, she knew it. It was impossible to feel the way she did without some sort of a climax or termination. It couldn't just peter out – it wasn't that kind of sensation at all!

And now as she sat beside him in the grass above the Pen Ponds, he told her that the moment had come. He'd been lying on his elbow, splitting the ribbed stems of her flowers with his pocket knife and carefully threading them into an outsize daisy chain.

"I'm sailing on the *Arcadia* next week for Colombo and Singapore," he said. And the thrust was so quick and so sure that she'd felt no pain – only a kind of numbness.

"How long will you be away?" she asked, conscious as ever of the dark shades of his eyes, flickering, searching her own.

"A year, two years – maybe longer. I'm to report on the North Borneo Trading Company holdings in Labuan, and I may go on to take a squint at Australia. If the place is all it's cracked up to be, there could well be some opportunities out there for me in iron or coal."

"To settle you mean – to stay for ever?"

"Forever is a long time for someone like me, Simmie!" His tone was sardonic. "But I've heard there are worse places to bring up a family, and we might give it a try if I can find something that interests me."

Then she felt it, the sharpness of the pain – and turned to Robert with all her soul in her face. It was the look that he'd been waiting for – that any man would wait for; and his words were the words that any man might use to seduce a girl like Simmie.

"We still have today," he said, gently looping the daisy chain around her neck and tucking a superfluous flower into the ribbon of her straw hat. "I want you very much, my dear, you know that, don't you? And you want me too – I can see that you do." His voice was deeper, thicker, more persuasive than she'd ever heard it. "So why not come with me now, Simmie – why not?"

The chain of flowers felt strangely heavy across her breasts. And the direct words that he used had cut through every protective nicety and convention that she knew.

"Let me give you something that you'll remember, that we'll both remember, Simmie, for as long as we live. Whatever else happens, I can promise you that at least."

There'd been a pleading, naked need in his eyes that she was unable to deny. All her life Simmie had responded automatically to the needs of others. And where Robert's need coincided so completely with her own, there was no choice for her to make. He was irresistible. If he'd touched her then she'd have melted. She'd have lain back in the grass like an animal, regardless of anything. But as it was she simply stood when he stood and walked when he walked, up the grassy hill to the Richmond Gate and the big gothic hotel that overlooked the river.

He was brisk, almost businesslike the way he went about it; and she didn't doubt that he'd trodden this path before, or one very like it. Outside the hotel he paid a raggletail urchin to mind the dog, with the promise of double when they returned for him. And although she felt uneasy about the arrangement, Simmie had been powerless to resist it. All her will had gone, and she must needs do as she was bidden. While Robert disappeared into the hotel, she waited limply outside. With one hand, incredibly slowly, she broke the daisy chain around her neck and dropped it to hang from the spikes of the hotel railing. She had quite forgotten the single flower in her hatband; and it was only much later, when she and Kit reached home, that she discovered it.

Simmie looked up from her mending and across to the bureau by the parlour window. In the second drawer lay her journal for 1890. And she smiled at the memory of herself completing the entry for that particular day – scribbling behind her arm in case Isobel should come in – the little daisy from her hat lying wilting on the blotter beside her.

The simple action of walking through the door of the hotel on Robert's arm, had been like passing through a wall of flame for Simmie. None of the heroines she'd read about had ever crossed this line, even in the most sensational novels. She walked mechanically into that echoing marble vestibule, looking neither to right nor to left but feeling the eyes of everyone on her. This was where dreams stopped and reality began. Outside in the street she'd shed the moral principles that had armoured her all her life, and now she was exposed. She was about to commit a mortal sin – worse, a social error. At twenty-three she had become an Abandoned Woman!

But as Robert closed the bedroom door behind her, he shut out the world for her too, and with it all sense of humiliation. She could think of nothing now but Robert himself, and her own violently trembling body. She stood with her back to him in the open window, groping for her hatpins. In the sunlight below she could see the shining curve of the river, and all the little rowing boats gay with coloured parasols. She saw them, but she ignored them. She opened her mouth to describe the scene, but she said nothing. She was listening for his movement behind her.

By the time it came, she was scarcely breathing. She had got the girl to lace her tighter than usual that day, and as his hands closed over her shoulders she really thought she was going to faint. She found herself panting suddenly, gasping for air – and when she felt the pressure of his body behind her, she leant back to it and closed her eyes – helpless, sinking, dying of love – or possibly something stronger. In a while his hands had been restless, and then busy; and almost before she understood what he was doing, he had unhooked the last of her back-fastenings and pulled her bodice forward over her shoulders. It was for her to free herself of the sleeves and the camisole, to step out of the skirt, the petticoat and the drawers – moving like a hypnotic beneath his gaze. But he wouldn't release her from her tight stays – not yet.

His coat was already on the door. Now he stood before her in the band of light that fell from the window, and unbuttoned his waistcoat. The sun gleamed bronze on his hair as he stooped to his boots and his stockings. But when he straightened to his necktie and studs she caught the look in his eyes – black, opaque, intensely self-absorbed – commanding her to watch him, as first the shirt and then the narrow breeches fell to the floor.

He had worn nothing beneath. And the sight of Robert Llewellen's naked body had shaken Simmie as nothing had shaken her, before or since. He was muscular and olive-toned, primitively rampant – smooth as silk. As he moved around and beneath her, to the lacings and suspenders and the last flimsy chemise – she scented the musky, masculine odour of him. She saw the swell of his thighs as he crouched and the fine black hairs between his shoulder blades.

And when she felt the brush of his moustache on her skin, Simmie had given herself to him unrestrainedly – wanting, longing to be conquered – to be bruised, to be ripped and hurt – desperate to drown herself in the depths of those ruthless black eyes.

That afternoon in Richmond, in the sunlight – on the floor and on the bed, he had brought her all the dissolution she craved, and more. He promised her a day that she'd remember as long as she lived. And even now, more than fourteen years later, there was hardly a gasp or a tremor of it that she could not recall. Sitting with her mending in her cosy Harpur Street parlour she thought shamelessly of the things that he'd done to her, that she had done for him – unconsciously arching her back at the memory, squirming and spreading herself in the seat of her button-back armchair.

"Anyone home?"

At the first sound of Ned's voice Simmie's guilty knees sprang together to send the mending flying from her lap.

"Ned – dear!" she gasped, with one hand on her heart. "Where on earth did you spring from? My goodness you gave me a start!"

He strolled in then in his overcoat and comforter, looking clean and wholesome and more than a little pink around the gills.

"I got away early," he said simply, "thought I'd come in for a bite and a bit of a chat." And he smiled that diffident, endearing smile of his as he weaved unsteadily towards her through the labyrinth of her furniture.

She smiled too with her head on the satin chair back, suddenly exhausted. As he reached her he brushed her cheek with his hand. It was a spontaneous gesture that on any other night might have passed without repercussions. But that night, at that moment, it touched Simmie in her loneliest most sensitive spot. Without thinking she caught his hand with her own, and turned her head to kiss the damp hollow of his palm. Then, shamingly, she began to cry.

Later, much later, Simmie turned up the lamp in her bedroom and returned to her mirror to do battle with the crushed bird's nest of her hair. Behind her on the bed, Ned sprawled like a great slain ox – so different to Robert, and yet so much the same. He had tried very hard to be slow and gentle, poor boy, and failed so utterly.

"Thank you."

Robert had never said it, not once; although God knows she had given him more of herself – a great deal more. And as she looked at Ned's reflection in the soft gaslight, Simmie felt a tenderness for him that she had never felt for the man she loved.

Chapter Six

It was a perfect jewel of a morning, a Sunday in the early spring of 1905. The sun was shining as if it had never heard of winter. The church bells were ringing, the birds were singing their hearts out; and in the tree-lined squares and in all the little city gardens the forsythia was in brilliant saffron bloom. Meriel Llewellen was thrilled to the marrow with all of it, with everything. With London in the sunshine and England in the spring – and most of all with her new walking costume, which was so obviously, so absolutely utterly suitable for both.

Practically everything that had happened in the past months had thrilled Meriel to the marrow – starting with the quay at Penco and their reunion with Da, as dashing and adorable as ever despite his new responsibilities. In Chile he was 'El Administador'; and as his daughter, Meriel had enjoyed the flattering respect of any number of attractive Chileans. She had begun to learn Spanish and ridden daily down the long sand beaches of Coronel. Until in December, on the recommendation of an unstable Santiago Government, Da had been offered two thousand pounds and the family's fare home to resign his appointment to a native-born Chilean. And that too had been a thrill. For now that she was eighteen and a woman of the world, Meriel felt differently about England. Now the prospect of London, with money to burn, seemed almost too good to be true!

Da had accepted the Schneider Company's offer, as she'd known he would, with a shrug of unconcern. "There are more fish in the sea," he said prosaically, "than ever came out of it." And of course Harriet had been beside herself with joy – until the steamer actually cast off into deep water.

For the rest of them, though, the voyage home had been splendid. In the Straits of Magellan they'd seen two canoes of Fuegian Indians – primitive, ferocious and rather fascinatingly naked. In Monte Video there'd been another unscheduled revolution. In Rio Meriel had seconded the world's opinion of the harbour as the loveliest anywhere, and purchased a scarlet Macaw parrot to fill her uncle's house in Pimlico with Portugese obscenities.

Now London itself! While Da scoured the City for the finance for some new overseas adventure, she and Vicky bullied their Aunt Alice into recommending them a good dressmaker. On the Atlantic crossing to Lisbon Vicky had somehow contrived to draw the eye of a chinless but affable and exceedingly well-heeled young man by the name of Reginald Baxter. And although Meriel had immediately pegged him as a drongo-of-the-first-water, she was alive to the opportunities that a connection such as his could create for her. Why, with the right dress on her back she could be the match of any insipid English debutante – of that she was quite sure. Besides, who could tell but that her beautiful Carstairs might not be lurking amongst Reggie's chinless friends, just waiting for her to sweep him off his feet!

The smart walking rig-out, her very first, was a huge success. It was a fetching shade of Violette de Parme, a hue that was all the go just now, so the dressmaker said and frightfully well suited, Meriel thought, to her own strong colouring. It had a high wired collar and belled sleeves. The bodice was blouse shaped, dipped in the front, with two rows of swinging violet fringes. There was a wide belt with a silver buckle, an elegant silk parasol, and a huge hat trimmed with masses of artificial violets and pleated silk bows. It really was the last possible word, everybody said so – an outfit to startle and kill! And Meriel simply couldn't wait to try it out on the world and his wife. That morning she and Gareth had ridden the length of Oxford Street in splendid prominence on the top of a bus; and she'd insisted on alighting at Coptic Street, to step out in style past the porticoes of the British Museum.

"Just to make sure it really is open on Sunday afternoons," she explained, hopping niftily off the tailboard in her new elastic-sided boots. "No good slogging all the way back again if it isn't!"

Not that Meriel imagined for a moment that Da could be wrong about such a thing. It was just that she couldn't sit still a moment longer. She had to be actually *doing* something, and had already had Garry in fits of laughter with her imitation of a fashionable English lady on esplanade – pushing out her bottom and wielding her parasol with devastating effect. Yes indeed, she intended to be noticed by as many people as possible on her way to Harpur Street and Miss Sims!

A brass band was playing in Southampton Row, and Meriel kicked up the violet flounces of her skirt in time with the music. She couldn't resist it.

'Such a stylish girl you see,
Just out in Society,
Everything I ought to be -
Ta-ra-ra-boom-de-ay!'

Never forward, never bold,
Just the very thing I'm told
That in your arms you'd like to hold -
Ta-ra-ra-boom-de-ay!'

"What do you think she'll be like, Garry, Grandmère's companion? Fat and jolly? Or skinny, with pince-nez and a flat chest?"

Ned was sitting in the little lime-washed yard at the back of Simmie's house. Later on in the summer it would become a kind of garden. She'd move her pelargoniums out here, and the jasmine on the trellis would fill the dark little downstairs hall with its perfume. For the present, though, it was just a place to sit quietly in the sun with his newspaper, and to relax.

He stretched lazily on his chair and rested his feet one over the other on the bench opposite. It was such a lovely day, 'Blackthorn hatchin' wather', that's what they'd call it down in Sussex. Gladys had propped the street door open to give the house an airing, and from somewhere outside he could just catch the brassy echoes of an itinerant German band. Otherwise all was peace. Matthew Starnes was away home as usual; and Andy, the other lodger, was still upstairs in his room sleeping off Saturday night. The women were at Matins, Gussie was snoring in his basket beside the range. To all intents and purposes Ned had the house to himself.

He closed his eyes and gave himself up to the sun. In a minute the church bells would start up again. Then his peace would be broken, beautifully. He'd hear Gladys' thudding footfalls on the kitchen stairs and fat little Gussie sounding the alarm – there'd be a breath of lavender perfume – and he'd look up into Simmie's gentle, smiling face as she raised her hands to her hat. Reassurance, security, and a feeling that took him right back to his childhood – to Cook in the big kitchen at The Bury and the smooth maternal scarps of the Sussex downs.

"This is it then, number nineteen!"

"But look here, Meri, we can't just waltz in," Gareth protested, as his sister's purposeful violet rear disappeared through the open door.

"Rot! It's meant to be a surprise, isn't it? So let's surprise her! Besides, impromptu calls are the coming thing, everybody says so."

A pair of substantial grey flannel legs were visible through a doorway at the end of a narrow hall. Meriel bore down on them like Nemesis. Their owner was asleep, it seemed, beneath an open copy of the *Sunday Times*. So she cleared her throat. A dog began to bark from somewhere down below, but the newspaper remained motionless.

'Lazy beast!' she thought, crossing the yard on a final flourish of the distant band music and twitching the newspaper impatiently from the man's face.

Ta-ra-ra-boom-de-ay!

The sun gleamed triumphantly on golden hair, on an incised, shaven upper lip and on the raised angle of a gloriously square chin: the face of her dreams, the hero of every *Girls' Realm* romance she'd ever read. He was smiling broadly too, as if he was expecting her, and his eyes when he opened them were too utterly blue for words.

'My godfathers, it's him!' Meriel was speechless with admiration and astonishment. But then, following hard on the shock of recognition, came a novel kind of fear. 'Careful,' she thought, 'careful now, Meri, don't muff it for God's sake.'

Ned felt confused and rather foolish. Squinting as he was into the sun, it took him a second or two too long to realize that there were strangers in the house. He was expecting Simmie not this over-dressed and forward young woman in mauve.

"Oh, ah – can I help you?" he said belatedly, struggling to his feet and folding his newspaper – and at the same time wondering why the devil people couldn't leave you alone at weekends. "Er, did you want to see Miss Sims?"

There was another uncomfortably over-long silence, while the girl continued to stare hard at him from beneath her preposterous hat. Then the freckled beanpole of a boy chipped in from behind her shoulder.

"Rather," he said cheerfully, "is she at home?"

"She's still out at church, I'm afraid. But if you'd care to step up and wait in the parlour, I shouldn't think she'll be very long."

His newspaper had somehow managed to crumple itself into a kind of fat parcel, and he hastily thrust it away behind his chair. She really did have extraordinarily uncomfortable eyes, that girl. They quite put him out of countenance. As he led the way upstairs he felt, stupidly, as if his hands had suddenly grown to twice their normal size, and his shoes squeaked quite horribly in a way he'd never noticed before.

"Well, she won't be long," he said as soon as he got them safely in through the door. "I'll tell her you're waiting when she gets in."

"But you're not going?" The girl's voice was surprisingly loud and conclusive. "I mean, won't you at least introduce yourself?" she amended, looking down demurely at the carpet.

"Oh yes I'm sorry – my name's Edwin Ashby. I'm, er – one of Miss Sims' boarders from University College."

'Edwin Ash-by,' Meriel thought to herself slowly. 'Mrs Edwin Ashby . . . Meriel Ashby . . .' It sounded too good to be true!

"How-do, I'm Gareth Llewellen," Garry was saying, for all the world as if nothing unusual had happened, "and this is my sister Meriel. Our grandmother used to live here, you know, in this house. Miss Sims was her companion for donkeys' years."

Meriel felt almost nervous as she stepped up to take the young man's hand. It was large and strong and rather moist – and damn and blast gloves! But when she looked up at him there was an awkward, restive look in his handsome face that was immensely reassuring. "But I thought you were in Australia," he said in that thrillingly husky English voice of his, "or South America?"

And then Meriel was back on familiar ground. Why of course, she'd tell him about her childhood in Queensland – of droughts and tarantulas and sleeping rough under the stars. Of how she'd crossed the Pacific Ocean under sail. When he'd heard it all he would see her quite differently; he'd have to, of course he would! And he'd smile the wide, lazy smile again that had so enchanted her when she first lifted the newspaper from his face. But just as she was about to speak, an uninvited spectre took substance in Meriel's mind, a perfectly horrid image of Captain McIntyre laughing at her for her obviousness on the starlit fo'c'sle of the *Catriona*. She caught herself in the bare nick of time.

"Why yes," she declared as coolly as she knew how, reluctantly releasing his hand, "how very clever of you to know, Mr Ashby. Indeed we have resided for some years in Australia, in the State of Queensland, and have but recently returned from the Republic of Chile. My father held the post of Senior Administrator, you understand, to a very large coal mining enterprise out there." She twirled her parasol handle as she spoke, as languidly as any bored English socialite.

Simmie had returned from church to find poor Ned caught in a web of relentlessly polite conversation. The change in Meriel Llewellen from the little girl in the park with the birthday and the tam-o'-shanter hat had quite taken her breath away – and Gareth of course was a dear. How lovely, she told herself, how splendid to find them here so unexpectedly in her little upstairs parlour!

Yet all the time she was fussing around them, telling them of their grandmother, trying to draw Ned in, working to set everyone at their ease, another insistent phrase kept drumming through her mind: 'He's back – back at last. Robert's back in town!'

They stayed to lunch, she insisted. Meriel had actually come prepared with an absurd little alfresco picnic for them in a paper bag. But Simmie refused to consider the idea of the girl's beautiful new ensemble on a grubby park bench. Besides, she said, she wanted to hear all about the family.

Gladys had complained, naturally. But despite her outspoken observations on the subject of visitors in the forenoon, she had been persuaded to see her way to stretching the roast mutton with plenty of extra onion sauce. And at one o'clock they all sat down to a very passable luncheon, with a clean white cloth and mitred napkins – and without any further hints of mutiny from below stairs. Andy had emerged by then, refreshed and affable, and patently taken with Robert's daughter. The meal developed into a voluble affair in which he and young Gareth battled to talk each other down, while Meriel monopolized the unfortunate Ned with her own excruciating line in cross-talk.

"Are your people in London, Mr Ashby? . . . Might I trouble you for the salt if you please, Mr Ashby? . . . Shall you be going to Ascot this season do you think? . . . Now tell me, Mr Ashby, what is your frank opinion of the aero-plane? . . . "

It amused Simmie to watch them, these young people, flexing

their social muscles. Moreover, by the time Gladys crashed the coffee down onto the chiffonier, she had managed to extract from them most of the information she needed. The Llewellens were putting up at Robert's brother's house in Pimlico, she gathered, at least for the time being. Today Meriel's father had taken his wife and elder daughter on the underground railway to visit relatives in Kew, entirely unaware, it seemed, of her nefarious designs on Harpur Street. And tomorrow, when he heard where Meriel and Gareth had been? Why then perhaps Robert would be the one to come knocking on her door!

Simmie should certainly have known better, but she never seemed to learn. It was exactly the same as on Robert's previous visit to London after his mother's death almost three years ago, and before he'd sailed again for Chile. From the Sunday of the young Llewellens' excursion to Harpur Street she once again began to take extra pains with her appearance; and every morning as she dressed she asked herself, just as before, if today was to be the day that Robert Llewellen would call.

Except that it wasn't quite the same, because this time there was Ned, and a new kind of moral dilemma to face. Simmie's own grasp of morals had been warped out of recognition in the white-heat of that afternoon in Richmond, she admitted it frankly. She could never recapture the clear concepts of virtue and sin that she'd acquired at her nurse's Victorian knee. And if she was honest with herself she must also admit that the adventure with Ned had meant less to her, a great deal less, than it had to him.

She had never really wanted him for herself – not that first time after the rugby match, nor later when he'd come to her straight from the laboratory still smelling of formaline, with that familiar pleading expression in his blue eyes. For all his sweetness he never stirred her as Robert had. But the giving had brought its own pleasure, because that was the way she was made. The mother in her had been touched by his youth, the loneliness in her responding to his need. She even felt a flutter of ridiculous schoolgirl excitement at the risk of discovery *in flagrante delicto* by a scandalized Gladys. And somehow it had all come together to make her feel real – a woman again.

The dilemma came later with Meriel and Gareth Llewellen,

and the disturbing news that their father was with them in London, no more than two miles from her own front door. And now Simmie found herself seriously worried that she had been wrong, morally wrong, to allow a boy like Ned to comfort her loneliness - dominated as she still was by her memories of another man?

Yes, Simmie – wrong, wrong! ! The answer had come to her dramatically in letters of fire. She had betrayed the trust placed in her by the university, and by Ned's own family. She was sure of it, absolutely, on the day that his grandmother announced her intention of visiting Ned's landlady in Harpur Street.

Margaret Ashby was making her usual end-of-term trip up to town to collect her grand-daughter from boarding school in Ealing, to shop, to pay a call or two and to visit her accountant in Chancery Lane. On this occasion a detour would be in order, she decided, to view her grandson's new lodging house. Her letter to Ned on the subject had been quite specific – and enclosed a personal note for his landlady in an uncompromising black hand.

'My dear Miss Sims,

I have heard a great deal about you from Edwin. Assuredly we must meet.

If it is convenient my grand-daughter and I will be pleased to call on you at 4 p.m. this Friday. If not, you may contact me on Thursday night at Brown's Hotel, Albemarle Street.

Sincerely,

M. L. Ashby'

She had not added that she'd be expecting Miss Sims' furnishings, linen and silver all to be in immaculate and pristine order. But Simmie certainly acted as if she had – working herself to a standstill and Gladys to within an inch of formal notice in an orgy of conscience-stricken exertion. It was a little late in the day to feel guilty, she realized that. A little ridiculous too under the circumstances. But there'd been a definite note of offended respectability in Mrs Ashby's letter, she was sure of it.

"My grandmother doesn't know, Simmie. I haven't told her, honestly."

But Simmie wasn't to be reassured. "My dear, she'd only

have to *look* at you to know," she cried. "It's written all over you, Ned! And now she's all agog, you see, to discover what kind of a loose-living household you've landed yourself in!"

It was all so very unlike her, and Ned hated it – Simmie in a tizwuz, Gladys in a stamping rage, the parlour smothered in antimacassars and reeking of furniture polish, and Gran breezing in like Dr Livingstone to bring enlightenment to Harpur Street – and to spoil everything.

"Feymales complicate, sure as fate!" Danny Goodworth had imparted that little bit of wisdom years ago, one night during lambing. He should know too; for despite the closeness of their ages Ned knew for sure that Dan had fathered more than one chance-born child on the gypsy girls of Crowlink, while he himself was still dreaming of Gaiety Girls in his bachelor dormitory at Lancing.

They'd all be lambing now, Bat and Dan and Jemmy Vine – quietly moving through the deep litter of the dig yard, getting on with the business in hand. And in all their faces, even in young Jem's, there'd be a remote kind of patience that you never saw in London. It was to do with livestock and regeneration and the timelessness of the chalk lands – a constant seasonal rhythm of ramming and lambing, shearing and sheep sales that took no reckoning of petty human problems.

Ned stood at Simmie's parlour window looking down into the bleak little street, waiting for the growler that would trundle Gran and Helen and their luggage to the front steps. He could hear a piano-organ in Theobald's Road, and on the corner of Harpur Street a flower seller was stridently advertising her merchandise: "Flahs – real flahs! All a-bloomin' and a-growin'! Real flahs!"

Behind him Simmie was humming to herself while she polished, a high tuneless little hum of bravado, and Ned wished himself to the world's end – or better still, away to the important, uncomplicated work of The Bury lambing folds.

Chapter Seven

"Better'n four hundred lambs so far, Ned, d'ye hear me – and from less than three hundred ol' muttons!" Margaret Ashby bellowed it up the stairs the moment she caught sight of her grandson's face at the top; and she waved a casual paw at him before bringing the weight of her attention to bear on the luggage.

"Not on the step, you lout! In here, in the hall where I can see it, *if* you please! And exactly where do you think your hold-all is, Helen? Confound it, girl, you've got arms haven't you? It isn't going to trot in on its own like a dear little dog, you know!"

She took charge of the house as a matter of course as soon as she entered it, dispensing parcels, walking sticks and outer garments with equal vigour, and automatically pitching her voice to the upper landing. It was a formidably deep voice for a woman and very little of its natural force was lost on Simmie, nervously waiting upstairs to receive her.

"Don't worry, Simmie," Ned had said bracingly as the cab pulled up, "her bark's far worse than her bite." But he'd omitted to warn her quite how terrifying the bark was going to be; and by the time Gladys showed Mrs Ashby into the parlour she'd fully imagined a Wagnerian Brünhilde of a woman, complete with horns and solid brass bosom.

The person who entered was in fact more like a Mrs Noah than a Valkyrie – short, blunt-featured, rigidly upright – eccentrically clad in heliotrope figured silk with an unsuitable biscuit-coloured homburg hat. And at close range the voice was more like a foghorn than ever.

"Margaret Ashby," she boomed before Gladys could forestall her. "You're Miss Sims, quite clearly, and this little mawk behind me is my grand-daughter Helen. Say how d'ye do, Helen."

"How do you do," Simmie repeated, courageously extending her hand. "I've been so much looking forward to meeting you."

"Now *that* I find hard to believe!" Mrs Ashby forced her way through to Simmie's own little button-back chair, seated herself heavily in it and motioned graciously for the others to join her. "And I'll thank you to stop 'Oh Granning' me, Helen, and to find yerself a perch somewhere," she said severely. "I've never been afraid to speak my mind as well you know – and I'm quite sure that Miss Sims here wouldn't want me to start at my age."

"Oh no, no indeed." On balance, Simmie thought she might have preferred Brünhilde. She did feel sorry for the wretched little grand-daughter, though. Helen Ashby was a shapeless creature, even by schoolgirl standards, with round shoulders and thick ankles, and a painfully obvious desire to efface herself from the adult world.

'Poor little thing,' Simmie thought compassionately, remembering the agonies of her own girlhood. 'I wonder if there's anything I could do to make her feel less of a lump?' "How about some tea?" she said aloud. "I always think a nice cup of tea is such a help in getting to know one another. Don't you agree?"

"No I don't, since you ask," Mrs Ashby replied remorselessly. "But I'll grant you that it's a middlin' good thirst quencher. And while we're waitin' for the kettle, Ned, you can take Helen up to see your room."

"Oh I don't know that she'd find it awfully thrilling, Grannie. It's only full of old textbooks and whatnot, you know."

"Kindly do as you're told, young man." The measured, quieter tone was if anything even more daunting. "Miss Sims and I would like to have a little chat on our own, if you don't mind, without the two of you garking at us like a pair of mooncalves. And you needn't worry, boy," she added gruffly, "I'm not goin' to eat your precious landlady – she's quite safe with me!"

But she smiled almost indulgently as the door closed behind him, nonetheless. "Great grummut! He thinks I'm goin' to get waxy and demand that you put your bed out of bounds to him, Miss Sims," she said. "An open book to me that boy – always has been!" Her eyes as she raised them to Simmie's in the silence that followed, were a clear, pale blue – paler, harder and altogether more penetrating than her grandson's.

"Come now, Miss Sims, there's no need to beat the devil round the gooseberry bush. You and I are both women of the world, I hope. We both know that a healthy young fellow like Edwin is bound to form liaisons of one kind or another. And far better with a woman of your type than with some undernourished drazel who'd take his money, and very likely give him a dose of the French gout in the bargain. Not a particle of sense in that, I'd say!"

'But how can she be so sure,' Simmie thought from the depths of her humiliation, 'how can anyone be so sure of their own judgement that they're prepared to risk such a terrible mistake?'

Mrs Ashby had been quite sure, though. That was only too obvious from the way her emphatic, resonant voice continued. "No, Miss Sims – dear me no. I can assure you that it takes more than a casual peccadillo to shock me! Just so long as nothing serious comes of it," Ned's grandmother allowed her inflexible blue gaze to rest for a moment on Simmie's face. "I am firm on the point, you understand?"

Simmie understood. And with understanding came a renewed sense of shame. She saw herself that afternoon as this old tartar saw her – as a harmless, middle-aged woman making a fool of herself over a boy little more than half her age. She felt an insane desire to spring up and run out of the room, to overturn the tea-table or pull down the mantelboard like Ned. But then of course, harmless middle-aged women simply don't do such things. So there was nothing for it but to incline her head with the best grace she could, and to ring for the tea.

In the weeks following Mrs Ashby's visit Simmie found herself distinctly disenchanted with the male sex; grateful to the Easter holidays for removing Ned and the other lodgers from Harpur Street, even grateful to Robert Llewellen for failing to appear after all on her doorstep.

Robert's children, on the other hand, were frequent and welcome visitors to her house since that first spring Sunday when she personally introduced them to the treasures of the British

Museum. Meriel in particular had proved an enchanting companion. Never more than skin deep, the girl's awkward social graces had vanished in Ned's absence. And without them she revealed herself as so confident, so alive and avid for new experience that it was virtually impossible to feel downhearted in her company.

It was rather a success that expedition to the British Museum, and Meriel had come back for more. A few days later she spun up to Simmie's front door with hoots of laughter on a spanking new Premier ladies' free-wheel bicycle, insisting then and there that Simmie should unearth her own battered Raleigh, and accompany her on a voyage of discovery to the Zoological Gardens in Regent's Park.

"But I haven't ridden it in years," Simmie wailed in genuine trepidation. "And I'm such a fool about traffic, dear, I'm simply bound to fall off!"

"No you won't." Meriel was already pumping up the front tyre for her. "Just pedal away for dear life as I do, and you'll get along famously, you'll see."

On the whole Simmie did too. She wobbled along behind Meriel, in and out of the traffic across the length and breadth of the city - from the Tower of London to the Kensington museums, from Hampstead Heath to the Crystal Palace – and she didn't fall off, not once! Her legs ached, admittedly, and her corsets were frequently agony. But she'd gladly have suffered worse for the pleasure of watching Meriel Llewellen discover London.

Meriel was delighted with the fine buildings and the parks, appalled by the foetid zoo and the black mud of the Thames and the stink of the city tanneries. She was in transports over the Art Nouveau furniture at Heal's and the underclothes at D. H. Evans and the Cinematograph in the Strand. She loathed the sooty hovels of Lambeth and Southwark, laughed uproariously at the bad horsemanship and precarious top hats on Rotten Row, and hotly pursued a coal dray to threaten the drayman with a taste of his own free-handed whip.

Watching her getting to grips with the metropolis, seizing her experiences with both hands, Simmie was reminded after all and more than once of the little girl in Richmond Park all those years ago, reaching out so boldly for Robert's shiny top hat. It no longer worried her to think of Meriel returning to her father each evening, a living link between them. All that was over now, she was sure of it, over and done with on the day that Ned's grandmother had confronted her with her own folly.

The problem of Ned remained. Of course she knew that his return to London for the new term would demand some kind of a formal statement from her, and at the first opportunity she bravely beckoned him into her parlour, closed the door and turned to face him with the worst. She would come straight to the point, as firm and forthright as Mrs Ashby herself. It was the only way. But then of course he had to go and smile that angelic smile of his and make the whole thing a hundred times harder.

"Ned – er, do you know what I'm going to say, I wonder?"

"No, Simmie."

"Oh dear, can't you even guess?"

"No I can't, Simmie, and I'm not sure that I want to try." He'd scooped up a brass elephant from the piano, and was shuttling it furiously from one hand to the other.

Simmie took a deep breath. "It's over, my dear, that's what I wanted to say. That's all really. It was splendid at the beginning, but now I'm beginning to feel ashamed, you see, and I couldn't go on with it feeling that way. You can understand that, can't you, Ned?"

"I don't feel ashamed – I feel jolly proud! And I don't think you should go and let Gran mess it all up, because you won't be seeing her again, you know. She won't be coming back here, Simmie, honestly."

"But it isn't just your grandmother, it's me, Ned. I'm too old, can't you understand? I just don't want the upset of it all any more. I don't want Gladys to find out, or Andy or Matthew, or anyone at the university. I couldn't bear that. Please try to see my point of view."

"You're not too old," he said, tossing the elephant into the air and catching it. "I'm too damn young – that's it, isn't it? I've only ever been a kind of first reserve, haven't I, for your precious Robert Llewellen!"

There was no point in contradicting him, in confusing him

with her own conflicting emotions. So she let him drop the elephant and replace it and go out and shut the door before she shed a single tear. And afterwards she concentrated on being nice to him – on trying to smile away the pathetically beaten look that kept creeping into his face, and on encouraging him to be civil to Meriel Llewellen.

If only the girl would help herself a little more! Her youth and confidence were exactly what Ned needed now, Simmie was convinced of it. For Meriel's part she clearly thought the sun rose and set behind him, plunging into dramatic appreciations of his quiet virtues at the drop of a hat. But maddeningly, as soon as Ned himself appeared over the horizon, the perverse child would mask her naturally ebullient personality with a nonchalant tea-hostess manner that was guaranteed to irritate – arching her eyebrows and picking her words with ridiculous care.

"Just be yourself, dear," Simmie advised her one afternoon, when Ned had seized the excuse of examination revision to make a bolt from the tea-table to his bedroom. "To be honest, Meriel, I really do think formal conversation is a little wasted on undergraduates. They do so dislike any kind of fuss. Ned especially."

"Tell me something I don't know!" Meriel retorted, flinging herself back in her chair in a deliberately inelegant attitude. "But don't you see, Simmie, that's the whole point. Men run like hares at the slightest sign of interest from a woman – why you practically have to walk backwards with a sack over your head to get them to look twice at you! You should try it," she added as a tactless afterthought, leaving Simmie with no alternative but to stand by and watch, helplessly, while the girl's terrifyingly offhand assault on Ned's bachelor state gathered momentum.

She buttonholed him regularly, doggedly, in the Harpur Street parlour, at the front door, even in the street outside – ever eager to demonstrate a decorous lack of interest in anything he might say or do. With Gareth or their portly mother, or even with Simmie herself as chaperon, she pursued him to university cricket matches and Sunday outings – correct, blasé, ostensibly bored to distraction, but there at his side, notwithstanding.

Poor Ned. First rejection, and now the life of the hunted!

It came as something of a relief to Simmie then when Meriel announced a midweek sightseeing expedition away from Ned and his tedious exams, and far beyond the sooty confines of the city.

"I haven't seen anything like enough of the English countryside," she declared, "and no more have you, Simmie. You're too lazy, you know you are! We'll take our bikes on the train, that's what we'll do, and make a proper day out of it."

Simmie had never been very adventurous herself. In all her years of residence in London it had never even occurred to her to put a bicycle on a train. But having once adjusted herself to the idea, she found it really rather exciting. Gareth Llewellen had recently been shipped off for his first term at the Redruth School of Mines in Cornwall, and Meriel's elder sister Vicky never bicycled; so there'd just be the two of them. They'd leave early, Meriel said, and spend the whole day in the country.

"And it's *my* outing," she insisted. "So you can leave all the planning and the tickets to me. You can bring the packed lunch."

"But where are we going?" Simmie laughed, "surely I have to know that, at least?"

"No you don't. Just meet me at nine in front of the refreshment rooms at Victoria Station – London and Smash'em Line. Don't forget your cycle, and try to bring a decent day with you, all right?"

The station was crowded to the point of lunacy, with trains coming in on practically every platform. There was smoke everywhere, trapped beneath the high glass roof and wafting down amongst the milling figures – and with it the important, coaly smell of stations the world over.

"Here we are then," Meriel shouted as soon as she caught sight of Simmie's hat. "This way – the train's just in!"

At the guard's-van all was sound and fury. Passengers and cabbies pointed and shouted directions, and porters trundled between them with long-suffering expressions on their faces. On the Guard's imperious instructions trunks, portmanteaus and Gladstone bags were still being hauled out onto the platform, stacked around with a variety of mysterious looking bundles tied up in canvas or brown holland. You'd think to look at it that the stack's dispersal would be the labour of hours, yet within a surprisingly short space of time the last laden cab had clopped out of the station, and the intrepid bicyclists were able to load their vehicles into the van and find themselves a convenient second-class compartment nearby. The train on the outward journey was a great deal emptier; and aside from a stout party in a feathered bonnet, they had the compartment to themselves.

"Ugh!" Meriel exclaimed, lifting a grimy glove from the window frame. "Soot – everything's covered in soot! Honestly, Simmie, the cities over here aren't fit for chimney sweeps to live in!"

She was looking quite particularly fetching, Simmie thought, in a belted cycling outfit with a knotted tie and an outsize parody of a gentleman's squashed motoring cap, secured with a large hatpin – the face beneath it reflecting every last shade of horror and delight in the scenes beyond her window, from the squalid tenements of Battersea to the fields and woods of Mitcham and the open country beyond.

It was June – hot, still, bee-swarming weather. There were butterflies in the meadows, and the pale discs of elderflowers and wild roses adorned the hedgerows. The sun was already high. In the shade that it cast beneath the oaks, groups of cattle and horses stood nose to tail, swishing at the flies. On a number of farms haying was in full swing and Meriel waved gaily at the haymakers as they paused to watch the train puff by – men in shirtsleeves, women in white aprons and Mother Hubbard sunbonnets. In some fields they were turning, laboriously, with long-handled wooden rakes, in others tossing the hay up to impressive heights from meadow to haywain, and from wain to rickyard stack.

Meriel exclaimed and pointed, restlessly crossing from one window to another – charged with nervous energy. Watching her vigorous movements, the flying hands and the sparkling eyes, Simmie thought that she had seldom seen anyone so attractive. If only Ned could see her now he'd be bound to fall for her, he could scarcely help it. But Ned was already far away, languishing with his textbooks in the stuffy city they'd left behind. At Haywards Heath the stout party alighted with a feathery nod to each of them.

"And thank God for that!" Meriel said, kicking her feet up onto the seat opposite and helping herself to an extra-strong peppermint from a bag in her pocket. "Isn't this a lark though, Simmie! Aren't you glad you came?"

"Very," Simmie replied truthfully. "And I'm sure I'd be gladder still, dear, if you'd only tell me where you're planning to put me down!"

"I daresay," the impossible child said blithely. "But look, do look, Simmie, it's just like a painting!"

The great agricultural panorama of the Weald rolled itself out of the woodlands of Haywards Heath in a green patchwork plain of pastures and standing corn, terminating in the distance in the long blue whaleback of the South Downs. At Lewes, where the River Ouse cut its own narrow channel through the downs, the railway plunged with splendid abandon straight into the chalk hillside on which the old town stood.

"All change!" Meriel cried, jumping up and releasing the window-strap when they emerged at the far end of the tunnel. "It's another train altogether for our bit of the coast – come on!" Simmie experienced a funny little thrill of excitement as they hurried back down the platform to retrieve their bicycles. Heavens, it was years since she'd been to the seaside!

The Seaford train was older and considerably shabbier – two or three forlorn old carriages working out their last days on a branch line. Once again they had to share a compartment. This time with a pungent odour of black shag tobacco and the antediluvian rustic from whom it emanated, sprawled in the far corner with eyes tight closed and boots akimbo.

"He looks like something out of *Punch,* doesn't he," Meriel whispered, pointing at the leather straps beneath the old man's knees and the archaic frill of whiskers that rose above his collar with every intake of breath. "You don't suppose he's called 'Gaffer Jarge' do you?" and she began to giggle. But it needed more than one comic character to distract Meriel for any length of time from the scenery beyond the window. Soon she was urging Simmie to admire cliffs of white chalk and sprit-rigged coal barges, and water meadows brimming with buttercups.

"And look now, Simmie, *do* look! It's positively *prehistoric!*"

In the lower Ouse valley, in the diked hayfields between the railway and the river, the wains were drawn not by horses – but by great black bullocks yoked in pairs, six to a team. Amongst the toiling haymakers, a number of individuals were still wearing traditional working smocks, loose frocks of homespun linen in black or grey or butcher blue.

"Oxen!" Meriel crowed, "and yokels – yokels in smocks! I don't believe it!"

"Wal p'raps 'tis aboot time ye made a start than, Missy," a sepulchral voice suggested from the corner. "An' I'll lay you'd git the idea of a roundfrock soon 'nough, wiv a hayseed or two under yer gusset!"

Meriel looked at him sharply. "Are you trying to be funny?" she said. He wasn't, Simmie could see that at a glance. But Meriel suddenly threw her head back and roared with laughter. She kept it up too, all the way to Newhaven, where the old man stomped out in a cloud of disapproving black shag, muttering things uncomplimentary about "ighty-flighty flarksy feymales!"

Unrepentant, Meriel turned her attention to the sailing vessels in Newhaven harbour, busily disentangling a forest of masts and spars to instruct Simmie on the practical differences between a brig, a schooner and a windjammer. But as the train steamed on across the salt flats that separated the fishing port from the prim little holiday resort of Seaford, Simmie looked out to the bleak horizon and sadly admitted to herself that she no longer found it exciting, the seaside. It was an alien environment to her, this world of winches and tar and mewing herring gulls, and she was beginning to feel such a long way from home.

The feeling persisted, despite the sunshine and the salty brilliance of the Sussex air. She must have been mad, she told herself, to have allowed Meriel to bring her all this way for a picnic in a field that would probably prove no greener than the fields at Swiss Cottage, twenty minutes by hackney from Harpur Street. But it wasn't until she focused on the finger-post at the edge of the town, and the name that it bore, that the full extent of her madness dawned on her.

"*Sellington 2 Miles*". How could she possibly have failed to guess it at that first blue glimpse of the downs from the railway carriage? And in the moment of her revelation, an all-too-solid vision of Mrs Ashby in heliotrope strode purposefully into Simmie's mind.

"Well, why not?" Meriel said robustly, taking off her jacket and strapping it to the back-stay behind her saddle. "He's always talking about it, isn't he? I just think it's high time you and I saw the place for ourselves. I'll race you down the hill, anyway," she added brightly. "Come on, it'll be fun!" Without looking to see if Simmie would follow, she launched herself over the brow and away in the direction that the sign was pointing.

Chapter Eight

Meriel liked Simmie very much. She was a great dear, anyone with half an eye could see that, but she did hope that the old thing wasn't going to prove an encumbrance now that they were here. They'd already had to walk most of the way up the hill from Seaford because Simmie hadn't felt equal to pedalling. Of course the Sellington sign had been a bit of a facer for her. Englishwomen could be such humbugs when it came to social calling – even the best of them. If you wanted them to do anything interesting or spontaneous, you just had to force them into it. Which was why she left Simmie stranded at the top of the hill, as a little incentive to follow on. And glancing back over her shoulder, she was pleased to see that it had worked. Simmie was there behind her all right, and doing famously – bumping down over the flints with both hands on the brakes, and the pedals of her old-fashioned bicycle spinning like catherine wheels. What a shame, though, that she couldn't relax and enjoy the view.

And what a whale of a view it was to be sure – so pale and bright and open to the sky that Meriel could almost believe she was back in Australia. Centuries of coastal traffic had etched the road deep into the surface of the hill. The chalk shone brilliant white on either side beneath a swaying fringe of grass-heads and scarlet poppies. As it spun them down into the valley, the banks drew back like curtains to reveal a new kind of landscape – a sweeping vista of blue water and deserted chalkhill downland that was different to anything they'd seen from the train. There was space here and freedom from hedges and stock-fencing and the endless little terracotta villas that characterized so much of this island. Away in the valley bottom, between the green bolsters of opposing downs, the Cuckmere river looped lazily to the sea. There was the sound of seagulls, the smell of hay and ozone in the air. Meriel could taste the brine on her lips, she could feel the wind tugging at her hat as she sped on down the hill to the river.

"Gee whillikins!" she sang out to the seagulls. "This is something like!"

He was a part of this uncluttered downland landscape, her lovely Neddy – she'd known that even before she came here. He loved it. And from now on so would she. Meriel slewed to a dusty halt at the bottom of the hill, and turned to watch the outcome of Simmie's perilous descent. What a pity, she thought irrelevantly, that Simmie had never had the gump to marry. Because anyone could see that she'd have made a first-rate wife and mother – even if she was a bit of an old hen sometimes.

"There you are then," she exclaimed, as Simmie jerked alongside her with glistening face and smoking brake-blocks, "I told you it'd be fun!"

Simmie hadn't spoken, she was still fighting for breath, but Meriel didn't seem to notice. "Not much further," she said encouragingly, "just over the top of the next rise, I think." She pointed to where a ribbon of chalk clung gallantly to the face of the opposite hill, narrowing to a faint white thread before it finally disappeared over the distant horizon. "That's our road. Here, have a peppermint – it'll give you strength!"

By the time they finally reached Sellington, the sun was at its zenith. Simmie was puffing like a steam engine; and even Meriel, in short riding stays, had to own that the hill had been fairly stiff work. The village occupied a sheltered combe in the heart of the downs between the Cuckmere river and Beachy Head. A dozen pairs of dappled flint and cobble cottages confronted their fellows across the path of some ancient glacier, following it higgledy-piggledy down into the elbow of a larger seaward-facing valley. On the chalky incline where the two converged a little green had been established – with a church and duckpond, and a huge windblasted sycamore tree to screen the eyes of the Lord from the profanities of the Lamb Inn taproom across the way. There was only one shop, a cottage like the others, with the legend J. J. PILBEAM above the door and a letter box beneath the familiar enamel plate.

"Post office," Meriel remarked as she sailed past. "We'll call in on the way back, shall we, and see if they've got any decent picture-postcards?"

It certainly was a quiet little place, she thought, this Sellington of his. And coming on it like this, slumbering in the sun, it was hard to imagine it in its heyday in the great old farming days of the previous century. One or two of the cottages were actually shuttered and derelict, with slates missing and nettles choking their gardens. There was an air of gentle decay about the rest of them, too, that was curiously appealing, even to Meriel. The eaves of all the houses were encrusted with the muddy shells of swallows' and martins' nests. Brick paths were mossy and uneven, the gardens on either side of them overblown with bolting lettuces and self-sown lupins. There were hens in potholed runs and ferrets in hutches against the cottage walls – a magpie in a wicker cage beside an open door, a cat asleep on a sill, a mongrel dog that ran out to bark at them as they passed. But of human life there was no sign.

"Where on earth is everybody, for heaven's sake?" Meriel wondered, taking the corner by the pond too fast and exploding a flock of quacking white ducks in all directions. "The place is like a ghost town!"

Then they saw them. From the Lamb Inn the two women looked directly down the valley to a range of traditional old farm buildings, and beyond them to the sea. A little to the right of the farm the gable of a big house was just visible through the trees, and in a yard to the front of it men were working between pens of bleating sheep, with all of Sellington, it seemed, leaning over the wall to watch.

'Yes!' Meriel thought, '*that's it!*' She stopped so suddenly that it was all Simmie could do not to cannon into the back of her. "That's it, that's The Bury!" she said aloud, with joyously shining eyes. "It's where he lives, Simmie, do you see? Look, they're shearing. Come on!" And she was off again before Simmie could stop her.

"Meriel!" She tried to call her back, then remounted, wobbling dangerously, to pedal after her down the track. "Dear, you won't try to see his grandmother, will you? Please Meriel, promise me that you won't." But the girl was already out of earshot.

A child astride the shearing-yard wall sounded the alarm as Meriel freewheeled down the hill from the village – to confront her with a whole row of staring Saxon faces, round and rosy, and hard with curiosity.

"Look out, you're sowing gape seed!" she called to them, returning their stares with interest. And she brought her bicycle to rest close against the flint wall, with one hand on the coping to steady her. In the yard beyond, a dozen or more men were working silently in shirtsleeves and dangling braces, shearing the sheep and neatly disposing the fleeces on prepared beds of scythed green nettles.

"They're very slow aren't they?" Meriel remarked loudly as Simmie panted up behind her. "In Australia one man can shear up to a hundred sheep in a day. But I doubt that this lot could get through more than half that at the rate they're going!"

"Bless yer Miss, are you a live Orstralian than?" a woman beside her said disbelievingly.

"Not exactly, but I was raised there," Meriel replied airily. "I've been spending my time in South America and in London more recently, as a matter of fact."

"There! Wal I niver!" The woman immediately nudged her neighbour, to spread the word on down the wall. "D'ye 'ear thad, Missus Armiger? This youn' lady's bin ter Orstralia an' all over – an 'er so young too!"

But Meriel had lost interest. "That man over there is the Catcher," she told Simmie, ignoring the village women's admiring glances. "It's his job to feed the sheep through to the shearers, you see; and I'd say by the look of that one that he must be the head shepherd around these parts."

After the initial relief of her discovery that Mrs Ashby was not amongst the spectators on the wall, Simmie herself was very much struck by the picturesque quality of the scene. It was as timeless, she felt, as the haymakers and the oxen teams they'd seen from the train. In London the 'Age of Progress' was upon them, with motor cars, the telephone and electric lighting following hard on each other's heels. But here, such a little way away in time and space, life was just as it had always been. The dignified sunburnt figure of the old shepherd Meriel had pointed to was probably very little different to the dignified sunburnt men who'd minded their flocks across these same hills in the days before the Romans. And the anxious bleating of the sheep, the wooden hurdles that penned them, they must surely be the same? And the way that the wool peeled back from the shears in a single perfect fleece, that must be the same too.

"He's the tar boy – has to dab a bit of lime onto any little nick that the shears make, to keep the flies off, you know," Meriel rattled on happily. "I've done that in Queensland tons of times, on a friend's sheep station, quite an important job actually. And he's the Winder, by the way."

Simmie watched, fascinated, as each complete fleece was opened up and spread out, looking easily big enough for two sheep – then expertly wound, folded inside-out, rolled from the tail and tied at the neck into a tight little self-contained bundle.

"And my God, Simmie, look, isn't he the living image of Ned?" Meriel exclaimed suddenly, forcibly dragging Simmie's attention from the Winder to the man who was ushering the freshly shorn ewes out of the yard. "It's his father – got to be!"

Simmie conceded that it had, for the man bore a striking resemblance to his son – a taller, older version of Ned, with a slight stoop and a droopy golden moustache. "Except that it's an unhealthy, bloodless kind of face," she thought. And having heard all the details of his father's tragic history from Ned, she felt she could sympathize with the man's careful movements and remote expression. Walter Ashby had been married several years it seemed, before he was found to be tubercular, too late for the young wife he'd infected, too late for his own right lung. Although he'd returned from Switzerland ostensibly cured, he had never recovered his interest or involvement in the Bury estate. He still kept the farm accounts, Ned said, and occasionally assisted with the livestock. But most of his time nowadays was devoted to shooting, to his library and to his Vice-Presidency of the East Sussex Naturalists' Field Club.

'Poor fellow,' Simmie thought, and promptly forgot him. He was that kind of man, Walter Ashby.

She could easily have stayed there all day, watching the shearers. But if she and Meriel had lost track of the time, the men on the other side of the wall quite clearly had not.

"Right, lads!" A man with two stars on his cap released one sheep from between his knees and signalled to the Catcher for another. "One more shi'p all round – than grub." As each man completed his final fleece, he straightened, hooked his braces back onto his shoulders and reached into his hip-pocket for his pipe and tobacco pouch.

"An' 'oo's agoin' ter git the beer than?" one of the team enquired pointedly, and an expectant ripple passed through the line of spectators on the wall.

"Tim'fy Tuff!" someone shouted. During the self-conscious laughter that followed, the shearers shuffled themselves into a rough circle in the yard, seating themselves amongst the sheep droppings and wilting nettles with their legs stuck out straight in front of them.

Simmie was enthralled. "Watch carefully, dear," she whispered to Meriel. "Do you know, I think we're going to be treated to something really quite special in the way of an old country tradition!"

Her attention was rewarded almost immediately by a sudden flurry amongst the shearers, as one of the men unexpectedly flung his legs back over his head, up and over, until the iron spelts of his boots embedded themselves in the nettles behind him.

"'Ere goes ol' Adam's bells!" he bawled. Then the man on his left followed suit with a different verse. "'Ere goes ol' Tim'fy Tuff!" he chanted, presenting a pair of equally impressive shiny corduroy buttocks to the assembled gathering.

"Oh, kin yer see my arse?" his neighbour enquired from between corduroy thighs.

"Oh yes – quite plain enough!" The fourth man was the unfortunate who'd have to draw the beer for the company, and he jumped up athletically to complete the chore, to a round of appreciative applause from the wall.

"Dear me, what a very quaint old custom," Simmie murmured, somewhat flustered. But when she looked at Meriel and Meriel looked at her, they both burst out laughing. It really was too absurd!

They ate their picnic lunch ravenously, with their backs against another old flintstone wall by the gate into the stable yard, and afterwards, of course, Meriel insisted on going to see the horses.

"It can't possibly be trespassing when we know Ned," she explained. "Not when you're his landlady, Simmie, for Lord's sake!"

Simmie was unconvinced, but what could you do with a girl like Meriel? She had already shot back the bolts on the nearest door, and disappeared out of sight inside. So, with an apprehensive glance behind her Simmie followed. If they had to get caught, she'd prefer it if they were together at least.

There were fifteen horses in all in The Bury stables. Meriel counted them: a couple of thoroughbred hunters and a barrel-chested cob, two matched pairs of carriage horses, and two four-horse working teams of docile great Shires with aristocratic Roman noses and feet like fluffy soup plates.

"Oh aren't they fine, Simmie, aren't they *lovely!*" Meriel cried, running from one stall to the next, standing on tiptoe to peer through the bars and closing her eyes to inhale the gorgeous horse-sweaty stable smell that permeated the place. "Wouldn't you just love to own all this, Simmie? To saddle your own horse up whenever you felt like it for a grand old gallop over the downs?"

"You wouldn't ask, dear, if you'd ever seen me on a horse! Besides, I'm never very likely to get the chance, am I?"

"That's what you think. When I marry Ned you can have that soft old bay cob, he should do you all right. And I'll have this handsome black devil here. Look Simmie, his name's Balthazar. I bet Ned rides him!"

But Simmie wasn't looking at the hunter's brass nameplate. She was looking at Meriel and thinking what a great deal she had to learn still – about love and life and her own limitations.

Meriel still thought that you had only to reach out to pick what you wanted. And when you watched her like this with the horses – that bright little face, that confident bouncing step – it was sad to think of all the frustrations and disappointments that still lay ahead of her. Sad to think that this child too would have to grow up like all the rest.

"He does look bored, though, don't you think?" Meriel was strolling across the cobbled alley from the black hunter's stall and into the tack-room. "Let's see, I wonder which is his saddle?" And she'd just reached up to lift a likely looking candidate from the saddle-horse, when a loud masculine voice behind Simmie's shoulder nearly sent her through the roof.

"Now than, Miss," it said, "an' what d'ye think ye'r adoin'?" The young man was so broad that he seemed to fill the doorway. As she spun round Simmie was conscious of a stern brown face, and two bare arms like hams covered with a fuzz of ginger hair. There was hair too in the open neck of his shirt, and a darker stubble on his throat and chin.

"What does it look like?" Meriel snapped back at him from the tack-room door. "We're looking at the horses, of course."

"Mus Ashby 'ent said nuthin' ter me aboot visitors."

"That's because we called in here on our way up to the house." Meriel was squaring up to him like a little ruffled game hen. "I'll have you know, young man, that this lady here is Mr Edwin Ashby's landlady in London. And she's come to pay an afternoon call on his grandmother while we're in the locality, so there!"

"Meriel!" Simmie couldn't help it – it just slipped out.

"Ah wal than," the man said, turning from one to the other with a definite twinkle in his eye, "ef thad be the case, Miss, I'd best see yer up ter the front door." He raised his cap to reveal red hair and a strip of snowy white forehead in sharp contrast to the dusky tan of the rest of his face. "Dan'l Goodworth at yer service, ladies, an' jes walk this way, if yer please." Leaving them no alternative but to collect their bicycles and to follow him on through the yards, past the cowsheds and up the short gravel drive to the house.

"What an impudent young man!" Meriel whispered to Simmie across their handlebars. "Sorry, but it was the only thing I could think of on the spur of the moment. Still, it'll be interesting to see inside won't it, Simmie?" And she pinged her bicycle bell with a smug little smile.

"But what am I going to say to her?" Simmie thought despairingly, "what *ever* am I going to say?" It was all very well for Meriel. She hadn't been conducting an illicit affair with the lady's grandson – and she hadn't been on the receiving end of those steely blue eyes.

"Do please forgive us for putting you out like this, Mrs Ashby. But we felt we simply couldn't pass by your charming little village without popping in to see you . . . " No it wouldn't do, she'd never swallow it, not in a month of Sundays. And if she'd thought Simmie a fool before, what on earth was she going to make of her now, in her shabbiest walking costume and just smothered in chalk dust?

As the impressive timbered façade of the house loomed up above them through the shrubberies, Simmie made some furtive attempts to brush herself down and to tuck her disordered hair into her hat. The front door was protected by a gabled porch, complete with bootscraper and walking stick stand, with an old stone mounting block to one side and a contorted trunk of wisteria sprawling like a serpent over the top. And as the man Goodworth reached out to tug at the bell, Simmie was taken back fifteen years, transported on the sound of that echoing doorbell.

She felt exactly as she had that day in Ham, trembling beneath the portico of Robert's mother's house on the common – just like this – like a naughty schoolgirl going in to see the Head. Robert's mother had been unbelievably kind, that other time, helping her as she fumbled for the words and stared at the swimming patterns of Mrs Llewellen's Persian carpet.

"Are you *enceinte*? Are you pregnant by my son, *ma chère?*" There'd been real compassion in the black bootbutton eyes, as she clasped Simmie to her own silk bosom and comforted her. "*Ce n'est pas la fin du monde, ma petite.*" She was that kind of woman, Mrs Llewellen.

Margaret Ashby, on the other hand, was most definitely not that kind of woman; and this time there'd be no excuse for tears. It just had to be got through. So Simmie straightened her back and faced the door, and pulled the corners of her mouth up into the facsimile of a smile.

To Ned's ears the sound of the doorbell had come as a bugle call, to break the fusty silence of the house and release him from his bondage. It was infernally hot and airless in his room at Harpur Street, and he was sick and tired of revision.

> As the male nucleus approaches close to the egg nucleus, the haploid number of chromosomes appears in each of the nuclei, and the nuclear membranes break down . . .

He had to keep getting up and pacing around to read any kind of sense into it; and had just completed his fourteenth circuit of the oilcloth when he heard the doorbell, shortly followed by a formal salvo of yaps from Gussie in the kitchen.

"I'm jest runnin' aht to the tinman to 'ave some knives reground, won't be a jiff." That's what Gladys had said. "So do us a favour an' kip an ear aht fer the door will yer, Mister Eddie?"

The doorbell was all the excuse he needed, and Ned was out of the room and down the stairs before it rang a third time. He hadn't the slightest idea who to expect, hadn't even bothered to think. But as he opened the door and looked into Robert Llewellen's swarthy face, it was as if he'd known all along.

"She's not here," he said bluntly. "She's out bicycling with your daughter."

"I know." The eloquent black brows were raised in exaggerated astonishment. "But the point to note is that you are, my young friend, are you not?"

Llewellen shouldered his way past Ned into the dark little hall, peeling off his gloves and turning to hand them to him at the foot of the stairs, along with his hat and his ebony stick.

"This way to the parlour, if I remember correctly?"

The man was sprawling drunk when they'd last met. But even then Ned had been aware of his extraordinary vitality. Now he felt inadequate to deal with it, as he dumped Llewellen's things on the hall stand and followed him slowly up the stairs.

"Look here, there wouldn't be any sense at all in your waiting," he said. "They've gone for the day, you know. I shouldn't imagine they'll be back for hours."

"Good God, it's hardly changed at all?" Llewellen exclaimed from the door of the parlour, as if he hadn't heard. "Same old pictures, same old carpet, same old fuss and clutter . . . "

His dark eyes were everywhere – enquiring, searching for instruction or amusement – like the eyes of every gipsy Ned had known. He'd seen them a score of times in the Bury yards – the Romanys from Crowlink – laughing with the men, giving cheek, while their eyes probed the farm for horses to be traded or gamefowl to be poached.

"Look, I honestly don't think there's any point in your waiting," he repeated. "Perhaps you'd like to leave your card, would you? Or is there a message of some kind I can give her when she gets back? I could write it down if you like."

"Whoa there – hold hard, Dobbin! Hasn't anyone ever told you, dear boy, that it's positively discourteous to throw a caller out on his arse in two minutes flat? And talking of cards," Llewellen said, "might one venture to enquire as to your exact status in this snug little household? The point does rather clamour for enlightenment, you must admit. Or perhaps you'd like me to guess?" He tossed himself back on the sofa and smiled up at Ned derisively. "Am I to presume that you acted on the inebriated confessions of our last meeting? And did you hasten with my calling card hot, er-foot shall we say to the lady's side, to offer her comfort and succour and any other little service that she might require?"

Oh God don't blush, Ned. Don't be the young ass he thinks you! Do something, blow your nose. Say anything . . . "Not at all – nothing of the kind," he said, hastily seizing a carved German pipe from the mantelshelf and pulling it in two. "I'm lodging with her, that's all, she's my landlady."

But it was too late, he'd thought about it, and within seconds he could feel himself glowing a sweaty puce from navel to scalp. Why, oh why did this always have to happen to him?!

"Hal-lo!" Llewellen whistled softly. "'He gilds his face withal, and it must show his guilt.' So that's the way of it, eh? And here was I hoping that she'd be pleased to see me again after all this time – deluding myself into believing that my first little note of assignation would rekindle the fire of our former passions. Ah well, so much for blighted hopes!"

He rose again with an easy, supple movement to cross the room to the little wicker waste basket that stood beside the firescreen. "I suppose you imagine that you love her too?" he enquired.

"Yes I do."

"Well then, there you have my official resignation." Llewellen took an envelope from his breast pocket, tore it neatly in four and dropped it into the basket. "Congratulate you, dear boy!" When he smiled with that debonair lift of the eyebrows, the force of his charm – and of his own awareness of it – hit Ned like a slap in the face. Never had he disliked a man more. He could so easily have told Robert Llewellen the truth then – "It's you she loves, not me!" But dash it all, why should he? The fellow was a Lothario, an out-and-out blackguard, married with grown-up children and likely as not enough mistresses to circle the globe!

"Do you have a message for her, then?" he asked flatly.

"By all means." Llewellen's voice was treacly with condescension. "Perhaps you'd have the goodness to tell her that the Stanhope Mining people are sending me out to South America again; to Colombia this time, to manage a new mercury enterprise for them. I'll be sailing on Tuesday. Tell her I came to say goodbye if you like – as I did once before." He turned again in the hall as he swept up his hat and cane and his grey suede gloves. "What's your name, boy?"

"Edwin Ashby."

"Well sir, I'll tell you again and hope that this time you'll remember it – it's our glands that rule us, Edwin Ashby, not our hearts or our heads. There are doubtless as many kinds of love as there are men and women to experience them. But not romantic love, d'ye see – there's no such thing in this unromantic world of ours. It's a delusion shared by old men who've forgotten and spinster novelettists who'll never know. By wives like mine who seek refuge from their own distaste for copulation – and by idealistic young men like you, frightened to death of the instincts that drive them."

He replaced his hat and tapped it into place as he stepped down to the pavement. A moment later he had gone.

Chapter Nine

"He came to say goodbye, Simmie, that's all. He'll be sailing for Colombia on Tuesday he said, on some crack-brained mining scheme or other. Won't be back for ages."

"Yes I know what his plans are, dear, Meriel told me all about them on the train home this evening."

Simmie had staggered in just after seven – lame, dishevelled and almost too tired to think. "But why did he call this afternoon?" she said, as much to the parlour furniture as to Ned. "Surely Meriel must have told him that we'd be out all day? And why 'goodbye' when he hasn't troubled to say so much as 'how d'ye do' in three months?"

Ned wavered for a moment between truth and inclination. "He came to leave a note for you, to propose some kind of meeting," he said heavily, "an assignation I daresay. But you see when he saw that I was here, actually living with you as it were, he tore it up."

"But that's absurd, Ned!" Simmie was in the act of removing her hat and as she turned back to him from the mirror with her hair floating around her face like a halo, her eyes strayed unconsciously to the waste basket. "He tore it up, you say?"

"It's no good looking for it, Simmie. It was there. But after he left I fished it out and burnt it in the grate!"

Simmie sighed, and wearily turned back to the mirror. "You mustn't imagine that a few hours in bed with a woman entitles you to run her life for ever afterwards, my dear," she said, busy with her hair. "Because it doesn't you know – it doesn't actually entitle you to anything, Ned."

And somehow she managed to remain like that, with her back to him, until after he left the room. One minute more and she'd have relented – held out her hands to him and undone all the good of the past weeks. But that was Robert for you. He had only to set one foot in her house to turn all her resolutions upside down.

"And one way or another you've had just about as much as you can take for one day haven't you, you poor thing?" she said to her bedraggled reflection. The face in the mirror gave a wan little smile. "Then there's only one answer, isn't there?" The reflection nodded wisely and together, in perfect accord, they climbed the stairs to the bathroom.

"A long hot bath" – why even the words were comforting! The bath itself was a magnificent commodious affair with a goffered flounce and ball-and-claw feet, and a great rearing shower-screen at the tap end that could spray you from above and from three sides simultaneously. Even now, as she watched the scalding water gushing down to meet the cold enamel in a fog of white steam, Simmie experienced a ridiculous sense of pride that such power could be hers at the mere twist of a dial. Mrs Llewellen had installed the new bath and the coke boiler that heated it soon after they'd moved up to London from Ham. But in all the years since, Simmie had never been able to forget the chilly hip-baths of her youth, never ceased to marvel at the wonders of modern plumbing.

"Enjoy, *ma chère!* Life is hard is it not? Therefore we must all take from it what we can, *n'est-ce pas?*" That had been very much the philosophy that guided Cécile Llewellen, formulated through her years as a French maid in the austere Welsh household of Robert's grandparents. She'd had a veritable passion for physical comfort, that dear old lady, and adored her *baignoire* – wallowing for hours in richly perfumed water, to totter off to her feather bed as pink and as fragrant as a little overblown musk rose. "Enjoy, enjoy, *ma chère...*"

Later, lying submerged with her feet on the brass column of the plug, Simmie pushed aside the soap-bridge to consider her own tired body beneath its luxurious canopy of heat and steam. It was strange, so strange that Robert had never seen the vertical white scar on her stomach, although it concerned him so intimately; his child, his poor little dead baby, his mother's charity in paying for the surgery that saved her own life – yet he'd never so much as seen it. And now of course he never would.

Such a wasted body, hers – good broad hips, nice thighs, so

pale beneath the water . . . enjoy, enjoy *ma chère*...Robert's, Robert's thighs, fine-drawn, long muscled and yet so strong, so heavy on hers . . .

"And that's quite enough of that, thank you!" Simmie told herself sharply, standing up to free herself from the bath's seductive embrace, seizing a bar of soap, and lathering herself briskly all over.

Meriel called in on Simmie early the next morning while she was still at breakfast. Clutched in her hand was a small brown envelope – inside it a pressed four-leaved clover.

"Found it last week on my uncle's lawn," she explained, "and I've been saving it to bring Ned luck in his Second Year exams. Meant to give it to him yesterday actually. So you will be sure he gets it this afternoon, won't you Simmie, first thing when he gets back from the labs?"

"Yes of course, dear, if that's what you want. A cup of coffee?"

"Thanks." Meriel accepted the cup automatically. "Now then, tell me what he thought of our trip to Sellington – I'm dying to know. Wasn't he surprised?"

"Well, to tell you the truth, Meriel, he was a little preoccupied with something else last night. I don't think we even discussed it."

"What! You are a cuckoo, Simmie, you really are! And I thought you'd be bound to tell him all about it," Meriel exclaimed, tipping back the coffee she'd just slopped into her saucer. "Especially when I went down so well with the old Grannie. I mean we got on like a house on fire, didn't we?"

Simmie had an unpleasant vision of Margaret Ashby smiling gruesomely at her over the top of an elegant silver teapot, while Meriel eulogized her grandson with a non-stop flow of superlatives. But fortunately, before she was required to comment, the girl's attention had already shifted elsewhere.

"Goodness, I almost forgot the other thing I came to ask you," she exclaimed. "We're all going down to Southampton by train on Tuesday, to see Da off, and I wondered if you'd like to come along for the ride? The others are longing to meet you, I'm sure."

92

"Southampton," Simmie murmured, playing for time, "how nice! But does your – er, do your parents know that you're inviting me?"

"No, but who cares? They'll be tickled pink, I know they will. Why, Da's always saying how kind you are, how good you were to Grandmère when she was ill."

"Oh but, in that case I couldn't possibly, dear. It's a family occasion, you must see that. Besides, I happen to know that I'm going to be extremely busy next week, what with the boys to see through their examinations and everything . . . "

"Well suit yourself, of course." Meriel sounded distinctly put out. "I'll have to run now in any case. But if you change your mind, Simmie, don't forget, we'll be catching the two thirty-five from Waterloo."

There were four days until Tuesday – something like one hundred hours of not seeing Robert to be got through. Simmie lectured herself bracingly on the subject every morning when she woke. Every night as she lay down to sleep, she congratulated herself on another day safely past. And when Tuesday finally came, she felt as if she personally had propelled every hour of time between. Tuesday was her achievement.

It was a dullish morning, threatening rain. After the strident bravado of her young lodgers gallantly setting out to do battle with their exam papers, the house seemed oppressively quiet; and Simmie drifted restlessly from one room to another in search of useful employment.

Three miles away at the Llewellens' establishment in Pimlico, neither quietness nor useful employment were greatly in evidence. And by the time the gig was brought round to take Uncle Vincent to the office, everyone had been up for hours, bumping into each other and stumbling over the luggage in the hall.

"Gareth, go upstairs this minute and clean your teeth, and bring me down your toothbrush and powder and your hairbrushes to pack. And listen – are you listening? I'm putting in three bottles of Chlorodyne for you, and Dovers Powders and castor oil. And quinine for fever, Gareth, and ammonia water for insect bites. Oh, and liquorice for constipation! Listen – are you listening, Gareth? One teaspoonful of liquorice powder every morning to keep you regular. Have you got that – *have* you?"

Harriet Llewellen was quite beside herself with anxiety for her one ewe lamb. Poor Garry! Heartlessly co-opted after only three terms at Redruth to accompany his father to Colombia.

"He's too young, Robert, I tell you he's too young and sensitive for such a hazardous journey!" But his mother's protestations had been unavailing. No one listened.

Gladys was out marketing, and Simmie had run down to make a pot of tea for herself in the kitchen. She couldn't work, she couldn't relax, couldn't even talk to Gussie in his basket without thinking of that confounded train. Her hand as she lifted the cup was trembling with suppressed emotion.

Robert used the new telephone in the kitchen passage to summon a pair of hackneys to transport them to the station; and after a somewhat sketchy cold luncheon, the family foregathered in the hall to await their arrival.

"I'm going with Da," Meriel announced in a voice that forbade contradiction. "And bags we have the first cab!"

Simmie had to get out of the house. She needed the distraction of people and moving things around her – she had to walk. On any other day she'd have taken Gussie and made for Coram Fields or Russell Square. But today she hadn't felt like his company, and instead of heading north she turned down Theobald's Road in the direction of Southampton Row. Not, as she told herself later, that she'd been thinking at all in terms of omnibuses and their routes. Far from it. Indeed, when a bus with a "Waterloo Station" placard on the front had trotted into view, the idea of boarding it had come as a complete surprise to her – or very nearly so.

There was no logic to it. She simply had to see him – just once more. She hadn't rehearsed anything to say to him. She wouldn't speak. She'd stand out of sight behind a cab or a pillar to watch him pass by, that was all. It surely couldn't do any harm – it couldn't matter to anyone but her.

Simmie had always enjoyed travelling by omnibus. As a child she'd sat up in the front behind the horses whenever she possibly could, and even now she much preferred the open view from the top deck to the stuffy overcrowding below. It was exciting to hear the chuckings and whoas of the bowler-hatted driver, to see the whip flourishing about in the air. And the way that the steeply cambered road threatened to throw you overboard when the vehicle pulled in to the side – that too was a thrill. A little like riding an elephant in India, Simmie imagined.

She hauled herself up to the nearest available seat on the aisle, two back from the driver, and sat down breathlessly. There was a cold void in her stomach like a pain, and she could actually feel her heart beating beneath her stays. Because she really was going to see Robert again, after all this time!

"I tell you, Meriellie, there's a fortune in mercury in those Andes, just waiting for someone like me to winkle it out!"

Robert fairly glowed with satisfaction, sitting knee to knee in the cab with his favourite daughter, his son at his side, their luggage on the roof, and above all the prospect of new fields to conquer. He looked like a great big schoolboy, Meriel thought, just off for the holidays. And really she couldn't help envying Garry his exciting trip out with Da, even if she did have other fish to fry.

"Your mother seems quite determined to come out and join us, just as soon as we're settled in the Company's hacienda," Da continued on a slightly less enthusiastic note. "And you and Vicky must come out too, of course, if only to prevent her from gambling away our savings and taking up with strange gentlemen on the boat!" He was so seldom serious. It was one of the chiefest things she loved about Da.

"Always provided that the mine really does turn out to be a going concern," she reminded him, laughing, "and that you can get the blessed natives to work."

"Work! I've worked the Irish in Australia, haven't I, and the Malays in Borneo? If I can do that, I should certainly be able to show the Colombians a thing or two, wouldn't you say?"

"Well, I hope you can. But to be honest, Da, I'm not all that keen on the idea of travelling anywhere just now, even if Mother does decide to go."

"Good God – can I believe my ears?" Da was genuinely surprised. "Now who would ever have thought that you of all people would prefer London society to a hike up the Andes! What's up, Meriellie? Not in love are you?"

"Well what if I am?" Meriel snapped. It was so important for her to clear all this with Da before he left. She needed his approval – his above everyone's. But somehow the thing wasn't going at all as she'd planned. "I am nineteen you know, Da, and you can't expect me to stay on the shelf forever."

"Oh quite." He was still smiling, but all the warmth had gone out of his eyes. "And might one be so bold as to ask who the lucky man is?"

"Garry knows – he's one of the undergraduates boarding with Miss Sims in Harpur Street. But I warn you, Da, I'm going to marry him, so you needn't jaw!"

"The dickens you will!" He had stopped smiling now and was looking her straight in the eye. "Listen to me, Meriel, you clearly know very little about this young man, or any young man I daresay, and I forbid you to see him informally until we've all discussed the matter further. Is that understood? You may be too young and innocent to realize it, Miss, but no man is to be trusted – and I do mean no man, not in affairs of this nature."

"Affairs of this nature!" She mimicked the pompous, preachy tone that sat so ill on him. "Honestly, Da, what more do you need – a certificate of good character? Well, for your information I already know all I need to about Edwin Ashby, thank you very much! I've seen his home, I've met his grandmother, and I'm jolly well *going* to marry him sooner or later, whether you like it or not!"

As the omnibus negotiated the High Holborn crossing for the downhill gradient of the new Kingsway thoroughfare, Simmie was wallowing shamelessly in the degradation of her defeat. What would he look like? How would he have aged? And would she feel the same about him as she had that last time in the solicitor's office in Boswell Street? He had written to her when he heard about the baby and the operation – hasty, scribbled letters, full of apology and abbreviated emotions. And of course he'd sent money. But there was precious little love, little real sympathy or understanding of her feelings in anything that he'd said. At the time she swore bitterly that she would never forgive him for it. But then she'd never been very good at feuds or antipathies of any kind. When Cécile Llewellen had unexpectedly left her the house in Harpur Street, and when she met Robert again after all those years to receive the deeds and sign the Assent document, she had forgiven him unconditionally. His was a nature that she'd never change – not in a lifetime. Moreover, if she was really honest with herself, she could even admit that his arrogance and ruthlessness were a part of Robert's appeal to someone like her. Why else should she cling to the memory of a day when he'd hurt her and used her, as he had that day in Richmond?

Simmie swiftly cast her eyes down to the raked floor of the omnibus, in case one of the other passengers should see her face and read her mind. But as she did so, something wet splashed against her neck. It was beginning to rain. From a dignified and almost silent little congregation, the top deck of the bus was transformed in seconds to a noisy rookery of flapping oilskins and black umbrellas. Passengers who'd never met before had perforce to share the omnibus company's waterproof covers, to co-operate in securing them from the pegs on their seatbacks. And since there was scarcely room for four umbrellas in a row, some sort of an equitable distribution of gamps had also to be agreed on.

"Do share mine," Simmie said to the woman in the mustard-coloured coat beside her. "It used to be my father's and it's easily big enough for two!" And she put up the clumsy great thing at arm's length to avoid poking someone else in the eye.

Down below in the Kingsway, umbrellas were sprouting by the score. The square roofs of the cabs, the awnings, the flanks of the horses – everything gleamed in the wet as if it had been polished. And as the bus rattled down the hill to the Strand, the cobbled granite setts of the street caught and reflected the light up through the moving patterns of the traffic.

*

"Typical!" Meriel gave up scowling at Da for a moment to scowl through the cab window at the rain. They'd spanked up the Strand in fine style for a four-wheeler; but now as they approached the Aldwych, everything slowed to a snail's pace. It always did when it rained, although for the life of her Meriel could never understand why. Five roads met at the Aldwych, in a chaotic new traffic scheme that so far seemed to have created more problems than it solved.

"Should've gorn by th'Embankment," the cabbie called back to them gloomily, and as he pitched his horse into the mêlée, Da pointed out the new Aldwych development to their left in an aloof, superior kind of way that would have infuriated Meriel – if she hadn't been looking the other way.

"Oh – ooh! Oh the poor horse! What's the fool playing at?" she shouted suddenly, leaping to her feet and scrabbling for the door handle. "Stop the cab – put me out! There's a horse down in its traces over there – the damn bus has run right onto it!"

Simmie hadn't consciously thought about the hill or the speed of the bus, or of the slippery road, for that matter. But very sensibly she'd put out a hand to steady herself, just in case. Which was actually what saved her from hitting the seat in front as the sudden impact threw her forward. She wasn't aware of her oilskin cover jerking from its pegs either, or of the umbrella handle leaving her hand. The extreme simplicity of her own rise and descent had been too painfully absorbing, accompanied as it was by a deluge of alien top hats and umbrellas, and by the alarming prospect of a small boy in front of her diving head-first over the rail and into the driver's lap. For a moment the world stopped spinning altogether and then lurched off again at double speed, with women shrieking and men swearing quite dreadfully, and the hideous sound of a screaming horse adding panic to the general sense of confusion.

The little woman in the mustard coat was moaning and clasping a crimson handkerchief to her nose, having rapped it smartly on the Nestlé's Milk advertisement in front of her. And Simmie was fully occupied with the problem of getting her down to the street when the Llewellens' four-wheeler, with Meriel still protesting loudly, turned away from the scene in the direction of Waterloo Bridge.

In the meantime a small army of passengers and pedestrians was straining to push the bus back off the lacerated body of the horse, while the conductor commandeered a passing cab to take the injured woman back down the Strand to the Charing Cross hospital. Simmie was convinced that the poor creature had broken her nose and naturally felt obliged to go with her to the hospital, to pay her fare and see her safely in.

"Lie right back, dear, across my knee," she advised. "It might help to stop the bleeding." And she patted the woman's hand sympathetically – trying nobly not to think of Waterloo.

As Robert Llewellen's elegant suede-topped boot touched the station kerb, his dark eyes eagerly raked the concourse for a plain straw hat and hair like sugar floss. But when he failed to find them, he merely tossed down his cigarette stub to grind it beneath his heel, and turned back with a shrug to see to the luggage.

Simmie trudged disconsolately back up the Strand from the hospital. She was wet and bruised and spattered with blood, and two of the spokes of her gamp were broken. But she didn't want a cab. She didn't want to talk to anyone. She wanted to lose herself amongst the anonymous pedestrians on the pavement.

As soon as she got home she'd go straight up to her room and shut the door – and bawl her eyes out like a child. Then afterwards she'd probably ring down to Gladys for some tea, and no doubt feel better. Life went on. But later when she did get home, when she finally, wearily climbed the stairs to her bedroom and shut the door behind her, the tears refused to come.

Chapter Ten

Harriet Llewellen wept continuously for the entire train journey back from Southampton, with Vicky and Aunt Alice buttressing her, like whaleboned bookends, one on either side. Meriel sat glowering at the three of them from the opposite corner of the carriage.

"So where does this leave me?" she thought resentfully. "In a pretty average ghastly hole, that's where! Without Da, without Garry and no forrarder with Ned Ashby than I've ever been." Why for two straws she'd embark on a crying-fit herself – and really give the Mater something to think about. She had so badly wanted Da's blessing on Ned. And although she naturally had every intention of proceeding without it, she was just now experiencing a moment of temporary insecurity – like a trapeze artiste who has let go of one strong pair of male hands but has not yet grasped the next. But then again, like most high fliers, Meriel was too sure of her own abilities ever to contemplate the risk of a fall for long. And in the end a glimpse of herself in her aunt's cloakroom mirror was all it had taken to restore her confidence.

"Listen you," she said with mock severity. "Make no mistake about it – you're *going* to pin that young man down, and you're going to do it before somebody else does!" She followed up the lecture with a hideous gargoyle grimace that she'd perfected as a child; and instantly felt five hundred per cent better.

The trouble with Meriel was that she never bothered to examine her own motives in any depth. Indeed she went to some lengths to avoid doing so – with the result that she was extremely bad at divining other people's. She recognized quality when she saw it, in men as in horses, and she'd grasped from the outset that Ned was a warranted genuine thoroughbred, with a thoroughbred's sensitive disposition. But how to attract him? How to rope him in without damaging his fine sensibilities?

That was the question. The answer came from her sister Vicky – an unexpected source – the very next week.

It would seem that the drongo Reggie Baxter was somewhat in awe of Da, since he had barely waited for the Atlantic Packet to be safely out of sight, before addressing himself to the tearful Mrs Llewellen to ask for her elder daughter's hand in marriage. Harriet had fallen over herself of course, to entertain the suit of one so charming and well set up, only waiting to cable Da for confirmation before announcing the engagement as official. And amidst the hugs and tears that such occasions seemed to demand, Meriel was forced to conclude that Vicky knew something that she didn't. She'd progressed from simpering idiocy to some more telling method of hamstringing a male. She must have.

"So how did you manage it?" she demanded, as soon as they were alone together in the double guest room that they shared in their uncle's house. "When everyone knows your inheritance won't be worth a row of beans!"

"My! And who's a lover-ly shade of pea green then, dearie?"

There'd never been any love lost between the sisters. As children they'd fought like Turks, always. It was clear to Meriel that the fruit of knowledge would have to be paid for there and then in self-control, so she simply bit her lip and waited.

"Well, if it's advice you're after, little sister, I do have to tell you that you're not nearly aware enough of your own appearance to get anywhere much with men."

"That's not true!" She wouldn't take that, not even for Ned. "Why, I was wearing that lovely Parma violet rig-out on the morning Mr Ashby first saw me, and even Mother thinks I look nice in that."

"Ashby!" Vicky was onto it like a terrier on a rat. "So that's it! I might have known you'd have something definite in view." And she smiled an infinitely knowing smile that made Meriel itch to slap her hard across her shapely little prunes-and-prisms mouth. "But to be candid, my dear," her sister continued sweetly, "that walking costume of yours is a little on the loud side of good taste. Not that it's the clothes that really matter, Meriel, it's what's underneath them that counts for most!" She smoothed the flimsy batiste chemise she was wearing down over her own generous breasts to illustrate the point.

"There are few things in this world that men put a higher value on than an alluring female form. And really there's nothing a girl can't make of that if she cares to! One has only to choose one's moment to stoop low in a skimpy little evening gown, shall we say? Or to hoist one's petticoats for the stairs, to have the poor dears on their knees," Vicky laughed that affected, silvery little laugh of hers, "exactly where one wants them, don't you see?"

"Right you are then, Ned my lovely," Meriel said under her breath. "If it's a body you're after – then nothing could be simpler!"

She and Aunt Alice were on their way to New Cavendish Street and to Madame Lena, the little dressmaker who'd made such a good thing of her walking costume. Across Meriel's knees in the cab lay a bolt of shimmering mahogany silk that made her spirits rise just to look at it. They'd purchased it at John Barker's the previous morning – although rather against Aunt Alice's better judgement.

"It's too dark, too conspicuous a shade for a young lady's evening gown. As a general rule, my dear, the lighter the tint the better; and personally I don't think a girl of your years can go very far wrong with white satin. It looks so fresh and – well, innocent you know."

If Harriet had been there, she'd have known by the set of Meriel's jaw that the battle was already lost. But Aunt Alice still had things to learn about her younger niece. She was a nice, well-meaning woman, no doubt of that. But at the same time it was clear to Meriel that she entirely failed to grasp the critical importance of this gown, despite all that she'd said to convince her of it. As far as Meriel was concerned, this was to be the first ball of the Season – because this was the very first to which both she and Ned Ashby had been invited. And if dear Aunt Alice imagined for one little moment that she would be prepared to lose herself amongst all those insipid whites and creams and shell pinks, then she needed her head examined! Besides, the colour was perfect – anyone could see that. Exactly the shade to bring out the warm lights in her hair and eyes, while at the same time dark enough to enhance the ivory whiteness of her shoulders and of her breasts.

Following her conversation with her odiously self-satisfied sister, Meriel had begun to appreciate the tactical importance of breasts as never before. Hitherto she'd tended to consider them mainly as conveniently adjustable mounting arrangements for a variety of attractive bodices. But now she appraised them more critically. While Vicky was in the bath the next evening Meriel stood naked before the wardrobe looking glass, her hands cupped beneath her breasts in a primitive gesture that went back – had she but known it – to the very dawn of civilization and beyond. They were soft, yet heavy in her palms. She'd feathered her small nipples provocatively, feeling them rise to the caress – then stooped to retrieve her chemise and drape it across them in the most daring *décolletage* she could possibly envisage.

"What a shame," she thought – experimenting, "that nipples are so hopelessly *outré*. Because I'm quite sure that mine must be pointier and nicer altogether than most girls'." She unveiled them again, slowly, and this time with the look of incredulous delight that she imagined Ned might exhibit when presented with the pair of them at point blank range. Then with a heartfelt sigh of regret, she snatched up the clean nightgown that had been laid out for her and dragged it ungracefully over her head.

So much for the body. Now, as the cab drew up at the dressmaker's door, Meriel moved into the next phase of her master-plan for the dress.

"Oh jinks! We've forgotten the lace, Auntie! And Madame Lena was so *particular* about having all the materials today if she was to run up the gown in time. Said she couldn't possibly manage otherwise!"

"Nonsense, my dear, we can drop the lace in later. Madame won't mind. It's only for the sleeves and trimmings after all; and she surely won't be doing those until last?"

"Oh no – no that won't *do!*" Meriel cried in a creditable imitation of her mother's histrionics. "I promised her faithfully that we'd bring it all today, and I know I'll never be able to show her quite what I want without the lace. Time's so short in any case, and it'll be *ruined,* I just know it will!"

"Well, I suppose if you think it's so vital, I could take the cab back for the lace," Aunt Alice suggested doubtfully. "Although I did assure your mother that I'd be there when you discussed the final pattern . . . "

"Would you – oh would you, Auntie!" Meriel exclaimed, sweeping the inconvenient assurance aside. "You're an angel, I've always said so!" And she planted a smacking kiss on her aunt's astonished cheek. "The pattern's all agreed, anyway, why even Mother thought it was too suitable for words."

The thing involved a small calculated risk. But by the time Aunt Alice returned with the prescribed eight yards of imitation antique lace, Meriel had everything well in hand.

"It's all settled," she said briskly, popping out of the dressmaker's doorway the instant that her aunt's hansom had come to rest. "No sense in letting the cab go, Auntie. I'll just nip this up to Madame and be back in two shakes!" And she was off with the lace and up the stairs before Aunt Alice could think of an objection.

The interim fitting proved no real problem – timed as it was for an afternoon on which both Harriet and Aunt Alice were officially At Home to callers. Vicky was detailed to accompany her to Madame's.

"And the least you can do is to keep quiet about it," Meriel said fiercely. "It's half your idea anyway!"

"Don't worry – the less said the better, I'm sure!" And again the maddening, silvery little laugh. "But you'll never get away with it, Meriel. There'll be a first class row, I guarantee. Mother will scream the house down as soon as she sets eyes on it, you know she will – and very likely forbid you to go altogether."

"Yes she very likely will," Meriel thought. "But it'll take a damn sight more than Mother to stop me on the night!"

The ball in Grosvenor Crescent was to be one of the last main events of the London Season, before society abandoned the free-for-all of the capital for the quieter pleasures of its country estates. Reggie Baxter was going, of course. He and his cronies practically made a profession out of that kind of affair, and he'd seen to it that both the Llewellen girls received invitations. At first Meriel had been less than keen; she'd been to swell events like this before. Everything would be "awfully" or "frightfully". The snooty English girls would stare rudely at her poor little primrose chiffon, while their brothers and cousins pestered her for dances and then laughed idiotically at every damn thing she said. Mother would be there to chaperon, getting gently tiddly on cold punch; and to cap it all Vicky would have a simply spiffin' time with Reggie and humbug about it for days on end, until everyone was sick to death with gowns and coiffures and all the latest titbits of society gossip. Oh Lord how dull!

But then she heard from Simmie that Ned Ashby had been invited through some London acquaintance of his grandmother's – and of course everything had changed totally. With Prince Charming himself in attendance, the ball suddenly became magic – the opportunity she'd been waiting for since that sunny Sunday morning in Harpur Street when she'd first seen her own destiny in Ned's blue eyes.

There'd scarcely been time to have the new gown made, let alone prepare the Mater for it, and under the circumstances Meriel thought it advisable to dispense with the final fitting, to arrange for the dress to be delivered on the afternoon of the ball itself. That way there would be no going back. And when the time came, she personally received the dress box from the hands of Madame Lena's assistant, commandeering Aunt Alice's maid to iron it out for her before supper.

"Be sure to use the box-iron, Effie!" she called after her, as she'd heard her mother do so often on such occasions. "And a flannel board – and paper, mind! And test the iron on your apron first, Effie, I don't want it scorched, d'ye hear?"

Vicky always bathed and dressed a good two hours before it was strictly necessary. So Meriel waited until her sister was well clear of the bedroom before emerging from her own hasty bath.

"Plenty of time – plenty of time," she assured Harriet, who was always convinced that everyone was going to be late, and had been anxiously rapping on the bathroom door. "For goodness sake, Mother, we don't have to leave for well over an hour – and Effie's going to help me."

"But I haven't even *seen* your dress!" Harriet wailed. "Why for all we know Madame What's-her-name has made it far too large – and there'll be no time to alter it!"

"Don't be silly, Mother, you know it'll be just fine. So why don't you go and stop Vicky sitting hers into creases – I'll be down in half a jiff, you'll see." She waved an airy hand at her as she crossed the landing. "Plenty of time."

Inside the bedroom it was a different story. "Hurry up, Effie, hurry *up,*" she hissed. "I'm late as anything, and at this rate we're never going to make it! No, not the corset – it's hair isn't it, *hair* first for heaven's sake! Have you got the curling tongs, then? And the spirit lamp? Well *light* it then – oh, give it to me – you start brushing out! Honestly, Effie, I thought you were meant to be good at this sort of thing? We really *are* going to be late you know if you don't get your skates on!"

Evening dress suited Ned, which was a good deal more than could be said for formal affairs in Belgravia. It was all very well for Grannie to pitch him into a ballroom of landed-gentlewomen and then sit back to await results. She didn't have to dance with the ninnys did she? Or to pretend interest in their inane chatter. Or to have to struggle first with ridiculously shaped bows that were next to impossible to tie! In the end he gave up, and took it down to Simmie in the parlour.

"Ned – how handsome you look, dear, quite the young dandy!" she said, reaching up to coax the recalcitrant bow into position. She said it in a favourite-auntie kind of voice that immediately made him want to do something passionate and shocking – anything to stop her from going calmly on like this, pretending that nothing had happened between them! And yet he knew that he wouldn't try to shock her, or hurt her in any way.

"I wish you were coming, Simmie," he said simply, and bent his head to kiss her slim fingertips as she gave the tie a final little tug for luck.

"Dear Ned." She dropped her hands quite casually, as if she hadn't noticed. "Do you know, I'm very glad that I'm not coming – because between you and me, dear, I never did care very much for dancing. And I'm sure I'd be quite out of my depth amongst all those titles and uniforms. Besides, you'll have Meriel Llewellen and her sister to dance with, Ned. Did I mention that they were going to be there?"

106

No of course she hadn't mentioned it! And both of them knew damn well why. Because he'd certainly have declined the invitation if he'd known, that's why. You couldn't talk to that girl – she said such ridiculous things. You couldn't look at her because she stared so. You couldn't even think about her without developing two left feet. Meriel Llewellen – that was all he needed!

"Well, here goes then!" Meriel gave Effie a conspiratorial smile and rustled across the room to open the door. The little maid-servant was still standing by the dressing table with her palms pressed tight together – an expression on her face that told Meriel everything she wanted to know.

"She looks like I always felt when we'd finished decorating the Christmas tree," she thought complacently; and slowly began her descent to the hall. The merciless diagonal-seam corset was so long in the busk that she could scarcely bend sufficiently to see her own feet. What with all the petticoats and the train and her two and a half inch Louis heels, the simple act of walking downstairs had taken on a new and exciting character. Meriel laughed aloud. If she fell and broke her neck it would be Ned's fault – and she'd never let him forget it! The shoes were of satin, dyed to match the dress, and as she lifted the hem, Meriel could just glimpse the contrasting white of her new silk stockings. Her kid gloves were white too, from fingertip to elbow, powdered inside and buttoned with twelve pearl buttons – while in her hand she carried a small, spangled gauze fan.

"Yes, oh yes!" she exulted. "Got him on toast!"

Down in the sitting room Harriet was doing her best to be amiable, with one prominent eye on the clock and the other on the open door. "I can't tell you how relieved I am, Mr Baxter, now that you and Victoria are engaged and no longer in need of a chaperon. I daresay these affairs are all very well for the young, but I'm afraid I find them insupportable – the noise and the crush you know, quite intolerable!" She pressed a plump little hand to her forehead, as if she could already feel the headache coming. "And I'm so very obliged to you for taking my little Meriel," she continued breathily, still watching the door. "She's thrilled, positively thrilled, Mr Baxter. We've had a new gown made especially, so you'll have to forgive her if she delays you just a little. You see she's . . . oh!"

Meriel swept dramatically into the doorway and remained there, posed, with head high and fan extended. Her dark hair had been dressed higher than usual, without pads or ornament, piled and twisted on itself – swept up from small ears to reveal Harriet's best pearl drop earrings, still dancing and swinging with the force of her entrance.

But nobody noticed Meriel's hair or her earrings. They were all too busy staring at her breasts – pushed up, pushed out and exposed almost to their nipples above the uncompromising tightness of the bodice. As Meriel watched, three mouths – the Mater's, Aunt Alice's and Reggie's popped open into three perfect O's. You'd think they'd all just heard the last trump to look at them, she thought, and that at damn close range. Then the scarlet macaw in the window began to whistle like a kettle, and everyone's mouth shut with a snap.

The pattern they'd approved at Madame Lena's had illustrated a charming little gown with a fashionably bloused front and modestly scooped neckline, with lace around the bodice and frilly, lacy elbow-sleeves. The reality as worn by Meriel had no neck and no blousing and no sleeves worth the name. Her shoulders and upper arms and the best part of her bosom emerged from it entirely bare. Two little puffs of gathered fabric stood out like wings on either side, just above her elbows – and from waist to hem the gown flowed sheer, in great sleek swathes of mahogany silk.

"The lace, Meriel? What have you done with the lace?" The first after the parrot to find her voice, Aunt Alice took refuge in a detail.

"Invaluable!" Meriel pronounced – and turned in the doorway to reveal a huge antique lace bow on her mahogany rump, trailing to the end of the train in an elongated swallowtail. "We made one or two little changes to the original," she added unnecessarily, rustling on into the room. "Do you like it?" She was looking pointedly at Reggie – and he jumped in gallantly, if a little late on cue.

"Aha – um, awfully swanky, what?"

If he hadn't been there or had shown the slightest hint of disapproval, it's certain that Harriet would have created the first class row that Vicky had predicted, and insisted that Meriel should change. Now she was forced to settle for a compromise.

"Well of course the wretched woman's made it far too low," she exclaimed, hurrying forward to drag at Meriel's *décolletage* as if she thought she could hoist it up by sheer force. "You'll have to wear a fichu." And she hustled her daughter away into the sewing room to fit her out with a Venetian point lace shawl, with a cameo brooch to hold it in position.

The makeshift fichu really looked surprisingly effective, Harriet thought, like Marie Antoinette; although the gown was still absurdly old for the girl. And one way or another she'd been so preoccupied with preventing her daughter from making a public spectacle of herself, that she entirely failed to wonder at Meriel's uncharacteristic co-operation – or to jib at the loan of the earrings.

"What a fool Mother is," Meriel remarked to Vicky twenty minutes later in the Grosvenor Crescent cloakroom – removing first her cape and then the lace fichu, and dropping the cameo neatly into her dorothy bag. "Righto – lead on, McDuff, I'm ready!"

The scene outside was one she was never likely to forget – arriving like a princess in Reggie's carriage, to have the door opened by a wigged and liveried footman and to step out onto a red carpet. There'd been a monumental doric portico with a red and white striped awning, guests and carriages galore, and a faint sweet smell of syringa drifting across from Belgrave Square. And inside everything had fulfilled the promise of that enchanted exterior. There was a tremendous crush of people in the vestibule, moving in and out of doors, up and down the shallow stairs like angels on Jacob's ladder – with candlelight gleaming on black marble columns and white satin cloak linings, winking and glittering on jewels and shirt studs and splendid military uniforms. And cut flowers – carnations, lilies and gladioli in every corner and alcove – and music, drifting down from the ballroom above.

It was far and away the biggest and most exciting function that Meriel had ever attended in London, and a far cry indeed from the Assembly Room subscription dances back home in Ipswich. At the top of the second flight of stairs awaited a long receiving line of unknown titled names and limp hands, and frosty eyes – all of them staring fixedly at her bosom. Beyond that, swacks and swacks of polished floor swishing with dancing figures. And beyond that, standing alone by a sculpted marble fireplace – there was Ned.

Chapter Eleven

He saw her advancing towards him. He could hardly avoid it, the way she swept through the pale tulles and chiffons of the dance floor in her devil-may-care dark silk – like a merlin through a flock of peewits. The *décolletage* was quite outrageous, and despite everything, Ned couldn't suppress a grin. It was somehow typical of Meriel to have to go one better than everyone else – and heaven only knows how she kept the dress up! The effect was pretty damn stunning, though that was certain, and when you saw so much of the girl's clear white flesh, it was impossible for any man not to think of what remained concealed. Personality aside, she was an immensely desirable girl – put all the rest in the shade. That had been only too obvious to Ned from the moment he'd first focused on Meriel's swinging violet fringes in the little back yard at Harpur Street.

But the trouble with Llewellen's daughter was that you couldn't leave her personality aside. It intruded on everything – strained contacts, killed natural conversation stone dead. She wasn't like Simmie, she didn't have any native tact or understanding. If she embarrassed or discomforted you – which she invariably did – she'd never look away or change the subject. She'd merely stare all the harder with those bold, striking brown eyes – as if she'd come upon you unexpectedly in pondwater at the far end of a microscope.

Ned had suspected all along that Meriel's awkward manner masked something infinitely more appealing, and the fact that she laboured so hard and so obviously to hide it from him, always set them off on the wrong foot. If only she realized it, the things she concealed were the very things he missed in her. He'd like to have taken her hand and climbed with her up through the beech woods to the Bury-house, to stand on the open roof of the downs square in the path of a sou'westerly off the Channel. Then perhaps she'd understand and let him see her too as she really was – when she'd watched the sea dashing against the chalk cliffs, and the pale sere grasses rippling across the hills, and the sky whipped into cloud fantasies of mountains and castles and billowing sails . . .

"Why, Mr Ashby – all alone? Permit me to present my sister Victoria, and her fiancé, Mr Reginald Baxter."

"Delighted to meet you," he said gravely.

The sister was tall and good looking, in a conventional doll-faced kind of way. The fellow was a poor stick though, and so typical that Ned smiled again for entirely the wrong reasons as he shook his hand. He had a figure like a hock bottle, patent leather hair and an eyeglass – and to think that this was the superior breeding that Grannie coveted for the Ashbys!

"Well now," Meriel said, flicking up a beribboned dance programme in a businesslike way and licking the end of her pencil. "Which engagements can we put you down for, Mr Ashby?"

And once again there'd been no escape. With ruthless efficiency she marked him down for three dances before and three dances after the interval; and then whisked him off onto the floor in a grip of steel.

"Delightful floor, Mr Ashby, don't you agree, and don't you just love to waltz? I could waltz and waltz all night, I assure you, and never grow tired!"

Meriel Llewellen clearly preferred talking to listening. She experimented then with a tinkling little laugh that set Ned's teeth on edge and she stooped at the first strains of the Valse Bleu to catch the loop of her train on her right wrist. As she did so Ned gazed straight down into the soft valley between her breasts. Then she looked up suddenly and caught him at it, so that he practically had to dislocate his neck from then on to avoid a repetition. She embarrassed him – she embarrassed him dreadfully with her meaningless chatter and her inescapable eyes, and her blatantly desirable body thrust against him. In his embarrassment Ned felt unmanned; and unmanned, he frankly wished himself anywhere but here dancing with Meriel Llewellen.

Ned had danced with her just as she planned, and danced well too. But he'd been stiff and unresponsive in her arms, and when he looked at her breasts there'd been nothing in his eyes, not even a hint of impropriety. They left him cold, dammit! And yet she loved him – she loved his wide smile and his strong arms. She loved his fair hair, darkened and shiny with brilliantine, and the romantic dreamy look in his eyes. She loved him to distraction, and nobody understood – not Da, not Simmie, not anyone! She loved him – she'd turned her back on her own father for him – and still Ned Ashby rejected her.

As they walked back across the polished floor, Meriel became irritably aware of the people around her – dapper little men in penguin suits and scarlet uniforms, dwarfed by their partners' plumes and henna-tinted coiffures, and overborne by the shrill cadences of their voices. They were the élite, the cream of London society, these people. They looked down their aristocratic noses at girls like her and called her "colonial" behind her back, she knew they did. Yet they themselves could talk only about Ascot and Cowes and the wretched bloody Season, as if that's all there ever was to life. They all seemed to know each other too, conversing in an extravagant jargon of their own – finding it screamingly funny to mispronounce things, to use exaggerated French accents or to tack Italian endings onto English words. "Lovelare darling!" they shrilled, "Marvellissimo – Fantisticamente!", waving madly at one another with their outsize ostrich feather fans. Meriel could cheerfully have throttled the lot of them.

To Ned Ashby and Meriel Llewellen that evening the ballroom in Grosvenor Crescent was an alien environment, with nothing in it, it seemed, to bridge the gulf that yawned between them still. But then few things are ever entirely what they seem.

Like most old-fashioned town houses with miles of wainscotting and no more than the odd elderly cat to patrol it, the mansion had a chronic rodent problem. There were mice in the cavities beneath the ballroom floor and above its crystal chandeliers, mice behind the gilded plasterwork of the dining room – and three or four prime specimens foraging at that very moment beneath the starched linen cloth of the running buffet. The clatter of porcelain and clink of silver overhead were all in a day's work to these socially experienced individuals; Reggie Baxter's plummy voice no more disturbing to their peace of mind than the swish of a housemaid's broom along the wainscot.

"Frightfully decent prog, what?" Reggie's foot beneath the cloth as he reached forward for the ices was another matter, however. The giant polished toe of his pump crashed into their peaceful rodent world with the force of a torpedo, and mice scattered in all directions.

Even so, only one mouse, the youngest, was foolish enough to abandon the twilit shelter of the buffet; and finding himself terrifyingly exposed to light and movement, he promptly took refuge in a convoluted embankment of white chiffon that lay in his path. Sadly, the lining of a lady's train proved no substitute though, for the stability of the dining room buffet, and after dragging the confused rodent the width of the room, Vicky Llewellen once again exposed him to the greater world as she swept in through the door of the ballroom.

The Contes d'Hoffman had just ended, and presented with the choice of a moving skirt or a stationary one, the mouse bolted for the imagined safety of the Hon. Aurora Gorrel-Smythe's oyster taffeta. In a commotion of piercing squeals and flapping frou-frou this refuge instantly yielded to another, equally unstable. And within seconds the floor was cleared of dancers, uniformed officers hard on the heels of their shrieking partners – to leave the mouse in sole possession for the two-step.

Meriel didn't stop to think, any more than the mouse had. Whenever a mouse or a tarantula had been discovered in their house at Ipswich, it was always Meriel who'd had to cope, and clearly things were no different here. The second she spied the creature scurrying towards her she left Ned's side and took four or five good strides out onto the floor to meet it. There'd naturally been no question of bending at the waist in the diagonal-seam corset. But she could still curtsy well enough – and with a single, accurate sweep of her arm she successfully caught the thing in mid-flight. The mouse bit her quite sharply as a matter of fact, clean through her glove. But as she rose and turned back towards the company, Meriel's face contained only that look of modest and maidenly virtue that she'd so often tried and failed to achieve in other circumstances.

"Up Australia!" she thought triumphantly, giving the unfortunate rodent a hard and fatal squeeze. The aristocrats had squawked and flapped all right, but it had taken a colonial girl to know what to do! And this time she'd got it right – she could tell by the undiluted admiration in Ned's blue eyes. Smiling demurely she hailed a lackey with an empty salver, and deposited the twitching corpse on it – face up.

"Horriblino," someone drawled in an inane Kensington accent; and the next moment everyone was roaring with laughter – her rare and lovely Ned included. She was the heroine of the hour, no doubt of that. Suddenly everyone wanted to talk to her, to listen engrossed to all the old tales of Australia and the Pacific and the South American continent. The men swarmed around her like bees round a honeypot, and best, best of all, Ned not only claimed every dance that she'd marked on his card, but demanded all the Extras as well. They danced waltzes and polkas together, two-steps and lancers. They danced to La Mattiche, 'the most wonderful tune in the world'. And at three in the morning they joined in the furious John Peel gallop that ended the ball – then spurned Reggie's carriage to walk home unchaperoned beneath a moon like a Japanese lantern.

Meriel had just about danced her hair down. Her feet ached like the devil and the red imprints of her corset stayed with her long after Vicky released her from it. But who cared! She pulled back the curtains and sprawled barefoot on the window seat – watching the sky pale and then fray into a long ribbon of peach-coloured light above the chimneys. And with one hand flat on her stomach and the other twined in her hair, she re-lived every word that Ned has spoken to her that night – every glance of his dear blue eyes.

"You've simply got to get your grandmother to invite me down for a weekend at The Bury as soon as ever you can," she instructed Ned over tea at Simmie's that afternoon. (Left to his own devices he might well take half the summer getting around to it – and that kind of patience she didn't have!) "Simmie will come with me as chaperon, won't you, Simmie? She adored that cycling trip, didn't you, Simmie? And this one will be forty thousand times more fun!"

"Oh no dear," Simmie said quickly. "Sweet of you to think of me, but I couldn't leave Gussie for a whole weekend. He hasn't been very fit recently, you know."

"That's right," Ned agreed, nodding hard. "And I really think we should invite your mother – awfully bad form not to."

"Oh very well, ask her if you must then – but don't blame me if you live to regret it!" Meriel felt altogether too pleased with life to be cross with them, even if they were being awkward. "Simmie, do you mind if I open a window? I'm sure we're all stifling to death in here – and you two have gone red as turkey-cocks, you should see yourselves!"

Ned met them at the station himself, in a funny little red and yellow governess-cart drawn by the portly bay cob Meriel had first met with in the Bury stables.

"Has to be light to get us all up the hill," Ned explained, "sorry if it's a bit of a squash." And he politely pretended not to notice how the shafts jerked up as he handed Mrs Llewellen in. He was informal in cap and plaid necktie, tanned from long hours in the hayfields – more real and alive than Meriel had ever seen him. In Harpur Street, in Simmie's parlour, he'd frequently stand with his fists in his pockets and his heels on the fender, or perch on the edge of his chair with his hands dangling between his knees, his eyes glued to the carpet. But here he was a different man. His head was up, his hands firm on the reins. He smiled and pointed and chatted to Harriet as if he'd known her for years. And all the time his eyes were scanning the bleached Sussex landscape with a joyful pride that made Meriel feel almost envious of it.

"The gap in the cliffs over there, do you see, Mrs Llewellen? That's Cuckmere Haven, where the old 'Fair Traders' landed their French contraband in exchange for the wool that my rascally ancestors smuggled out. It used to be big business once here in Sussex, you know."

"Smugglers! And in your own family, Mr Ashby? How simply thrilling!"

"And have you noticed the way the thorn trees all grow in one direction down here, Mrs Llewellen – all away from the wind? There's nothing between here and France to turn it, you see, they get the full force. And up there, right up there near the top – do you see the speckles of white? Do you see them, Miss Llewellen? That's part of the Bury ewe flock – purebred Southdowns, every one of 'em – best sheep in the world for this kind of land. My family had quite a hand in breeding them too . . . "

"I'll have a go now if you don't mind," Meriel interrupted him suddenly, reaching over for the ribbons. The cob had been taking the downhill gradient at a regular snail's pace and if someone didn't light a fire under the stodgy old thing, why they'd be all day getting nowhere! "I always used to drive the wagonette to fetch Da home from Brisbane, didn't I, Mother? I'm a dab hand at this, you'll see!"

"Now, Meriel!" Harriet's voice was squeaky with alarm. "You always drove that wagonette too fast, you know you did – in heaven's name, girl, you're doing it now! Oh don't let her, Mr Ashby, it's only a trotting road and she'll have us over in the ditch any minute. Why look, she isn't even wearing the right gloves!"

"Anyone would think it was Mother and not us who had to get out and walk up the hill – the way she created!" Sitting on the beach at Sellington Gap that afternoon, Meriel regaled Ned's sister Helen with her version of the journey to the farm.

"Ooh Meriel! I'm going to fall out, I know I am! Can't you do anything about the angle of this vehicle, Mr Ashby, are you sure this door's safe? Oh no it's too steep – I can't bear it. I'm getting out! I tell you I'm getting out!" Her imitation was hilariously accurate, somehow managing to convey Harriet's looming bulk beneath the clutching hands and rolling eyes. Helen was giggling uncontrollably, between nervous glances up the beach at her grandmother. She had never heard anyone say anything so irreverent about a parent before, even at school – and she thought Meriel Llewellen most frightfully daring.

"A Gap day, most definitely," Ned's grandmother had decreed at lunch. "In this climate of ours you have to take your opportunities where you find them, Mrs Llewellen. And take my word for it, a day without wind is a rare and wonderful thing in Sellington. We'll go at half past three and take a picnic, shall we?" The "shall we?" had been for form's sake only, because no one would have argued.

She was right in any case – it wasn't a day to be missed. The governess-cart with the same sober old cob between the shafts had creaked and rattled down the track to the sea, laden with deck chairs and camp stools and all the essential paraphernalia of a full scale Bury picnic. Mrs Ashby drove herself, with the house-parlourmaid behind her and Harriet squeezed in opposite them beneath a large striped gig umbrella – while Ned and the girls made their own way on foot through a blazing corridor of barley.

There was a five-barred gate at the end of the track beside a pair of limewashed coastguard cottages, and beyond it a delapidated bathing machine drawn up above the tidemark. On either side the chalk cliffs rose abruptly to form the Gap itself, with tufts of thrift and purple knapweed clinging to their crevices and hosts of summer butterflies rejoicing in their glare – whites and gatekeepers, and dozens upon dozens of tiny chalkhill blues.

"Last one in's a giddy-goat!"

Meriel waited to chant it until she was almost in the water. But Ned could dive, and she couldn't in her new bathing cap – and to her fury he'd whooped past her at the last minute to fling himself in with an almighty splash. He was still out there now amongst the seagulls and the skimming swallows, while she sat with Helen on the beach impatiently waiting for the moment when he came in – shivery and shiny and wet all over. Seeing him out of his clothes like this made her think of other men – of men generally – of Da, of the corded brown arms of a Queensland cattle drover, of the sprouting red hair in the neck of Daniel Goodworth's shirt. And now she rather wanted to see him again, her Ned, all of him from head to foot, coming out of the sea to her in his wet costume like a lovely stripey Greek god.

From the water, Ned's view of Sellington was reduced to a series of horizontal bands of colour, compressed between the blue masses of the sea and the sky – grey for the beach, white for the cliffs, green and gold for the downland and barley fields between them. On the beach he could see Gran and Mrs Llewellen settled in their deck chairs, and Bridget, busy with her collapsible spirit stove and tea caddy. And Helen down by the water's edge in her navy worsted bathing dress – with Meriel Llewellen beside her.

She was sitting on a rock, like a siren, with the long stems of her legs squeezed together, bare to the knees, and a wedge of wet fabric folded in tight between them. She was talking, waving her slim arms in the air while Helen gawped and giggled. But even at this distance he could tell that her eyes were on him, exulting in her power over him – irresistibly drawing him back to the shore.

Margaret Ashby watched her grandson swimming in to the girl, shaking the water from his eyes, and vaulting up onto the rock beside her in as fine a show of exhibitionism as she'd seen in the young addlepate.

"You're makin' a regular fool of yourself over that girl, Ned, d'ye know that?" She waited until the Llewellens retired after dinner, and then summoned the boy to her bedroom. "No background, Ned, none at all. Great-grandfather Welsh . . . " and for all her London education, Margaret said it exactly as Bat would have said "furrin" . . . "a Taffy who made his money in coal, if you please! Grandfather married a French maid – father's a ne'er-do-well, mother's a nincompoop. Rag, tag and bobtail – that's what they are, rag, tag and bobtail."

"You've absolutely no right to pass judgements like that, Gran, no right at all. I'm twenty-two now, you know, and old enough to choose whom I please for my friends."

"Old enough my eye!" His grandmother snorted with amusement. "Old enough to choose a doxy p'raps, when you've only yourself to please. That girl's unstable, Ned, and socially impossible – sticks out a mile. And just remember this, boy, you'll be choosin' for your heirs and this valley of ours when you marry – not just for your own pleasure."

Chapter Twelve

It was unusually warm and close the next morning. Ned had kicked the covers from his bed to lie naked, staring at the cracks on the ceiling and listening to the sudden echoes of his father's shotgun knocking over rabbits in the wood. He was thinking of the other time he'd lain like this, in the winter – reflecting how different things might be now if he'd left Llewellen's calling card where it was in the pocket of his old Norfolks.

His fantasy that other time had been of a faceless golden Venus with a soft belly and enveloping thighs – a physical ideal with no life of her own outside his pleasure. But that wasn't how it had been with the real Simmie. Nor, as it turned out, was it what he really needed. He needed to give not just to take, he knew that now. The warm fountains of love welling up inside him carried with them more than the seeds of his body. They carried the need to give of himself – to love and be loved for the rest of his mortal life. Something too committing for Simmie, who still lived with the memory of Robert Llewellen; something too emotional for Gran, who thought only in terms of bloodlines. Now the chain of events that had begun with the calling card had led him on to Llewellen's daughter; and Ned couldn't help wondering if Meriel too would draw back at the critical moment, as Simmie had done, to leave him exposed in his need for her.

He slid off the bed and walked to the open window. On the croquet lawn beneath, the grass was cauled with a web of dewy gossamer, catching and refracting the morning sun in a dozen points of white and emerald light. The ramparts of the downs beyond were pale and indistinct, the trees dark in their summer foliage – the barley ripening, bowed to its own weight. Even the birds seemed subdued and replete. It was a time of pregnancy, of coming fruition. Next week the binders and teams would be out, swishing and racketing through the oatfields. Then all too soon the Sheep Fair would be on them and ploughing, and the first mists of autumn.

As Ned stood with crossed arms contemplating the changes he felt in himself and the season, a figure moved out from the shadow of the house and onto the wet grass. It was Meriel – hatless, coatless with her hair looped and plaited and tied with a black ribbon; Meriel, slashing at the daisies with Gran's favourite blackthorn walking stick. Ned stepped back hastily to grab for his dressing gown and smooth his own hair into some rough sort of order, all else forgotten. "Hello there," he called down hoarsely. "I say, you're up early."

She looked up without surprise and smiled at his smile, enchantingly. "You don't call this early, do you? You're disgustingly late, that's all – and I thought you farmers were all supposed to be up with the lark!"

"Ssh – you'll wake Gran, and then there'll be the devil to pay! Wait there, I'll be down in two minutes." He broke all records for dressing and hair-brushing and peeing and getting downstairs, chortling to himself like a fool and wondering how he could ever have felt nervous of that slender, smiling girl down there. It was summer, it was Sunday and the sun was shining – and here she was in Sellington to share it all with him! He'd take her down to see the milking and to watch Bat and Jemmy move the folds. They'd explore the farm together, and the house and have a cuppa in the kitchen with dear old Cook. And hearing her enthuse over it, and seeing her adore it all as he did, Grannie would have to admit that she'd been wrong about Meriel Llewellen.

"Gawd a'mighty, you look as if you got dressed in a hurricane! Here, let me put you to rights." She hoisted his tie for him and actually reached up to brush his hair back from his forehead. "You'd look a lot better, you know, with a centre parting like Da's – you'll have to try it."

Ned glanced up at the house. "There'd be a first class stink if they knew we were out here alone together at this hour of the morning," he said.

"Pooh – who cares what they think!"

She'd stopped pretending with him now and he loved her for that. But he couldn't relax himself until he'd manoeuvred her out of sight of the windows and onto the steep little back path that led down from the kitchen door to the dairy. At the bottom, where the track up from the Gap skirted the ivy-clad wall of the cowshed, they met the milking herd slouching back to the fields – red and piebald and strawberry roan. Dan Goodworth was behind them, whistling "Annie Laurie" and lobbing pebbles at the laggards.

"Morning, Danny. I was just bringing Miss Llewellen down to watch the milking, but I see you're all through."

"Yup, milk's down 'smornin', Mus Ned. "Bent overmuch grass jes' now – an' whad ther is ent thad flush. Poor lit'le mouse-eared stuff, I'd call et." He gave Ned a broad, friendly smile and winked at Meriel as he passed her. "Marnin' Miss – tarrible swelt sorta day fer the race wouldn' yer say?"

"Good morning, Mr Goodworth." To his surprise Ned saw that she was right back on her old high horse again, as cold as a January moon. "And what race might that be, may I ask?"

"Why bless yer, Miss, the 'uman race ter be sure!" Dan chuckled pleasantly and flung another pebble at the cows, leaving Meriel to glare after him, fuming with silent rage. Nor did she fare any better with Bat Vine. The old shepherd stood very patiently with his hat in his hand to listen to her lecture on the superiority of the Australian Merino sheep. Then he returned it gravely to his head with a nod at Ned.

"Baggered ef ther wus iver a wooman 'oo knowed the fust thing aboot shi'p," he remarked philosophically. "Hee-ar! Dang ye, come in Lass!" And off he went, following the hummocking rumps of his ewes with the same unhurried stride as the cowman.

Even Cook was too preoccupied with her breakfast to give Meriel more than a fraction of her attention. "Pleased ter meet yer I'm sure, Miss," she said as she shaped and crumbed another fishcake for the pan. "An' now Master Ned, run along, will yer kiddy, 'afore the bell goes fer prayers. Unless you want me ter pin a dishcloth on yer tail, thad is?"

"Wun't be druv", that's what they always said of Sussex folk – and reluctantly Ned supposed that he couldn't actually force them to see Meriel as he did and accept her into their world. But they would in time, he was sure of it – and Meriel would grow to love them too when she knew them all better.

It was sweet, Meriel thought, the way Ned kept pushing forward everything and everyone he'd grown up with for her approval. But she did rather wish he wouldn't. It cramped her style so to feel him watching for her reactions all the time – begging her to endure the interminable Sunday service in Sellington Church, willing her to show an interest in his ineffectual father's discourse over luncheon on the disappearance of the Great Bustard from Sussex. All she was actually interested in was getting him on his own again, without Mother or the doglike Helen trailing after them.

Her chance came immediately after lunch, when the older ladies toddled upstairs for their afternoon 'peace hour', as Mrs Ashby called it, and Ned's father retired to the library with the *Sunday Times*. A quiet little game of mah-jong or a jigsaw puzzle was suggested for the younger folk, and it had only been necessary for Meriel to whisper in Helen's ear that she'd prefer to ride, to ensure some time to themselves while the simple creature went off to find the groom and help him saddle up.

"Come on, lazybones," she said to Ned as soon as his sister disappeared down the drive, "let's get out of here while the going's good. You can show me that little summer-house place up on the hill if you like. I bet she won't find us up there in a hurry!"

The sun barely filtered through to them as they climbed the steep path up through the shrubberies and into the tall colonnades of the Bury wood. Here and there it struck red on the carpet of last year's leaves, or pink like flesh on the smooth shaft of a tree. The dank smell of moss and leafmould was overpowering in the gloom, and the throaty song of a solitary blackbird echoed through the silence. They were there together, illicitly and in more intimate circumstances than ever before. Meriel could scarcely breathe for excitement, and when a wood pigeon had noisily clattered out of the branches above them, she reached for Ned's strong hand.

"Isn't it topping!" he said with shining eyes and looking, Meriel noticed, not at her but out through the wood. "You should see it with the bluebells though, over there where the oaks are. It's so beautiful you'd never believe it!" He whistled to call Bess back to him from her explorations of some distant rabbit warren.

'And you should see me in my birthday suit!' Meriel thought sourly. 'Then perhaps you'd forget about the confounded bluebells, and actually do something about *me*!'

"We're almost at the top now, Miss Llewellen – and look, I want you to close your eyes and keep them shut until I say, all right? I want you to see this for the first time just as it should be seen." He pulled her up onto the level as he said it and turned her to face the south. She shut her eyes obediently, exalting in the feeling of his body guiding hers, his hands on her shoulders. She leant back against him. In a moment he'd stop all this silly jaw and spin her round to take her in his arms and kiss her. She just knew he would!

"All right, you can open now." His voice was low and vibrant with pride. "Don't speak though, don't say anything – just feel it!"

'Just as well,' Meriel thought, 'can't think of a damn thing to say anyway!' In her opinion Ned was making a great deal too much fuss altogether over a collection of treeless hills and a bit of chalk and a distant view of the sea. But she stood for a moment nonetheless, pretending to take in the details of the scene before adjusting her own features to the required expression of rapture.

"And this is the summer house?"

"The Bury-house," Ned corrected – as if it mattered two farthings.

"Well it's most romantic, I must say. A kind of a Greek temple, isn't it? But what's the mound that it's built on – that isn't natural, surely?"

"Nobody really knows. It could be neolithic – or part of a Bronze Age hill fort, or a Saxon burial mound, perhaps? There's even a legend about a golden calf buried in these chalk hills, and our foreman Shad Caldwell says it's under here for sure."

"Better dig it up then! Da would do it for you – just up his street."

"You can't, that's part of the legend – if you dig for the calf it disappears. They used to come up here from the village, though, in the old days. Gran remembers it from when she was a girl. Every Easter Sunday the village girls had to dance around the Bury-house mound and sing a little song that was meant to ensure that they'd marry and have children – a leftover from some old fertility rite I suppose."

"What was the song – do you know it?" Meriel was genuinely intrigued.

"Well yes, but . . . "

"Sing it then!" She pointed at him like a queen, with the mottled pink and white sceptre of a foxglove that she'd just dragged up by the roots from beside the Bury-house steps. "Come on, spit it out!"

He looked at her silently for a moment. She saw his adam's apple bob up and then down again as he swallowed. Finally he sang the ditty for her self-consciously and barely above a whisper:

> "Hey diddle derry, dance round the Bury—
> Hey diddle derry – da-nce to the man."

"Bravo – love it!" she cried, and pranced off on her own around the mound, waving the foxglove and chanting the rhyme at the top of her voice:

> "Hey diddle derry, dance round the Bury—
> Hey diddle derry – da-nce to the man!"

"Miss Llewellen – shush, they'll hear you down at the house!" But he couldn't help laughing. "As a matter of fact there still is a fertility rite of sorts attached to the Bury-house. We Ashbys are all meant to propose in there, you see. They say that Grannie nearly gave my grandfather a heart attack trying to get him up the slope in time!"

"Really?" Meriel stopped dancing right away, and started up the steps instead. "Let's go inside then. And for heaven's sake stop calling me Miss Llewellen!''

'Come on – *come on!*' she thought, settling herself on the rough-stone bench and practically jiggling in her impatience as she beckoned him to sit beside her. 'Now he's *got* to kiss me, that at least – and with any luck he'll come right out with it and propose!'

But he didn't come out with anything, anything at all. He just sat there dumb as a fish with his hands between his knees, staring out at the wretched view – and at the dog, Bess, lying at the foot of the Bury-house steps with her nose on her paws. She might have known he'd need prompting, even in this. What a case!

"We had a cable from Da last week," she said with sudden inspiration. "He's all cock-a-hoop about this new mercury mine. The Colombian Government have given him a six-year extension on the lease; and when Mother goes out to join him, he's asked me to go too to see her safe." She paused and allowed a second or two of silence to elapse before continuing. "Realizing of course that my sister could never agree to go – not now she's officially engaged to Reggie, don't y'know. Heavens, they'll be man and wife this time next year!"

There, she'd said it, so now it was up to him. Meriel cleared her throat and waited, but only for a moment. "Well then, what do you think? Shall I go or not?" She turned to Ned pointedly. When he looked up at her with that earnest, boyish expression on his handsome face, it was all Meriel could do not to lean over and damn well kiss it out of him!

'Say it, *say* it, can't you?' she thought, exasperated, tapping the ragged foxglove against her riding boot. Before he could open his mouth, though, Ned's expression changed. His eyes flickered past her to the entrance of the Bury-house, and Meriel turned to see the wretched Helen, of all people, panting towards them through the wood.

"There you are, I've been looking for you two everywhere!" Ned's sister called out enthusiastically. "The horses are all ready. Aren't you coming, then?"

In the end the Llewellens had to hire a private carrier to convey their seven trunks from Pimlico to Waterloo – not to mention innumerable cases, hat boxes, parcels and packages of every description. Just as before, the family followed on in four-wheelers; except that this time they were met by Simmie at the barrier, with an appropriately glum-looking Ned at her side.

In the four months since her abortive weekend in Sussex, Meriel had not only reconciled herself to Ned's failure to propose, but by some back-handed reasoning of her own had actually convinced herself that it could be for the best. Da's letters had revealed Colombia to her in vivid primary colours. Never one to throw up a good opportunity, she now perceived the place to be the best possible showcase for her own particular talents. She'd write at length to her old stick-in-the-mud Ned, that's what she'd do, to describe herself hacking her way through jungles, fording piranha-infested rivers, shielding poor, helpless Mother from every conceivable danger. And then he'd simply have to love her! He'd realize what a perfect dolt he'd been to let her go, and write back to her on his knees from the Buryhouse begging her to return – and to marry him . . .

Besides, she couldn't help recalling that he still had another boring year of study to get through at the university. And as an alternative to bicycling round London with Simmie while she waited, Da's description of the journey out to his mountain hacienda was practically irresistible – two weeks on a passenger steamer, nine hours on mountain railways, seven days in a river paddleboat, six days on horseback – and three days on mules, straight up into the central range of the Andes!

"Mother couldn't hope to make it without me, in any case," she assured herself, and that had clinched it.

It was only when she came to say goodbye to Ned on the deck of the Royal Mail Steam Packet that she experienced her first qualm. When she saw him standing below her on the quay with Vicky and the others, and Simmie in tears clinging to his arm – why then for two pins she'd have called the whole thing off. She'd long been planning her goodbye kiss, she'd even practised it in the mirror – a soft lingering kiss to remember her by the whole year through. When she had actually come to feel his arms around her, though, and to taste the taste of his mouth on hers, she'd clung fiercely to him like a little bear, unwilling ever to let him go.

But sensations of taste and touch are hard to retain in the

mind, particularly for someone like Meriel Llewellen; and by Barbados her worst regrets had been elbowed out of existence by the sheer thrill of the adventure ahead. The new year of 1906 and the rapid change of climate from a bleak English December to the intense heat of a Caribbean January, combined to produce in her a feeling of exciting unreality. The physical impressions of Ned's arms and lips faded beside images of palm trees and multicoloured shanty-towns, and Trinidad negroes in spotless white.

Reality of a kind returned with the Steam Packet's arrival at the Colombian port of Cartagena; and with the serious business of packing and getting Harriet up on deck while the ship still lay against the wharf waiting for the customs house to open.

"Do you know, dear, I think I feel a little better," Harriet conceded, now that the ship was safely anchored. "How do I look, all right?"

"You look at death's door, Mother, as always, and scarcely a day under eighty-five." Meriel was in no mood to humour her after the disgraceful way she'd behaved on board – forcing everyone to fetch and carry for her, too exhausted to come ashore in Barbados or Bridgetown or Port of Colombia, too sick to lift a finger – but not too jolly sick to consume quantities of champagne and candied cherries and wafer biscuits spread with caviare!

"And now Mother dear, if you feel strong enough to carry your own valise I think we should disembark, don't you, before the captain gives up on us and carries us on to Panama." It wasn't going to be easy, this commission of Da's to transport a woman of the Mater's bulk and temperament one thousand miles into the uncivilized interior of Equatorial America. But if anyone could do it she could. 'And the sooner we get started,' Meriel thought, 'the better.'

From the deck of the Steam Packet, Cartagena looked like something out of the Arabian Nights – a white walled city with a great cathedral dome, rising from a green phalanx of coconut palms. 'The Pearl of the Indies' they called it. One of the other passengers told Meriel that it had once been the principal Caribbean stronghold of the *conquistadores* – the harbour in which Spanish galleons had taken on gold, precious stones and indigo from the Isthmus and the plundered cities of the Incas. Drake had invaded it in the reign of Elizabeth, the buccaneer Henry Morgan a century later – and now Meriel Llewellen, armed with a fair smattering of Spanish and six pages of closely written instructions from Da.

From the rackety little wharf tram, she and the Mater took a *coché* to the Hotel Americano within the walls of the old city. Da's instructions on the subject had been graphic and Meriel knew what to look for: 'a lightweight American buggy,' he'd said, 'drawn by a pair of ratlike ponies, and driven by a negro in a sombrero with a speculative look in his eye'.

"Oh no, Meriel, I can't be expected to travel in a contraption like that, not over these roads!"

"Get in, Mother, or walk, it's entirely up to you." It was their first little trial of strength. In view of what lay ahead, Meriel could hardly afford to lose. And in the event, they'd both been surprised at the skill with which the black *cochero* skimmed them over the potholes and boulders that littered their path.

Inside the old city it was quite suffocatingly hot. The narrow canyons of its streets were pungent with cigar smoke and roasting coffee, intermingled with cooking smells and the stench of putrefaction that rose from the gutters. Overhead, the flaking walls of the houses met in a chaotic interlace of jutting pantiles and balconies, gutter spouts, birdcages and brilliantly painted shutters of scarlet, turquoise and canary yellow. On the balconies and in the doorways, and on the corners of the streets, men in sombreros waved and grinned and shouted after the two Englishwomen as they passed. The Hotel Americano was a typical Spanish colonial building of whitewashed wood, built around a central patio with the severest possible economy of furniture, doors and interior walls.

"It's a stable! Your father's landed us in a stable after all we've endured to get here!" Harriet practically dragged her daughter into their bedroom in her haste to catalogue her complaints. "No door – there's no door, I never heard of such a thing! Brick floors, iron beds, barely a stick of furniture and – I ask you Meriel – an Irish manageress!!" And Meriel watched her flick a disgusted handkerchief across the seat of her chair, before creaking down onto it with a prolonged sigh.

"It isn't filthy, Mother. If you bothered to look around you before condemning everything in sight, you'd see that it's perfectly clean. The driver told me that it's far and away the best hotel in Cartagena; and we can always tack a sheet up if you're that worried about the doors." She was too hot and tired herself to be bothered with Harriet's dramatics. "Mrs Walters is a pretty decent sort, in my opinion," she said firmly, "so you'd be well advised to be civil to her while we're here. She'll be sending over tea in a minute – and after that she's agreed to lend me the hotel *coché* to check on our luggage at the Customs."

"But the driver's black! Surely you can't be contemplating driving out alone with a black man, Meriel?" Harriet was aghast.

Meriel laughed. "His name's Antonio, Mother, Mrs Walters says he's perfectly trustworthy. And if the worst comes to the worst, I've always got my little revolver, haven't I?"

But as it happened, Antonio hadn't required shooting. On the contrary, he proved most useful in explaining to the Customs Officials the purpose of the drilling equipment Da had ordered from London, in making it clear to them that a British woman *never* gives bribes, and in conscientiously translating Meriel's final and heated ultimatum: "The Señorita wishes to make it clear that she will require your intestines for securing her stockings if her freight is not cleared within two days".

Afterwards she made him drive the *coché* down onto the beach beneath the palm trees, and to wait there while the Royal Mail Steam Packet steamed out. Antonio pulled his sombrero down over his eyes and affected sleep. But for the best part of an hour Meriel sat bolt upright on the seat behind him, shaded by the large green holland parasol that she'd bought in Trinidad, watching the ship until it was no more than the merest speck on the horizon.

She wasn't at all sure that she couldn't feel something of a lump in her throat at the breaking of this final link with England. She tried to picture Ned's face in this outlandish location – his eyes, his dear blue eyes. And his mouth – how was his mouth? She knew it, of course, she must do – and yet she couldn't see it. All she could recapture of him was the photograph that she herself had taken on the steps of Simmie's house in Harpur Street, and now carried with her in her bag. Curiously enough, when she thought about it she found that she could recall Da's face perfectly – and the bass tone of his voice, and the way he showed his teeth when he smiled. But not Ned's. Ned was reduced now to the man in the photograph – in his off-the-ankle tennis flannels and dashing new reefer, with his hands in his pockets and his eyes for once looking directly towards her. A splendid icon in a silver frame – as handsome and as two-dimensional as the Carstairs of her girlhood dreams, and now very nearly as remote.

Chapter Thirteen

Via New York
Señor Don Edwin C. Ashby,
19, Harpur Street,   'Casa Inglese',
London. W.C.   San Lorenzo,
Inglaterra   Rep. of Colombia
                                                     January 25th 1906

My dear Ned,

I wrote to you last from Cartagena just before we left. So there's a *great deal* to catch up on and I give you fair warning, this is going to be a fearfully long letter. You'll be suffering from brain-fag before the end, I shouldn't wonder!

Here we are then, safe and sound in San Lorenzo, which is quite something, isn't it? Mother isn't so chipper – thinks she's dying and all that. But apart from being very brown from the sun and having all our digestions permanently ruined, I really think we're none the worse for wear.

According to Da's instructions we left Cartagena by train early on the morning of the 13th – and *what* a train! – a miserable little engine half the size of nothing, and just two carriages with seats 'vis-a-vis' like a London underground train and an open door with a little balcony at the back. As soon as we were under way the dust just poured in on us from the line. Within minutes my hat was a miniature Sahara, I promise you. And what with that and the cigar smoke, I don't think Mother stopped coughing and spluttering for the entire five hours it took us to reach Calamar. There we were invaded even before the train stopped by a dozen or more beastly great Colombians, all fighting madly amongst themselves and with us for the privilege of carrying our traps to the river boat! One of them even tried to get the Mater's sealskin bag off her. But she hung onto it like grim death, screaming like a banshee – although it wasn't until I brought my parasol handle into play that the fellow could be induced to relinquish his grip. Thank goodness for hockey and fencing lessons at school, that's all I can say! You've got to be firm with foreigners, haven't you?

The river boat when we finally reached it was quite furiously hot, with hardly a breath of wind to disperse the heat from the funnel. So as you can imagine it was quite a relief to get out onto the water. The Magdalena River is still the only means of reaching the interior of this country. So anyone bound for almost anywhere must resign himself to at least a week on one of these slow old tubs. Ours was called the *Enriqué*, and really rather picturesque to look at – a real Huckleberry Finn paddle steamer – if a little short on comfort. It was built on three decks, with paddles at the rear and an enormous wood store in the bows to keep the boilers going. The cabins were quite tiny, with tin floors, like rows of little ovens – and totally uninhabitable from eight in the morning until after sunset. So our seven days on the river were mostly spent slacking around on deck, gasping in the heat and watching the forest slide by.

I can't tell you what a strange feeling it is passing through uninhabited swamps and forests for days and days on end. Out here in the back-of-beyond you sometimes feel as if you've lost touch with civilization altogether, and with everyone you're fond of. It's hard to believe now that I'll ever get back to dear old, chilly old England. I will though, you may be sure of *that!*

Meriel stopped for a moment, frowning and gnawing at the end of her pen. How to put it without giving too much of the game away?

Really I'm all at sixes and sevens just now, I have to confess, and feeling horribly uncertain about my own future . . .

Well that should set him thinking at least.

Not that there aren't plenty of distractions out here. You should just see the Rio Magdalena, Ned. In some places it's almost a mile wide, but when the boat came close enough in to one bank or another it quite often sent up big flocks of yellow and green parrots, shrieking their heads off. There were lots of little squirrel-monkeys too, leaping amongst the forest lianas – and literally hundreds of *huge* alligators lying in rows on the sandbanks, motionless as logs.

But the sunsets were the thing, Ned! The Magdelena's famous for them – and I do so wish you could have been there with me to see just *one* of them. I can't write for nuts (now don't contradict me!), but picture me standing at the rail in my white tropical outfit, looking out across a sheet of crimson water to a great flock of pink and white flamingos wading in the shallows – and above them a sun like a blood orange slowly sinking into the forest. Or come a little later to stand beside me when the moonlight's on the water, and the fireflies, the *candelelias,* move like tiny lanterns along the river banks. And listen with me to the rhythm of the paddleblades, and the strumming of Spanish guitars from the crew-deck beneath our feet . . .

And if that didn't get him going nothing would, she thought with satisfaction, returning the cap to her pen and shutting up her writing slope with a snap. There'd be plenty of time to finish the letter after dinner. No sense, though, in mentioning mosquitoes the size of elephants – or the perspiration, or the blisters on her face and arms, or Mother's diarrhoea. In fact the less said about her tiresome parent the better. No, she'd tell him instead about their train journeys up through the mountains from the Magdalena landing stage to the half-way rest house that Da had rented for them at San Lorenzo. And she'd describe herself with Da's *inventaria* in her hand, standing beside each little train to check every item of baggage on and off with proper British efficiency.

I do hope that you don't find this too 'egotistical' an account. But it's so hard to keep oneself out of one's own letters I find . . .

Whether she cared to admit it or not, a fundamental change had taken place in Meriel during the past few months. In the days before London and Ned Ashby, it had been nothing for her to go for weeks on end without giving either her behaviour or her appearance more than a passing thought. But now she was constantly, acutely aware of how she might appear in Ned's eyes, if only he could be there to see her. 'If only he could see me – if only he could see me *now!*' The wilder and more exotic her surroundings, the more persistently nagging was the thought. Whenever Meriel knew that she made a particularly pleasing picture – on the beach at Cartagena staring out soulfully from beneath her sea green parasol, or at the rail of the riverboat in the moonlight – Ned's own lack of substance became almost insupportable. In fact she never seemed to enjoy anything so much nowadays as when she was describing it to him, with suitable embellishment, in one of her interminable letters.

They had arrived at San Lorenzo the previous afternoon, to find a pleasant adobe hacienda all ready and waiting for them on a little rise at the edge of the village – the 'Casa Inglese'. A Union Jack fluttered bravely above the door, and on the verandah a negro cook and two hatchet-faced Indian maidservants waited to receive them. It was just like the story of Beauty and the Beast, with everything in readiness but no Master – only a letter in Da's handwriting lying on a cane table inside the door.

"But I thought he was going to be here to meet us, and Garry too!" Harriet protested for the tenth time since alighting at the station. "A nice example I call it – a nice example . . . !"

She was building up steam for another bout of tears, Meriel could tell; so she ripped open Da's letter to forestall her. "He says there's some difficulty up at the mine – he can't get away. But, but wait, Mother, he's sending Garry down with some horses, and mules for our baggage. They'll take about a week to get here, but Da says we'll be quite comfortable until they arrive. The cook's good, he says, and the maids willing – and they're all to come on with us when we leave to join him."

"But he's no right to send your brother down alone – a boy like that on a man's errand. It's sheer folly, Meriel! Why anything could happen to him – cut-throats, sunstroke, anything! And to think that he expects us to ride on to him, on horseback, alone and unprotected – while he sits up there on his mountain like some little tin god! Well I'm sorry but I'm not a strong woman and I can't do it, I'm quite decided . . . "

"But that's the whole point, Mother, you don't have to do anything yet." Patience had never come easily to Meriel, but she was doing her best. "All we have to do now is to sit tight and wait for Garry to arrive – and for the rest of our baggage to come up from Cartagena. Why Da's even arranged for a bullock waggon in the village to fetch it up from the station for us. He's thought of everything."

She was too late, though, the waterworks had already started. "You always take his part," Harriet sobbed, "never mine. But you'll learn, my girl, you'll learn one day that your precious father doesn't give a rap for any of us, not a rap! Just so long as he's doing what Robert Llewellen wants to do, that's all he's ever cared about."

Meriel looked down at her mother's fat heaving shoulders – at the outdated teapot-handle bun and over frizzed grey fringe, and the inevitable lace handkerchief dabbing ritualistically at streaming eyes. Unexpectedly she felt a kind of pity. It really must be quite tiring, she supposed, maintaining oneself permanently at the extremity of despair. And poor Mother was probably no worse than thousands of other silly women, undermined from childhood by Victorian precepts of feminine weakness.

"But if you feel like that about Da, why do you stay with him, Mother? Why on earth did you insist on coming out to him in Colombia, when you could quite well have stayed in London?"

"Why?" Harriet looked up at her daughter, with wet cheeks and a pathetic dewdrop on the end of her nose – and even Meriel could see that she was groping for an answer. "Why –

because I'm married to him, that's why. Because my place is by his side . . . whether he wants me there or not." At the thought of her own undesirability, she shuddered into a fresh paroxysm of tears.

'Poor Da,' Meriel thought, 'pursued to the ends of the earth by fat, faithful, weeping old Mother!' And it hadn't occurred to her for a moment, then or later, to compare her own relentless pursuit of Ned with anything so depressing.

Harriet had cheered up in any case when she discovered that one of the Indian girls was to act as a ladies' maid – a luxury that was not to be afforded in London. And as she closed her writing slope, Meriel could hear her mother impressing the evils of maize liquor on the girl in loud and ringing tones – as if nothing more than emphasis and volume were required to drill the King's English into any Indian. The older Indian girl, Maria, had been sitting at Meriel's feet on the cane matting of the hallway while she wrote her letter to Ned. Now, as she rose, Maria rose too like a dusky shadow.

"I'm going down to the river for a swim, Maria, *un baño.*" Meriel tossed it over her shoulder and walked straight on outside, in the certain knowledge that the girl would follow with a sunhat and a chair and a mat, and everything else that she needed. It was nice to be waited on, of course, but she did wish Maria wouldn't be quite so proud and serious about it. You'd think she was handmaiden to the Queen of Sheba or something, the way she strode along behind with her great beak in the air. And if Ned had happened to be watching just then – well, he might just have thought the pair of them faintly ridiculous!

Maria apart, stepping out into the heat of the San Lorenzo afternoon felt exactly like stepping back into childhood for Meriel. With her back to the 'Casa Inglese' and the thatched huts of the Indian village, it was easy to imagine herself back in Ipswich – riding down through the banana plantation to surprise Da on his way home from Dinmore. The glare and the dust and the constant shrill of the cicadas were so like dear old Queensland – in fact all she needed now was the horse.

"Wot-o Meri, how's tricks?" The horse had shivered up out of the heat more or less to order the following week – a fine high-stepping little grey, ridden by a gleeful Gareth at the head of a long train of pacing ponies, riding mules and contract pack animals.

Delighted as Meriel was to see her brother so lean and sunburnt, and so obviously full of himself for getting through to them in one piece, she'd been gladder still to see the horse; and quietly appropriated it on the afternoon of his arrival, while the Mater was still hugging her last-born child and besieging him with questions about Da and the mine. Because whatever Garry himself might have to say on the subject, Meriel was quite positive that Da had intended that horse for her all along. Of course he had. They were two of a kind, she and Da – everyone said so. And now that the transport had arrived she could barely wait to see him again – to discover him on the verandah of this mountain stronghold of his, or to surprise him riding home down the trail from the mine. To catch the spark of recognition in his black eyes, before they creased and crinkled into the familiar pattern of his smile.

"It's Meriel – it is by jove! My own little, brave little Meri-ellie!" And to run to him – to become again the carefree, spoilt little Daddy's-girl she'd once been.

But she had to wait as it turned out, they all had to – for rain. During the Colombian dry season the Magdalena river-boats were necessarily reduced to minimum cargo for fear of running aground. The Llewellens' four hundred-odd separate items of baggage had therefore to be sent up from Cartagena in instalments – the third of which encountered a more than usually obdurate sandbar, and remained there for ten days until a 'fresh' from the mountains finally lifted it clear. Not that the time had been totally wasted – Meriel had seen to that.

"All right then, Mother, riding practice for you!" she announced when they'd first heard the news. "And it's no use saying you can't do it, because if you intend to keep up with us on the next leg you're going to have to." It was the only way to handle the parent, she was convinced of it; and come hell or high water, she roped in the smallest and slowest of the riding mules each day after siesta, and called all hands to hoist Harriet into the sidesaddle.

At first she limited their expeditions to the village and the sandy track that called itself the main road, in the belief that

Harriet would make more effort in the face of the solemn-eyed Indians and feel less inclined to fall off amongst the fowls and the dogs and the hooves of the passing mule trains. To a great extent she'd been right too. Harriet moaned and closed her eyes and swayed dangerously from side to side, but nine times out of ten British Imperial pride and a rudimentary sense of self-preservation had been enough to keep her in the saddle. And gradually the scope of their rides increased – down through the cane fields to the sugar factory, up into the ravines and thickets of the mountain foothills, back and forth through the white-washed village of San Lorenzo until the poker faces of the Indians began to crack into huge horsey grins as soon as *la Inglesa grande* lurched into view.

It hadn't been nearly enough tuition. Not for someone of Mother's excess of temperament and paucity of aptitude. But it had to suffice. And when their expedition at last set off across the great Plain of Tolima on its journey south to the Andes, Harriet was there on her mule in the midst of them – in a huge and unsuitable hat trimmed with artificial cherries, her absurd little sealskin handbag dangling from her arm.

They made an impressive sight, Meriel thought, idly kicking her grey riding horse forward to the head of the procession, and good for at least three pages of her next letter to Ned. Immediately behind her Garry's servant, Avriliano, strode barefoot, leading a string of seven spare horses and riding mules, followed by Garry himself on a pacing horse and Harriet on her little mule. Behind them an untidy file of eleven pack mules straggled out across the baked yellow surface of the plain. Despite the heat, the two muleteers were also on foot and constantly at the run, weaving in and out of the line to adjust uneven packs and keep the animals moving; while at the rear, the negro cook tramped stoically along with a large cigar in his mouth and an impassive Indian maid on either side of him.

In a way it was like putting to sea again, launching out across that vast empty plain, with the snow-capped peaks of the Central Cordillera ahead of them like the cliffs of some distant shore. Garry and Avriliano were the pilots, having made this voyage before. But Da had entrusted the baggage and Mother to Meriel's care, which made her the captain; and it was this conviction more than anything else that kept her hands steady and her spurs idle against the grey's flanks. She longed to give him his head and gallop free of the tedious convoy, to tear away across the savannah with the dry grass crackling beneath her – leaping creeks, dodging termite hills, making a beeline for the Quindío mountains and Da. But instead she led them at a sedate pace by the established bridle path, humming with the cicadas and trying not to look too often to the shimmering, beckoning line of the mountains.

At noon she called a brief halt for lunch in a little copse of stunted sandpaper trees. Then on they pushed again, ignoring Harriet's objections, to ride until dusk. Da had allowed them four days to cross the plain, but if they made good time Meriel saw no reason at all why they shouldn't make it in three.

By five o'clock Harriet was calling down every kind of malediction on her daughter's head and seriously threatening to fall off her mule. By six the light was beginning to fail.

"Oh come on, Meri, be reasonable. It'll be pitch dark before we get all the tents up as it is, and the Mater's dead-beat." It was Garry's fourth attempt, and Meriel knew he was right. But their route just then was passing through an outcrop of rock, with large boulders on both sides of the track – and she felt uneasy. It wasn't just the darkness. There were bandits on the Plain of Tolima, everybody said so. 'And I'll feel a lot happier about pitching camp,' she thought, 'with a nice open space around me!'

"Tell Mother that we'll just keep on until we're clear of the rocks then – and tell her about the *banditi*, Garry. That should be good for another mile or two." And she tried not to feel too lonely as he turned away to canter back down the line.

"Rocks and shadows – rocks and shadows, that's all they are," she repeated to herself and to the nervous horse as she edged him forward. "Avriliano's behind us – I've got my gun – I'm a big girl now!" But her heart was beating furiously, and she had to force herself to keep her eyes on the narrow exit to the plain she could see ahead.

"*Cuidado, Señorita! Cuidado!*" It sounded like a child's voice, a child's or a woman's – whispering a warning to her from somewhere in the rocks to her right. Already tense as a crouched cat, Meriel acted on it instantly. And when a moment later a dark, moustachio'd figure stepped silently out into her path and fumbled for the grey's bridle, he found himself staring straight into the trembling muzzle of a shiny new five-chamber revolver.

"*Pardonamé, Señorita, pensaba que era un amigo*" – "I thought you were a friend."

"A good job for him that you weren't, though," Gareth remarked a little later, between mouthfuls of cocoa and hard boiled egg. "Because any Colombian friend I've ever known would have shot him between the eyes first and asked him what he wanted afterwards."

"Well, his eyes were so close together, I'm not sure I could have got a bullet between them!"

Meriel had laughed about it then, in the relative safety of their camp on the plain. But she still insisted that Garry and Avriliano take it in turns with her to sit up on guard through the night. And at first light she roughed out a racy account of the incident for Ned, deliberately omitting the quaking knees and the feeling of nausea that followed it.

For the next two days the plain stretched its hot emptiness to the horizon, and the Llewellens were tormented by heat such as none of them had experienced – not in the hottest Queensland summer, not even on the fearful *Enriqué* with the furnaces going full blast. There wasn't a tree or a creek or a single scrap of shade for as far as the eye could see. The ground was baked and crazed into a network of cracks, endlessly glaring beneath them to bounce the heat up under the brims of their hats and blister their faces. Their lips were cracked, the saliva dry and sticky in their mouths. Their clothes clung wetly to their backs. Gareth and the muleteers were soon down to vests and cotton breeks; and Meriel discarded her riding stays and opened her blouse two or three buttons below the lowest limits of decency. When even your breasts were par-boiled, it hardly seemed to matter.

Only Harriet refused to compromise with convention – with

long sleeves and wide revers and enough whalebone beneath to refit a small whale – her florid features contorted with effort and running with perspiration.

"I can't, I can't – I can't go on," she croaked again and again, without any real hope of recognition; while Meriel, holding in the grey alongside her, constantly leaned across to steady her and push her up in the saddle.

"Brace up, Mother, it can't be far now to Ibagué, and then you can sleep until doomsday in a real hotel bed, think of that! So just hang on and we'll get you there, you'll see." 'Dead or alive!' she thought grimly.

By noon on the third day, just when Meriel had decided on some kind of a device to lash Harriet to her mule, Gareth gave a wild blood-curdling, dog-howling whoop from the front of their long train.

"Waah-ow-ooh! Land ahoy, Cap'n – look!" And he pointed to a shining white speck at the foot of the distant mountains, like something out of a magic lantern show on the Eastern Empire. "Ibagué!"

"We've made it, Mother, we've done it, we've crossed the plain!" Meriel couldn't keep the triumph out of her voice, and hadn't tried. For the first time in days she could feel a faint breeze fanning her face – and with it came the steady, tinny chime of the cathedral bells.

Chapter Fourteen

Ned was having another ugly day. For a start he had the most awful cold, a real stinker. He felt rotten, he felt depressed – but worst of all he felt a fool. It was plain as a pikestaff that Meriel had been expecting him to propose that day at the Bury-house. But instead of acting on his own masculine instincts, instead of taking her in his arms to tell her how he felt about her and beg her to become his wife, he'd been as cautious and circumspect as ever Gran could have wished. He'd paused to consider his own youth and inexperience, his final terms at university. And he'd basely seized on Helen's arrival as an excuse to avoid answering her question, to put off his own decision for another year.

Looking down from Simmie's window he could see the grimy frontages of the houses opposite, the prim repetitive pattern of iron railings and triangular pediments and dark panelled doors. At the end of the street the traffic of Theobald's Road ground past in a monotonous stream – grey vehicles, grey horses, grey faces – London at its most oppressive. And all because Meriel Llewellen had gone.

Her letters to him were written in a bold sloping scrawl, with numerous underlinings and exclamation marks. They overflowed with her personality. It burst the seams of her narratives and all the romantic images she strove so hard to convey. He saw through her. He saw through her letters to the selfish core of vitality that characterized her – and that he loved.

It was true – he loved her. She was the only girl in the world for him, and he'd let her go.

> Hotel Central,
> Ibagué,
> Rep. of Colombia
> March 4th 1906

My dear Ned,

You must forgive me for writing with this *fiendish* pencil, but Garry and Mother are scrapping over the inkpot!

Well, Ibagué at last – and what a journey! We finally arrived here yesterday at four o'clock in the afternoon to find your letters waiting for us at the hotel and one from Da – the greatest treat, I assure you! And today being Sunday, we have put Mother into dock for repairs, for our ascent of the Quindío range of the Andes first thing in the morning.

I have so often wondered what you did when you and Simmie left the quay at Southampton, and now I know! But fancy you being so down in the dumps? I really had no idea Mother and I meant so much to you. Mother was most gratified to hear it!

Garry sends 'chin-chin'. And tell Simmie that I'm *disgusted* not to have heard from her yet. I know she loathes and abominates writing letters, but I simply *won't* have her forget me. Besides, I've quite set my heart on having her come out to look after Mother in a month or two, so that I can come back and see what you've been getting up to!

Ibagué is quite a large modern place (but a Spaniards' town, you know – and the Spaniards will never become wholly civilized, I think). And the *crowds!* We haven't seen so many people since leaving Cartagena, and most of them seem determined to follow us wherever we go. We Llewellens seem to raise quite as big a crowd in Ibagué as the suffragettes and Hyde Park orators do in London (as some of the photographs I've taken with my little Kodak will show you). When we went down to see our horses and mules corralled last night, why half the town came with us – men, women, children, dogs – even one or two bristly little *pigs!* And this morning I caused another sensation by attending mass in the Cathedral in a borrowed mantilla. I'm not a Roman Catholic as you know, and I can't say I enjoyed it much. The whole place reeked of tallow and raw onions. But I do think the mantilla suited me most awfully!

Mother is spending the entire day today resting and writing letters. She's quite fagged out. I don't know what sort of a person I might be though, for after three days in the saddle I seemed less tired than anyone, even Garry. I can't say that I found any part of the journey particularly taxing, except perhaps the final hour or two when I had to hold Mother onto her mule. But even then I soon recovered.

I will tell you all about our adventures on the Plain of Tolima in my next letter, when we've completed our journey through the mountains. There will be time then for a really full account, and perhaps even to get the daylight developer going (I wonder what you will make of my photofying?). But just now we have to negotiate for another six mules, and a third muleteer to cope with our cabin trunks (which were sent on ahead of us to Ibagué by bullock cart). And can you believe it – we are also having to have a special *litter* made for Mother!! We have heard that the road up into the mountains is in an almost impassable state, due to heavy rains. So we really can't risk her falling off her mule eight or nine thousand feet up, now can we?

The litter is to be a kind of gimcrack sedan-chair affair on two long poles, with a waterproof roof. We will have to engage eight peons, we think, to carry it in two shifts of four (poor fellows). I simply can't *wait* to see Mother in it! It promises to be the funniest thing imaginable . . .

The people of Ibagué had to be up early the next morning to see the mules loaded up in the hotel courtyard – and they'd lined the roadside six or seven deep to wave *los Inglesos* on their way. Riding near the head of the cavalcade, Meriel reacted to the reverential awe in the rows of upraised faces by arching her back and raising her chin – imagining herself encased in flashing silver armour. She felt like Joan of Arc or Elizabeth at Tilbury, or Queen Isabella riding out against the Moors. If only, if *only* Ned could be there amongst them to see her ride by!

She hadn't looked back down the long procession of men and animals behind her; it hardly seemed the thing to do. But if she had, Meriel might have seen Harriet – clutching at the supports of her covered chair seventeen mules down the line – and coming in for an even greater share of native admiration than herself. The hat with the cherries on it had been dusted off and rein-stated, and the handbag. Hoisted on the shoulders of her bearers – so large and black and sedate in her Nagpore silk and jet beads – Harriet lent an almost religious significance to the cortège. Like the effigy of some inflated Virgin of the Andes. The additional bearers, shambling self-consciously behind her, enhanced her likeness to a goddess with attendants. And at the tail of the procession the cook and the two Indian maids had risen to the dignity of the occasion, marching proudly – still barefoot, but this time with the cigar in the mouth of the haughty Maria.

"Whoop-ah! Whoop-ah!" The old Spanish road up out of the town was sufficiently steep to warrant some vocal encourage-ment from the muleteers; and more than sufficiently potholed to have the Virgin of the Andes squealing with fright, as her chair pitched and rolled and threatened to run aground on one or two of the larger boulders in its path.

Beyond the foothills the gradient became steeper still, doubling and redoubling on itself until they could look down on the spire of Ibagué Cathedral and the barren surface of the plain five hundred feet or more below them. Meriel and Gareth were both forced to dismount and exchange their horses for riding mules, and the Mater's bearers began to show signs of exhaustion. At the first precipitous hairpin their passenger sat chalk-white and rigid, peering out owlishly from beneath the gabled hood of her litter. At the second acute bend she closed her eyes. And on the third she finally lost her nerve, heaving her considerable weight back and away from the declivity, with a suddenness that had buckled the knees of both offside bearers and threatened to pitch them all to their doom.

After that all eight peons had been pressed into service between the shafts of the litter – to fore and to aft and on either side of it – jostling shoulders, treading on each other's heels, and gradually dropping back behind the pack mules and the servants until the leaders of the procession were several loops of the road above them.

"It's no-go, Garry," Meriel declared at last, at a point where the road dropped away again down into a mountain valley. "One of us is just going to have to stay back to keep an eye on Mother. They'll dish her over the edge otherwise, sooner or later – bound to. I know I would in their place!"

And Gareth was persuaded to be the one to stay back, without too much unpleasantness.

As Meriel and Avriliano rode on into the valley, she tried to imagine Mother as she must have been once as a girl. In an old portrait study at the time she and Da married, way back in the year dot, Mother had actually looked rather pretty – plump as a partridge, with round dark eyes and hair swept up into rows of fat curls on the crown of her head. Yet even then there'd been something feeble about her face, a helplessness that made one wonder how Da could ever have failed to see how little character there was beneath the prettiness.

'He's going to feel as old as Methuselah when he sees her on Wednesday,' Meriel thought. 'I bet he's forgotten what a perfect fright she can look nowadays when she puts her mind to it! Not that it'll ever be like that for Ned – or for me,' she told herself resolutely, automatically kicking her mule into a sitting trot as she reached a level stretch of the path. 'I won't stand for it. I'll never let myself get fat – or wispy like Simmie. And my Ned will stay handsome until the day he dies!'

"*Aguardase! Aguardase, Señorita!*" Avriliano's voice entreating her to wait called Meriel back to the present, and reluctantly she checked her pace to allow the others to catch up.

The road up out of the valley was spectacular beyond words – a continuous rocky ledge spiralling up the green face of the mountain, with glimpses between the leaves of orchids, hibiscus and crimson fuchsias, and of lupins the size of young trees. As they gained altitude a magnificent panorama of Andean peaks and ranges opened up before them to the south. With altitude, however, came a dramatic change of climate – a cold wind blowing off the snowfields of the Nevada del Tolima and clouds closing in around them, obscuring the way ahead and muffling the yells of the muleteers from the slopes below. Until finally, as they drew level with a solitary Indian hut on a high pass of the mountains, it began to rain.

It continued to rain all that night – in buckets and tank-fulls, just like Queensland in the Wet. They struck camp the next morning in the aftermath, a dismal English drizzle. But when they came to resume their journey, it was to discover with dismay that their road had been all but obliterated. Landslides had in places reduced it to half its width or less. Waterfalls gushed over it to erode what was left, and everywhere great heaps of mud and loose shale obstructed the way.

Clearly a change of tactics was called for. This time Gareth, Avriliano and the servants went ahead with shovels to clear the path as best they could – followed by the muleteers, riding animals and pack mules in single file – with Meriel, Harriet and her bearers bringing up the rear. The climb up from Ibagué had broken the Mater's bearers in body and spirit, all eight of them. So now, perforce, she must ride – with nothing more substantial than her handbag to be borne in the litter behind.

"But just remember, Mother, if you fall off you'll be travelling non-stop for a very long way indeed! We've all got ourselves to look to now, and the path simply isn't wide enough for me to ride alongside to hold you on."

"There's no need to take that tone, Meriel," Harriet replied huffily. "I'm sure I can ride as well as the next woman if need be." And amazingly she squared her large shoulders and proceeded to do just that, while behind her Meriel rolled her eyes heavenward in silent gratitude. 'Halleluia!'

One problem solved. But now a clarion call from somewhere near the head of the convoy presented another.

"*Sacio la mula! Sacio la mula* – the mule is down!"

Meriel thrust her reins at one of the bearers and gingerly edged her way on foot past a jam of fifteen stationary animals, to a point where a plank bridge carried the track over a regular delta of swollen mountain streams. And there, lying in a stream bed with her precious cargo beneath her and all four feet in the air, was Antonia – the largest and certainly the slowest witted of all the pack mules. She'd fallen from the slippery bridge and now seemed resigned to death by high-altitude drowning.

They had to cut the girth, some of the mackintosh that covered the pack and most of the rawhide thongs that held it together. But even then it was more than half an hour before Gareth and one of the muleteers, over their boots in water, were able to persuade the foolish creature to find her feet again.

Meriel had progressed no more than six mules back down the line to Harriet, however, when the cry went up again: "*Aguardase – aguardase! Sacio la mula!*"

This time Antonia *mula* had really excelled herself. The track here crossed an earth-slide of sticky yellow clay – and the wretched animal had somehow contrived to fall so that she now lay with her hind quarters dangling over the edge. Below was a four foot drop to a steeply falling scree, covered in undergrowth and thorns and terminating abruptly in a sheer cliff. Realizing that the least movement would send her over, Antonia lay perfectly still with an expression of philosophical resignation on her long face.

"Crikey, what a mess up!" Meriel and Gareth looked at each other blankly across the mule's body.

"What's she carrying, Garry, do you know?" Meriel had a horrid suspicion that she recognized the big black rectangular package that counterbalanced the mule and held her to the road, but she had to be sure.

"We gave her one of the cabin trunks – what's the number? I say, here's a go!" Gareth grinned nervously "It's yours, Meri!"

Inside the trunk, amongst other things, was Ned's photograph. She'd put it in for safety in Ibagué. There was also the new pink coutil corset she'd bought in D. H. Evans the week before they'd left London. She couldn't possibly lose that. Mules were two a penny in Colombia, everyone knew that. But corsets with bust-bodices were few and far between, even in London. Why, she doubted that there was another one on this entire uncivilized continent!

"You grab hold of that end, Garry," she said grimly, setting to work right away, "I'll cut her loose."

Everything was harder at eight thousand feet. She was puffing like a grampus, concentrating fiercely on freeing the trunk and closing her mind to the consequences. Later she'd tell herself that she tried to save them both, the animal and the trunk. But just now she was concerned with priorities. Deprived of her counterweight, the mule lay for a moment held only by the mud between her forelegs. Then, very slowly, she began to slip backwards. Meriel and Gareth hauled on her bridle with all their might while she struggled for a purchase, and the image of Antonia's straining neck muscles and her brown eyes starting with fear, remained with Meriel for many weeks afterwards. But in the end they had to let her go, or go with her; to watch while she fell and continued to struggle, silently, head towards the track – sliding down through bushes and saplings, fast gathering momentum until suddenly, with one terrified guttural bray, she was gone.

'It could have been one of us.' That's all Meriel could think of. 'It could have been Mother – it could even have been *me!*' And she left Garry to reallocate the trunk. It was safe, that was the main thing. "I'll go back for my mule now," she muttered to herself as she made her way back down the line. "Then as soon as I get a chance, I'll damn well pass them all and ride on to Da like billy-o, that's what I'll do." Garry said that they'd get a view of the hacienda through the valleys in an hour or two, but wouldn't reach it tonight. Well she *would*, that's all. She'd been sensible for jolly well long enough. The condors were already circling the place where Antonia had fallen and at the first twinge of guilt, Meriel felt an almost desperate need for reassurance. She wanted someone stronger and braver than herself to lean on – she wanted Da.

"But Meri you can't go on your own!" Gareth actually put out a hand to restrain her when she announced her intention later that afternoon. "You could fall or anything. You know there'd be no one to help you; and Da isn't expecting us anyway – not until tomorrow."

"I can go, and I *will!*" Meriel's voice rose stridently. In their contests as children it had always been her best weapon. "Look, I can see the house from here, and it's mostly downhill. So what's to stop me – tell me that?"

"Well what about the Mater? What's she going to say when she hears you've done a bunk? She'll do her block!"

"That's all you know!" Meriel smiled, a sisterly smile. "I've already told her, clever-dick, and after what happened to Antonia back there she's too damn busy sticking to her mule to care about me! You won't hear any more complaints from Mother, I guarantee it, not until she's home and dry. So enjoy your evening won't you now?" she called back cheerily from a little further down the track. "Da and I will be thinking of you all tucked-up snug in your little camp beds. So long!" And she waved to him casually before disappearing out of sight amongst the trees.

From their vantage point on the ridge, the hacienda had been clearly visible as a conglomeration of grey roofs on a distant hillside, looking absurdly close despite their diminutive size. But once she'd descended into and climbed out of the first of the steep little valleys in between, Meriel began to understand something of the steeplechase she'd taken on. Often no wider than a man's shoulders, the mule track dipped and climbed on a constant incline, down into dark pools of jungle foliage reverberating with the cries of unfamiliar birds, down through the mud, slithering and squelching, to cross the inevitable stream at the bottom. Then up again, to throw her back in the saddle as the mule scrabbled for a footing amongst the roots, up above the creepers and tree-ferns to the thorny scrub of the higher slopes and to another glimpse of the hacienda, scarcely nearer than it had been an hour, two hours before. Occasionally stones shifted and rattled on the slopes above her. Leaves rustled and twigs snapped in the undergrowth of the forested valleys. There were bears in these mountains, and pumas and wild boars – and doubtless *banditi* as well.

Meriel wouldn't have admitted to feeling nervous, not even to herself. But she was never exactly sorry to regain the open mountainside – and she rode with her revolver in one hand resting before her on the pommel of her saddle. 'A droopy moustache on legs', that's how she'd describe her Tolima bandit to Ned in the gripping account of their journey that she'd compose at the hacienda. She'd make fun of him and reveal herself as the natural heroine, in perfect command. Yet the incident had shaken her. It disturbed her still whenever she caught sight of a native hut or a moving shadow amongst the lianas, and she spurred her weary mule whenever the track allowed it.

"Because I've got to reach Da by nightfall," she told herself, "I've just got to – I'll never find the way, otherwise." And she sang to herself at the top of her voice to awaken the silence of the brooding ranges.

> *"Such a stylish girl you see,*
> *Just out in Society,*
> *Everything I ought to be –*
> *Ta-ra-ra-boom-de-ay!"*

The path occasionally branched in the valleys, on one side of the stream or the other. But with her intermittent views of the hacienda from the slopes above, Meriel found that she could plot her course in advance of each descent. And so far she hadn't gone wrong – if only she could reach it by nightfall.

"Three more valleys, two more valleys – just one more!" She pretended she was talking to her mule, spurring him on to a last effort. "Then we'll see Da, you and I Señor Mula, and give him the surprise of his life!"

As they began their final descent the sun sank with them, away behind the furthermost range. 'The Valley of Anaime', it was comforting to know its name. The shadows deepened around them, and the *candelelias* darted and flickered between the trees. In place of the usual stream there was a regular river to ford at the foot of the last incline. The mule floundered more than once in the water, wetting Meriel's legs and the soiled skirts of her riding habit. But she didn't care – not a bit. Because on the far bank, on a little isolated hill of its own, stood the hacienda.

A track like an English driveway wound up the hill, past a line of sentinel poplars, to the cluster of buildings at the summit, and Meriel dismounted to lead her mule in. She no longer felt the slightest bit nervous. Suddenly she wanted to walk. The moon had risen dramatically to illuminate immense mountain peaks on all sides, with pale, fleecy clouds clinging to them like necklaces. There were *potreros* – paddocks with neat rail fences, and a garden with coffee and orange trees, cypresses and spikey date palms. And up above them at the top of the steep drive, there was a verandah just as Meriel had imagined it, with wooden uprights and bamboo railings – and yellow lamplight streaming out into the garden.

It was so silly, but she actually felt tears pricking at her eyes. It was such a fitting end to the adventure somehow – civilization in the very heart of the wilderness. Inside there'd be Da – the most civilized man that anyone anywhere could hope to know! She tied the mule to a fencepost a few yards from the house and stepped onto the verandah stairs, with the shrill of the cicadas beating on the air around her like a fanfare. A wooden bead curtain hung over the door – and inside, a degree of comfort that was astonishing to Meriel after the bare Spanish interiors that she'd become accustomed to.

'This is something like!' she thought proudly. 'Like stepping into Liberty's of London – only not so damn stuffy!'

It smelt of cedar wood and Da's Egyptian cigarettes – a kind of salon, with real carpets on the floor and unbleached canvas stretched across the rafters to form a ceiling. There was a table with a fringed paisley cloth, and a shaded lamp just alive with flying insects – and around it a set of solid-looking calfskin chairs. At the windows hung the heavy lace curtains Meriel remembered so well from the dining room in Ipswich. On one wall there was a bookcase and a framed oleograph of the King, on another a cabinet of family photographs – including the study of Vicky and herself that Da always thought so amusing, with their arms around each other like the cover of some ghastly free almanac. Da's military chest secretaire was there too, heaped with papers and ledgers just as she'd pictured it. Except that Meriel had rather expected Da himself to be sitting at it, with his hair ruffled and his long legs stretched out before him.

"Aah! Ah-ahh!" A sudden violent cry rang out from behind the cedar wall – and at the sound of it a shock passed through Meriel like an electric current.

'Ginger!' she thought, 'he's ill!' Without a moment's hesitation she dashed out onto the verandah and into the lamplit bedroom next door – to yank back the mosquito netting from Da's bed and his poor, tortured, writhing body.

And there she remained, rooted to the floor, with the netting draped around her like a shroud.

Da's face on the pillow was feverish, wet with perspiration. His eyes were wide open, astonished, black as the hair of the Indian girl who straddled and pumped at his loins so assiduously.

"It's Meriel – it is by jove! My own little, brave little Meriellie!"

He didn't say it.

Chapter Fifteen

There was nowhere to run to, nowhere to hide from the rotten, filthy beastliness of it all – and Meriel's headlong flight from the bedroom pulled her up short at the verandah rail. With the most solid of all her illusions in ruins she felt lost, sick and utterly betrayed. Vaguely she knew that somehow she would have to find a way of reinstating Da, of understanding and forgiving him. But she had no idea how to begin.

She moved her hand to feel the rough joints of the bamboo verandah rail – she clung to their texture. They were real, she could mark them with her fingernail. Then she looked down to where her poor old knocked-up mule drooped beside his fencepost, disconsolate in the moonlight. She could understand him all right. He'd have to be unsaddled and watered, and turned out into a paddock somewhere. Now that was something she could do. Meriel had already started down the verandah stairs when she heard Da's step on the boards behind her.

"Meriel? Where are the others – Gareth and your mother?"

Facts. Yes, she could cope with facts – if only he'd stick to them. "They're camping tonight, out there in the ranges somewhere." She waved at the mountains across the river without turning to him. "They'll be along in the morning."

"Well, well, so I'm not the only one to abandon her, then?"

He wouldn't help her by pretending to sound ashamed. There was amusement in his voice, she could hear it. What's more she knew that if she turned around, she would find him smiling down at her with one eyebrow lifted quizzically. It was his most charming expression, she'd always thought so. To her utter confusion Meriel felt a sudden and scandalous desire to smile herself, to laugh even – and with it a curious sense of familiarity, as if the whole thing had happened before.

"How could you? How *could* you behave like that, Da?" she said, turning and glaring at him in a sudden fury, "when you knew perfectly well we were on the way!"

He was wearing his embroidered kimono dressing gown – and as far as she could tell, nothing else. And his black eyebrow was raised, just as she thought.

"You mean that you disapprove of my carelessness rather than my morals?" he said smoothly. "You think I should have guessed that you'd personally establish a new record for scorching through from Ibagué, and covered my tracks, as any good philanderer should? And of course, my dear, in that you're absolutely right."

Irritatingly, she couldn't think of an answer. The anger, even the inclination to laugh, had left her – because now the whole thing really was beginning to feel familiar. Da getting the better of her once again, Da in command, one step ahead as usual.

"I am grieved, naturally, that you should have to see your father in such a wretchedly undignified posture," he continued, unabashed. "But carelessness aside, you must surely have known that I couldn't hope to remain faithful to your mother for all the months and years that we've spent apart. It wouldn't have been practical, my dear. Call it a weakness if you will, but we mortal males simply aren't made for celibacy."

"Some men are! I know some men would be faithful through anything!" It was only a comment though, something she'd like Ned to have heard her say – rather than any real criticism of her father. Because Meriel understood that nobody could seriously be expected to stay faithful for very long to someone like the Mater.

By the time that Gareth and Harriet and the rest of their muddy retinue forded the river the next morning, she and Da had declared a truce – the Indian girl having already departed at first light for Anaime village.

As everyone who knew her had anticipated, Harriet collapsed with ruthless totality as soon as she set eyes on her husband's tall figure on the far bank of the river. Harriet Llewellen had known for some years that pity was the only positive emotion she could hope to stir in Robert, and now she demanded it as a right. The frightful overland journey from San Lorenzo had been more, she said, than any woman of her fragile constitution could be expected to endure. For once in her life she really was suffering in fact. She complained of severe headaches and lay moaning in a darkened room, or on a chaise in the salon – entreating her husband to sit with her, to talk to her and hold her clammy hand. Until, at the end of a week of ill-concealed impatience, he announced that he and Gareth must return to the mercury mine to check on progress and interrogate their Colombian Manager. It was a longish ride into the mountains, and he fully expected to be away for several days.

Meriel's promised account of her epic journey from San Lorenzo to the hacienda at Anaime finally arrived at Harpur Street in early June, together with a more recent letter from her to wish Ned luck in his Finals at the end of the month. He read extracts from both to Simmie in her cluttered little parlour, crouching on the edge of his chair with an excitement in his voice that she found almost absurdly reminiscent of the writer. As if something of Meriel's own bold spirit was rising from the page to dispel his self-doubts and examination nerves and make a new man of him.

153

"Listen to this, though, Simmie! I mean isn't this just typical?":

. . . I often wonder how you would have liked the experiences and episodes we have been through, and what you would think of me now if you met me out on one of my rides – with my Mexican saddle and lasso, my hair in a long horse-tail and at my belt a dangerous looking revolver (just in case!)? In this quiet little valley of ours, it's often hard to believe that we're deep in the interior of one of the wildest continents of the world – more than a thousand miles from the sea and three weeks' journey from the nearest railway. And it's only these little details that recall one to the fact – every Indian with a machetta hanging from his belt, and every *gringo* like me with a revolver at the hip.

But to resume what I was saying. Barney was saddled and Avriliano held his bridle while I mounted. Then a plunge, a cloud of dust – and we were away at full tilt down the *potrero!* It was still early, so I rode to my most favourite place round here – a longish ride by the usual goat tracks 'til you come to a *dear* little plain right in amongst the mountains just like a natural racecourse. Barney knew of course, the villain, and began to toss his head and pull at the bit even before we'd cleared the trees. Then you may be sure he was off as hard as he could lick, just at the slackening of the rein – round and round and round and up and down until we were both quite out of breath. But do you suppose my Barney was tired – not a bit of it! As we were coming up the hill to the house (and it had come on to rain a bit, so we weren't exactly *walking!*), an Indian woman who lives on the *estancia* stepped out to ask me for some quinine for her son. But do you think Barney would stop for her? *Four times* he reared up, pawing the air with his hooves, while the silly creature prostrated herself emitting a never-ending stream of 'Ave-Marias' (and I said a few short words in jolly old English too, I can tell you!). So there was nothing for it then but to give up and come on home.

When I got in I immediately understood why Barney had been in such a hurry. Of course – he'd known all along! You see Garry was there waiting for us with *piles* of English letters from Anaime – and in amongst it all, *three* letters from you! SO THREE CHEERS FOR THE ROYAL MAIL!! . . .

Ned sat back and beamed at Simmie, with love and pride written all over his face.

"Can't you just see her, Simmie? I know I can! And what I wouldn't give to be able to chuck up the Finals and pop out there to watch her holding up bandits and tossing dud mules off cliffs and terrorizing the Indians!" He laughed delightedly at the thought.

"She's so splendidly unsinkable, isn't she, Simmie? Do you know, I don't think there's anything on this earth that could get the better of her!"

He was wrong of course. Ten days after Ned received that letter from her, Meriel sat hunched at her father's chest secretaire staring hopelessly at a blank sheet of notepaper. She'd come in to write to Ned – she wanted to write to him, but the right words wouldn't come. She felt exhausted, drained of energy and emotion. Even the action of lifting the pen and forming the successive words on the page seemed too great an effort . . .

She hadn't been entirely honest with Ned. The stirring scenes she recorded for him in her letters had reflected only a part of her existence in the Anaime Valley. She had written to him vividly of her wild rides on the 'racecourse', of cases of dynamite in their salon, of bullocks setting off from Anaime with detonators and tramway wheels for the mine and returning with precious distilled mercury in crates of leaden retorts. She described the forest that bounded them on all sides, with its monkeys and squirrels and gorgeous purple orchids. She sent him her own photographs of the hacienda and the village of Anaime, and of the wretched Indians who traipsed daily to her door for medication. And she'd racked her brain for adjectives to describe the thrills of nightly thunderstorms, of earth tremors and landslides, and of swollen watercourses that washed away the roads to the *estancia* to cut them off from civilization for weeks at a time.

What she had omitted from her letters was the intense

boredom of the Colombian rainy season, with the clouds down on the mountains and the mud over your boot-tops whenever you ventured out. She'd written of Da singing 'The Bells of Aberdovey' so beautifully to her own accompaniment on their portable American organ. But not of the long wet afternoons when the four of them sat around playing halma or dominoes and snapping each other's heads off. And she'd joked as usual of Harriet's 'habitual unwellitude', glossing over the increasing frequency and intensity of her headaches.

By the end of May the wet season was over as far as the *país caloroso,* the hot-country of the plains and the Magdalena river, was concerned. But in the ranges and valleys of the Andes the rain still beat into the mud of the mule tracks, the thunder still rolled menacingly overhead. Up at the mine the levels and sluices were flooded. Work had stopped on the new sulphide furnaces that Da was installing, and to his disgust, Robert was cooped up in the hacienda with the rest of them to await the return of drier weather.

Inactivity suited Da as little as it did Meriel. As Harriet's condition worsened and her emotional demands on him grew, he became increasingly irascible himself. While the rain thudded against the shingles of the salon roof and gushed out over the verandah, there was no escape from the carping invalid. Her patent remedies no longer seemed to have any effect on the terrible, blinding headaches that tormented her. Yet still she insisted on remaining in the salon – prone on her chaise with a damp cloth on her forehead, whimpering and grizzling and constantly trying to catch her husband's eye. As she watched her father reaching repeatedly for the whisky decanter, Meriel actually felt envious. As always, men held all the best cards.

Things had come to a head one night in June, in the middle of the most violent electric storm. The atmosphere in the salon was unbearably hot that night. Yet despite the thunder and lightning, not a drop of rain had fallen.

'If only it would – if only it would rain!' Meriel thought, slapping her double six down against Garry's six and four. 'Something's going to happen otherwise – something dreadful, I just know it!'

"Oh Jesus the pain! Oh Jesus, Jesus I'm dying – I'm dying I

tell you, and none of you care!" Harriet's constant querulous complaints from the chaise sawed against their nerves through the splintering crashes of the thunder, until her pain seemed to have entered the storm itself and become part of its violence. So far Da had succeeded in ignoring her, sitting at his desk with his back to the chaise and the whisky bottle at his elbow. But he wouldn't for long. Meriel could see the sprung tension in the curve of his spine, poised like everything else in the room on the verge of some fearful climax.

Then, quite suddenly, an explosive flash of blue lightning scorched their vision, centreing on the table lamp beside Da and searing its negative image onto every retina in the room. A heartbeat later Harriet began to scream at the top of her voice, and the rain followed with the next almighty clap of thunder. "*Stop it!*" Robert Llewellen's voice cut through it all like a sabre – Harriet's shrieks, the thunder and the drumming hiss of the deluge. "Stop it, stop it, I say, you goddam fool of a woman! Or so help me I'll take you by your fat neck and make you!"

The screams subsided almost immediately. But Robert had already passed the point of no return – striding across the room, kicking a cane chair aside to stand above his wife and berate her for a lifetime of shortcomings.

"That's right, spoil it!" he shouted. "Spoil any chance I've got of making a success of this jossing place! Because that's what you do isn't it – you block me, undermine me, drag me down whenever I've a chance of succeeding?"

Beneath him on the chaise Harriet sobbed hysterically with her hands to her head, twisting from side to side like a great spiked eel.

"Christ, you can't bear it, can you? You can't bear me to be happy or successful or to feel younger than my age. You have to be ill don't you – old, unhappy? That's it, isn't it – to drag me down with you?"

"No, Da, she is ill, really. Look, can't you see how ill she is?" Meriel tugged at his arm and then tried to force herself between them, anything to stop him. "Garry – help me for pity's sake!"

But nothing could stop Robert now. He brushed them aside, both of them, to continue the barrage – flinging the words down, bludgeoning his wife with an invective that came to him spontaneously in the whisky, without the need for thought. "By heaven you're grotesque! Look at you – look at yourself, a failure in everything you touch – with your pathetic ideas of 'continence' and 'abstention', cold as a frog in bed – ignorant – incompetent – unwanted . . . !"

"*Da!*" Meriel couldn't take it, not another word. She saw her mother cringing grey-faced, trying to fend off the terrible words with her hands – then helplessly vomiting over the cushions that supported her and the crumpled silk of her matinée gown. And she launched herself at her father, shoving him, striking him with her clenched fists and all her strength behind them.

The unexpected violence of her attack caught him off-balance and sent him sprawling, down on his knees in the vomit. For a moment she was glad. But then he was up again, the veins standing out from his forehead just as they had the night she surprised him with the odious Indian girl. She thought then that he would kill her. But he merely settled for destroying her happiness.

"Well if it isn't our gallant Defender of the Faith! The little lady who believes in love and fidelity and all the conventional virtues!"

Meriel ignored him, pushing past contemptuously to do what she could for her mother. But Robert hadn't finished. He turned to Gareth with glittering bloodshot eyes. "She has a young man back in London, has she not? A white hope who she swears will be faithful to her for ever and a day?" He laid his finger against his nose in a deliberate caricature of a drunkard's confidence. "But I know, and you know, Garry, we know because we're men of the world – that even now that young fellow of hers is exercising the quim of his ever-so-charming landlady!"

"Rot! Absolute rot!" He could say what he liked, Meriel was damned if she'd give him the satisfaction of an argument.

But he wouldn't leave it at that. "You don't believe me, do you, my little innocent?" he said, gripping her by the arm and dragging her round to face him. "You think that those two are above such things? Well, let me tell you that I've known Beatrice Sims for a number of years – you didn't know that did you? – and I can assure you that she's less of a lady and more of a human being than you give her credit for. As for your young Ashby – you may as well face it, Meriel, he's been her lover ever since you've known him, my dear. Admitted as much to me himself when I called at Harpur Street last summer."

"*No!*" But even as she heard it, her own voice harsh against the rumble of the receding storm, Meriel recalled Ned and Simmie as they'd been on the quay at Southampton – her arm through his, her wet cheek against his sleeve. She'd seen Simmie's face discountenanced, blushing at the prospect of a weekend at Ned's home in Sussex. She remembered a glance across a luncheon table, a smile, an atmosphere of physical intimacy that she'd never really understood. And she knew with a sickening certainty that it was true.

Early the next morning they hoisted and strapped Harriet back into her ridiculous litter, to carry her down to the doctor in Ibagué. From the verandah of the hacienda Meriel watched the little procession fording the river and climbing the far bank – unable to feel pity or revulsion, unable to feel at all.

The news of Harriet Llewellen's tragic death in Colombia of a brain tumour caught Simmie in a strange unsettled frame of mind – although it was some little time before she could admit to herself that she had acted uncharacteristically.

It was just that she too had come to a watershed in her life that June of 1906. She was losing her first, her original student lodgers. Andy had already gone down. At the end of their Final examinations Ned and Matthew Starnes were to follow – and none of them would be returning to her at the end of the summer. There'd be new coats in the hall next term. In May her little dog Gussie had died in his basket beside the kitchen range after more than twelve years of faithful companionship. Worse, on her own next birthday Simmie herself was to attain the age of forty – that most obvious and unavoidable landmark of middle-age. Change was all around her, unsought and unwelcome. So in a way there was something almost appropriate about a telegram in this month and this year of her life to announce the death of Robert Llewellen's wife.

The fact that the telegram had been addressed to her personally, and came from Robert rather then Meriel, had not at first struck Simmie as peculiar, and in other circumstances it might never have done so. But as it was, her new restless mood convinced her of its significance within a matter of minutes. 'There can be only one answer,' she told herself with quickening pulse. 'He's got to be offering me the chance I've never had, to go to him freely of my own choice! Or why else would he have troubled to send it to me?'

It wasn't a considered, responsible, middle-aged reaction. It was the last wild cry of departing youth: a chance to be rash and daring that would never come again. Suddenly Simmie found that she wanted – actually needed – the sheer physical hardship of the journey to Anaime, and to triumph over it as Meriel had done. She wanted the heat, the cicadas, even the *banditi*. She wanted to don a pith helmet and gallop madly across the Plain of Tolima to Robert! And never mind her performance on a bicycle – under providence she could do it, she knew she could. There was no family now to hold her in England; since Papa's death Isobel had returned all her letters unopened. The house in Harpur Street could be sold if need be, and a maid of Gladys' experience could always find employment. For the first time in her life Simmie was a free agent, responsible to no one, and to nothing but her own happiness.

So the next morning – without thinking, without allowing herself to consider any of the problems or practicalities – she took the underground to the Bank, hurried up Moorgate Street to the R.M.S.P. Company offices and booked a six months' return passage to Cartagena – to depart from Southampton on October 22nd, via Cherbourg, Barbados, Trinidad and Port of Colombia.

"And why ever not, Gladys?" she added defensively, after finally summoning the courage to break the news to her maid. "I've never had a chance to go abroad before, you know, and you're always telling me yourself that we only live once."

"Too true, an' we only die once an' all." Gladys had an unnerving habit of jerking her chin at one when she disapproved. "An' what if yer ketch maleery out there then, Mum? Or go an' git yerself skelped by them injuns? Where would we all be then, I should like ter know?"

In her heart of hearts Simmie knew the idea to be fantastic, and after a week or two of Gladys' jerking chin all her old uncertainties came crowding back – the dangers of the journey, the possibility of Robert's rejection and the extreme likelihood of her making a guy of herself at the end of it all. Yet still she clung to it, this fantastic idea of hers, this one last chance. She wouldn't write ahead, she wouldn't plan anything beyond the clothes and the money she'd take with her. She'd go, that's all. This time she'd do it, she really would – and the rest was in the lap of the gods.

At the end of July, after Ned's final return home to Sussex, a letter from Meriel Llewellen dropped through Simmie's door. It had been written, she discovered, on the very day that Robert's wife was carried down to the *médico* in Ibagué and three days before the telegram announcing her death. The writing and style of the letter were shocking, almost unrecognizable. Six un-numbered pages filled with the agonies of loneliness and lost confidence: the smudged, inky heartpourings of a daughter abandoned, a lover deceived – childish vilifications of Simmie herself, the friend who had betrayed her, degenerating pathetically into entreaties to give Ned up, to send him out to her in Colombia to fetch her home.

'I *need* him so much, Simmie, and now that I've lost Da I can't lose Ned too – not both of them, Simmie! I know I'll just *die* if I do . . .'

Simmie adjusted her reading spectacles with a hand that shook, willing herself to stifle self-pity, not to flinch at Robert's treachery or the hurtful accusations that leapt out at her from the page, to think instead of poor little Meriel, of Ned and their future together. But even so, she had to remove her glasses more than once before she finished the letter. Afterwards for a long moment she sat silently, staring at the wall. Then she crossed to her writing desk to rummage for a sheet of her own ribbed cream notepaper, and for the old-fashioned quill pen she still used.

My dear Ned, (she wrote)
    The enclosed booking receipt and note of transfer for my return reservation to Cartagena comes to you with my love. I hope that you can use it, my dear, and think that you

should. The deposit has been paid. But I believe that you will be required to reaffirm and complete the transaction sometime before the end of next month. (The R.M.S.P. people in Moorgate Street will advise you.)

I had thought that I might be brave enough to undertake the trip myself – and to take a peek at them all up on that mountain of theirs. But I have come to realize that I am too old, after all, and too timid for such an adventure . . .

"*Más fuerte, Maria – más!*" "Come on, Maria, pull harder!" Meriel added in English. "Harder girl – much harder than *that*. I'm not made of porcelain, for heaven's sake, I'm hardly going to break in two!" It was the very first time she'd put on the new pink coutil corset – there hadn't seemed a lot of point before. But now that she'd left it so late in the day to introduce Maria to its mysteries, Meriel was having the greatest difficulty in getting the girl to lace it tight enough.

"Just because you Indians can't grow your own waists, you think we should all go round looking like cow seals," she muttered, knowing that she couldn't be understood. "Come on, Maria, *más fuerte!*"

Meriel's confidence and all her old energy had returned to her on the instant with Ned's first glorious telegram and the long-awaited proposal it contained. Now there was no time for Garry's tomfoolery, or Da's inebriated sarcasm. So much to be repaired, cleaned, laundered, weeded – to be seen and appreciated as Ned would first see it when he rode down into the Anaime Valley. She had to be everywhere at once. She had to run from the gardener to the painter to the little Indian carpenter who was mending the roof – urging and harrying in a voice that sang with the sheer joy of living.

"He's coming out, he really is!" She had to repeat it to herself a dozen times before she could even begin to believe it. And next year, in the English spring, Ned would take her home and make her his wife – Mrs Edwin Ashby! She might just burst with happiness!

The first practical thing she'd done after replying to his telegram was to find a mount for Ned at the Ibagué horse fair – a strong, well-mannered pacer to carry him safely to her across

162

the plains. Her grey Barney was far too wicked. Then she packed Garry and Avriliano off to meet him from the *Enriqué* with heaps of time to spare. She'd have gone herself – God knows she wanted to. But Da had been so strange and unpredictable, drinking so heavily since Mother's death, that she judged it unwise. She'd encountered the Indian girl, Rosita, more than once on the track up to the mine – and she wouldn't put it past Da to re-install the wretched creature in his bed as soon as her own back was turned.

Preparing for Ned's arrival was like waiting for Christmas for Meriel – crossing off the dates, opening the little doors of the advent calendar one by one – and all the time wrestling with an unreasonable anxiety that the great, the final day would never come. Then suddenly it was upon her, and the weeks of waiting had become hours and minutes. Why, even now they must be packing up their tents and their camp beds and preparing for that last long descent to Anaime.

'And is your heart thumping like mine, my darling? Is your mouth dry and your throat burning like mine – and all your insides like hot blancmange?'

The bust bodice was a spectacular improvement, lifting and cupping her breasts above the rigid busk of the corset – and Meriel could scarcely wait to wriggle into the plain white sheath of her dress to study the full effect in her bedroom mirror.

"*Perfecta!*" She said it aloud for Maria's benefit. The hair was good too, as smooth and glossy as a well-glazed cottage loaf, with no loose ends and no rat-pads visible. A little rouge and a little lip salve (enough to turn the poor Mater in her grave!) – 'And yes – yes, good enough to eat!'

For the final confrontation she was to be discovered, she decided, out on the verandah and quite alone. It had been cleared of everything but two enamalled cane chairs, and Meriel arranged herself in the one by the steps, in full view, with her work basket on a table at her elbow. Da, in the blackest of moods, had long since taken off for the mine. The maids, Maria and Gabriella, were instructed to stay inside and out of sight. Even poor Garry, who'd travelled for eleven days to fetch her fiancé to her, had orders to stay well back with the baggage mules. And the Señorita had sent word to the village that no sick were to be treated today. It wouldn't do to have a gaggle of malarial Indians cluttering up his first sight of her (and nor on reflection, would it be at all a bad thing to be seen dispensing to an unusually large and grateful congregation the following morning!).

She was out there in position long before it was strictly necessary. But Meriel wasn't for taking chances. And when he arrived? Why then she'd look up from her needlework, startled – but not too much – then rise elegantly from her chair, to float down the steps towards him; cool and lovely, an apparition in white with an impossibly tiny waist. She would smile up at him in picturesque confusion, and perhaps raise her hand to the horse's bridle . . . waiting for him to sweep off his hat, and to lean down . . .

The Indian maids peered through the venetian sunblinds at her, their heavy immobile features candy-striped in the shadows, while their mistress sat for hour after hour in her uncomfortable cane-backed chair. The first ten minutes she devoted to sewing a blue ribbon around the big sombrero she'd bought for Ned in Anaime.

'And I'll jolly well force him to wear it, too,' she thought. 'Fair skin like his is bound to burn easily – and the blue will go just perfectly with his eyes!' But the rest of the time she spent flexing and twisting the hat between her hands until she'd entirely ruined it.

A faint faraway 'Whoop-ah!' jerked her to her feet. A minute later a solitary figure appeared on the far bank of the river in a white duck suit and panama hat, and on his face – she was sure she could see it – that familiar, dear, shy attempt to quench an unquenchable smile.

One look was enough for Meriel. She gave a wild incoherent yell and bounded off the verandah to meet him – pounding down the hill with her hair flying loose from its pins and the tears of happiness streaming down her face.

Chapter Sixteen

In the big Bury kitchen, Cook lowered her newspaper to stare hard at the gardener over the top of her reading specs. "Come in if ye'r acomin', Zacky Cheal, an' set down them dratted greens. Or cut yer stick an' clear out of et, man, one or t'other. 'Cos there's some in 'ere as wants t'ear aboot Master Ned an' all, even ef you doan't."

The little man ducked his head respectfully, sidled a few steps further into the room and set his box of vegetables down on the floor beside him. Then, cautiously, he removed his cap and clasped it tight against his waistcoat, waiting with shifting eyes for the reading to continue.

"Right than, start agin shall I?" Bridget and the new between-maid nodded obediently, while Cook rustled the newspaper back into shape and cleared her throat.

"At the Church of the 'Oly Trin'ty, Sloane Street, Lunnon, on Toosday thirteenth inst., the weddin' took place of Mr Edwin Charles Ashby, B.Sc., only son of Mr Walter Ashby of The Bury, Sellin'ton, Sussex, ter Miss Meriel Alexandra Llewellen, younger daughter of Mr Robert Llewellen of Colombia, South America.

"The bride wus charmin'ly dressed in a robe of ivory Liberty satin wiv a corsage of old lace, the skirt bein' looped up wiv orange blossoms, an' wore a wreath of myrtle an' orange blossom an' a Brussels net veil. She wus met at the door of the church by the clergy an' surpliced choir singin' the 'im 'Come Gracious Spirit 'Eavenly Dove'. In the absence of 'er farver, 'oo wus detained abroad, the bride wus given away by 'er brother, Mr Gareth Llewellen.

"Mister an' Missus Edwin Ashby left the reception in a victoria kerridge soon after five o'clock fer the Langham 'Otel. The bride travelled in an 'Arris linen coat an' skirt of a partic'ly pretty an' becomin' shade of saxe-blue. The 'oneymoon is ter be spent bicyclin' in Kent. Weddin' presents comprised a gold bracelet an' case of silver brushes from the bridegroom ter the bride, a gold signet ring an' carbuncle scarf pin from the bride to the bridegroom, a canteen of silver from Mrs Margaret Ashby, cheques from Mr Ashby an' Mr Llewellen, an' a variety of very 'andsome an' useful articles from relatives an' friends of all ranks – *includin' an 'andsome salad bowl an' servers from the Ashby staff in Sussex,* an' a gentleman's free-wheel bicycle from Miss Beatrice Sims, a friend of both families . . . "

"There!" said Cook, removing her spectacles with a flourish and beaming all around her kitchen.

'There's nothing, nothing in all this world like an English spring!' Ned thought joyously. The past six months had made an explorer of him in more ways than one. But now he was back, with the cuckoo calling and all the springtime flags flying, pacing and racing his energetic young wife through the twisting green lanes of Kent. Cycling honeymoons were all the rage just now. And with good reason, for there was surely no nicer place to be alone than in the heart of the English countryside. You could cheerfully bump along for miles without meeting anything beyond a chicken or two or a white-tilted baker's van. Discounting the towns, he and Meriel had seen no more than half a dozen motors in so many days, most of them stationary and one with its innards out all over the verge. The railways had finished country roads for traffic they said. 'And a jolly good thing too,' Ned thought.

Against the normal convention of advance booking and railway freighting for baggage, he and Meriel had opted for travelling light. They cycled where they pleased when they pleased, each with a small suitcase strapped to the back-stay pillion behind them and a lunchbox and waterproof cape in the basket in front; and neither with any kind of definite plan in their head. Sometimes they covered vast distances. Sometimes no distance at all when they chanced on a village or an inn that appealed. When it rained they scrambled for their capes and dashed for the shelter of a barn or a church. Often as not they got wet, but they didn't care – because afterwards there'd very likely be a rainbow, with everything beneath it brighter and greener and even more perfect than before. And all the time, every hour of every day, Ned studied his wife with a secret sense of disbelief.

HAVE PASSED STOP MAY I COME OUT TO VISIT AND PERHAPS BRING YOU HOME STOP ECA

CONGRATS AND YES YES TO BOTH YOU OWL ML

He hadn't believed it even when he held her reply telegram in his hand, even when she hauled him down from his horse on the river bank at Anaime. She still seemed to him too impossibly wild and glamorous ever to be really his. And now that she was, he felt as he had all those years ago, catching his first butterfly in the net that Father had given him on his eighth birthday. At first he felt sure that he'd lost it, and looked up to see it fluttering free. But then he looked down again to find it held within the meshes of his wonderful new net. A tiny, perfect Chalkhill Blue – as if he'd caught for himself a piece of the wild blue sky.

For some reason he'd never told Meriel of the original source of his ticket to Colombia. There seemed little enough point at the time, and now even less. No place for a past in a present that smelt of warm earth and wild flowers and burgeoned with new life.

In Sussex there were so many sleepy little villages like Sellington. Places that could barely recall the heyday of the great pastoral and arable farms they'd once served. But here in Kent there was a settled prosperity about the village communities that came of regular employment for the villagers in the orchards, hop-gardens and nut plats that surrounded them. Their houses crested the hilltops shoulder to shoulder, white faced, with neat ridge-bone boarding and white picket fences and honeysuckle around the doors. On the slopes below them sheep grazed beneath a pale quilting of fruit blossom – orchards of blown white cherry and apple still pink in the bud – with porcupine hop-gardens between them, a fresh green bine twisting up clockwise at the base of each wooden quill.

"Isn't it grand – isn't it splendid, darling?" He was struggling to express the inexpressible, and they were the only words Ned could find. "Honestly, we couldn't have picked a more perfect week!"

She laughed at him for his hopeless English complacence – for forgetting the rain as soon as the sun came out again. "Listen, there's the cuckoo again," she cried. "Turn a penny in your pocket and you'll be a rich man!" What did she care though, whether he was rich or poor? As the smile faded from her face her great copper-brown eyes bore down on him with a message of far more import. "More to the point, my handsome Nednog," she said softly, "where are we going to find a bed tonight? Have you thought?"

He knew, of course, that she was thinking, as he was, of another old inn with a beamed ceiling and clean white sheets. Of a bed that would creak and groan and bear them away on its back to a world where every dimension was one of sensation. Even the memory of those nights made him gasp with pleasure – and at the thought of another his front wheel began to wobble dangerously, refusing to answer to the helm.

"We'll try the Star and Eagle shall we, at Goudhurst? The man at the White Lion said it was most awfully good – and it isn't far." He tried to sound casual. But his eyes wouldn't behave – his body wouldn't either, and his ears were burning like the very devil. It was ridiculous to feel shy of her still after all they'd been through together abroad and on the voyage home, and during this last madcap week of honeymoon. He didn't feel shy when they touched – when he could burrow his face in the hollow of her neck and taste the salty sweetness of her skin. But a few feet away from her like this – desiring her from the seat of a bicycle – he suddenly felt the need to duck down behind something, to hide from the intensity of his own emotion.

"Stop!"

"Why whatever is it? What's the matter, darling, is there something wrong with your bike?"

Meriel had braked so sharply that her straw boater jerked forward on its elastic and now tilted crazily over one eye. "Come here," she commanded, making no attempt to straighten it. And as he edged his own bike alongside, she reached up to take his face between her strong little hands.

"Listen you great pook-noodle. I already love you more than any woman has ever loved a man – do you know that? And I intend to love you more still . . . "

"Oh darling . . . "

"Don't interrupt – this is important! See here, Ned, if you were to say you wanted me now, over there in that orchard, or in the ditch, or in the middle of the damn road, you could have me – and I'd love it. I'd revel in it, do you understand? I wouldn't care if the whole world was looking on! We were made for each other you and I, anyone with eyes can see that. And I simply won't have you looking at me like someone else's maiden aunt, d'ye hear? Now then!"

He felt the end of her handlebar hard against him as he kissed her – and that wasn't all. "Over there in the orchard then, please." And he kissed her again, lingeringly, just to make sure. There was a padlock and chain on the gate, so he lifted the bikes over, out of sight behind the hedge. Then she shook out her hair and pulled him down amongst the dandelions and cuckoo-flowers – and in a moment he saw the gleam of her white skin and felt the earth damp and yielding beneath his knees.

The first time they had made love in the stuffy hotel in London, they'd almost fought with each other in the violence of their need to possess and to be possessed – and Meriel had cried out, as much in surprise at the nature of her victory as in pain. Later, in the old coaching inns of the Weald and the Romney Marshes, in Maidstone, Canterbury and elsewhere, they had learned to give and to take much more from each other – and with less urgency. Each time it had been different, quite different – as if they themselves had been altered, refined in some way each time they passed through the flame.

And this time, the first time for them in the sunlight and fresh air, Ned was less aware of the separate demands of their bodies than the common lifeforce they shared. As Meriel stirred and sighed in the grass, he felt a sense of perfect fitness – no longer certain of where he himself stopped and where she and the orchard began. He smelled blossom and the scent of warm hair. His flesh beat against warmth – in the earth, in the air and in Meriel – the pulse of his blood, her blood, birdsong, breath, it had become a single sound – a single feeling – expanding, rising – taut – dammed – deafening – deafening – *deafening*...then pulsing – then separating – gradually, into shuddering breath, and heavy, thudding heartbeats, and the individual songs of a dozen wild birds.

In Goudhurst that night, at the Star and Eagle, they slept quietly in each other's arms with the innocence of children. While in the bar-parlour below the locals nudged each other and trotted out all the worn old courting and honeymoon stories, and listened in vain for the sound of a creaking board. Mrs Noakes, the publican's wife, told them roundly that they ought to be ashamed, so they ought; although at seven in the morning, when she herself bustled through to open up the parlour for her visitors' breakfast, she had been unable to ignore a noise from above like a busy garden swing, and a fine drizzle of dust shaking down between the crossbeams.

"Geemeny – at it 'ell fer leather already!" she exclaimed, but not without satisfaction. "An' 'im lookin' as if butter 'ouldn't melt, bless 'is 'eart!" And for a moment she stood at the open window, smiling – and recalling her own honeymoon in Hastings, when her Bert had yelped so loud one morning that a group of fishermen had called up from the street to ask if he'd been took ill – the great chouse!

They bundled downstairs an hour later, all kitted up in their smart new knickerbocker suits like a couple of spring lambs. Mrs Noakes took a vast delight in stoking them up with triple helpings of bacon and eggs and tea so dark and strong you could trot a mouse on it, chatting about the likelihood of rain and sportingly suppressing her broadest smiles. Every time the good lady left the room, Ned and Meriel collapsed – it was all so dreadfully, transparently obvious. And each time she returned with more toast or tea, it had been to see them leap apart and scramble back into some kind of facetious substitute of their own for conversation.

"Did you know that Sussex is only about an hour away from here, my little one? We could be there before ten."

"You don't say – only an hour? Is it really, Nednog?"

"Indeed it is, old thing."

"But surely we're not due back until Sunday, my own dear heart?"

"Well, I thought perhaps that if we asked her nicely, my sweeting, Mrs Noakes might put us up a picnic lunch to eat at

Bodiam – so that we could take a squint at Lord Anscombe's old castle there. It really is very fine, you know. Then if you like we could spend the night at the George in Battle and see the Abbey – and wire Gran to expect us home for luncheon on Saturday? How would that suit you – Meri-ellie-issima, my dear?"

"Pshh-shsssh! Oh Noggin you *idiot* – now look what you've made me do!" He'd caught her awkwardly in the middle of a swig of tea which Meriel proceeded to spray all over Mrs Noakes' clean apron.

"Oh crikey, I'm sorry. But he made me do it, didn't he, the devil? You saw him, Mrs Noakes."

"'Oneymooners!" that lady remarked a little later in her kitchen behind the bar – as she crammed an entire coburg loaf of sandwiches into their lunch boxes, with hunks of cheese, and enough sweet Kent pippins to last them through to Battle. "Think they *invented* it – eh Bert?"

They did too, and the orchard had confirmed it for them – its memory reverberating like a song between them, set to the whirring music of their free-wheel bikes as they cycled down to Sussex. They crossed the Rother river by a stone humptyback bridge, and wheeled their trusty steeds up through the buttercups to the romantic old ruins.

"Oh yes – that's what I call a castle!" Meriel exclaimed as she caught sight of the moat and the massive battlemented towers that it reflected. She left Ned to juggle with both bicycles while she ran on ahead for a better view.

They were to return to Bodiam a number of times in the years that followed, these two. But whenever he pictured this old castle to himself in the future, Ned was always to see it as he saw it now – with buttercups and grazing cattle, and a radiant Meriel unpacking their lunch boxes at the edge of the moat.

"If I lived in there you'd have to swim across for my favours, you know, Sir Nednog, and climb up the ivy to my window at the top of that tower."

"Or then again you could swim across and carry me off into the nearest orchard!"

"Vile beast!" She buzzed a piece of bread at him, and hit him exactly where she intended. "They'd spot us from the battlements – bound to. Then my noble father would have you drawn and quartered, and nail the best bits up over the gate for all the ladies to gloat over!"

She chattered on happily about the castle over lunch. While he told her what he knew of its history, Ned lay in the grass beside her, watching her squander her sandwiches on a family of downy moorchicks and wondering how he'd feel tomorrow – taking her home at last. Through all the excitements of Colombia and shipboard, and the bustle of Kingston and New York, that thought had been his most constant beacon – the thought of bringing Meriel home to The Bury, and of openly taking possession of her in the house where he was born.

"Can't wait to get her back, can you?" her father had observed, on one of the few occasions that she'd dared to leave them alone together at the hacienda. "You think it's all going to drop into place, don't you, the moment she commits herself to that cosy English inheritance of yours? You think my Meriel will be content to bear your children and run around behind your grandmother picking up useful hints on domestic felicity?"

Ned sensed unhappiness, jealousy even, behind the sardonic black stare. The man had done nothing to prevent his marriage to Meriel, nothing to keep her in Colombia, and yet he opposed them, you could hear it in his voice.

"No, not necessarily," Ned replied stoutly. "I expect to love her and to be loved back, that's all. I imagine that the rest will follow on naturally enough in its own good time."

"Ah love! Dear me, we're back to love, are we? But how very curious, Ned – I may call you that, mayn't I, now that we're to be related? But how curious! Forgive me if I'm mistaken, dear boy, but as I recollect the last time we discussed that interesting and variable emotion, you were professing undying affection for an entirely contrary lady!"

Meriel's father clearly had no faith in the durability of love – possibly because he'd never really experienced it. Grannie still thought he and Meriel were wrong for each other – possibly because she knew less about her own grandson than she imagined. But at Bodiam that afternoon, just twenty-four hours away from home, Ned himself was in no doubt at all about the future course of their life together.

"Do you know what I think when I look at that castle, Meri?"

"Me in a chastity belt?"

He smiled, sucking at a pink sorrel stalk. "I think of life and civilization stretching in both directions, with us in the middle. So I can sit here with you on the edge of this moat and look back five hundred years to the feudal knight who built those walls and towers, and to the lady who brought him this land as her patrimony, and to the child who inheritied it from them. Then I can look into your eyes like this and look forward five hundred years to our descendants, caring about each other and about the timelessness of places like this just as I do. Love, reproduction, continuity, that's what this place is about, and The Bury and you and me and everything else, don't you see? It's the only kind of permanence there is."

But she saw only the eyes that looked down into hers – soft as butter, unfocused, distant dreamy blue. They made her want to shock him, to shake him into reality – yet at the same time to protect him, to stand between him and all the violence and ugliness of the world – to bolster him in his lovely dream of life, whatever it might be.

'God but he's beautiful!' she thought. 'And he's *mine!*' Looking up into her husband's face, waiting for him to come-to again and take her in his arms – that was all Meriel asked of life. That and a top-to-tail exploration of the castle across the moat.

Book 2

(1913–1925)

Chapter Seventeen

If Meriel Ashby had ruffled the smooth surface of her husband's life in the Sellington Valley, then he had only himself to blame – or so she frequently told him.

Like many another healthy young bridegroom before him, Ned surprised even himself with the constancy of his physical appetite during those early years of marriage, with gratification continually inflating desire until his expectations of Meriel often exceeded even her capabilities in that direction. Meriel, on the other hand, had taken to the marriage bed quite as easily as she had to the saddle, curbing and giving-head to Ned's passions as she considered necessary, and frankly insisting on artificial means of birth restriction after the arrival of her second son Robert in May of 1909.

"'Demoralizing to character' my foot!" she retorted in response to the Lambeth Conference's notorious pronouncement on the subject. "A damn sight more demoralizing to end up with a dozen screaming kids, I'd say, or a misplaced husband and a sopping wet bed! And what the blazes do a bunch of Anglican bishops think they know about modern women anyway, I should like to know?" With which she'd promptly mailed off to the Leicester Rubber Company in London for a sample packet of the latest thing in protective sheaths for Ned to try. A system which – after the briefest of altercations with her husband – she declared entirely satisfactory.

"A hundred times better than all those fiddly syringes and sponges and whatnot, at any rate," she confided to a flustered Simmie on one of her flying visits to Harpur Street. "Or than relying on the wretched man to do the right thing, for heaven's

175

sake. Any woman who pins her hopes on *that* deserves everything she gets!"

Nor had Meriel's reactions to The Bury and its farm proved noticeably more conventional. On their return from honeymoon Ned had been all for converting a pair of flint and cobble cottages in the village into a snug little home for the pair of them. But his wife refused to hear of it.

"Really, Noggin, there's no need to be so old-fashioned," she declared after a brief speculative tour of the old Bury nurseries and schoolroom. "A 'flat', that's the modern thing. Look, don't you see, darling – a wall there, another across here, a bath and a sink in your Nanny's old parlour, a new front door over there and Bob's your uncle! Oh come on, Ned, this house is your *home*, isn't it? Tell me where else your children should be born!" And not only had she gone on to supervise personally the structural alterations, but demanded a free hand with the decor and furnishings as well – hectoring local carpenters and painters and the Manager of Heal's furniture store in London into creating an undeniably modern interior for her, with white paintwork and pale colour-washed walls. English winters were quite dreary enough, she said, without smothering the windows in velvet and everything else in dismal patterns and depressing colours. Pictures were for walls, she said, not table-tops. Photographs were for albums, pot-plants for glasshouses and horsehair for horses, for God's sake. Simple decoration and room to swing a cat – that was the modern idea, Meriel said; and 'modern' was Meriel's latest word.

Ned's grandmother had been patently unimpressed. "If you plan to live in a servants' attic, then I'd say you were goin' the right way about it," she remarked privately to Ned after her final inspection of his new home. "All this *nouveau* nonsense is no more nor less than an excuse for cheap, manufactured furnishin's, if you ask me." But she'd taken care, nonetheless, to modify her comments on the subject to her new grand-daughter-in-law. For however she might personally disapprove of Meriel's taste in furniture, Margaret Ashby was keenly alive to the advantages of settling her grandson and his family under her own gabled roof.

Ned had liked it all right, though, after the initial shock.

When he came to think about it he actually did prefer plain English oak to mahogany or rosewood, and cane to velvet plush. If the rather spartan atmosphere of their new sitting room reminded him more of a Colombian ranch-house than of Gran's own comfortable upstairs den or Simmie's crowded little parlour in Harpur Street, well then that wasn't necessarily a bad thing. Besides, if it was what Meri wanted, then he was only too happy to indulge her.

Her plans for the farm were another matter. Almost as soon as she'd grasped the outlines of the traditional downland agriculture that the Ashbys had practised for generations, Meriel had begun to bombard Ned and his foreman Shad Caldwell with revolutionary ideas for ploughing up more chalk, for boosting the efficiency of the milking herd and increasing the size of their stocky little Southdown sheep. "You simply can't stand still, you've got to move with the times," she told them. And when Ned patiently tried to explain to her something of the professional pride and hereditary expertise of men like Caldwell and the shepherd, Bat Vine, the proven success of a farming system that had withstood the test of time, she called him a hopeless old fuddy-duddy like his father and threatened to buy her own breeding rams over his head at the very next sheep fair.

In the end it had been Margaret Ashby who advised Ned to let his wife take over the Bury poultry enterprise, if only to keep her from pestering the men. And both of them had looked on with some astonishment while Meriel proceeded to establish a small village of modern Sussex poultry arks on the sloping meadows beyond the dig-yard, and to replace the old barndoor fowls with a new type of hybrid pullet that increased egg production by more than two hundred per cent within the space of three months.

But Ned had known all along that the hens could prove no more than a temporary diversion. Denied the wider influence she'd hoped for on the farm, and with her two young sons in the capabale charge of a trained nursemaid, it was inevitable that Meriel would begin to look beyond the narrow confines of the valley for her interests and amusements. Ned had accepted the truth of her father's predictions long before he married her – hers was a spirit that could never be curtailed.

So when she took herself off to spend his money for him in Brighton, when she covered the floor of their sitting room with magic lantern slides of Australia for her latest lecture to the Seaford Girls' Friendly Society, he did nothing to discourage her. When she had scandalized Gran by captaining a Downland Ladies' stoolball team that was soon the scourge of the Sussex villages, or when she stayed away from him for weeks at a time with her aunt or her sister or with Simmie in London, he simply grinned and bore it as he knew he must. It was the price one had to pay for that bouncing step of hers, for those snapping brown eyes and for the joy she so frequently brought into his life.

In their first six years of marriage Meriel had regularly provoked her husband to intense feelings of pride and exasperation, ecstasy and frustration. She provoked him constantly. But Ned was honest enough to admit to himself that he would never have married her in the first place if he'd been prepared to settle for other men's ideas of pallid femininity. He recognized Meriel as the stimulant he'd always needed to enliven the quiet life that was prescribed for him in the Sellington Valley. If, as so often happened, she overstepped the mark with Gran or the servants or with some local village worthy, why then he could draw on reserves of tact and patience from within his own character to meet the situation. And when at the end of each working day he said goodnight to the two little boys she'd provided for him and for the future of the valley, when he lay beside his wife in the extraordinary lotus design bed that she'd had sent down from Heal's in London, Ned Ashby was content.

> "It is now –
> We have ploughed –
> We have sowed –
> We have reaped, an' we have mowed,
> And provided for the valley next year!"

Ned felt like singing – he so often did nowadays. The sun had already disappeared behind the Bury wood, drowning the buildings ahead of them in shadow. But the sky still glowed, and behind them the shorn yellow barley stubble caught the last of the light from the sea. It wasn't the last of the harvest for that summer of 1913. But it was the last load from the fifteen acre laine, the last for the week. The binders would lie idle now until Monday – and that at least called for a celebration.

> "We 'ave carried our last lo—ad,
> An' niver overthrow—ed,
> An' provided fer th'valley next year!"

The rest of the harvest gang joined him enthusiastically for the chorus, belting it out over the steady jingle and cloppet of the team and the uneven rhythms of iron-shod wheels and creaking cleat boards. It was a full load, stacked high above the corner poles, with an extra course of neatly butted sheaves all round and the two lads on top to bind them in. From below Ned could just see the peaks of their caps bobbing up and down to the lilting old song – young Jemmy Vine and Cook's nephew, Shaver Tinsley, released from their normal duties in the sheep folds and the kitchen garden to lend a willing hand with the harvest.

In recent years, and despite diminishing cereal acreages, they'd inevitably found themselves short-handed at The Bury around harvest time. In the old days there'd been cheap Irish labour to call on through July and August – but not any more. For two or three hours that afternoon Ned had pitched-up on his own while Dan and Pyecroft attended to the milking. In the barn the foreman, Shad Caldwell, had stacked on his own too, with the other three taking it in turns to load and impitch, or to shunt the trace horse and shuttle back and forth with the wagons. Not that any of them objected to the extra labour. Ned enjoyed physical exertion – always had. Unlike Father, he was never sorry for a chance to demonstrate his prowess to the men or to share their pride in the work. It helped to see him through all those other times when he merely delegated and they performed. And if he strained a little harder and sweated a little more freely than they did, they forebore to mention it. All but Dan Goodworth, who seldom missed an opportunity of pulling the young Guv'nor's leg if he could help it.

"Wouldn' be amazin' ef yer slep' sound tonight, Mus Ned," he observed as they creaked slowly down past the dairy and into the yards. "I'd swear we ent seen yer so stalled since last year's 'arvest." And it wasn't until Ned cuffed him sideways into the wall of the cowshed that he condescended to crack a grin.

"All right, Danny! We all know you're never fagged, but I have loaded up the odd barley-stock in my time, you know, without actually falling apart at the seams."

It was true though, nothing ever did seem to tire Dan – even the flowery wreath of trumpet-bindweed he'd twined around his hat looked disgustingly fresh. Nothing and no one was ever able to outface him either, not even Meriel, and despite their social differences, he and Ned had always been aware of each other's worth – always friends. As boys they'd swum together at the Gap. They'd smoked tom-bacca clematis stalks together behind the pigscots and pooled their wool collections from brambles and hedges to earn a few extra coppers at shearing time. On dark winter evenings they'd crept out together with the batfowling net, to 'spadger' sparrows in the rick yard for Mrs Goodworth's famous 'Spar' pudden'. And later on, their batting partnerships had been justly celebrated through a whole series of Sellington Sheep Fair cricket matches. It was an unstated and slightly uncomfortable alliance, now that Ned's wife had taken such an obvious dislike to his cowman. But the fact that their friendship survived even that had been a measure of its durability.

"And don't go telling everyone that the Guv'nor's flogged himself to death now, just because I've got to leave you to stack this lot on your own," Ned added, with a wink at Stumpy Pyecroft's abashed face. "You know my father-in-law's landed himself on us for the weekend – and I rather think Mrs Edwin will have something to say if I don't put in an appearance for dinner."

"Bless yer, Mus Ned, the very idea!" Dan regarded him with mock horror. "Now I arsk yer – would I iver do anythin' so oudacious? No you jes' doddle along an' see ef me an' the boys doan't 'ave this lot in the ol' barn afore ye've 'ad the time ter shuck yer boots off."

Ned smiled. "Well don't be in too much of a hurry, old son, because I was thinking of setting aside a jar or two of ale for young Shaver to fetch down to you when you've finished. Pity if you beat me to it, don't you think?"

"Crim'nal," Dan agreed. "Ah but thad's different, ent et? I'd say we cheps'd be willin' ter stop on fer a bit ter drink yer 'ealth, Mus Ned – an thankee. Seein' as it's Sunday tomorrer an' we're all of us dry as kex." He touched the brim of his jaunty flower-wreathed hat with just a trace of impertinence in his smile, and the others chipped in with their own thanks. "Thankee – thankee, Mus Ned." As the Guv'nor saluted them and turned up to the house, they led the weary team on across the cobbles and in through the lamplit portals of the great barn.

Outside the back kitchen door Ned shed his cap, his boots and his sodden socks, and as much of the barley straw as he could – pulling his wet shirt tails out of his trousers and doing a little dance on the bricks to shake the chaff and the barley-beards through. Everything about him felt good, including the muscles that ached and the grey patina of dust and sweat that coated his face and forearms. It was the visible evidence of a good day's work – gritty in his ears and eyelashes, and ending abruptly in a black brim-line across his forehead.

"Lord in 'eaven – it's a blackamoor!" Cook cried as he padded across the kitchen flags. "Run an' fetch the copper-stick, Gertie, an' see 'im orf, gel!"

"Sorry about the mess, Cook. Have they gone in to dinner yet?"

"They 'ave not!" Cook was immediately up in arms. "Mrs Edwin wus jes' in, wantin' ter hold the 'ole thing up 'til *nine* if yer please! 'Nine?' sez I – 'them spring chickens'll be dry ol' broilers afore half-eight!' But she doan't care, not she. She's a quick 'itter, Master Ned – always a word an' a blow wiv Mrs Edwin. 'Nine, Cook!' sez she – an' hout she goes!"

"Oh I am sorry, Cook," Ned said diplomatically, "it's all my fault really. But look, I'll nip up and have a lightning splash in the old tub and be dressed and down in ten minutes – how about that? And if I skipped the soup course you could send them in right away."

"Not my good soup you ent skippin'." Cook turned back to the range to work out her disapproval of Master Ned's wife on the gravy lumps. "You'll eat at nine wiv the rest of 'em an' do et proper justice. But ef et's an 'ot bath ye'r after, ye'r outta luck. What wiv Mrs Edwin's bath an' Miss Helen's, an' another 'ot bath fer them lit'luns o'yourn, thad ol' boiler ent dishin' out no more."

"Oh, that's all right, Cook, I've had enough heat today anyway – a nice healthy cold bath will suit me just fine. And I'm sure that chicken dinner will be A1, whatever you say. I don't believe you could come within a mile of spoiling a meal, even if you took lessons at it. Oh and Cookie," he stuck his head back round the door to catch her smiling helplessly at the housemaid. "That young nephew of yours will be up presently for some harvest ale for the men – if Gertie would draw a jug for him?"

"Will someone be good enough to explain to me what Bulgaria thinks it's playin' at?" Gran's voice – deeper, fruitier than ever.

As he trudged barefoot up the front stairs, Ned could hear Robert Llewellen's drawling reply. A charming, simplified view of Eastern European politics that Father – who lived for his morning *Times* – could certainly run rings around, if ever he could raise the energy.

"Dog-eat-dog, my dear Mrs Ashby. That's the name of the game, always has been," Llewellen was saying. "Bulgaria bites off a chunk of Turkey. Then Serbia and Greece each take a little nip out of Bulgaria, you see. Austria devours Serbia – and our old friend Kaiser Bill glides in out of the shadows to snap up the lot of them by way of an *appétissant*, don't y'know, before moving on to the Middle East for the entrée."

When he first married Meriel, Ned had fervently hoped that her father would steer clear of Sellington. The happiness that she brought to him here, to this place that was so dear to him, had seemed altogether too perfect for the cynical eyes of the infidel. That's how he'd felt in those early days. But as the seasons turned and the years passed, and his happiness incredibly survived the constant gyrations of daily life with Meriel, the prospect of a visit from Llewellen no longer seemed threatening. And now this evening, still glowing from his day in the fields, Ned knew that at last he could look his father-in-law in the face across the dinner table and laugh at the ludicrous irony of their relationship. Natural adversaries, that's what they were – oil and water, coexisting in a state of intimate discord – forever bound by an obscene shared joke and the affections of two extraordinary women.

Robert Llewellen had returned to England at the end of June, following the Colombian government's decision to withdraw their concession and take over the Quindío mercury project themselves. Gareth, who'd returned to Anaime soon after his sister's wedding in 1907, had been asked to stay on as Manager; but Robert Llewellen had clashed too often with the Bogotá government to have recommended himself to their agents in any kind of administrative capacity. 'And after seven years in that goddam hole, I shall be only too glad to return to civilization,' he declared in a letter to his daughter. 'I think I can say as a matter of principle that I have now finished with the Latin American Continent for once and for all.'

From the moment of her own departure from Colombia, Meriel on the other hand had decided to view everything South American through rose-coloured spectacles, including the offending parent who remained there. As soon as he arrived back she dashed off to lunch with her father in town, eager for his promise to spend a weekend with them all in Sussex as soon as possible. It wasn't that she'd consciously forgiven him, that would have been impossible. It was simply that she refused to call the more unforgivable of his sins to mind.

After a number of interviews in the City and convivial lunches at Simpson's in the Strand, Robert Llewellen had rapidly found himself another post abroad, curiously enough as Consultant Engineer to a British company involved in the recovery of ancient artefacts from the bed of a lake no great distance from Bogotá, in Colombia.

> "Almighty providence fashioned us hollow
> So that we might our principles swallow!"

He'd recited it to them in The Bury front hall as he tossed his coat over Gertrude's extended arm, ignoring Mrs Ashby's frigid stare and flashing a near perfect set of white teeth at his awestruck grandsons. He was to sail again in early September, he said. And somewhat to his own surprise Ned now realized that he no longer particularly cared one way or the other.

Llewellen's voice was clearly audible from the first landing, still holding forth authoritatively on the Balkans. But behind the closed door of the Flat, peace prevailed.

The water for Meriel's white painted bathroom was heated by the same boiler as the rest of The Bury. So Ned's bath that evening was quite as refreshingly chilly as Cook predicted – and he towelled and dressed his weary limbs to an encouraging ragtime tempo, madly syncopating 'Hitchy Koo' under his breath to avoid disturbing the children. 'They should be well off by now, anyway,' he told himself. 'But perhaps I'll nip in just in case.' It was still only a quarter to nine, and it'd be a poor kind of father who sneaked off to dinner without so much as an attempt at a tucking-in or a goodnight kiss.

"Oh Mr Edwin, sir, do try to settle Master Patrick if you can. He's that worked up, what with his new grandfather an' all, I despair of ever gettin' 'im to sleep, and I don't know what Mrs Edwin won't 'ave to say if she 'ears he's still sparkin'." The children's nurse, Betty, met him at the door of the night nursery, all starch and Pears soap and raw-boned anxiety. "Miss Helen's in with 'im now, sir – said she'd stay 'til you looked in. But to tell you truly, I think the little lad's got somethin' on 'is mind. Won't tell me though, not for all the tea in China. You ask 'im, sir."

"Leave it to me, Betty, I'm an old hand with Master Patrick." She was a good-hearted methodical type, Betty, and the boys liked her. But at times like this he did wish that Meriel had let him bring old Nanny Jefferies back to the nursery.

The first thing he saw as he stepped into the room was Helen's giant shadow thrown up onto the wall and the ceiling, bending and swaying with a grace that owed everything to Patrick's flickering night-light with the glass off, and alas nothing to poor Helly herself. She was slumped on the edge of his bed like a sack of potatoes, reading with some difficulty against the hearty concerto of snores that issued from little Robbie's cot across the room.

"Hunca Munca tried every tin spoon in turn – the fish were

glued to the dish." Helen's voice was childishly high, and by now a little weary. "Then Tom Thumb lost his temper. He put the ham in the middle of the floor, and hit it with the tongs and the shovel – bang, bang, smash, smash . . . "

"Daddy!" He'd been spotted. Patrick had heard the boards creak and wriggled up in bed to peer around his auntie – his brown hair smoothly brushed across the dome of his forehead, his eyes in the candlelight quite as round and dark as Tom Thumb's in the story.

"I knew you'd come."

"Well of course Daddy's come, I told you he would." Helen straightened her back automatically and smiled at her brother, her finger still in the book. "We'll leave the rest of *The Two Bad Mice* until tomorrow then, shall we?"

"Um, all right." Patrick had scarcely heard her. "Daddy, Daddy look – something to show you!" He leant out of bed in his sleeping-suit to scoop a small box off the top of his chest of drawers, and to hold it out to his father. "Gran'farver Ll'ellen brought it!"

Ned sat down on the bed beside Helen and took the box gently from his son, acutely aware of the child's eyes on his face as he opened it. "Let's see, what is it? I wonder what can be inside?"

It was an old cardboard cigarette box of Llewellen's, lined with tissue paper and still reeking of Egyptian tobacco. Inside, a tiny Colombian hummingbird with a cap of brilliant ruby feathers crouched on a nest of moss and thistledown no bigger than a crown piece. Ned had seen dozens just like it in Cartagena, on sale to tourists for ten cents or less – the price of a cup of coffee. He lifted it carefully by its fragile beak. Sometimes there were a couple of minute white eggs in the nest, delicately blown. But this one was empty. Ned turned the little bird into the candlelight, the irridescent feathers on its throat changed from topaz to emerald. The eyes were just visible as empty white sockets. Two thin claws clenched pathetically beneath the tail, and from the vent between them a wisp of cotton wool protruded.

"It's dead," Patrick said stonily. Little Robbie wouldn't have cared. He'd have laughed at the bright colours, and very likely gone on to crush the scrap of bone and feathers in a strong, careless little hand. But at five, Patrick had already developed his father's sensitivity.

"It's dead, Daddy," he repeated in a voice that was suddenly stricken. "An' Gran'farver must've killed it."

"No, Patrick – I think he bought it in a shop." Ned smiled, just a fraction and mostly at Helen, looking at him with exactly the same expression of helpless distress on her face as his son. "I expect it had already died of old age when they found it. Everything does in the end, you know."

"But it's got a nest!" Patrick's soft little lip trembled. "So – so what happened to its babies when it died, Daddy . . . ?"

"*Patrick!*" At the sound of Meriel's voice all three of them jumped guiltily; even Robbie's snores were arrested for a moment as he turned over in his sleep.

"Patrick, what in the world are you doing awake at this time of night? You know perfectly well that you should have been asleep hours ago – even if Daddy and your Aunt Helen don't." She glared at them fiercely. But Helen had already sprung to her feet, dropping *The Two Bad Mice* on the floor and standing on the hem of her own evening dress, in her efforts to kiss Patrick and get out of the room before her sister-in-law decided to make an example of her.

Meriel sailed on past her without a glance, and up to the bed. In a panniered gown of peacock crêpe-de-Chine, with a slit tango skirt and a fringe of silvered glass beads, she looked superb and knew it.

"Not another peep out of you now, Patrick, understand?" She stooped to smooth his covers and to kiss him briefly on the forehead – replacing the glass shade on his night-light, returning the cigarette box to the chest, pulling her husband to his feet and moving on to Robbie's cot – all on the same continuous wave of motion that had carried her into the room, and that within a very short time would sweep her out of it.

Patrick lay still, wide-eyed and wordless. "I'll nip up again after dinner to see if you're still awake," his father whispered, and the little boy nodded gravely. "And listen, old fellow, now I come to think of it I'm sure that bird would have been too old to have any babies or anything – probably an old nest too, left over from last year, I expect." His instinct then had been to take this little offshoot of his in his arms and hug away the last of his fears and uncertainties. But the boy's mother had already reached the door, and was standing there tapping her foot. So he had to compromise with a fatherly wink and a kiss on the top of Patrick's smooth brown head.

Outside on the landing Meriel grabbed him by the sleeve and dragged him unceremoniously to the nearest lamp. "Right then, let's have a look at you. Just as I thought, a dog's breakfast. In here!" And ignoring his protests and snorts of laughter, she pushed him on into the bedroom, to haul him out of his dinner jacket and force him down onto her dressing table stool. "There – now don't you dare move!" She disappeared into his dressing room, to re-emerge a moment later with his comb and brushes and a flat tin of hairdressing.

"Really, Ned, I've told you about that parting. It doesn't suit you, and I can't think why you will persist with it."

He smiled. "I suppose I must do it just to annoy you."

She looked at him sharply in the mirror. "There's no need to be sarky," she said, slapping a greasy white lump of hairdressing onto the back of his head and briskly massaging it in. An over-powering smell of coconuts filled the room. "And it's no good making that face either, Ned Ashby. There's more to life than tossing barley-stocks about and trudging around behind cows, you know. You're an important man now. Not a bad looking one, either, when you make a little effort; and you simply can't go about the place looking like any old country bumpkin, not any more."

He did so love Meriel! If she treated him like some prize possession – like her horse or her dining room table – always polishing and sprucing him up and wanting him to look his best, he really didn't mind. He knew that she disliked him in his smelly old farm togs, hated to see him unshaven, positively loathed it when he was ill. But the unholy glee that sparkled in her great brown eyes now, as she parted and smoothed his hair so hideously flat and shiny, was worth almost any indignity. It was her way of keeping him up to the mark – of loving him. And if she took such pleasure in dressing him up like a lounge-lizard, it was still very frequently worth it for the undressing.

Chapter Eighteen

"We'll take our coffee outside." Margaret Ashby's voice at full volume automatically killed any other conversation at the dinner table stone dead. She thrust her chair back peremptorily and beckoned Ned to help her out of it. "You can serve it in the rose garden, Gertrude, in fifteen minutes' time. Fifteen minutes, gentlemen," she repeated sternly from the door. "We mustn't keep the servants up, must we? And you may as well bring the croquet things, Edwin – moon's far too good to waste."

If it occurred at all to her to consult her family or her guest on the choice of venue, she certainly gave no sign of it. Tea, luncheon, even breakfast at The Bury were frequently taken out of doors. As a dinner hostess, Margaret Ashby saw nothing at all odd in taking coffee in the rose arbour at a quarter to eleven, or in playing croquet by moonlight. It was a part of the tradition of life she'd been born to. "And five hours' sleep is more than enough for anyone," she declared.

It was precisely fifteen minutes after leaving the dinner table that Mrs Ashby plucked her blackthorn stick from the porch stand and launched herself out into the garden, with her granddaughter Helen tiresomely clinging to her free arm.

"Oh I say, Gran, isn't it a heavenly night!" Helen exclaimed. "Have you ever seen such a brilliant moon? I'd swear you could read a newspaper by it, you really could!"

"If you were idiotic enough to want to try!" Her grandmother twitched her arm away irritably. "You know, Helen, in my young day we were told that it was better to remain silent and be thought a fool than to open your mouth and remove all doubt. Now where's that goose Gertrude got to with the coffee?"

As the two women approached, Robert Llewellen and Walter Ashby tossed back the last of their brandies and surreptitiously wiped their moustaches, rising politely to settle the ladies into vacant basket chairs under the rose arbour. And Gertrude, watching discreetly from behind the drawing room curtains, scuttled off to Cook for the coffee tray.

"Nice evenin'," Margaret conceded with a curt nod at her guest. "'Print moonlight', that's what we call it in Sussex, Mr Llewellen – meant to be the sign of a good harvest, which I'd say was only too damned obvious. But then I daresay you'll tell me it's nothin' to the moons you see in the tropics, if all we hear about them is true?"

Robert had been watching the youthful figures of his daughter and her husband out on the croquet lawn, weaving between the hoops, calling, laughing, absorbed in each other and in the violent percussions of their game. The moon elongated their shadows on the lawn, silvering the slates of the farm buildings beyond and the curving sweep of the downs across the valley. Bats flickered. A little owl tooted tunelessly, like a child on a penny whistle. In his nostrils the comfortable domestic odours of the stables and the cattle byres blended with the sweeter perfumes of the rose garden; and when Robert turned to reply, his hostess just caught the tail of a wistful expression as he whisked it out of sight.

"Why certainly! Dear me, even our stars out there are as big as gas lamps. And as for our tropical moons, my dear Madam, I assure you that you English farming types could harvest your corn by any one of 'em!"

Mrs Ashby's stays creaked ominously.

"Ah coffee!"

"Coffee, Gran!"

Her son and grand-daughter spoke in unison and with loud relief – each to be treated in turn to a blue basilisk glare.

"Thank you so much, Walter, thank you, Helen. I do have eyes in my head, however, and I think I can just about recognize a coffee tray by now when I see one at close quarters. Thank you, Gertrude," she added to the maid, with an instantly gracious smile. "Set it down there if you please, and then run along up to bed." And miraculously the smile remained on the old lady's face, as at that moment a hiccupping snatch of song drifted up to her from the barn on the mild night air.

> "Now lads need no persuasion,
> But send your glasses round . . . "

"Their wives'll serve them a rare ol' dish of tongues tonight," she remarked as she poured the coffee. "But I'll own that it does me good to hear it. In the old days now, Mr Llewellen, they'd be good for the best part of a night after a harvest supper. You could hear 'em up in the house with the windows shut, plain as you please. In fact I don't mind tellin' you that I've learned a good number of new words that way in my time!" And she chuckled richly as she handed him his cup.

They were all of them celebrating in their way, that still night of 1913 – the Ashbys in their rose garden, the Sellington labourers down in the great aisled barn below – celebrating a long Indian summer of order and security that had come to seem as much a part of the English way of life as the land itself. Fads and fashions blew in with the March winds of one season to melt away with the January snows of the next. Balkan wars and Irish Home Rule, suffragettes and hobble skirts – all seemed transitory, irrelevant almost, beside the moonlit permanence of the chalk hills and the ancestral laines they sheltered, and the red-faced sons of Sussex who sung of them with such lusty confidence.

> "Now lads need no persuasion,
> But send your glasses round,
> And never fear invasion
> While barley grows on ground!"

Ten months later two squadrons of the British Navy moored in friendly German water, alongside five of the Kaiser's latest dreadnought battleships, for the festive occasion of the Kiel Yachting Week. The Kaiser himself had donned the uniform of a British Admiral of the Fleet to visit His Majesty's flag-ship, only to be called away unexpectedly before the end of festivities – recalled to Berlin with news of the assassination by a Serbian of his friend and ally, the Archduke Franz Ferdinand of Austria.

It was the latest of a succession of Balkan disturbances that made little enough impact on the farming communities of Sussex. While the issue of Austria against Serbia was joined by the great powers on a European field that spread out in alarming vistas on both sides, Ned and his foreman inspected the meadows for their second hay cut and declared them fit for mowing.

The demands of the agricultural year took no account of diplomatic bickerings and newspaper politics. An unusually hot July made for an early harvest, with the oats bleached white before the end of the month; and an early harvest meant virtually continuous fieldwork through from shearing at the end of June to the Sellington Sheep Fair in early September. So Ned left his father to worry over *The Times'* gloomy political outlook, and Meriel to bait Gran with her scorn for the idea of Britain supporting France in the event of a conflict. He was responsible for his own family, for The Bury estate and the people of the Sellington Valley – and that was enough. His business just now was with reaping and carting, with corn sales and store lambs, and with the hay and straw that would see his livestock through to the spring of 1915.

Towards the end of July, still five weeks away from the local Sheep Fair that represented the end of his shepherd's year, Bat Vine was tending his ewe flock on the open downland to the west of Sellington Gap. It was noon. He had already finished his bread and cheese and stoppered up his tea bottle for later, and his dog lay watching him shake out the last crumbs from his dinner bag for the birds. She knew what he was about. Her eyes followed the movements of his rheumatic knotty old hands, as he punched the canvas satchel inside out and half filled it with water from a second bottle. She'd been told to 'lay-down' and she durst not move – nothing but her eyes and the expressive gingery tufts above them. Not until he gave the command.

"Lass." One quiet word that carried far beyond the dog to the nearest of the grazing sheep. As they raised their mousy faces from the grass, she scurried forward to lap the water from the bag, never looking up until she finished. Afterwards he fondled her ears for a moment and extracted a bur from the long hair beneath her chin. She responded in silence with a flick of pink tongue and a perfunctory movement of her tail, for neither of them was over-demonstrative.

Bat remained leaning on his crook – a Still Man as they said in Sussex – a timeless solitary figure silhouetted against the vast summer sky. A woman from Eastbourne who'd once encountered the Bury shepherd in a weekend ramble across the downs, had described him to a friend as an 'arcadian Elijah'. But the proud, all-seeing expression that she'd noted had not been that of a visionary or a prophet. Far from it – Bat never dwelt for long on abstract concepts. It was simply that he worked a great deal with his eyes, and took pleasure in doing so.

The ewes were his first and main concern. As those keen, deepset grey eyes swept across the flock, he automatically divided them into groups, piercing avenues through their ranks and telling them in pairs with a speed that a bank clerk might have envied. Here, there and everywhere he picked out individuals that he knew – 'Shut-in-the-twist', a young animal with an unsteady lopsided gate, an old draft ewe with knees heavily calloused from seasons of grazing in a kneeling position, a six-tooth with an unsightly ridged back, a young four-tooth with a foxy face and a receding lower mandible. ('Hogjaw' he called that one, and had fixed her up with a jangling old horse bell – for she could only graze on the longer grass and was bound to wander.) And many others that he recognized – dozens of them – from the notches in their ears, from the individual set of their limbs, and from peculiarities of locomotion and facial expression he could not have put words to. He simply knew them. And knowing them, watching them, listening to the settled clucking and clanking of their bells, Bat was assured that all was well with the flock.

Satisfied, he turned his attention to the outer perimeters of the sheep run – to the valley and the slopes across it, to the white flint doole stones that marked the boundaries of Ashby grazing, and to the high, scalloped shoreline of the Channel. For here too there were signs to be read and considered. Even as Bat's grey eye traced the scattered pattern of the dry flock on the far slope, it was measuring the area of grazing that young Jem had allowed them. He calculated from its progress through the oats the likely achievement of the reaper-binder for the day. And as he watched the rippling movement of the breeze on the distant hill, he noted its direction – a light sou'westerly set fair. But at the conclusion of that long perceptive glance, it was the motionless figure on the cliffs that finally captured and held his attention.

The duty coastguards were familiar features in the elevated landscape of Bat's downland world. He could have set a clock by their cliff path patrols to west and to east, to meet and exchange news with the coastguards of Crowlink and Cuckmere. Occasionally, when the ewes were on a southern slope, he and Lass would waylay one of them on the return journey, to chew the quid for a minute or two of companionable conversation.

The sight of a coastguard on the cliff was nothing out of the ordinary in itself; but when after twelve minutes by Bat's watch the trim figure of the bluejacket still failed to move in either direction, the shepherd left the sheep to his dog and walked down the hill to investigate. Bat had always been accountable to a tidy mind.

As he neared the cliff edge, he announced his arrival in the way of a working countryman who himself disliked surprise, with the whistled snatch of a melody. 'Sons of the Sea' it was, in deference to the old sailor. The coastguard glanced briefly over his shoulder and nodded to the shepherd, before returning his glass to the ocean.

"Good day, Vine."

"Good day t'ye, Mus Etheridge."

The sea was azure, pale as a butterfly's wing, without so much as a fishing smack to disturb the calm or to show where the water bled out of the sky. But Bat had already followed the line of the glass to discover its quarry, even before it was placed in his hand.

"Look, but doan't ask, Vine. 'Cos ther ent nothin' I can tell yer, an' thad's a fac'."

The round window of the telescope sped like a swallow from the deserted shore, up over the surface of the water – to come to rest on the ghostly outline of a great battleship, suspended as it seemed in mid air. To the left were two more. To the right a fourth – and more, many more, parading in Indian file across the skyline from Beachy Head away down the Channel to Newhaven and Brighton and beyond. The distant vessels were foreshortened steel castles of towering superstructure and tripod mast. But on the nearer ships the outlines of funnels were visible, belching black smoke, with white ensigns fluttering above the sterns and massive guns to fore and aft.

Bat considered them in silence. "Fair 'nough," he said at last, handing back the telescope. "I doan' like 'em anyways, blamed ef I do." And he turned to go.

The coastguard stared after him, outraged beyond all caution. "British Ironclads," he shouted at the shepherd's calmly retreating rear. "King's ships, solid from 'ere to Shoreham – near on twenty miles of 'em I rackon! An' as valiant a sight as ye'r iver likely ter set eyes on, Bartholomew Vine, ef you live ter be an 'undred an ten!"

"No sir," Bat turned once out of politeness on his way back to the flock, but only once. "No sir, t'ent – not fer a feller as sees the dawn come up over the downs reg'lar iv'ry marnin'. An' look'e 'ere, Mus Etheridge – ef we're in fer a start-up wiv they ol' Germins, 'tis ter be 'oped them tippytoppy gurt pike-bungs o'yourn doan't go an' make a boffle of et, thad's all!"

The First British Fleet reached its war station at Scapa Flow on the evening of July 31st. On August 3rd, the day Germany declared war on France, the British Government delivered an ultimatum to Berlin demanding respect for Belgium's neutrality – to be confounded the next morning with the information that six German columns had already crossed the Belgian frontier near Gemmenich.

On August 5th Simmie's copy of *The Times* discreetly murmured the news to her across the breakfast table – in column two, in undramatic, understated lower-case type:

> We have been at war with Germany since midnight last night . . . The immediate interest of the campaign for us centres in the naval operations, and especially those in the North Sea during the next week . . .

So it had come; and they said it never would, not so long as

British battleships could match those of the Germans. Everyone seemed to welcome it too – everyone except her. Over the extended August Bank Holiday London had been thronged with people, marching around waving flags and working themselves up to a fever pitch of patriotic enthusiasm over the war that now seemed inevitable. Even Gladys had been infected by the general mood, bursting in on the Monday to report that Charing Cross was jam-packed with sailors.

"'Arf the bloomin' Navy I shouldn't wonder – an' soljers too, 'udreds of 'em – Frenchies an' all sorts, all dressed up like a circus! You want ter go an' see fer yesself, Mum!"

But Simmie hadn't gone, or even wanted to. The concept of a European war involving England still seemed quite as unreal to her as Ladysmith and Mafeking had done. So did the flushed, excited faces in the street outside. There was no place in her life now for such upsets – all that had gone eight years ago with the mail that had borne her Colombian passage transfer to Sussex and to Ned.

She had committed herself to middle-age that day, irremediably – and to the penance of proving herself a capable and circumspect landlady to the succession of undergraduate lodgers who'd followed Ned Ashby. She still undercharged for their meals, still darned their socks and sewed on their buttons when need be. But the fastness of her upstairs parlour was out of bounds to them now. She no longer ate with them in the dining room, no longer wished their shirts to smell of anything but starch and clean linen. Commonsense had prevailed.

She still had the 1890 journal – she'd never quite been able to destroy that. She even knew where to find it, amongst the jumbled letters and photographs in the bottom drawer of her writing bureau. But she hadn't done so. She hadn't looked at it for years – and wouldn't, not now. The echoes were too faint.

Simmie had heard of Robert's brief return to London in 1913. Dear Ned had written to warn her of it – and Meriel actually called in at Harpur Street on her way back from lunching with her father in the City. But Simmie hadn't expected or wanted Robert to call. It was like the time when a cousin from Yorkshire had treated her to a trip down the river to Hampton Court. On the way the pleasure steamer had passed right beneath Richmond Hill, and she'd looked up to see the gothic spires of the old hotel above the trees. But as they'd disappeared from view she'd felt a sense of relief – the same relief she was to experience when Robert Llewellen sailed away again without seeing her. She still wanted to remember – but that was all.

Life for Simmie was peaceful and pleasant enough. Twenty years in Bloomsbury had brought her a wide circle of friends and acquaintances. She played bridge regularly twice a week; and although she remained unbelievably bad at it nobody seemed to mind. Everyone liked her. Everyone confided their innermost secrets to her at the drop of a bonnet. Friends, lodgers, tradesmen, nannies perambulating their charges in Bloomsbury Square – they all had a good word to say for the lady with the vague, kind smile and the sympathetic ear, and the hair that refused to stay put in any weather.

Beyond an occasional bus ride to attend a rummage auction, or to watch some suburban cricket match in which her lodgers were performing, Simmie seldom strayed abroad from Harpur Street. Meriel was forever pestering her to come down to Sellington for a day or a weekend, or a little summer break. But she'd always declined. It wouldn't have been fair on Ned.

Ned seldom came to town nowadays, but the little that Simmie had seen of him in the past few years was more than enough to convince her that marriage had changed him, and for the better. He'd matured and gained confidence. Although he still looked like a bull in a china shop when he came to tea with her in her upstairs parlour, there was a deliberation in his movements now, and a calm steady light in his blue eyes that augured well for her breakables.

But neither marriage nor motherhood, nor even the passing of the years, had succeeded in slowing Meriel down. She still raced through life like a small human tornado, boasting of her children, boasting of her beloved Ned – but spending little enough time with them, Simmie noticed, at home in the Sellington Valley. The way she dashed from Heathfield poultry higgler to Seaford lecture hall, from Brighton to London to her married sister in Bedfordshire, it sometimes seemed almost as if she was running from the valley itself. And when she spoke of Ned's decrepit old farm or the illiterate Sussex yokels who helped him run it, there was a note of resentment, even of jealousy, in her voice that Simmie found disturbing.

During the early years of Meriel's marriage she had also felt more than a little constrained by the shadow that still lay between them:

'Give him up, *please*, Simmie! . . . I can't lose him too – not both of them, Simmie . . .'

And Meriel's insistence on acting as if that letter had never existed had been hard to take for someone as honest as Simmie. There was so much still that needed saying. She wanted to be trusted again – to get the whole thing into the open and to clear the air. And on one of Meriel's frequent shopping visits to London she had tried.

"Darling, I want you to understand about me and Ned," she'd said suddenly as they turned into Harpur Street one afternoon, after a miserable bus ride from Oxford Street spent screwing herself up to speak. "It was over, you know. Everything was over between us long before that ball in Grosvenor Crescent – even before our bicycling expedition to Sellington, Meriel. I do want you to understand that, darling, and to believe it." She looked at Meriel beseechingly.

Meriel looked back at her for what seemed to Simmie an eternity of silence, before she finally spoke.

"Tell me honestly, Simmie, did you ever see anything so utterly damn foolish as those hats in Fentons? You'd have to be an ostrich yourself to go in for all those blessed feathers – and a pretty short-sighted one too, I think!" And she juggled her hatboxes onto one arm to ring the bell of number nineteen, hopping about like an impatient child while she waited for the door to open. "Here we are then, Gladdie, safe and sound and stony broke – and absolutely *gasping* for a cuppa!"

Simmie hadn't the courage to try again. Life settled back into the comfortable, undemanding round of activities that she'd come to expect, and to welcome – until Gladys' Bank Holiday revelations of troops at Charing Cross had finally forced her to take this wretched war seriously.

Last night crowds of exuberant straw-hatted East-Enders had surged down Theobald's Road to congregate in Whitehall and

Trafalgar Square, and sweep like a great tide up the Mall to Buckingham Palace. Then in the early hours they'd come straggling back, cheering and singing 'Land of Hope and Glory' and 'Tipperary' at the top of their voices.

"Are we downhearted?"
"No! No! No!"
"Shall we beat 'em?"
"YE-E-E-S!!"

Listening to them as she lay in bed, Simmie felt horribly lonely in her inability to share their confidence and jubilation. This morning's hastily set *Times'* commentary filled her with misgiving. She read it again, absently stroking George – the tortoiseshell tomcat who sprawled in the sun on the chair beside her – deriving a little comfort from his complacent sensuality.

. . . The campaign begins under favourable conditions for us, since we have a just cause, a Navy mobilized and at its war stations, and powerful friends. The country will set its teeth and prepare to conduct the war with the tenacity and perseverance that have distinguished it in the past . . .

"Never you worry, Mum," Gladys said in much the same vein as she stalked in for the breakfast things, jerking her formidable chin, "if it's a fight they want, they'll git more'n they bargained for from our boys – no mistake abaht it!" And she slapped a sticky sideplate down on her tray with a robust defiance that sent George streaking for the door, and broke the inoffensive plate clean in two.

Chapter Nineteen

Glady's aggressive optimism was matched in dining rooms and kitchens, on buses and trains, in offices, stable yards and cornfields throughout the country that momentous morning of August 5th. The Foreign Secretary's pledge to stand by France and Belgium had united all political factions; and it was clear to all that the German bully needed a lesson that only Britain and the united force of the Empire could teach him. War to the British was something rather dashing involving scarlet uniforms and gallant cavalry brigades – nothing that could possibly last. It was widely held that by autumn, or Christmas at the very latest, the whole thing would be over – with the Union Jack flying triumphantly in Berlin and the pattern of life elsewhere returned to normal.

The Navy and Regular Army had already been mobilized. Including Reservists and Territorials, it was announced that there'd be a magnificent total of six hundred thousand men under arms within a week. And when Lord Kitchener called for an additional one hundred thousand unmarried volunteers between the ages of eighteen and thirty, the urban recruiting offices had been literally overwhelmed with eager sporting young men, desperate to prove their fighting worth before the war was over.

In the chalk hills of Sussex and across all the vast tracts of rural England where August still meant 'harvest' first and foremost, the call to arms was less fervently heeded. The march of the seasons was set to an older, more compelling rhythm, and it was to be a demanding season that year, with unusually heavy crops and changeable weather mid-month. But many enlisted, nonetheless. Several families in Sellington had sons in Newhaven or Brighton who'd responded to Kitchener's beckoning finger; and it was fortunate for Ned that of the ten men in Bury employ, only two were strictly eligible for the New Army. The foreman, Shad Caldwell, was married and well over age. The same applied to Bat and Zachy Cheal and Henshaw the groom. Dan Goodworth was the same age as Ned himself, both thirty-one now. And although the youngsters – Jem and Shaver Tinsley and the stable boy, Warry Hurst – were all anxious as Toddy to join the colours, none of them would be eighteen for at least another year.

Ned thought the whole thing was likely to prove a flash in the pan in any case. Everyone had long known that war with Germany was a possibility, some said an inevitability, for the future. But despite his father's pessimistic predictions of a protracted engagement, Ned himself was still convinced that the powers would extract themselves by diplomatic means from a massive conflict that none of them could afford. So when Jake Armiger and Stumpy Pyecroft, the two eligible Bury men, began to talk of enlisting he'd done his utmost to dissuade them.

"The way things are going," he said, "old Kitchener will have his hundred thousand before anyone's even had time to look you out a uniform. So why not just sit on the fence for a while and see what happens? God knows there'll be plenty of other opportunities to volunteer later if they still need men. And how the hell do you think we'd all manage without you through harvest? The country needs good men on the land too, you know."

Little Stumpy, who hated upsets as much as Ned did, shifted his weight from one foot to the other and back again, blinking nervously and avoiding the Guv'nor's eye. But Armiger was made of sterner stuff. The way he saw it, not even a Sussex-bred Ashby could dictate to a Sellington man on matters of personal integrity – and he pushed his cap back off his face to emphasize the fact.

"Thad's as mebbe, Mus Ned, but t'ent whad they're askin, is et? Wars want men ter fight 'em, ther's no gainsayin' thad – an' the more the merrier, I rackon."

Poor Stumpy had dumbly nodded his agreement. But if Ned felt sorry for him then, he felt a good deal sorrier when the man sheepishly returned a day later with the information that he'd been rejected on account of his height. Out of his boots he stood little more than five feet, admittedly. But he was broad with it – and although he was frequently called 'short-arse' behind his back, no one had ever before questioned his physical capability.

"Wouldn' tek me, Mus Ned," he said with a brave attempt at a smile. "Man sez t'were jes' as well, as I'd more'n likely be needed fer 'arvest, whad wiv Jake joinin' up an' all. An' I sez, ef they go an' lose the bleddy war wivout me than, they'll only 'ave theirselves ter blame!"

Not that the harvest had proved any real kind of problem that year, despite the heavy crops. The weather cleared and settled again. Four or five young lads from the village had more than compensated for Armiger's absence – with Helen shocking-up or acting as standfast for the horses, and Meriel in new corduroy trousers and an old shirt of Ned's, insisting on driving the waggons.

In addition to Armiger's services, the Ashbys were also obliged to contribute their hunters and carriage horses to the local Military Remount Service, at forty pounds apiece complete with harness and tack. But they were permitted to keep their working teams and the old bay cob, Archie, for carriage duty.

Inside the house, Margaret Ashby voluntarily sacrificed her 'peace hour' to preside over a ladies' sewing circle, manufacturing a variety of outsize flannel dressing gowns and pyjamas for the troops. And Ned's father, Walter, bestirred himself to the extent of offering his services to the Voluntary Home Defence Corps, to assist the coastguards with their patrol of Sellington Gap.

Down the coast at Newhaven, the Channel ferries were requisitioned as troop carriers and auxiliary warships, and the port itself entrusted with a primary role in the transport of stores and munitions to France. On the downs around Seaford huge army camps were established to train troops in all aspects of infantry warfare – and to electrify the prim little resort with mass nude bathing from its beaches.

In the wake of the shocking news that Liège had fallen to the enemy, a flood of homeless Flemish refugees had descended on boarding houses and private homes in Eastbourne and Brighton and other large coastal resorts. And everywhere committees and sub-committees sprouted like field mushrooms at the end of a wet summer – a War Refugees Committee, a Committee for Red Cross Supplies, War Savings and War Distress Fund committees, and the euphemistically named 'Emergency Committee' – charged with preparations for a possible German invasion of Sussex. Daily newspaper reports of events across the Channel were uncertain, out-of-date and hopelessly confusing. Stirring accounts of Belgium's heroic defence made each engagement sound like a victory. Yet manifestly the German host was continuing to advance.

In the absence of any more definite instruction, there was nothing for Ned and his men to do, however, but to heed the

Government's demands for increased agricultural production, and to prepare for the coming Sheep Fair.

Sellington Sheep Fair was the single event in the farming calendar to which the entire population of the valley was still committed. For this one day the eyes of several counties were to be focused on them – and the responsibility was keenly felt. For the weeks running up to the event Helen Ashby was busy turning out Useful and Fancy Work for the traditional Bury bric-à-brac stall, working with clumsy persistence in the media of pipe-cleaners, seashells, crochet, lacquered fir-cones and passe-partout. Up in the village the cottagers were also hard at work. Drunken cabbages were staked upright, yellowing onion-tops combed into line, curtains laundered, windows cleaned and polished with newspaper, and every item on the shelves of Pilbeam's Post Office and Stores laboriously dusted and replaced. At the Lamb Inn a special consignment of Tipper Ale was ordered well in advance from the brewery at Newhaven for the greatest influx of the drinking year. And down in Sellington Meadow the area laid-off for the cricket pitch was freshly mown and rolled.

One way or another most of the other old village fairs had fallen by the wayside in recent decades. Less land under the plough meant less folding, fewer sheep on the hills; while cheap New Zealand lamb and rail access to the great sheep fairs of Lewes and Chichester had made cross-country droving less of a profitable proposition. But Sellington Fair survived. In the days of Ned's great-grandfather, Jonas Ashby, it had been a purely local event – a time at the end of the shepherd's year for the eastern downland flockmasters to foregather to exchange rams and cull surplus ewes, and sell off store tegs for fattening. But in Sellington's case the coming of the railways in the eighteen forties had actually brought new buyers for Southdown stores from the big arable farms to the north and the west. Sellington's position at a junction of chalk ridgeways that now linked it with the railway goods yards of Eastbourne, Polegate and Seaford had ensured not only its survival, but its expansion.

"Waste o'bleddy time ef y'arsks me, Mus Ned," Bat muttered in mock disgust as he surveyed a pen of square-trimmed wether tegs with an artist's appreciative eye. "Bloomin' furriners doan't know the bleddy back end frum the front, anyways."

"Hardly surprising I'd say after all you've been doing to them," Ned retorted, crossing the shearing yard with a new batch of wattles. "Still, so long as they're prepared to pay thirty shillings or more apiece, they can drive them out backwards as far as I'm concerned, and welcome!"

But Bat had already moved on to the final stage of the beautification process, and wasn't listening. "Now than, Jem m'boy, look slippy an' run an' fetch us the wat'rin' pot an' raddle shaker," he commanded, with the air of a head chef calling for the Hollandaise. "An' let's us see what a bit o'colour bloom'll do fer matching' 'em up, eh? Thad's et, boy," he added as Jemmy returned with a large zinc-plated watering can and a perforated tin canister like a giant pepper pot, "rain furst, than sunshine." With which he'd hitched up his smock and climbed into the first of the lamb pens – watering the animals to right and to left like so many coldframe cucumbers, then dusting them all liberally from the shaker.

"Ef ther's one thing thad improves an ornary ol' wather Down more'n summat, et's a pountle good colour. Puts a shillin' or two on the price, an' thad's sartin'." He whistled a flat little tune to himself through his beard, as he massaged the red ochre dye into the fleeces and up his own arms and down the homespun skirts of his working smock. Some years he used a yellow shaker to bring them up a bright, uniform canary. But on the whole he preferred the deeper, richer tones of the raddle.

While Bartholomew Vine was trimming and colouring-up the last of the Bury store lambs in the shearing yard, and raddling himself rusty red in the process – Ned and the others were putting the finishing touches to the parallel ranks of sheep pens that now occupied the meadow beyond. The six long ranges of wattle enclosures had been erected back-to-back in the traditional way, with supporting spines of driven chestnut stakes and open access lanes between each double row. But as always there was plenty of scope still for soul-searching and head-scratching over the number of smaller pens to be allocated to rams and ewes, and over which of the better outer store pens should be reserved for Harding, Gilbert and Paul and other favoured local flockmasters. By the end of a long, hot day of earnest deliberation, Ned was ready to introduce almost any alternative topic of conversation – even the war. "Has anyone heard the latest from Belgium?" he said, reaching for one more pitch-bar and bashing it home into the chalky subsoil. "I didn't get a squint at the papers this morning. Did your Missus have anything new to pass on at lunchtime, Shad?"

"Not a lot." Shad Caldwell was wiring name-signs to the gates of the farside pens with a look of professional gloom on his long, lugubrious face. "She knows I ain't so tarrible wrapped up in this 'ere war, doan't she?"

"An' doan' yer be so choice, y'ol bugger!" Dan Goodworth called across to him good-humouredly, as he strode up from the milking shed with little Stumpy trotting at his heels. "Didn' you tell me as Missus Pilbeam 'ad et thad another five 'undred wounded come in yisterday?"

"Wul, whad ef I did? T'ent nuthin' ter go cluck over is et? We 'ad three 'undred more'n thad the day 'afore, didn' we?"

"Thirteen hundred wounded in two days?" Ned's eyes met Dan's, questioning, as they had so often in childhood adventures when Dan had given the lead. "And that's only the beginning, isn't it, Dan?"

"Mons." Dan confirmed it without a flicker. "Rare ol' losses fer our boys up there they say, Mus Ned – an' many more ter come in yet, I rackon. Kitchener's askin' fer another 'undred thousand, ent 'e, ter stop up the gaps? An' ther's some as say 'e'll tek 'arf a million of us 'afore 'e's through."

"My bible oath, ye doan't say so? 'Arf a million fer sure?" Stumpy was all agog.

But Shad remained stubbornly unimpressed. "Wul our boys 'ave got them off-scourin' Germins by the bollocks," he said, methodically wiring up another sign. "They can't 'ardly 'ope ter best our Empire, can they, Mus Ned? An' anyways – t'ain' agoin' ter rain fer the Fair is et, so thad's one comfort."

On the morning of Sellington Fair everyone was up at dawn, or soon afterwards. The air was soft and still, and a thin grey mist creeping in from the sea confirmed Shad's forecast, it wasn't going to rain. Up in the village every cottage step shone chalky-white as the first rays of the sun broke through; and every cottage wicket stood closed and latched against the four-footed invaders. Down in the Sellington Meadow the striped poles and dappled horses of Harris's steam-driven merry-go-round reared out of the swirling ground mist. And in the warm, bovine fug of the Bury milking shed the alternating milk streams fizzed and frothed in waltz-time, to Dan's slow bass rendition of 'After the Ball'.

As he walked down from the house, Ned could already smell the odour of warm wool that would presently fill the valley – an infallible cure, some said, for all manner of physical ailments. And with it had come the thrill of expectation that always characterized Fair Day morning.

Bat's rusty wether lambs occupied five of the pens in the meadow – those nearest the farm. But the others stood empty still, and waiting.

"Hee-ar! Hee-arr!" The first incoming flock announced itself as a muffled echo from somewhere in the mist above them – and then within a matter of minutes the business of the day had begun. The mist lifted like a curtain to reveal half a dozen tightly-knit little flocks, advancing over the hills to Sellington by ridges and sheere-ways that had borne sheep since the Bronze Age, when villages hereabouts still lived in fear of wolves. Between the flocks the racing shadows of the dogs were visible, circling to keep them apart. As they descended unwillingly from both sides of the downs, the air was filled with shouts and whistles, clouds of white chalk dust and the drumming scuffle of thousands of small hooved feet. From the head of the valley, through the village itself, came the lowland flocks of Cuckmere and the Weald – trotting down between the cottages, scattering droppings like squashed currants and leaving wispy smears of wool on the flints of the garden walls as they hurried to join the bleating throng in the meadow below.

By twelve noon most of the real business of the Fair had been completed. In Sellington all transactions were still conducted in the old-fashioned way, by private treaty – beginning with pipe-chewing, belittling comments and pointed excursions into the pens to feel the backs and view the teeth – progressing through the standard gamut of exasperated cap-adjustments and astounded appeals to heaven – and ending with an abrupt hand-shake, cash on the nail and a smile or a wink on either side.

And if one or two surplus rams and the odd pen of lambs had to be driven home unsold, the majority could still be reasonably sure of finding their worth.

Long before the last hard bargain had been driven in the sheep pens, a brisk trade in crooks and sheep bells and gypsy remedies for foot-rot and blow fly had started up on the far side of the cricket pitch. And for those to whom a country fair was simply a better-than-average excuse to enjoy oneself, there were the usual coconut shies and catchpenny stalls, and the Italian mechanical organ of the merry-go-round thumping out 'Oh, oh Antonio!' for all it was worth.

All the Useful and not a little of the Fancy work on the Bury bric-à-brac stall had quickly sold, and in less than no time they'd been down to Helen's pipe-cleaners and fir-cones and the worst examples of the Seaford Girls' Friendly Society's crochet work. Margaret Ashby, who'd presided over more Sellington Fair bric-à-brac stalls than she cared to recall, had long since departed in the direction of the bull-pen – to exhibit the cylindrical splendours of her champion Sellington Magnate to a fellow Red Sussex breeder. Meriel had just decided to abandon Helen to what was clearly a sinking ship, when she caught sight of her husband loping up from the sheep pens to intercept Betty and the boys at the Punch and Judy show.

"Give me sixpence out of the War Distress Fund, Helly," she said on a sudden impulse. "Come on you goose, they can afford it!" and she twitched the sixpenny bit out of Helen's doubtful fingers to make a beeline for the ice cream float. By the time she reached them with the penny ices dripping from her hands, Ned had already hoisted little Robbie up onto his shoulder for a better view. She watched them chuckling together at the puppets, both so flushed and handsome and so ridiculously alike – and Patrick laughing too, clinging to his father's sleeve. Her children! Never more dear to her, those two, than when they were with Ned – her menfolk!

"Here you are, chickabiddies – ice creams!" she called out to them, as casually as the pride and the happiness within her would allow. "One for Daddy too, and one for Betty. And who's going to run this one down to poor old Auntie Helly on the bric-à-brac? Patrick?"

Major Rab Attwood was nobody's fool when it came to recruitment. In the chance offer of motor transport from the rally at Hove back to Eastern Divisional Barracks at Colchester, he recognized an opportunity that was too good to miss – and planned his route with the foresight of an experienced strategist. Seaford at eight, to the station and all along the bus route to intercept the clean-collar men on their way to work. Sellington Sheep Fair at noon for a ready-made audience of brawny shepherds and men of the soil. Eastbourne at three to catch the holidaymakers on the promenade and in Devonshire Park, and to confront them from the Grand Parade bandstand. On to Bexhill for another captive audience, and a pre-arranged evening amongst the pierrots of the Kursaal Pavilion. Then an early start again in the morning for more clean-collar workers, and for St Leonards and Hastings, before finally turning inland through Kent.

'Dash – enthusiasm – initiative!' Attwood repeated to himself the effective words that he employed so often with his subordinates. 'And if the Battalion isn't a hundred men the better by this time tomorrow, then by George I'm not the chap I think I am!' And he permitted himself a tight, bristly little smile at the thought of such unlikelihood.

Seaford, he had to acknowledge, had been something of a disappointment – with women by far outnumbering men on the pavements and on the railway platform, and no kind of an audience to get one's teeth into. He'd felt sure that his own particular combination of rank and experience, the substance of his message and his friend Butterwick's chauffeur-driven Belsize motor would prove well-nigh irresistible to potential recruits; but the patriotic ladies of the town had already been busy awarding white feathers for cowardice to every able-bodied man they could find out of uniform. The few hardened cases that Attwood himself succeeded in running to earth had been stubbornly entrenched in their resistance to his appeals to honour and duty. A dozen or so had undertaken to consider enlisting, when pressed. But when it came down to it, he could only feel confident of one definite recruit from the town – a poor stick whose wife listened intently to all the Major had to say, and then announced her decision not only to part with her Alfred, but to escort him to the Recruiting Office personally there and then.

From Sellington, however, Major Attwood had reason to expect a good deal more. As the Belsize chugged and simmered down through the village and out into the open valley, he ran a professional eye over the gaily dressed crowds around the cricket pitch, and noted with approval that almost half of them were men. Men in archaic smocks and gaberdines and unbleached drill jackets – men in corduroy suits and salt-and-pepper tweed – a pair of muscular wrestlers stripped to the waist – cheapjacks, booth-men, paper windmill hucksters with impudent polka-dot hats and floral waistcoats. Rude, healthy-looking fellows, every man jack of 'em – and a good many of them quite respectably young.

'By Jove,' Attwood thought, 'they may be undisciplined bucolics now, but the material's there, right enough. Get them into uniform and give 'em a fortnight at Colchester with a first-rate Sar' Major to lick 'em into shape, and we'll have a platoon or two of tolerably fine soldiers out of that field. Damned if we don't!'

The moment they spluttered to a halt, the Colour Sergeant jumped smartly down to distribute the broadsheets they'd had reprinted from the Battalion's newspaper advertisement.

APPEAL. 7TH SERVICE BATTALION, THE ROYAL SUSSEX REGIMENT.
This battalion of Lord Kitchener's Second Expeditionary Force of 100,000 is forming at Colchester, and is SHORT OF MEN.

Major R. B. Attwood appeals to ALL SUSSEX MEN, including ex-N.C.O.s and Soldiers to COME FORWARD NOW WITHOUT DELAY, to join the Battalion and fill the ranks with men of Sussex, who will sustain the honour of the Regiment abroad.

The age limit for enlistment has been extended from nineteen to thirty-five (or in the case of ex-soldiers, forty-five). Height 5′3″ and upwards, chest 34″ at least.

Report at the nearest Recruiting Office, and INSIST ON

SERVING IN THE 7TH BATTALION FOR THE PERIOD OF THE WAR.
GOD SAVE THE KING!

Ned had a leaflet thrust into his hand by the pugnacious little sergeant before he could realize his duty as an Ashby, and push through to receive the Military in a proper manner. By the time he'd collected himself, the Major had already slipped Fred Harris a half-sovereign to stop the merry-go-round, and stepped up to address them.

"Men of Sussex – will you answer your country's call?" Ned felt Patrick's sticky little hand jerk in his at the raw challenge of the man's voice, and smiled down at his son in reassurance. The words were as intrusive and unwelcome as the corseted khaki figure who projected them, and every bit as pompous. Although it occurred to Ned as he listened that the Major in his uniform was as much a puppet in his way as the policeman in the Punch and Judy show he'd just been watching. His speech was a formula, already tried and tested and set to the authorized refrain of the military Pied Piper.

"I think that perhaps many of you here do not fully understand the nature of that call – and it is my purpose and duty to enlighten you. I have no doubt that all you able-bodied men would have hastened to enlist before this, had you felt that England herself was in danger. But, gentlemen, I am here today to assure you that England *is* in the most perilous danger – together with all that she stands for in the way of liberty, peace and honour. Do not deceive yourselves into thinking that we are in for a swift or an easy victory over the Hun. I tell you, at this very moment our Empire is poised on the brink of the greatest war in the history of the world. And it is for us gentlemen, for you and me, to determine its outcome.

"It was my privilege on Sunday last to attend at Hove Town Hall the first of many great recruitment rallies that are to be held in the months to come. I should like to quote to you from the eloquent speech that Sir Arthur Conan Doyle made on that occasion. 'The enemy,' he said, 'is almost within sight of our shores. We have had to change the base of operations, and there is a possibility of disaster.' *A possibility of disaster,* gentlemen! And perhaps those words will seem more real to you if I tell you that you are in fact less distant from the Flanders battlefield here in Sellington than you are from your own English cities of Plymouth and Derby!"

The Major paused for this information to take effect, standing dramatically with one hand resting on the arched neck of a merry-go-round horse – his pale boiled-gooseberry eyes inviting reaction. But there were no oohs and ahs from his audience. The farmers and stallholders in Sellington Meadow regarded him to a man in unwinking silence. But if the speaker himself was disappointed, Ned had seen that blank, buttoned-up look on the faces of too many interested buyers at too many stock markets and sheep fairs to be deceived. The Major had caught their attention all right.

"Business As Usual might be a good maxim for you farmers to adopt," the Major continued on an even more abrasive note, "but Happiness As Usual is something that we none of us any longer have a right to expect. Not when our gallant boys are returning wounded to our shores, anxious only to be well enough to rejoin their comrades at the Front! Lord Kitchener himself has spoken of a long and arduous struggle, of sacrifices beyond any that have been demanded of us in the past. I am not here, gentlemen, to offer you an easy choice. I am here to take you from your families, and from the peace of these pleasant hills. To take you to a place where *men* are! To set you a task which will demand sacrifices of you and your loved-ones, and all the selfless courage and endurance that you have. For no price is too high to pay when honour and freedom are at stake!"

"Rot!" Meriel exploded, with one eye on her husband's infinitely precious profile. "Don't listen to him, Ned. He's talking through the back of his head, you know he is!"

"We are not a militaristic people like the Prussian Guard, who enjoy fighting for its own sake," the Major was insisting. "But when it's a question of fighting a bully to preserve our own decent way of life, then by God you know as well as I do that we are the hardest people on earth to beat! We hate war. But that is the very reason why we must fight. For if we win – and make no mistake, gentlemen, we *shall* win if we set our

210

minds to it – the finest of our politicians are pledged to see to it that *there will be no more war!* This sacrifice of ours will be the sacrifice to end them all! Yesterday and the day before, each day, thirty thousand valiant Englishmen have rallied to their country's call. But we need more still, many more, for today and tomorrow and all the tomorrows to come.

"So step forward, step up, men of Sussex," the Major cried, automatically adopting the fairground cheapjack's pitch. "Step up and answer that call! *Your King and Country need you now!*"

"Yes I daresay they do," Meriel exclaimed with rather more violence than she intended as the merry-go-round spun back into motion and 'Antonio' reverberated down the valley once again. "But if you're thinking of making the sacrifice-to-end-them-all, Ned Ashby, then you can just think again, that's all!" She pounded her palm with a small, clenched fist as she said it, unconsciously hammering at the fear she felt inside her. "Because your own family and this blessed valley of yours need you more, a *damn* sight more than they ever will, you can take that from me!"

Chapter Twenty

The cow's brindled roan coat was warm against her cheek – and shifting her position to strip out the back quarters, Meriel nestled in closer to its flank, staring down into the brimming bucket. Her fingers ached but Phoebe was her final cow for the afternoon milking, so there was an especial satisfaction in feeling the great veined purse of her bag relaxing and contracting until the powerful milk jets finally reduced to trickles. "Right-o then old girl, you're done," she said at last, and more to Stumpy than the cow – deftly extracting her stool and pail and decanting Phoebe's contribution into the nearest four-gallon bucket. For although Pyecroft regularly milked twelve cows to her eight, Meriel could never quite resist racing him to the finish.

After Dan Goodworth's enlistment with the Royal Sussex back in 1914, Meriel had surprised everyone by demanding to take his place in the milking shed. Ned had better things to do, she said, in trying to meet the War Agricultural Committee's impossible demands for increased cereal yields with reduced manpower; and in any case it was high time he allowed his wife to do something useful. Besides, she'd milked in Australia heaps of times – in Colombia too, for that matter. Why what she didn't know about milking could be written on one side of a threepenny bit! In the event she'd proved such an apt pupil too, that only Stumpy – who instructed her – realized quite how limited her previous experience had been. In Queensland she'd very occasionally addressed herself to an ancient Jersey house-cow who was light in both front quarters – and then only when Mulvany was off on a bender. And although she'd sometimes made butter at the hacienda in Anaime, she'd only ever actually milked there once or twice out of sheer boredom.

Not that such technicalities daunted Meriel herself in any way. The Bury shorthorns had fidgeted at first at the sound of her unfamiliar female voice; three of them refused outright to let their milk down for her, and one old cow, Marigold, had persistently flicked over her pail with a swift and fiendishly accurate hoof. But Meriel persevered, rising before Ned at five each morning to coax and cajole the reluctant cows – milking Marigold for the first fortnight with her hocks roped together – and finally emerging triumphant as she knew she would.

"Another eight gallons up there for the cooler then, Stumpy," she said in the monotone they all used for the cattle ('talkin' thin' Stumpy called it). "I'm all through, now." She stretched her back surreptitiously while the cowman's face was still hidden from her by Victoria's bony red and white pelvis. He made a curious gnome-like little figure on his stool, did Stumpy – like something out of the Middle Ages, Meriel always thought, with his lank hair and bandy legs. And even after almost two years of working side by side with her, he was still quite painfully shy. He couldn't even bring himself to call her 'Mrs Edwin', without blinking madly and dipping his head like a nervous moorcock.

"There now," he murmured to Victoria in polite admiration. "Milkin' wants feelin' an' method, doan' ert? An' I rackon as she've got 'em right 'nough – same as you ol' craturs do, the way ye lets down fer 'er."

"No thanks to the Government and this ridiculous Summer Time idea of theirs!" Meriel snapped, forgetting the monotone. Servility always irritated the hell out of her. "Perhaps they'd like to send down one of those clever-dick Food Commissioners of theirs to explain the War Effort to the cows, and why they suddenly have to come in an hour earlier, eh?"

The substance of Pyecroft's reply was lost in the grumbling depths of Victoria's rumen. And by the time Meriel had shed her wrap-over and scoured out her pail in the dairy, she could hear him droning into one of the objectionable little lullabys that all cowmen swore helped the milk to flow:

"O we doan' wan'ter lose ye, but we think y'oughtta go,
For yer King an' yer Country bof' needs yer so . . . "

The limitations of Stumpy's memory unfortunately confined him to the choruses of no more than a handful of popular songs, which he was in the habit of repeating again and again until Meriel could scream with exasperation.

"O we doan' wan'ter lose ye, but we think y'oughtta go . . . "

Silly little man! Meriel slammed her pail onto its drying stump outside the dairy window and marched off towards the house. Well, he could damn well take the cows back on his own then, for all she cared! She was fed up to the back teeth with this wretched war dominating every conversation and newspaper and song. It would be just the same inside! Father-in-law in the library, wasting his time with his maps and packets of coloured flags – plotting minute fluctuations through unpronounceable villages up and down the zig-zagging line of the Western Front; Grandmother-Margaret in the drawing room, bullying the Rector's wife and Madame Waedemon and her other sewing ladies into producing more and more stinking anti-vermin underwear for Helen to rush through to the War Hospital Supply Depot at Southover; Cook and Gertrude in the kitchen, converting old socks to mittens and brewing up great vats of *Soupe aux choux* for the villagers; and Cheal in the garden, producing successive bumper crops of cabbages and potatoes to the exclusion of anything more palatable. It was all part of the War Effort, as they kept telling each other so smugly – as if running the farm wasn't a hundred times more important. The whole world had gone mad!

Meriel slipped in quietly through the conservatory door, determined to avoid an invitation to tea with the ladies, and yet another tedious discussion on the new Allied 'push' they were all getting so hot under the corset about. After twenty-two months of war, Meriel knew all about 'pushes'. They began always with triumphant announcements of victory in all the newspapers. Then came vague and confusing qualifications. Then interminable casualty lists – and finally a map that showed no detectable alteration in the five hundred miles of trenches that still bisected Northern France. And she certainly wasn't about to get involved in all that again!

The cellar door effectively blotted out the sound of Grand-mother-Margaret, belling away like an old bloodhound in the drawing room. As she lit a candle and pulled the catch to behind her, the delightful coolness of the place rose up around Meriel. After the sticky heat of the cowshed, she plunged gratefully down the stairs to meet it, to immerse herself in its pool of darkness and dusty stone and malty, beery odours. There was a gallon Sussex-ware jug in an alcove at the foot of the stairs; and she wiped it out carefully with the hem of her skirt before filling it to the rim from the tapped barrel. Despite its weight, she was able to lift it easily with one hand, milking had done that for her, but she had to support it against her body to take up the candle again. The men would have to do without mugs, and be grateful!

In the front porch she set the jug down again to collect an old garden hat of Helen's from a peg behind the door. The chaplet of tattered blue cornflowers around the crown reminded her of Mother's infamous hat with the cherries. But appearances be damned, she was only wearing the thing as an example to the boys to keep their sunhats on in the hayfield, and it was plenty good enough for that. Outside, the sun was nearing the topmost beeches of the wood, washing the whole valley in butter-yellow light. In the stable yard Meriel paused again to pour off the top three inches of beer and to rest for a moment. It was heavier than she'd thought. More than half the stables were empty now that the Remount people had taken their second working team, and with Warry Hurst in France and Henshaw assembling trench howitzers in Eastbourne, the place had a neglected look about it. The mayweed had got a hold between the cobbles – the whole yard reeked of it. There were thistles on the maxon, already making heads; and Meriel made a mental note to fetch a swaphook to them after morning milking tomorrow. These days there was always something extra for tomorrow.

They were haying up in the Sellington Meadow this week – in the place where they'd erected the stalls and the merry-go-round for that last Sheep Fair at the beginning of the war (before the Ministry introduced size-grading for lambs, and made the whole thing pointless). Shad Caldwell was stacking with his usual deliberate method – and Pierre Waedemon chewing tobacco and loafing at the horse's head with an expression of *ennui* on his fat Belgian face that made her itch to snatch off his silly glasses and stamp on them. Ned was pitching-up and managing to do the dog's share of the work as usual. It really was too bad the way he let the men exploit him.

She did nothing to attract his attention as she toiled up the meadow, concentrating on holding the jug steady. But there was something about her husband's body that told Meriel that he knew, that he'd seen her coming – something overt in his stance and the quality of his movements as he stooped and flexed and strode towards her through the haycocks. The show-off! He reminded her still so much of that young Adonis who'd bobbed up out of the sea to her in his stripey bathing costume the day of her first picnic at the Gap. At thirty-three her Ned was still the best looking, quite the loveliest man she'd set eyes on. And climbing up to him through the scented hay, Meriel felt a familiar knot of apprehension tightening inside her.

He was standing just about on the spot where that idiotic Gilbert and Sullivan major had stood and bawled that nonsense at them about relinquishing the right to happiness – as if he had some godgiven right to involve them in his posturing, bugle-tooting prescription for self-sacrifice. And she couldn't help wondering if Ned was thinking of him too as the haywain rumbled on down over the site of Fred Harris's merry-go-round.

After those first repetitive arguments while Dan Goodworth

was still training at Colchester, they'd never been able to discuss the war calmly. Meriel was adamant, Ned was *not* going. She said it again on the day he received his National Registration Certificate; and unexpectedly, his grandmother had backed her up.

"She's right, there's nothin' to be served by schoolboy heroics in a man of your responsibilities," Grandmother-Margaret bellowed at him across the drawing room. "Take a leaf from your wife's book, boy. It's not what you'd rather do, it's what you ought. And you *ought* to stay and work the land; that's your job so long as the U-boats are tryin' to starve the country out. You and Meriel have got all you can handle here on the farm, Ned, without taking on the Military's problems for 'em." And long before they'd got around to extending conscription to her grandson's age-group, Mrs Ashby had personally seen to it that the Local Tribunal were acquainted with his second class degree in zoology – and consequent indispensability to the Land Army.

But even then, even after Ned had been starred as officially exempt, they found ways of getting at him – the rats. They'd printed taunting yellow cards for display in cottage windows: '*A man has gone from this house to fight for King and Country*'. And they'd sent char-a-banc loads of military wounded from the Eastern General Hospital in Brighton, to parade through the valley applauding the gallant farm workers. 'Blue-boys' they called them – confoundedly cheerful creatures in shapeless royal blue convalescent uniforms, with bandages around their heads, or white slings, or empty flapping sleeves. She'd seen Ned's face as they called out to him, seen his fist gripping the handle of his shovel like a crutch. And afterwards she'd run straight down to the gateway he'd been chalking, to seize him by the forearms and shake the frightening expression out of his eyes.

"No, Ned – no, I won't have you see them as heroes – because they really aren't. They're pathetic. My idea of a man starts with someone who has two good arms and two good legs, and all the right bits in between. My kind of man wouldn't want a wife who pitied him – do you hear me, Ned? And he wouldn't come home maimed or crippled either – unable to eat without dribbling or to function properly as a husband and a father!"

Then later, in the Flat in the dark, she offered herself to him blatantly, as she had so often in the past – ruthless in her choice of weapon.

Oh yes, she knew how to win him round all right, her Ned. And when he smiled at her as he was smiling now, coming down to meet her through the hay, she knew why she had to. Everything in his face lifted when Ned smiled – the corners of his mouth, his nostrils – the lines beneath his eyes criss-crossing and fanning out above his cheek bones. Each dear line under-scoring her own purpose and joy in living.

"There you are then – not that you deserve it," she said roughly, thrusting the jug into his hands. "You haven't the ghost of a hope of getting this lot in tonight, at the rate you're going – and I wouldn't be at all surprised if it rained later on."

Ned extracted a long yellow bent from the corner of his mouth and leaned forward, stooping beneath her hat brim to kiss his wife on the very tip of her nose. "Darling, you're a bally marvel. And if there's any justice at all in this world, the District Sub-Committee will mention you in dispatches." With which he passed the jug straight on to the wretched, bone-idle Belgian! Meriel could scarcely believe her own eyes, for two straws she'd have snatched the beer back and thrown every drop of it in her husband's soppy face!

After the fall of Antwerp she'd felt as sorry as anyone for the dispossessed Belgians. One heard such pathetic stories of them camping in bathing vans at Ostend – drowning even in their attempts to reach England. She by no means disapproved when Ned's grandmother had written to the local Relief Committee to offer a Belgian family houseroom at The Bury, long before anyone else in the neighbourhood received their allocation of refugees. But that had been eighteen months ago. Her sympathy had survived less than a week of the Waedemons, who seemed to accept board and clothing and local social clubs as no more than their due – eating like horses, immediately relinquishing all responsibility for two ghastly little boys who peed in the rose garden, obdurately refusing to speak English, and having to be bullied into doing anything remotely useful around the place themselves. And here was Ned deferring to Pierre Waedemon like an honoured guest! As if she'd slogged all this way out with perfectly good beer, only to have half of it wasted on a rotten loafer!

Betty and the boys (her two and two horrid little Belgians) playing havoc with the haycocks were all the scapegoat she needed. "*Leave – that – hay – alone!*!" She could compete with Margaret on volume when she put her heart into it. "Betty – what do you mean by allowing the children to get in Mr Edwin's way? And why aren't they in at tea, pray? And where in the name of goodness is Master Robert's hat?!"

"It's all right, I told them they could play in the hay if they didn't scatter it too much, and Gran gave them the all-clear for a picnic tea. Cook sent it up an hour ago." Ned was clearly going to be obstructive, so she ignored him.

"*Robbie!* If that sunhat isn't on your head by the time I've counted to ten there'll be no supper for you, and no story either. *One...two...*"

"It's up there!" Robbie smiled engagingly and pointed to a sheep-trod that tacked steeply up the side of the valley. "I was Amu'sen, Mummy, an' Patrick was Scott an' the Belgies were huskies – an' I had to leave my hat on the South Pole, you see, to prove I'd got there first. Look, there it is!"

Meriel looked. High above them on the knap of the hill the sun illuminated a tiny parasol of white starched cotton, perched on an upright stick. "Oh for pity's sake! I blame you for this, Betty! How *could* you let him leave it there – what can you have been thinking of?" (The girl was witless, she'd always said so.)

"Don't worry, Mummy, me an' Patrick can fetch it directly. Shall we? Shall we, Pat – yes let's!" Robbie was already halfway to the foot of the path. At seven he was the living image of his father – Ned's hair, Ned's smile and Ned's blue eyes. But there was something of her in him too – something in the boy's breezy attitude to life that invariably took the wind out of Meriel's sails at times like this. He was such a little charmer, Robbie – so different to his brother. Somehow she always found it hard to believe that she had really given birth to Patrick. It was a constant surprise that she could ever have grown within her something so alien to her own nature. He was so quiet, that one, so hard to understand. Whereas Robbie – why she'd understood him perfectly from the moment he stretched up out of his crib and yanked her little silver locket from its chain around her neck!

She pretended to consider the sheep-path and the sunbaked South Pole, and her son's eager little face, but the child in her was right up there behind him already, treading on his heels.

"Well then you rascal, we'd better get a move on, hadn't we?" she said. "Before the blizzard sets in eh, and cuts off the Pole for the winter? Not you, Patrick," she added sharply, as the older boy started forward to follow them. "You'll have to stay and help the others hatchel those haycocks back into some sort of shape. And you had better hold the horse, Betty. Then Mr Waedemon will be free to help Mr Edwin pitch-up, and that way, with a bit of luck, you might just get in two more loads before dinner."

She was holding Robbie's hand as they started up the path. But he soon wriggled it free and scrambled on ahead, elbows thrusting, short little legs working furiously. And at the sight of his linen shorts caught in the crease of his bustling little bottom, even Meriel had to laugh. "Not so fast, Amundsen! You've already won the race, remember?" But on the path above her, Robbie paused only for the time it took to look back over his shoulder, and to smile that enchanting open smile of his, before hurrying on towards his goal.

On the lower slopes the sun was still hidden from them behind the Bury wood, and the colours of the wildflowers glowed like gems in the long grass – spikes of deep blue bugloss, mignonette, church-steeple and purple knapweed – sapphire, topaz and amethyst. But crossing the line that divided the shadows of the valley from the sunlit hillside was like entering another world – a lighter, brighter realm of butterflies and buzzing bumbledore bees and aromatic wild thyme. And from somewhere higher still, from the sky itself, the liquid crystal notes of a skylark cascaded down to them.

Meriel, searching for the singer, finally located him as a tiny hovering speck far away up in the blue. What was it they were meant to sing? What did Ned say? 'Christ is risen!' – that was it – 'Christ is risen! Christ is risen!' As her glance descended from the ecstatic little skylark to the bobbing golden head of her son, she thought then how good it was to be alive. A minute later the advance party of her expedition reached the Pole and uprooted it with a hoot of triumph. "Got it, Mum! Can we go back now?"

"Robbie, for goodness sake hold on – just stop for a minute and let me get my breath! Look at the view – just look at all the things you can see from up here. Look, there's the house down in the trees, do you see – and that's your nursery window."

"I can't see – which one?" The little boy screwed up his whole face to look into the sun.

"That one there, with the bolsters over the sill. Look darling, surely you can see it – the idiot maid hasn't taken them in yet." But it wasn't a game that appealed. Robbie threw himself back onto the turf with a heartfelt sigh of impatience, while his mother shaded her hat brim and continued to stare down the valley.

She could hear the seagulls quite distinctly above the cliffs of the Gap, and the voices of the haymakers. She could see Vine and his ewe flock on the bare slope beyond the Bury-house. She could even detect the old field patterns in the Rough above the Brooks laines, where they'd ploughed up the chalk during the wheat shortages of the Napoleonic wars. They'd be ploughing them again soon, for more corn, if the new Agricultural Committee had its way. 'But with dairy products at the price they are, we'd all be a lot better employed putting in new ryegrass leys and doubling the size of the milking herd,' Meriel thought. Why, Land Army girls were two a penny these days – and she rather fancied the idea of a couple of subordinates in the cowshed. She'd have another go at Ned on the subject this evening, she decided. In bed perhaps!

Meriel's gaze returned to the endearingly solid figure of her husband in the meadow below – still showing off, still tossing up four shocks to the wretched Belgian's one – with his big Clumber spaniel, Puck, padding along devotedly at his heels. It was strange to think that once she'd actually have turned away from a sight like this, in the days when Ned's absorption with the farm and the valley had so rankled with her. It had been something in those early years of marriage that he shared with his men, with Goodworth, but not with her; something of him that she couldn't control or possess. Then there'd been that last

Fair and the recruiting officer, and Danny Goodworth marching off to war. And on the day Meriel realized that her husband was no longer completely content to remain where he was, she had seen Sellington in a totally different light – the farm, the valley, even the Bury labourers – no longer as rivals, but as valuable allies in her struggle to keep Ned out of the army.

A faint breeze rustled the ripening grassheads at her feet, some of them already seeding to cheat the returning flocks. Everything up here was scaled to the wind and those constantly nibbling sheep – an aerial pasture of miniature grasses and creeping herbs – bents and clovers, trefoil, burnet and chicory, flowering and seeding flat to the soil. And miniature blossoms for the insects – thyme, rock-roses and great yellow splashes of horseshoe vetch, the food source of the gay little blue butterflies that would outnumber all the others in a few weeks' time. Just now the butterflies were brown, almost all of them.

'How odd,' Meriel thought as she watched them. 'Now I've never seen butterflies do *that* before!' They were rising in unison from the blossoms and in time to a kind of regular pulse that she felt in her own body – settling raggedly, only to rise together again as if to an agreed signal. Meriel turned to draw Robbie's attention to the phenomenon, but he spoke first. He was lying flat on his back with his short little arms flung wide, like a butterfly himself spreading his wings to catch the sun.

"Bom!" he chanted loudly, "Bom! Bom! – there's a giant in this hill, Mummy, I can hear his heart beating!" The things the child came out with! "Come on, Mummy, you listen. Bom! Bom! Bom! . . . "

"Well all right, just this one game then. But after that we must go down and see if we can't do something to help Daddy. I don't think Mr Waedemon is ever going to be much use, do you?" And she pushed back Helen's hat to make a proper pantomime of putting her ear to the turf . . . to remain there, perfectly still, while Robbie laughed with delight at the change in the expression on her face. Good God – oh good God, he was right! The entire chalk hill was quivering and thudding with a life of its own! She wouldn't panic or act like a fool. She'd stand up – that's what she'd do – and stop shaking. There was bound to be a rational explanation of some kind – bound to be.

But it was instinct rather than intellect that prompted Meriel to turn towards the Gap. As she did so, a fresh gust of wind carried the sound to her ears – like someone dropping a whole library of Mrs Beetons, one by one. Down in the Sellington Meadow the haymakers heard it too, and Puck began to bark. The men stopped and conferred together as she watched, leaning on their prong forks – and then turned slowly, as she had, to face the sea.

It was the sound of guns – of a great artillery bombardment across sixty miles of water.

Chapter Twenty-One

By the time Meriel and Robbie returned with the missing sunhat, Ned had already left the meadow. He went directly to the stables to find a head-collar for Archie and canter him down to the Gap, with poor old Puck panting along behind. He'd done it a thousand times in his youth, in summer holidays and university vacations – riding bareback like this with a towel across the horse's neck. But those days had gone now – long gone.

Etheridge was out on the mown slope beside his cottage; and as Ned looked up at him he nodded gravely. "Sounds like they've started than, Mr Ashby sir," he said. "Chaps down there say et's the Somme this time – Al-bert or summat." He indicated a group of soldiers, grouped a little self-consciously around the old bathing machine. "Niver thought as we'd be able ter 'ear them, though, not from Sel'ton! Mus' be a middlin' bannickin' our boys are givin' they ol' Germins, wouldn' ye say, sir?"

"Yes – I'd say so." Ned managed a crooked smile, before turning Archie through the gate, down past the soldiers with their inadequate barbed wire defences, and onto the beach.

"Evenin' sir – started then?" The Royal Defence Corps had recently taken over patrol of the Gap from Father and his amateur Home Defence people. They were decent enough fellows, and the sergeant would clearly have welcomed a discussion on the new Allied offensive. But Ned didn't want to hear his views – his or anyone else's. Not now.

"Started, Sergeant, but not finished," he said briefly, and left the man staring after him as he made his way down over the shingle to the sea. It was low tide. There were sandhoppers in their thousands at the water's edge, and dotterels feasting on them – pretty little grey and russet birds running hither and thither on the wet sand, oblivious of horse or dog, or of the persistent rumbling vibrations from across the Channel. Archie dipped his head to a skein of oarweed that had washed in from deeper water, pulling out a long brown ribbon of the stuff and munching it with obvious satisfaction. Puck explored the shallows, never straying far from his master and keeping a wary eye on the eccentric horizon. Ned simply sat and listened, while the water surged back and forth beneath him and the sun sank slowly towards the sea. With the breeze in his face he felt and heard the percussion of the guns simultaneously. They came to him muffled, as if through some physical barrier. But he knew that there was none – nothing but distance now between him and the fighting.

He had been waiting for days now for news of the new offensive. Everyone had – except Meriel. Helen had heard through the Supply Depôt in Lewes where she worked that the wards of the 2nd Eastern General in Brighton were already cleared of all convalescents, to prepare for a great influx of wounded. Ever since Kitchener's drowning, Father had spent hours in the library, staring fixedly at his map of the Western Front. And the universal silence of the newspapers on the subject of the coming 'push' had only added to the tension through those hot, haymaking days of June.

Now it had come, not only to the Somme but to Sellington Valley, and to all the downland valleys and villages to whom the actual noise of battle was now audible. And no one who heard it, as Ned heard it on the beach that evening, could ignore its implication. Not even Meriel!

There were men dying out there at this very moment. Men being torn apart, dismembered, shattered – bones thrust through living flesh by British shells, many of them prepared in sunny

Sussex holiday resorts like Brighton and Eastbourne, or by rosy-faced Sussex girls, shift-working at the great munitions factory at Willesden. After the preliminary bombardment would come the push itself – the 'big push' – with thousands, tens of thousands more British lives tossed down like gambling chips in a game of war that had long since outgrown its players.

How many thousands this time for a few miles of devastated campagne? Fifteen thousand like Mons and Le Cateau? Fifty thousand like Gallipoli? Sixty thousand like the first battle of Ypres, where the exhausted remnant of poor old Kitchener's expeditionary force had given their lives for Calais. It was slaughter on a brand new scale – by armies who calculated victories and defeats mathematically, in numbers of men. In terms of casualties the battle of Neuve Chapelle alone had been greater than Waterloo. Allied losses in five weeks of the Dardanelles campaign exceeded those of the entire South African War. And God only knew how many French and Germans had already died at Verdun – three hundred thousand, half a million, more?

Yet still it went on. Both sides had rejected outright the American President's offers to mediate for peace – and now there was the Somme and another fresh New Army. Thousands more expendable young conscripts to be waved off to the Front. Thousands more gleaming new shells to be shipped out from Newhaven. Thousands of waiting beds – thousands of wooden crosses – thousands of hearth-rug strategists like Father, ready to plot another precarious little salient in the Western Front that in all likelihood would prove impossible to hold.

It was sickening for Ned to have to admit that man's natural violence should have such an immense destructive force, when compounded. But in a way he supposed he'd always known it to be true. Meriel, on the other hand, had declined to grasp it, any of it, right from the beginning. The numbers, she said, were greatly exaggerated – they had to be. She'd long ago written them all off as fools – soldiers, generals, politicans, Germans, she made no distinction – fools the lot of them! She could still pretend, too. She could still refuse to speak of the death of her brother Harry with the Anzacs at Suvla Bay. After the collapse of her father's prospecting company in Colombia, she could still describe him – even think of him – as 'iron mining in Pennsylvania' – deliberately turning her back on his profiteering activities as a purchasing agent for American minerals and nitrates, to be used in British munitions. The war, war-consciences, the whole thing was indigestible to Meriel. So she spat it out.

But for Ned it wasn't so simple. He could no longer believe in the old shibboleths of Justice and Freedom as applied to this war. Nor could he share the General Staff's scorn for a negotiated peace. In fact he'd begun to suspect that it was British Imperial pride as much as German militarism that was keeping the thing going now – in a reckless 'fight to the finish' that would finish far more than one fanatical Hohenzollern. But he also saw – as Meriel couldn't, or wouldn't – that life had already changed irretrievably. Dan had gone to fight, and the boys Hurst and Tinsley and Jemmy Vine. They were all out there somewhere behind the guns. And Armiger in Belgium – in his grave now for fourteen months.

> And Bill has left his woolly flock,
> And Tom has left the farm;
> And Jack deserts the farmyard stock,
> And Jake throws off the Sussex smock,
> He too now leaves his master's flock
> And answers the alarm.

Arthur Beckett's verse in the *County Herald* had spoken of Sussex's tribute of men to the holocaust. But there was more to it than that.

"The ol' ways are goin', Mus Ned, wather you an' me likes it or no." That's what Dan had said to him at the cricket match after the Fair, while they sat together waiting to bat. It was true enough, for in the months since, the war seemed to have penetrated every aspect of life – as poisonous and corrosive as the yellow gas that killed poor Armiger at Hill 60. You could scarcely take a step beyond the farm now without passing one of the encampments of dismal huts and canvas stablings that marred the smooth contours of the downs; or a Sea Scout airship droning slowly overhead; or a brake full of noisy convalescents, flourishing their dressings like banners.

They were everywhere these days, the convalescents, spilling out of the military hospitals into Nissen wards and drill halls, seaside boarding houses and all sorts of unlikely private residences. Simmie had written to say that they'd even invaded the great house in Grosvenor Crescent where Meriel had once captured a mouse, and rather more. It had become an annexe of the King Edward VII Hospital, she said, with rows of iron bedsteads scarring the surface of the dance floor, itself a casualty of the war.

Ned couldn't pretend like Meriel – not any more. He couldn't ignore what was happening in France, or here at home in Sussex. He couldn't go on devoting his energies to producing food that was to be rationed and denied to so many who needed it. Nor could he turn a blind eye to those who were lining their pockets from its sale, or from the wartime boom in resort hotels, or from the proceeds of iron foundries and private munitions works – profiteers like Meriel's unscrupulous father, who cared nothing for abstract ideals.

"I wouldn' go fer choice," Dan had confided to him quietly that day of the Fair, "not fer all the beer in the brew'ry. But there ent no mortal sense in bellickin' about it, neither. Fer ef blokes like me didn' go a-soldierin' ther'd be no armies ter fight. An' ef blokes like you didn' stay, Mus Ned, why ther'd be nuthin' left ter fight for, surelye? T'wouldn' make neither fat nor wool, thad wouldn'."

But too many had died since – too many ordinary fellows who hadn't wanted to go. And too many had stayed to profit by their destruction. The evidence of another phase in that destruction was still pounding in Ned's ears as he rode back up the valley to the rickyard – thudding up through all the comfortable summer evening noises of rooks and ring doves and clenking sheep bells – the callous, senseless destruction of human beings with high explosive – the only sound he really heard.

There was no point in telling Meriel of his decision, not until he was sure he could pull it off; and Gran was bound to give him an argument. So he took it to his father instead.

"Mind if I put on a pipe, Father?" Ned held the library door open for Puck to come through and closed it behind him, fumbling for his tobacco tin and trusty briar as he followed

Father across to the fireplace. "I've been dying to light up all evening."

"Dear boy . . . " Walter waved a dismissive hand. Yet there was something unusually alert in the faded blue eyes, as he watched his son packing down the tobacco and stooping to light a spill from the fire – almost as if he knew.

Ned took a few quick sucks at the briar stem to make sure it was drawing, stirring the logs with the toe of his boot and watching the sparks fly upward. In here with Father and Puck – with the smell of books and woodsmoke in his nostrils, and a good meal in his belly – the war seemed scarcely more real to him than the maps on the wall.

"It's no use, Father, I can't dodge the column any longer." A sentence, once uttered, that must surely change the course of his life. "I've known all along that I'd have to go some day, if the war lasted. I'd never have stuck it out for this long if it hadn't been for Meri."

"Then I expect you'll be wanting a note from me, Ned, to send with your letter to the Tribunal? Some kind of assurance that I'm fit and willing to run the farm in your absence?"

He hadn't expected it. His father had always been such a neutral figure in his life, so totally overshadowed by Gran. He'd expected him to recoil from the emergency – to take refuge in silence or evasion as he normally did. Now it seemed that he'd misjudged him all along.

"I don't suppose it'll be that simple, Father. I should think old Wilmott would want to come to see you personally in his capacity as Inspector, to be sure in his own mind, you know. And I'm afraid we'd have to try and keep it under our hats until it's all settled. There'll be the devil of a shindy as it is when Gran and Meri find out. Do you think you can bear that?"

"My dear fellow – do you imagine that I've survived all these years of your grandmother without being able to weather a squall or two of that kind?" Walter hesitated awkwardly on his way over to his writing desk, to pat his son on the shoulder.

'Sending me off to school,' Ned thought, 'with a bright new sovereign in my pocket.'

"You're not to suppose that I want to lose you, my boy, any more than they do," his father muttered, echoing the words of that frightful recruiting song. "You're a trump, Ned, always were. Best thing I ever did fathering you – or ever will do, I daresay." He moved off again without meeting his son's eyes, standing with his back to the room and busying himself with the papers on his desk. "I expect you think I'm a pretty poor fish, Ned. But I have my good faults as they say, as well as my bad ones. And I do understand – because I'd have gone to the Front myself, you see, if I could."

If Father was unexpectedly supportive, the Local Tribunal and the Royal Sussex Regiment itself had been almost indecent in their haste to smooth Ned's path for him to a commission – and to France. Unprecedented casualties on the Somme had streamlined procedures wonderfully for shipping new men out to the Front, it would seem.

Meriel's reaction, however, had come as no surprise at all. "Of course I always knew you were soft in the head," she declared. "But I was foolish enough to think that you had more consideration for your family than to go and get it blown off in France for the benefit of the bloody War Office!" After the first hasty sentence she began to puff and blow like a little opera singer working up to a top note, hands clasped before her, bosom heaving. "You promised, Ned! You *promised* me you wouldn't go . . . !"

"Now, Meri, you know that's not true . . . "

"You *did,* you promised – and if you didn't, you certainly led me to believe you had. Of all the vile, sneaky, underhand . . . !"

"Steady on old thing! You know you're going to regret this later."

"*Regret it!* Are you trying to be funny? I'd damn well regret it all right if I didn't tell you exactly what I thought of you here and now, Ned Ashby! I suppose you think it's honourable and brave, to abandon us when we need you most – to go swaggering off to play at silly war games all got up like Vesta Tilley? Is that your idea of *fun?* Well *is it?*"

"Meri – darling, I know you're upset and I'm sorry. But why do you have to say things like this, when we both know you don't mean them?"

"Why – *why*? Because you *will not learn to do as you're told*, Ned Ashby, that's why!"

When he smiled at her then for her appalling presumption, and tried to fold her in his arms in loving forgiveness, Meriel tore herself away from him to stamp out of the room and slam the door behind her. And after that, right up to the moment he left for Shoreham Camp, she treated him with an aloof indifference that hurt him more deeply than anything she could have said in anger.

The camp was more like a first term at school than anything else. Ned learned how to salute correctly, how to dismantle a Short Magazine Lee-Enfield rifle, and how not to lace his boots crosswise. He became reasonably proficient in Field Service Regulations. He could use a Mills Bomb in theory, and a light machine gun, and disembowel a straw-filled German with a bayonet. But somehow he lost sight of the real war in the process, and of the bracing sense of resolution that he'd felt that day on the beach at Sellington Gap. He felt childishly homesick amidst the aggressive cheerfulness of the assault course and the officers' mess – lovesick for Meri on his uncomfortable folding camp bed. And on the parade ground, in his pristine Temporary Second Lieutenant's uniform, he felt a thorough-going fraud – drilling squads of convalescent trench-veterans who understood the reality of war only too well. There'd been a hag-ridden expression deep in the eyes of those men that gave the lie to the recruiting officer's description of wounded eager to return to the Front. But they wouldn't speak of it. They knew as Ned did that the average life expectancy of a junior officer at the Front was no more than eight weeks. And like the Bury farm workers of his youth, they tolerated his ignorance of their business without rancour.

He arrived home on leave one cold Friday in early December, with orders to report back to camp, to entrain for Folkestone via Victoria first thing Monday morning. In practical terms it meant leaving The Bury after tea on Sunday.

On the Sunday morning they all wrapped-up-warm and trooped up to the church on foot – where Ned was forced to endure Mrs Pilbeam's face staring woodenly up at him, as he read the lesson from the pulpit in his sham Second Lieutenant's uniform. Her son Tony had died on the very first day of the push that followed the Somme bombardment. So had Bat's grandson, Jemmy Vine. And so, in a single day, had fifty thousand other young Britons, in the tragic misapprehension that their guns had smashed the German defences.

After church they walked the farm as they did each Sunday, Ned and Shad Caldwell, with Walter and Meriel in tow – and the unsuspecting Puck running around them in circles, so glad to have his master home again. They inspected the cledgy furrows of the ploughlands and the seedcorn in the barn to confirm the rotation for next year. They pondered the possibility of taking on some Land Army girls from haymaking through to harvest – and Ned walked on up alone to say so-long to Bat and the Southdowns, his spirit shrinking within him with every step he took.

By luncheon it had compressed itself into a tight hard fist high under his ribs, and it was only the presence of the boys at table that enabled him to keep up the performance they all seemed to expect. There were no awkward silences. Father and Helly, normally so quiet, fell over each other to fill the gaps with any topic they could think of, even engaging the Waedemons in conversation. Meriel nagged the children ceaselessly on their table manners. And dear old Gran in her long black cardigan at the end of the table, went on cutting them all down to size out of sheer force of habit – while she watched her grandson with a look of ferocious tenderness in her eyes.

Discounting their detour through the apple orchard on honeymoon in Kent, in all the years of their marriage Ned had never once made love to his wife in the afternoon. Whatever they expected downstairs, it would have embarrassed him to suggest it to her then, had he been given the opportunity to do so. As it was, Meriel herself took the initiative, drawing their bedroom curtains with a businesslike clash of brass rings that robbed him of all say in the matter.

Someone had the foresight to order a fire for them, despite the coal shortages. But the sheets were icy cold – and so was Meriel when he reached over, tentatively, to touch her. It wasn't going to be any good. It wasn't going to be any better than the last two nights – he could tell immediately. It was as if the war that had claimed him was already reaching forward into his relationships to destroy unsoldierlike emotions. But there was something it couldn't touch, and he wanted her to know it.

"If I should die out there, Meri . . . "

"For God's sake, Ned, don't say such things!" She was instantly galvanized. "And look, just get used to the idea of *living,* all right? Because you can take it from me, that's what you're going to be doing!"

"But darling we have to talk about it," he persisted. "I'm not immortal, you know."

"Ned, I'm not listening!" She clamped her hands over her ears, and screwed up her eyes as well so that she wouldn't have to see the earnestness in his face.

"Meri, you must," he insisted, tugging at her hands and holding them back hard against the bolster. The elevated position of her arms lifted her small breasts clear of the counterpane – creamy, soft shadowed, rose-tipped as a girl's.

"Darling, you've got to face the possibility, at least . . . "

"Why? Why must I? It *isn't* a possibility – and I won't think of it as one. I *won't,* do you hear me? I just *won't!*"

She wrenched herself free to wriggle out and over, pressing herself against him, smothering words, using her body as she had so often before to vanquish his resistance. Then as he began to stir beneath her she slid aside again – all but her hands – for they were with him still, flat on his belly, warm now and smooth – sliding upwards to his chest and his shoulders and the fluttering pulse in his neck – down the length of his arms to his wrists and his broad, veined hands. Beyond to the shifting hollows of his thighs – and on downwards, lifting, kneading, caressing him with her fingers until he arched and stretched like a cat in ecstasy, and turned over to her, groping for the centre of her being.

Her hands were there before him, ready to guide and enfold – wet to wetness, warmth to warmth, softness for rigour. And for Ned that first sweet moment of sheathing was like a summation of all the moments they had shared. He'd wanted so badly to make her understand that nothing in the future – not even his death in this senseless war, could rob her of those. Their memories were a part of them both, of what they had become – a reason to feel privileged still in the face of anything the future might bring. But now the words were superfluous, for his body had found a way of telling her. And then another way, deeper and more emphatic – and another, and another – until he was perfectly sure that she understood.

If only love's certainties could survive its climaxes. As it was, all the miseries of parting returned with the first sight of his soldier's uniform laid out ready for him in the dressing room. Cook had been squandering her privileged flour on scones for tea and one of her famous Sussex 'plum biscuit' teacakes. But he couldn't eat. And when he slipped back to the kitchen to say goodbye to her, and to be hugged to that broad, print-covered bosom, Ned felt the last dim flicker of his childhood snuffing out inside him.

They all stood on the chilly twilit front step to watch him down the drive – Father's restraining hand on Puck's collar; and he turned at the bend to wave, and to catch a final glimpse of The Bury before it disappeared behind the trees. As Meriel turned Archie up the valley road towards the village, the side-lamps of the cart glinted briefly on the knapped flints of the stable wall. All the browns and beiges and listless greens of the winter landscape had deepened now to indigo; and although the night was fine, the moon was visible only as a thin rind on the dark circular shadow of the earth.

"Look, Daddy, it's following us!" Robbie whispered, peering up out of the woolly cocoon Betty had wrapped him in. "The moon's coming to say goodbye, too!"

Gran had strongly disapproved of taking the children out in the cold and the dark. Betty too – although she knew better than to say so. But Meriel was adamant.

"They're coming to see their father off, of course they are." And there was a brittle quality to her voice that made it clear even to Gran that further argument was inadvisable. The boys were thrilled, though – particularly Robbie, who went on whispering excitedly all the way up the valley and through the spooky shadows of Sellington Village, snuggling close into the crook of his father's arm.

"Will there be Christmas in France, Dad – an' presents for all the soldiers? An' mummers an' carol singers an' a big turkey? I've seen the one we're going to have – he's as big as *this!* An' Cook's going to make a great big cake, too – with icing an' holly on the top, and an apple-stuckling an' mince pies and lots an' lots of sandwiches. And we're going up to London next week on the train with Betty! Simmie's going to take us to the Toy Fair at Gammages, isn't she, Mummy?"

"Well, she might, if it doesn't snow too much to get to the station. They've got it up north already, I hear, and I wouldn't be a bit surprised, chickies, if we woke up one morning soon to find everything white outside the windows!"

"Daddy won't, will he – they don't have windows in trenches."

Poor Meri, trying so hard to be cheerful. Ned leant across to squeeze the driving apron that covered her knees. He'd handed her the reins to give her something else to think about. But of course Archie knew the road well enough on his own, even in the dark, and driving had always been second nature to Meriel. It was certainly cold enough for snow. The potholes and puddles of the village street were already paned with thin ice, tinkling and crackling beneath their wheels. But the wind that caught them as they emerged onto the open downland was a sou'wester off the sea, and the sky was still clear.

"Pat, look – we're up in the stars! Let's pretend we're flying – shall we? Let's be airships chucking out bombs onto the U-boats!" Robbie was gleefully impervious to his parents' misery and to the anxious, haunted look that had crept into his brother's pinched little face.

He was right about the sky, though. One was more aware of it than anything else up here on the downs on a winter night. The wind soughed through the bents and the stunted upland gorse, bearing with it the rasping bark of a dog fox from some-where below in the combe. The yellow gleams of their sidelamps flickered along the verges of the track and on the shaggy flanks of the horse. But as they jogged on down to the frontiers of Ashby land, it was the great starry hemisphere of the sky that dominated.

Lighting restrictions were still in force in Seaford, despite the recent reduction in Zeppelin activity; and Ned automatically jumped out as they approached South Camp to turn down their lamps. "Like smugglers!" Robbie whispered, as they joined the mysterious shadowy throng along the whitewashed station kerb. "'Baccy for the clerk' Pat – 'member?"

There was the choice of an illuminated and very public ticket office, fuggy with cigarette smoke, or the freezing anonymity of the station platform. They chose the platform, standing close together with their backs to the metals to shelter the boys from the wind. Someone down at the far end was whistling 'The Girl I Left Behind Me', and at the sound of it Meriel began talking rapidly, just as Father and Helly had done at luncheon, racing from one trivial subject to the next – from the leaking cowshed roof to War Loan dividends to a workhouse Christmas party at East Dean – her hands thrust into coat pockets, twisting and writhing like prisoners, her breath gusting white on the frosty air. He tried to help her, tried to join her in this last, desperate game of deception. But his mouth was dry, and there was a gripe, a kind of cold cramp inside him that made it impossible for him to speak naturally.

A signal clattered somewhere. Then they could hear the train putter-puttering towards them across the shingle from Newhaven – and the constriction moved up into Ned's throat to choke him. They embraced, he and Meriel, with the two little boys clinging to their legs and nothing in the world left to say. The blinds were drawn down in all the carriages, but as the train doors opened to disgorge its passengers, he saw her face in the light – just for an instant – before she pushed his children at him and stumbled blindly away into the darkness.

Chapter Twenty-Two

Ned's first letter from France arrived by afternoon post on Christmas Eve, with a whole batch of Christmas cards. To Meriel's rage and disgust it carried a large red label on the envelope, EXAMINED BY BASE CENSOR, and at the top of every page an intrusive purple stamp, '*Contrôle par l'Autorité Militaire*'.

Confounded busybodies!

Base Camp, Étaples.
Tuesday, December 19th 1916

My darling girl,

Here am I lying on my stretcher bed in this chaotic place, trying to make love to you by candlelight with the stub of a copying pencil! As a matter of fact I'm dog-tired – half asleep already, in spite of the guns and the motor lorry convoys. I can still hardly conceive myself to be a soldier, and quite feel that I'll wake up at any moment to find myself back home in bed with you. And darling, *how* I wish that I could! Everything's so disorganized and unreal, and so totally different out here that England already seems light years away – it barely seems possible that only two days have passed since we were all together on Seaford station.

Simmie came to see me off at Victoria as arranged. But there was such a mob of officers around us that we really weren't able to say goodbye properly. I was at least able to give her a wire to send you, though. Did you get it all right?

Our crossing to Boulogne was a fairly good one I think – although I felt bilious anyway. But no one seemed to be expecting us at this end. So we spent the entire afternoon being passed from one weary-looking official to another, filling in forms and being told to go away and come back in an hour or so. Eventually we put up at the Hôtel du Louvre, with instructions to proceed to The Base at Étaples the following morning, to await further orders there. Proceeding, as we later discovered, consisted of jerking by stages down the coast railway, often sitting for ages quite stationary in a freezing compartment and literally taking hours to travel a distance of no more than twenty miles. I tell you if it hadn't been for the other officers in our first class compartment (all of them rattling good sorts) I think I should have gone mad with boredom. As it was we played 'nap' and took it in turns to read the *Strand Magazine* – and of course I talked a great deal about you – and somehow the time passed.

Things were no more organized here at The Base when we finally reached it. In fact nobody seemed to have heard of any of us. And as I write this I'm still 'awaiting further orders'. I haven't yet been able to get any news at all of my battalion and their whereabouts. So when, or even whether, I'll be permitted to join them remains a mystery. Who knows, perhaps I'll still be here for Christmas? In the meantime I've been allocated a tiny corrugated iron shanty (like an allotment hut) all to myself. Just the kind of place you'd like to sleep in I think – with any amount of fresh air available! There's a bitter north wind blowing now, and it's all I can do to keep my candle alight. I wonder if you've got your snow over there yet? Everything's frozen solid here, including all the outside taps and most of the drinking water.

The Base is an absolutely vast place outside Étaples town and slap on the Boulogne-Paris railway – about ten times as big as South Camp at Seaford I'd say, although quite as dreary to look at. The Tommies call it 'Eat-apples' in honour of the various hospitals here, which have wards in dozens and dozens of huts and tents for wounded of all nationalities – including Germans. It seems so pointless, doesn't it, that we should do our outmost to kill the poor blighters in any way we can at the Front, and then try equally hard to nurse them back to life again behind it! I'll never understand war.

Have you forgiven me yet, my darling, for joining up? If I don't fully understand my own motives for doing so, I know I shouldn't expect you to – but please try! You know that whatever comes, I love you more than anything. And whatever I have to get used to out here, I don't ever want to adjust to not having you physically near me. Nothing and no one else will do. My weaknesses need your strengths, Meri, just as my body needs yours (and just now that's a very great deal!) It helps to write – makes me feel that I'm talking to you – and in a way that brings you closer.

I will write as often as ever I can. But I'm afraid you must be content with few details of what I'm actually doing – because that's all the censors out here will allow. I'll write a postcard each to Patrick and Robbie as soon as possible. (I find that I'm allowed to send picture postcards of Étaples town, since no one supposes the Boches to be ignorant of our Base positions.) I will also try to get some lines off to

Gran and to Simmie. It was good of her to come and see me off, wasn't it? Although naturally upsetting for both of us.

I live in hopes of hearing from you tomorrow, or the next day at latest. It would be such bad luck to have to go on without any mail. And the way things are (or aren't) organized over here, goodness knows when or where it would catch me up!

Goodnight now, sweetheart. Please give those two little imps hugs and kisses from me (yours are all being stored up), and tell them not to forget their Dad. I know I don't have to tell you to be brave – it's your second name, isn't it? It's a very wretched business, but perhaps it won't be for much longer after all. They're saying over here that the war will be over by spring – quite the latest rumour! Meantime, take care of yourself and those two little ducks – and don't overdo things on the farm. The land will survive, it always does. Ask old Bat.

I do so wish I could have you in my arms – just for a minute, or an hour or a decade or two. Then I'd give you the rest of my news all right!

You know you're as much loved as you possibly can be, by your own absolutely devoted and adoring, and lonely old

x x x x x Nednog x x x x x

P.S. Do you realize that it'll be exactly ten years ago next Monday that I set out on another momentous journey – back across the Plain of Tolima and thence home to England? But what a difference. We were together then weren't we, for the first time in a way. Now who knows when we shall be again?

The Bury, Sellington.
January 16th 1917

My dear old frozen old exile,

The only mail from you this morning, sad to say, was a card to Patrick (and you know I had to go all yesterday without as well!). Never mind, I'm keeping my fingers crossed for this afternoon's post. I only hope to goodness your letter hasn't gone astray like that one last month. I have to tell you that they've let some *moron* loose out there with a little rubber stamp – insists on plonking his blessed 'Army' and 'Field Post Office' nonsenses bang on top of my name and address! As if it isn't quite bad enough having them nosey-parkering through the contents! I really don't know how you can bear to do it for your men. Not that your letters have ever been censored yet (other than by Second Lieutenant E. C. Ashby, that is!). Now I know you're not allowed to tell me where you are or anything like that, Ned, but I do think you could give me a *few* more details. It's quite impossible to get any real picture from the little scraps you've been dishing out since you left Étaples. Your letters really aren't a *patch* on mine to you from South America. (Oh yes, I know they're written under difficult circumstances and all that – but then so were mine!!) By this post I'm sending you two writing blocks and some envelopes, anyway. So make *good use* of them!

Patrick was over the moon with his card. Honestly, Noggin, you should have *seen* the look on his face when I handed it to him. Words utterly failed him! And after he'd finished reading it he stuck it up his school jersey (having no pocket in his knickers), where as far as I know it still resides.

The last thing I heard from you was that your outfit will be moving again soon, which I suppose could account for the delay with the mails. You make no mention of it in your card to Pat (do *try* to be more helpful, dearie), but of course we're all hoping it won't be anywhere too lively. And remember, Ned, whatever happens, *take no risks*. I should hope I don't have to remind you that your *first* duty is to yourself and your family. It seems to me that there are a great deal too many people sounding off about self-sacrifice and the common good nowadays – and I wouldn't want anyone to begin to take them too seriously.

It's cold as charity over here, with snow frozen into ruts and icicles hanging from all the gutters – so no more ploughing, I fear. The cowshed is just about the warmest place on the farm, as you can imagine. So I spend as much time down there as I can spare. We can't ever have much of a fire in the house now – coal really is too dear for words, and we need all we can get for the threshing tackle. And although you talk so fondly of 'home comforts', I can assure you that they're not much in evidence these days!

In one of your letters last week you said that you wished I was more affectionate in mine to you, and I've been wondering ever since how best to reply. The truth is, Noggin, that if I once started being sentimental I'm afraid that I might lose control – and I just can't risk that. I'm a *pig* I know. But never mind, I'll make up for it all one fine day soon – see if I don't! And for what it's worth I can tell you that every time I see the postboy with a telegram my heart simply stops. I'd go crazy if anything happened to you.

Talking of going crazy – you should see your father now! The War Effort really has given him a new lease of life, everyone says so. He dashes about all over the farm, puffing and panting and red in the face, but happy as Larry all the same. He was down at the barn all yesterday morning supervising the men on the steam thresher. Then in he came to luncheon – right into the dining room, Ned, smothered from head to foot in dust and briffen-chaff! Talk about a row – for a moment I quite though GM was going to put him across her knee!

Well that's about it for today. I'm enclosing with this a letter I got from Simmie yesterday morning (wonders will never cease!). You see even our mails over here must be pretty hopeless, since I wrote her a good long letter last Friday which she clearly hasn't received. I can't spare the time to traipse up to town, of course, and she refuses to come down here – although naturally she'd be much safer in Sussex with all those beastly Zeppelins and things buzzing about. But you know Simmie, she *won't* be told!

Keep your tail up, old bean and take *good* care of yourself – and write, write soonissimo!

I do love you,
Meri

The post-corporal had sent her letter up to Ned's billet half an hour earlier, and he'd already read it three times. He knew it was from Meriel the moment he caught sight of the Ridouts Economy Label ('*Not to be used on foreign correspondence*'), which she habitually pasted over his own field service envelopes with her usual scorn for regulations. And as always, he'd deliberately postponed the moment of opening for as long as he could possibly bear it. That was the best moment of a letter from Meriel, the act of breaching the illegal Ridouts label – like the act of love itself, when you felt her need reach out for yours from the written page. Because afterwards, always, there was anti-climax. She admitted it herself, she was afraid to be sentimental, and the endearments he so badly needed to hear had been precious few:

"My dear . . . dearie . . . old bean . . . "

Oh Meri!

"I'd go crazy if anything happened to you . . . I do love you . . . "

That had been something to hold on to, at least. And of course he knew that she felt like that inside. Love letters simply weren't Meriel's style. If you wanted emotional support from her – well then, you just had to fall back on those old memories, the things that the war couldn't spoil. You had to snuff the candle and open the shutters as Ned had just done. To stand at the window in the darkness and force yourself to face the war that was waiting for you out there beyond Arras, while you groped for the images that would comfort and carry you through it.

It was a tall window, tall and narrow, with heavy lace curtains and a dim view of the crossroads below. He could see the shadow of a cat crossing between the houses, black against the frosty treads of a stairway . . .

. . . Meriel bounding down the hacienda steps, tearing down the hill – crying out her love for him . . .

A black-robed *curé* on a bicycle, turning the corner from the church, bumping home across the frozen cobbles . . .

. . . Meriel in a cycling outfit with her boater all skew-whiff

– and "*Listen you great pook-noodle – I already love you more than any woman has ever loved a man, do you know that? And I intend to love you more still . . .*"

. . . Meriel in the orchard, on her back amongst the cuckoo-flowers – and a pulse, a heavy pulse – and a bursting brightness . . .

He was listening to the ponderous muffled thump of the artillery on the Front somewhere to the east of Arras. He was watching a parachute flare curving up high above the grey slate roofs of Wanquetin, to burst and bathe the landscape in a ghostly greenish light. Then another, crimson this time like a blossom – and beneath it the drifting red smoke of exploding shells. The windows of the *estaminet* below him were blacked out. They couldn't see the flares, the men at the bar down there. And if they could hear the shells, it surely wasn't for want of singing loudly enough.

"*Auprès de ma blonde, qu'il fait bon, fait bon, fait bon,
Auprès de ma blonde, qu'il fait bon dormir . . .*"

. . . Meriel asleep beside him in the lotus bed from Heal's with her brown hair spread across the pillow – Meriel relaxed, compliant in a way she never could be awake – nestling, fitting to the curve of his own body – warm against him . . .

But then another soaring white flare burst high in the sky to the east – and for a moment, at the wavering climax of its arc, it was like daylight. He could see every mesh of the lace at the window, every tile and brick and cobble of the village street – and the road that left the village, chalky white, winding across the downs to Arras.

It was the way they'd march tomorrow, the road they'd take to the Front. Ned closed the shutters and re-lit the candle, tucking Meriel's letter away with the others in his valise, to be read again later. He wasn't unwilling to go. After the weeks of waiting and exercising at Sibiville, the prospect of action came almost as a relief. He'd endured the brass-polishing and parades and all the pompous petty militarism of the rest camp in the knowledge that he was witnessing a resurrection – the painful reconstruction of a battalion that had lost more men on the

Somme than it could now muster in total, despite continuous infusions of new recruits. But none of that had made the waiting itself any easier.

"Funny thing is, it never does, Mister A, never does get any easier," his platoon sergeant, Davey, had once confided on the strength of a proffered Woodbine. "Although Gawd 'elp us, after this lot you'd think we'd be glad to get back to our own pitch in the shootin' gallery – if only fer a bleedin' rest!"

They'd finally left Sibiville in the late afternoon – a fifteen mile route march over the treacherous, icy *pavée*, pausing for ten minutes in every sixty to rest at the dusky roadside in huddled groups of glowing cigarette ends. The billets at Wanquetin had been cramped and rather uncomfortable for the most part, and although Ned was lucky enough to secure a single room in the *estaminet* for himself and his batman, it had been at the cost of interminable choruses of '*Auprès de ma blonde*' and 'When this bloody war is over' from immediately beneath his bed. Not to mention a hostile *ménagère* in carpet slippers, who patently cared more for the polished surface of her hall tiles than for any of the greater issues of war and peace.

"*Messieurs! Ça ne vous dérangerait pas de vous essuyer les pieds!*"

Arras and the line came five days later, although scarcely in a form that any of them could have anticipated. For a city under siege there'd been a puzzling silence about the place on the day that they entered it. Many of the houses they passed were still undamaged. Others had been carefully patched with canvas and iron sheeting. Yet they already looked quite dead, all of them – abandoned, with drawn curtains and snow drifting across their door sills. The shop windows on both sides had been boarded up or stuffed with old mattresses in anticipation of the new offensive. But although the sound of their boots rang through the streets as the battalion marched smartly to attention down the Rue Gambetta, there were no grateful citizens on the pavements to wave them in. In the Place de la Gare a couple of tattered posters advertised the delights of the *Côte d'Azur* and *Bruxelles Historique*. But there were enemy trenches now across the Brussels line less than a mile away in the eastern suburbs. And apart from a solitary military policeman, the station itself was deserted.

The flares and Very lights were up again soon after dark, and one or two loud detonations shook the walls of their billet near the railway station – although no one seemed inclined to take them too seriously.

"Only the night shift signin' on," Davey remarked philosophically after the second explosion. "Jerry's got the 'ump, same as us, Mister A. 'E'll send over a couple more 'friendlies' an' then pack it in – see if I'm not right." He was too. For by the time Ned and the other platoon commanders had made their way to the Grande Place for an operations briefing, the German lines had reverted to silence.

As far as the city itself was concerned, the reverse applied. Under cover of darkness, previously deserted pavements now jostled with soldiers and civilians. Convoys of hooded motor lorries shuddered out of side streets to converge on the five cobbled acres of the Grande Place. Houses that had looked empty now showed light discreetly through chinks in curtains and shutters, while it was obvious from the queues outside a number of boarded-up shops and *estaminets* that soldiers' francs were still considered worth the risk of remaining open. Arras-Sur-Scarpe was alive, it seemed, after all.

The centre of military operations, the Grande Place and the Petite Place that adjoined it, were faced on all sides by a series of arched colonnades said to date from the Spanish occupation of the city three hundred years earlier. Some of the arches and the tall gabled houses above them had already sustained shell damage and were heaped with rubble. The rest were sandbagged and cluttered with the incoming freight of the lorries – and of a special goods-train that disgorged directly into the Place itself. No wonder the Tommies called it 'Barbed Wire Square'. For the whole area, every arch, was crammed with A-frames, duck-boards and galvanized trench revetting, barbed wire gooseberries, screw pickets, angle-irons and God only knew what else besides.

Yet despite every ugliness and indignity that modern warfare could inflict on them, they still retained a kind of grandeur, Ned thought, those stately Spanish cloisters. And when the runner who'd seen them up from the Place de la Gare beckoned their group through one of the archways, and into the sandbagged entrance of an old wine cellar, he anticipated some equally impressive vaults beneath. He was in for a shock.

An NCO of the Royal Engineers, waiting to receive them at the foot of the staircase, broke into the hectoring patter of a tour-guide as soon as their first man came into view. "That's it, come along, down this way if you please – 'urry along, gentlemen, we don't 'ave all night."

A brassard identified the man as a 'Caves Officer', and although he only actually ranked as a sergeant, Ned and the other subalterns were sufficiently impressed by his manner and by the general atmosphere of the place to file down and form an obedient semi-circle in front of him.

"That's the ticket – all 'ere then, are we? All present and correct? Well now – I s'pose you've bin told you'll be bringin' your blokes up in support, 'ave you? Sweatin' it out in commy trenches an' the like?"

He raised his eyebrows enquiringly at Ned, but didn't wait for an answer. "Well o'course you' ave! Couldn't 'ardly be otherwise, could it? Jerry 'as big ears, too blinkin' big, an' Caves is 'ush-'ush, see?" He indicated a crude representation of an owl painted on the wall at the head of the stairs, with the words, 'THE MORE HE HEARD THE LESS HE SPOKE' neatly printed beneath it.

"That's where I come in – for briefin' on the spot. Jerry 'asn't cottoned onto us yet, see? An' Staff aims to keep it that way – 'til we're ready to shove our Third Army through, toot sweet, an' right up 'is teutonic arse!" He smiled benignly.

"You see, gentlemen, these 'ere Caves under Arras *are* the commy trenches to the Front, so to speak. We don't 'old with none of your rabbit-scrape surface runs – not down 'ere we don't! Close-on twenty miles of tunnels an' quarries through solid-blinkin'-chalk, that's our communications – from Barbed Wire Square slap through to the Jerry line. Electric lights, runnin' water, 'ospital, telephone exchange – you name it, we've got it down 'ere. An' livin' accomodation, gentlemen, for *twenty 'fousand* Allied troops! I tell yer, there's never been nothin' like these 'ere Caves – not even in 'istory!"

Chapter Twenty-Three

If the war seemed less than real to Ned before Arras – that night in the chalky catacombs below the old town it entered the realms of total fantasy.

They began their subterranean journey through the long avenue of connected cellars that ran directly beneath the cloisters of the Grande Place.

"'Boves', that's what they call 'em – mostly used as workshops an' ware'ouses in the old days, with wine cellars underneath," the Caves Officers explained, pointing to a trap-door in the floor with 'KEEP OUT – THIS MEANS YOU!' daubed across it in white paint. "Some of them cellars go down two, even 'free more levels below this – 'ardly credit it, would you? Romans began 'em for Jul'us Caesar, so they say. Then they chucked up a bit more when the Dagoes invaded, an' a bit more again when our old Marlborough rolled up with 'is lot. An' now 'ere we are at it again for Jerry! Bloody marvellous!"

He paused again then, digressing in the manner of any professional tour-guide to highlight an interesting point of detail. On a narrow door behind him Ned deciphered 'NO! WE DON'T KNOW WHERE YOUR UNIT IS. ASK THE TOWN MAJOR.', before it swung back to admit a hurrying khaki figure – and to reveal a glimpse of a crowded smoky mess-room, with a Soyer stove and picture-postcards on the wall and a splendidly inlaid chiffonier groaning with wine bottles.

"Quarries," their guide was saying, "that's 'ow it all started in the first place. You 'ave to go down a good forty feet to get chalk 'ard enough for building, see? So there's quarries under the town an' quarries outside it – 'undreds of bally great caves, all nice'n 'andy between us an' Jerry – at Ronville an' St Saviours and under the Rue St Quentin. So we've been busy little moles 'aven't we – joinin' 'em all up an' pushin' 'em out under Jerry's wire? This way please, gentlemen." He turned sharp left down a slight incline, following the mainstream of the foot traffic –

soldiers scurrying like rats down the white chalk tunnel, their shadows circling around them as they moved from the orbit of one bare electric light bulb to the next.

"You don't want to take any of them side passages," he added, turning right and then left again and indicating a delta of branching tunnels – all of them illuminated and one, signed to the Petite Place, quite as wide and as busy as their own. "You'll get maps tomorrow – but they don't 'ave 'arf this perishin' lot on 'em. So unless you want to get lost for a week, I'd advise you to stick to the main roads an' follow the signs."

Ned had been trying to follow the signs ever since they'd left the Grande Place, but without a great deal of success. Because, apart from those that pointed to the Cathedral or the railway station or the various battalion HQs, the signposts of the Arras Caves were quite evidently a law unto themselves. Some of them merely consisted of incomprehensible combinations of letters and numbers – BM.67.25., W.13., H.41.B. and so on. Others advocated highly unlikely geographical alliances – NEW OXFORD STREET TO INDIA, BURMA AND CEYLON – GODLEY AVENUE TO AUKLAND AND WELLINGTON – GUERNSEY, GLOUCESTER TERRACE, INNS OF COURT AND ALADDIN'S CAVE. And all of them added considerably to his feeling of unreality.

"Your blokes'll be working for the Kiwis at the start-off, up at the end of the Strand," the Caves Officer said, pointing to the relevant sign, and leading them on ever deeper into the ancient chalk of Artois. As the sloping passageway veered again sharply to the left, a draught of warm, putrescent air drifted up to meet them.

"Crinchon Sewer," he explained. "Proper old shit-stream she is too."

Several of the other officers were already holding their noses and showing a marked lack of enthusiasm for the Crinchon. 'But actually,' Ned thought, 'if it wasn't for the pong, it really would be rather splendid.'

The bridge that spanned the sewer at the end of their tunnel offered them a long perspective view of vaulted brick, stretching away into the distance – its moist surfaces gleaming like a reptile's scales in the electric glare – and beneath it volumes of black water, silently gliding through the underworld.

"More than a mile and an 'arf of 'er all told," their guide said, and not without a note of pride in his voice. "All under the main boulevards she goes, clear through the city an' down to the River Scarpe."

' . . . where Alph the sacred river ran – through caverns measureless to man – down to a sunless sea . . .' A fragment of Coleridge, force-fed to him at school in Lancing, worked its way up through Ned's mind.

> Then reached the caverns measureless to man,
> And sank in tumult to a lifeless ocean:
> And 'mid this tumult Kubla heard from far
> Ancestral voices prophesying war . . .

On the far bank of the sewer a group of men were loading cartridge and fuse cases into what appeared to be a miniature version of the goods-train in the Place. "Looks like a railway, don't it? T'ain't though," the Caves Officer was pleased to inform them. "It's a tram, see – electricity all laid on an' two separate tracks up to the Front, with a link-line under the Boulevard de Strasbourg. I tell you the Piccadilly Line's got nothin' on us down 'ere! All aboard for Imperial Street, then."

For want of anything else to sit on, they perched on top of the cartridge cases in the open trucks, with less than a foot of clearance on either side as they jerked off into the narrow tunnel of the St Saveur gallery. "So keep your blinkin' elbows in!" the Caves Officer shouted back to them. "We're under your own battalion's billets now, comin' up to the mainline and the Rue Emile Breton – next stop Glasgow!"

It was hardly how Ned had pictured himself going to the Front. There had been a certain fearful glamour about the idea of creeping up a communication trench with the shells whistling overhead. But balanced precariously like this with your knees under your nose? Lurching up to the line on an underground toy tram? If only Meri could see him now! He could almost hear her hoots of laughter echoing down the tunnel after him. "You numbskull, Noggin – you great pook-noodle! Didn't I always say you were soft in the head? Well, didn't I?"

"The conduits above your 'eads are for mains water and for the signals wires to the Front," their guide's commentary continued remorselessly. "The lay-bys are for foot-sloggers caught short, so to speak. And 'ere we are in Glasgow, gentlemen!" With which the tunnel opened up into a great chalk cavern seething with troops.

"Kiwis," the Caves Officer shouted, "New Zealand Tunnelling Company. You'll be with them up the Strand and Imperial Street this week. Not a bad bunch neither – so long as you steer clear of the Maori Pioneers. Rumour 'as it they bleedin'-near ate a Boche prisoner last week! Whatto Fernleaf, 'ow's business?"

"Cushy, mate – fuckin' cushy!" A tall New Zealander in a goatskin jerkin raised a dixie of tea to them as they rattled past. But his companions scarcely bothered to look up. The whole place was buzzing like a hive with movement and conversation. Dozens of untidy cubicles and sagging tent affairs had been slung up around the perimeters of the cave between massive chalk pillars. Burlap walls everywhere bumped and bulged with moving figures; and from a roofless tin shanty near the track the delicious smell of frying sausages assailed Ned's nostrils. In the caves beyond there were more chalk pillars, inverted cones like huge stalactites meeting to form archways above the track – and other concentrations of men, New Zealanders and 5th Northamptons, working with mattocks and shovels to level heaps of chalk and spread it out across the cavern floors.

"Supplies go up the line, chalk comes down for spreadin', see?" the Caves Officer explained. "Can't afford to chuck it out up there. Shows up too blinkin' white on the air photos. You should see what we've dumped in some of the caves in the Ronville sector. Christchurch Cavern's damn near as big as Barbed Wire Square – an' we 'ad to 'arf fill the perishin' thing to bring the floor level up. Room for four 'fousand Tommies in there now – no trouble!"

The tram had been passing through a virtually continuous string of subterranean quarries and caverns for perhaps half a mile, when, suddenly they were back to the narrow tunnel again – rising in gentle gradients now towards the Front. Ned listened for the sound of the heavy guns that he'd first heard at haymaking in Sellington Meadow, and so often since. He was coming to them – close to them at last. But all he could hear was the hum and the rattle of the toy tram, and the crackling of the pick-up arm – and the irrepressible voice of their guide.

"Jerry's quiet tonight. P'raps 'e's done a bunk – I don't think! Oopsy-daisy, 'ere we are then – end of the line, gentlemen. This way then please, through the gas door. Got your box-respirators 'andy? That's the ticket!"

The door was airtight, gas-tight, muffling the sound of the men unloading the cartridge case – intensifying the silence: and the slope was steeper now, colder, earthier, flickering in uncertain candlelight. The Caves Officer hadn't said how close they were to the line and nobody asked. But Ned guessed its proximity from the sudden proliferation of gas curtains and dugout entrances, and from the whispered conversations of the sentries they passed along the way. He was glad it was cold too, because it gave them all an excuse to shiver.

"Who'd like to meet Jerry, then?" the Caves Officer said quietly after a walk of five or ten minutes in near silence. "There ain't a lot of room through 'ere, an' I can only take two at a time – so 'oo's first?"

It was precisely because he'd been so long in meeting Jerry, that Ned volunteered. Anonymous, the enemy was infinitely more frightening than he could ever be in the flesh. Now he wanted to see for himself what the German line was like at close quarters – and to try to understand. Now the time was coming to kill or be killed. The tunnel here was too low to stand in without bending, pitch black, and so narrow that your sleeves brushed against both walls.

"Russian sap," the Caves Officer hissed. "Not a lot above us just 'ere. So better 'ope we don't get a crump, eh? Our own line's back there be'ind us," he added as an afterthought. "We're out in no-man's-land now, see – 'arf way to bleedin' Berlin."

Ahead of him Ned could see a dim oval of light, with the familiar mushroom shape of a Tommy's tin hat outlined against it. They had to crawl for the last few feet. "All quiet," the sentry whispered, slithering back to make way for them at the entrance. "Must be Fritz's night off!"

The mouth of the tunnel opened into the end of a deep shell

crater, or the craters of two shells more probably, falling in line with each other. For there was a dividing ridge of chalk across the centre of the thing some twenty yards away, reinforced with a glinting bluish entanglement of concertina wire.

"'E's up the other end," the Caves Officer said in Ned's ear. "Sap just like this one – you can see it in the air photos." And as he spoke, someone cleared their throat out there beyond the wire. The chalk walls deflected and channelled the sound to them – an apologetic human sound that was the same in any language.

Looking back at his guide, questioning, Ned could just see the Caves Officer's lips moving to silently form the word 'JERRY'. From somewhere above them and to the right came the crackling stutter of a machine-gun – then the throat-clearing again, nervously, from the far end of the crater.

"*Ade zur guten Nacht...*" It was a youth's voice, crooning to himself something sad and nostalgic – and unmistakably German.

"*Jetzt wird der Schluss gemacht*
Dass ich muss Scheiden . . ."

"Blow me, you're in luck!" The sentry sounded really quite gratified. "'E don't usually perform to order, you know!" But he must have said it too loudly, because the singing stopped instantly. For a full minute all they could hear in the crater was the metallic rattling of the wire. Then it came again, that nervous little cough.

"Hello, Tommy!"

They didn't answer. The Caves Officer frowned and shook his head, and beckoned them back into the darkness of their own tunnel. But Ned had wanted to, had desperately wanted to answer – to shout back some kind of a reassurance to the frightened young man. 'Hello, Jerry – you're not a monster are you? And no more am I! We British can sing too, you know, and dream of our homes just as you do. I don't want to kill you. I don't want to fight in this crazy war any more than you do . . .'

Yet such is the effect of military routine, that within a few days

Ned stopped asking himself what business he had on the Front in a war in which the protagonists actually seemed to tolerate each other, and settled down to the troglodyte existence beneath Arras as if it were entirely normal. There was no requirement for intelligent thought, in any case, in the business of transporting chalk and stores. No one in the Caves was remotely interested in Second Lieutenant Ashby's mental and emotional preoccupations – only in what his orders were, in what his working party was doing and in how long they'd take to do it. And they all talked blithely of the coming push, as if it were no more than the deadline for the completion of their latest tunnel system.

By the time Ned and his battalion were sent up the line to relieve the West Kents at Blangy, the memory of the boy's voice in the crater no longer disturbed him. A number of German soldiers carried pocketbooks of folksongs into the trenches, he learned. He was shown one that had been captured on a recent raid. It had a little man with a guitar on the cover and romantic silhouette illustrations between the songs – pictures of arcadian figures, birds, butterflies and twining wildflowers. The Germans weren't officially allowed to sing on stand-to, of course, any more than the Tommies were, but you often heard snatches of song drifting across from their dugouts and support lines. It was accepted as normal, just like everything else.

In Ned's sector of the Arras Front the names of all the communication trenches began with the letter I. And beyond Iron Road and Ingle Lane, in the ruins of the Blangy suburb itself, the opposing front lines were said to be closer than anywhere else on the Western Front – no more than forty feet apart at one point, with a Kiwi tunnel actually passing beneath the German front trench. In the mornings, sipping tea that tasted faintly of petrol, you could smell the superior smell of Jerry's breakfast coffee across the road. If you felt so inclined, you could probably lob a Mills or an egg bomb right into his lap – to scatter coffee and drinker to the four winds. But nobody had recently. There was a quiet permanence about the Front here that discouraged undue aggression. Small-arms fire was still permissible, and occasionally a stray bullet ploughed into the snow behind the trench. Sometimes you saw the silver flash of an aeroplane's wings – or an observation balloon, swaying on its moorings like a girl's parasol. But that was all. Further down the line there were 5.9 shells and the blinking red sparks of trench mortars. But never in Blangy.

"We're laughin' 'ere, Mister A, an' that's the truth," Sergeant Davey declared from the depths of a dugout that stank of mouldy serge. "Jerry 'arf asleep, mud frozen 'ard – blimey what more could you ask? Bleedin' 'ome from 'ome, an' no mistake!"

Yet perversely the knowledge of his own surprisingly good fortune didn't prevent Ned from feeling cramped and cold and fairly thoroughly bored by his first experience of the front line. The battalion's trench duties consisted of four days' stint in the line, alternated with four days of working parties in the Caves. Ned very soon found himself counting the hours to the times when he could move about freely below ground, without stumbling into sumps or barking his shins on wooden firesteps every two minutes. Time and space were both grotesquely magnified in the trenches. Five minutes could seem like an hour, a journey of thirty yards like a five-mile hike, a glimpse through a peephole or a Vigilance periscope like a walk in the campagne. And to Ned the luxury of stepping up and raising his head above the parados every once in a while seemed infinitely worth the risk.

"I shouldn't do that just there if I were you, Sir." They never seemed to tire of saying it – and he always did move, if only out of respect for their concern. But he went on stepping up and raising his head just the same. Partly because he never did get shot at on a trench watch. Partly because some daredevil in him actually enjoyed the stimulation of a genuine risk. But mostly because he needed more to look at than parapet and wire pickets and geometric strips of sky. He really did need those little glimpses of open downland landscape.

They reminded him so much of Sussex, those snowy hills of Arras – a part of the same great spine of Cretaceous chalk that formed the South Downs across the Channel and the valley he called home. Over the Scarpe river the long whaleback of Vimy Ridge rose white and smooth, flawless against the sky – like Seaford Head over Cuckmere, or Mount Carmel across the flats of the Ouse. And you'd never guess to look at it that hundreds of thousands of men had already lost their lives for its possession.

The snow hid so much that was unacceptable. It smoothed over the smaller shell craters, blanketing shattered *pavée* and the twisted rails of the old Brussels mainline – and the narrow fields of a medieval agricultural system that had been strafed out of existence during the original formation of the line back in 1914. It couldn't disguise the wire, or the corkscrew pickets, or the truncated trees and fallen telegraph lines. But on winter mornings even they had their grim beauty – glittering with crystalline hoar frost, with the sun rising through the mist behind them like a huge crimson balloon.

"Fair clemmed wiv cold!" That's how a Sellington man would have described their condition in the trenches that winter. And as he practised his duckboard-glide between the firebays with the ice crackling on his puttees, Ned often liked to turn himself to the north west, in the direction of the English Channel, and to think how things would be back home. Meriel's letters were full of fuel shortages and frozen pipes, and the impossibility of warming a house like The Bury. But it was left to him to imagine the Sellington villagers, with their hats jammed down over their ears in the face of a cutting nor'easter gusting down the valley. He pictured the sheep clustering in the lew of a drifted furze bank – and the neat pad prints of foxes and rabbits criss-crossing each other along the hedgerows. He could almost hear the steady slicing rhythm of the beet-cutter, smell the strawy cosiness of the cowsheds. And he could miss – how he could miss – that particular winter pleasure of seeing his own beasts warm and well-fed, despite the worst that the weather could come up with. A stockman's reward that Dan Goodworth had graphically expressed as 'racked-up an' fother-snug!'

He'd heard from Dan himself recently in a characteristically self-possessed letter from somewhere down the line – maybe from no more than a few miles away, for all the censor and military communications would allow. "So now I am a second lieutenant as well, Master Ned," he had written in a careful schoolroom hand.

"I don't say I looked for anything like this, and when it comes down to it I would just as soon be back in Blighty milking the old moos. But there, we can't always do what we would like or be where we would wish in this life, can we? It wouldn't be good for us. And I daresay things could be worse . . . "

Good old Dan, he'd make a first rate subaltern too, Ned had no doubt of that. There'd always been a natural authority about him, even as a cowman, and an orderly rural attitude to life that was bound to recommend itself to the Military.

It often seemed to Ned in the frozen lines of Blangy that system and orderliness were all that Staff ever really cared about, as if warfare, even on this gigantic scale, was no more than an incidental to the efficient running of an army. In the absence of any kind of enemy bombardment, the trenches were assailed instead with salvoes of communiqués – contemptuous memoranda from professionals to rank amateurs, from Brigade Headquarters or from GHQ itself at Montreuil-Sur-Mer far beyond the stars. Incessant petty requests in indelible pencil concerning the exact number of 'BOOTS, GUM AND BOOTS, THIGH – SOLDIERS FOR THE USE OF' in each platoon. Stock returns to fill out on screw pickets, wire cutters and entrenching tools. And optimistic Intelligence Summaries – 'comic cuts' Davey called them – demanding details of Enemy Activity and Enemy Deposition; as if anyone in Blangy had the faintest inkling as to what Jerry was up to on the other side of the wire.

It was with the scarcity of information on Enemy Deposition that Brigade revealed greatest dissatisfaction. And towards the end of February, one of the exclusive little chits fluttering down the Front to their neighbours of the 11th Middlesex Battalion, demanded a daylight raid 'for identification purposes'.

"Fuckin' marvellous!" Davey commented bitterly as a sentry's warning whistle announced the inevitable enemy retaliation. "'Old tight for the bump, Mister A, 'ere comes Krupp's blinkin' iron-foundry now – COD!" And a range finder shell swished over their heads to explode with a hideous twang between the trenches. "Bloody-fuckin'-marvellous! They 'ave to go an' pull Jerry's short-arm, don't they, just when 'e's settled lovely? They 'ave to make sure 'e's still there, see, to give theirselves somethin' definite-like to fill in on their Casualty Reports, when 'arf of us poor bastards 'ave bin shelled to shit!"

A trench mortar canister fell with a crash, spouting earth and chalk high above the parados – then something larger, a Woolly Bear, tearing down at them like an express train, to crack the world apart in an explosion that filled the trench with black smoke and sent shards of steel scything into the sandbags.

"Lay still, chum." Davey was impressively calm. "It's only a demo – this lot wouldn't knock the skin off a rice pudden'."

Choking in the reek and the fume, terrified by the noise and power of the explosions, Ned found that he couldn't lay still. He couldn't just sit there and wait for another of those screaming shrapnel shells to fall on top of him and blow him to Kingdom Come.

"No – I'll check sentries on stand-to. You stay, Platoon Sergeant, no sense two of us going . . . " The words came out in ridiculous jerks; and when he moved his limbs felt weak and uncontrolled. But at least he was moving – forcing his fear into action of some kind – and that seemed to help. In the next firebay the sentries' faces were the colour of putty – looking towards him, all of them, with the fearful expression of sheep waiting to be driven. Confronted with their fear, Ned felt his own diminishing.

"Soldier on lads," he said, "it's only a demo – be over in a minute."

"Tooter the sweeter," one of them responded with a watery smile. "Roll on Duration, eh Sir?"

"You can say that again!" But another Woolly Bear said it for him – louder and closer than the last. Ned went down to it like a ninepin, face-down on the boards, flattened by a great fist of foul air punching down the trench. The others were coughing and swearing and beating at the black, nitrous smoke as he hauled himself up again. But it wasn't until he saw the damage to the traverse behind him that Ned remembered where he'd left Davey.

The blast had flattened the Platoon Sergeant too, in amongst the frozen chalk and splintered boarding. But Davey hadn't got up. Something had neatly flayed the serge and woollen underclothing from him, and beneath them the flesh from his backbone and part of his ribcage. There was blood, but not much. A red hot fragment of shell-casing hissed like a serpent in the chalk beside him; and Ned noticed irrelevantly that it was melting the silver carapace of ice from the pebbles closest to it.

"Poor bloody sod!" Someone else said it – words from the standard litany that Davey himself had quoted a few minutes earlier. But Ned could feel nothing but resentment, a dull kind of anger with the unfairness of it all; with Davey for having bought-it like this, and with himself for somehow failing to grasp the incredible finality of death. Inside Davey there was a red and white carcass of flesh and bone – one minute alive, the next not. All so simple and obvious. Here was the body for all to see, opened like a clockwork toy to reveal the workings. So why couldn't he understand where the laughing, grumbling, everyday lifeforce that was Davey had actually gone to?

It was as if he knew, almost – but couldn't quite put his finger on it. It was there in the back of his mind, in the corner of his eye, on the tip of his tongue. Yet somehow it still eluded him.

Chapter Twenty-Four

"Ah tea – the cure for all possible ills!" Simmie dropped a barely level scoop of tea leaves into her smallest teapot and leaned forward to inhale the aroma as she poured in the boiling water. She could bear anything – ration cards, sugar queues, daylight air raids, anything – just so long as she could still have her tea. The grocer in Lamb's Conduit Street was a particular friend of hers, and slipped an extra quarter pound of Government Control Blend into the bottom of her shopping basket whenever he could. But even his supply was precarious and unreliable now, and recently prudence had limited Simmie to a single spoonful a day at teatime – normally made up extra weak, and shared with her maid. She was lucky to have Gladys with her still after all these years, all her friends said so. But this afternoon, Simmie thought gaily, she was luckier still. Gladys was out to tea at her niece's – and that meant a spoonful all to herself, good and strong!

While she waited for the tea to infuse, Simmie replaced the black japanned tea caddy on the dresser and made up a little tray for herself, with sugar and a milk jug, a lace doily, two Marie biscuits and an extra saucer for George. Then she strained the tea into one of her best bone china cups and started up the kitchen stairs. It was absurd, this afternoon tea ritual, of course it was, all alone in the house with no one but George to see her perform it. But then again it was something rather nice, something unchanging to hold onto amidst all the sacrifices and sadnesses of this changing world.

"And we enjoy it, don't we, George?" she said aloud as they turned past the yard door and into the hall passage. The cat had shot out from beneath the clothes horse at the first little chink of cup meeting saucer; and he was already crabbing ahead to the foot of the stairs, his tortoiseshell tail fluffed and quivering with anticipation.

Indeed, it was principally on account of George that his mistress failed to notice the post that afternoon – a black-edged letter lying face-down on the doormat. One could no longer expect mail these days, paper was so short. Simmie's attention was caught instead by the sight of her cat bounding up the stairs two-at-a-time just as her student lodgers had done – Ned and all those other poor young men – as if they thought life were some kind of a steeplechase. Andy had been one of the first to volunteer in 1914, to die six weeks later at Ypres; and Matt Starnes, another of that original trio, had lost an arm and part of a leg on the Somme. Of the twelve who'd boarded at Harpur Street over the years, eight were now dead and buried – three on the Somme, two on the Ypres salient, one at Loos, one in Salonika, and the last – Richard Drew, still two months short of his twenty-first birthday – in the fierce fighting to the south of Arras in the spring.

George was prowling and meowling over by the parlour fireplace, agitating for his milk, so Simmie poured it for him first to keep him quiet, before subsiding with her own tea into her favourite old button-back armchair. Her little parlour had changed very little over the years, that's what she liked so much about it. The pictures on the walls were all of them old friends, and the place still smelled of potpourri and furniture polish just as it had in Cécile Llewellen's day. The room still rustled with memories.

A bluebottle buzzed against the window pane, a comfortable drowsy sound for a September afternoon. Simmie smiled and dropped her free hand to the cat beside her chair. That was her trouble, she supposed. She was always too ready to romance over old memories, to pore over them like fading photographs; instead of taking life by the horns as Meriel did, to create new memories for herself day by day.

'And face it, Simmie,' she told herself sternly, quite forgetting to savour the precious tea, 'that's not a weakness you can blame on the war or on Robert Llewellen – or even on Isobel as the wicked stepmother. You know perfectly well that you've always been a hopelessly timid creature. You could have got that black-eyed scoundrel back if you'd cared to, if you'd had the nerve. But you didn't, did you? You had your chance, and you let it go, to settle for living second-hand through your college boys and people like the Ashbys.'

The tea had gone, she'd drained the cup without even tasting it, and with it the brief little flutter of gaiety that she'd felt, brewing it for herself so greedily in the kitchen. It had been a mistake not to take in more students this autumn, she could see that now. Without even the anticipation of their cheery voices and thumping footfalls, the house felt empty – a lonelier empt- iness than weekends or holidays. But after young Richard's death at Arras, she hadn't the heart for any more. She felt too old, too old and tired to go through the hoop again. She was fifty-one. She'd weathered the Change, the climacteric that shut the door for once and for all on her romantic aspirations. At the time the prospect of having to cherish and grieve over even one more young life had seemed too much to ask. Just too much . . .

"Oh Gladys, is that you? Dear me, I suppose I must have dropped off for a moment . . . " She had been slowly revolving in her comfortable little armchair to the sound of the buzzing bluebottle, when something prodding and intrusive jerked her awake and upset the empty teacup in her lap.

"So you 'ave, Mum," Gladys confirmed, miraculously fielding

the cup and saucer before they reached the floor. "An' no 'arm to that neither, I'm sure." It was an unusually charitable reaction for Gladys; and looking up into her battered old face, Simmie could tell immediately that something was wrong.

"What is it, Gladys? What's happened?"

In place of an answer a letter was thrust at her with disconcerting suddenness from the folds of Gladys' apron. It was a small, overfilled mourning envelope, of cheap, shiny paper and heavily bordered in black. Simmie held it for an age, stupidly reading and re-reading her own name and address in Meriel's hasty scrawl:

MISS BEATRICE SIMS, 19 HARPUR STREET, THEOBALD'S ROAD, LONDON W.C., . . . 19 HARPUR STREET, THEOBALD'S ROAD – 19 HARPUR STREET . . .

Meriel was the only person she knew who crossed her Ts afterwards like that, in continuous horizontal lines. It was something she'd always noticed.

"Would you pass me my reading glasses please, Gladys, from the work-table? And the paper knife?" Her voice was all right, quite calm and clear, but she was all thumbs when it came to opening the thing, fumbling hopelessly while the clock ticked away on the mantelpiece and the bluebottle buzzed at the window – with Gladys looming over her relentlessly like an angel of death. She tried not to think, not to panic, but her mind galloped on ahead of her, regardless; and it took time to force it back onto the track of Meriel's letter, to assimilate what she'd written.

The first thing Simmie saw when she looked up was a great fat tear coursing down her maid's ravaged cheek. Old fraud that she was!

"It's all right, Gladys – it isn't Mr Edwin," she said gently. "It's his father, Mr Walter Ashby. Mrs Edwin has just written to say that he died most unexpectedly of septicaemia yesterday morning."

Gladys gave a sniff in response that racked her angular body from top to toe, surreptitiously wiping the tear with the back of her hand as she stooped to retrieve the teatray.

"Shame!" she declared. "Wicked – an' 'im such a proper, quiet sorta gent by all accounts. Thanks-be Mister Eddie's safe though," she added gruffly, but with something uncommonly like a tremor in her voice. And the next moment she whisked herself and the tray out onto the landing, expertly hooking the parlour door to behind her with a large and highly polished black boot.

You couldn't mourn them all, Simmie reflected, returning to Meriel's letter. One simply hadn't enough tears for all the mourning this interminable war demanded. As a case in point, Meriel seemed to be facing up to her father-in-law's death with a degree of stoicism that at any other time might almost have seemed callous.

"No one but *himself* to blame for it of course," she wrote in her usual emphatic style.

"You know he only had one good lung, Simmie, and the doctor warned him *ages* ago that he'd crock up if he went on trying to work the farm in his condition. GM and I both had a go at him – and I told him we could manage perfectly well without him (better actually!). But do you think he'd listen to reason? He could be quite as stubborn as Ned you know when he chose. And on Tuesday he actually tried to lay a barley headland all by himself – if you can imagine anything so damn foolish – ending up with a septic reaphook gash on the ankle that killed him *dead as a dodo* within forty-eight hours! Hard lines, of course, and most distressing for the children, but I *ask* you! When all's said and done I doubt if he'd have had the strength to throw off a severe cold, let alone septicaemia. And once it took a hold there wasn't a damn thing that any of us could do to save him."

'Oh poor man,' Simmie thought, struggling not to smile at Meriel's absurd way of putting things. In his own way Walter Ashby was surely as much a victim of the war as any of the poor boys who'd died for their country out there in Flanders. 'And there's nothing very funny in that, is there?' she reminded herself sharply – really quite shocked at her own want of feeling.

"So much for the sad news," Meriel continued briskly over the page.

"Now, Simmie, what do you think? *Ned's coming home!!!*

The military authorities in France haven't had time to confirm it (they don't know yet, actually), but he'll *definitely* be coming! We telegraphed him this morning to tell him about his father, and are now requesting a Special Leave for him 'for Urgent Private Affairs' through the War Office. They can hardly deny it either (when they're sending men home for the *mumps,* for Lord's sake!), and once I've got him back you can bet your boots that this time I'm going to keep him!! They've accepted Pyecroft into the Bantams Battalion now – and I swear Caldwell and that useless Belgian get slower and more impossibly unwilling with every day that passes. So now that Father-in-Law's gone, there's no question that Ned will have to stay home to run things – even the Executive Committee will have to agree. Apart from anything else there's death duties and whatnot, and masses of accounts work that I haven't time for. And of course the boys are still too young to be anything but a hindrance.

Which brings me to the other thing. Now look, Simmie, I want you to think again *very seriously* about coming down here to us in Sellington. You know how marvellous you are with the boys, and once Ned's back, and demanding his own attention, I really don't know how I'll manage. So don't just sit there shaking your head and dreaming up piffling excuses (oh yes, I know you!), come on make a decision, Simmie! There is a war on and you can't hope to stay up in town with air raids all around you and munitions factories blowing up at the drop of a hat. I've always said you'd be better off down here, haven't I and GM agrees with me.

Gladys could come too, if that's what you're worried about. There's no earthly reason why not. We've *masses* of room, and she's bound to get on famously with Cook – they're both such frightful old stick-in-the-muds!''

It wasn't the first letter Meriel had written to ask for her help, and as always when confronted with a direct appeal from someone she cared for, Simmie found herself longing to respond. She'd never really worried about the air raids, nor even the Silvertown munitions factory explosion that had shaken the house and threatened to repeat Ned's famous trick with the mantelboard. In spite of Gladys' highly coloured accounts of blood and gore in Bishopsgate and bombs in Hyde Park, it all still seemed to her unrelated to anything that could possibly happen here in Harpur Street. But Meriel and the children were another matter. She'd been seriously worried about the Ashby ménage ever since Meriel's previous letter announcing the departure of the boys' nursemaid, Betty.

"You know I never cared for her in the first place, and of course as soon as I realized that the children were becoming fonder of that pudding-brain than they were of me, their *own mother*, I knew she'd have to go. Good riddance too! But honestly, Simmie, you should have seen Patrick when I told him I'd sacked her. 'Who's going to Betty-us now?' that's what he said – and *such* a woebegone little face. You'd think that he'd just taken all the cares of the world on his shoulders."

It was the vision of that woebegone face in relation to his mother's exclusive preoccupation with getting his father home and keeping him there, that concerned Simmie most. She didn't see how she could possibly leave Harpur Street for any length of time, what with Gladys and George and all of Cécile Llewellen's precious treasures. But on the other hand that child, those children, needed her, she truly believed they did. And that surely was more important?

She and Gladys ate early that evening – fried eggs and mushrooms on toast from the last food hamper Meriel had sent up by carrier from Sellington. By eight o'clock Simmie had retired to her bedroom to do what she'd been wanting to do all evening – to brush out her hair and stare into her mirror, and to think. She was still sitting there with her elbows on the mirrored surface of her dressing table and her fingertips pressed against her eyelids, when her thoughts were interrupted by the aggressive bark of an anti-aircraft gun, followed within seconds by the booming of the air raid maroons from Holborn Police Station.

"'Ere's the air raids, Mum!" Gladys' voice yelled up the stairwell, for all the world as if she was announcing the laundry woman or the afternoon post. And the next moment Simmie was catapulted to her feet by an almighty explosion, followed by the sound of tinkling glass and a squawk of outrage from the hall below. Then silence.

The bomb had fallen four streets away in Southampton Row, killing twelve people outright and injuring dozens of others with flying glass. Gladys went over there at the crack of dawn to report that the police actually had the bloomin' 'ide to close the street to law-abiding citizens.

Later, after breakfast, Meriel was on the telephone, shouting as always to compensate for the distance the message had to travel.

"Are you there – is that you, Simmie?" Despite the fact that she'd forced Simmie to install the telephone at Harpur Street soon after she'd bullied the G.P.O. into running a wire down through the Sellington Valley (and currently used the instrument approximately twice as much as anyone else) it was obvious that Meriel still distrusted it. "Simmie, is that you? Can you hear me?"

"Yes of course I can, dear – there's really no need to shout."

"Well what about this bomb? Are you and Gladys all right? I *told* you something like this would happen if you insisted on staying in town. Come on, admit it! And now I suppose you're going to stand there and tell me that you *still* aren't prepared to leave? Well, listen to me – can you still hear me, Simmie? What was that you said?"

"I said I can hear you perfectly, darling."

"Right, then I'm coming up on the eleven o'clock train this morning to help you close up the house, and to fetch you and Gladys and your traps back to Sellington. Now don't argue, it's all settled. Gladys had better clear things with her niece this morning, all right? And I'd advise you to start looking out your dust sheets right now. Oh, and I'll need a hammer and some nails and anything in the way of timber that you can lay your hands on. Have you got that? Did you hear me? Simmie? Hello – hello . . ."

Meriel could ill afford the time it took to winkle Simmie out from her overcrowded little den in Harpur Street, what with

Father-in-Law's funeral to organize, and the hire of Harris's steam-thresher from Polegate, and all the details of Ned's homecoming to rehearse and gloat over.

'But if I don't get her out of that house today,' she told herself as the train sighed into Victoria, 'then I never will!' And she jumped down onto the platform, brushing the porters aside and stepping it out for the barrier. On reflection she'd thought it wise to bring along her own hammer and nails, together with a lidded wicker maund-basket for the wretched moggie and a set of sticky labels for the trunks. 'A bottle of smelling salts and a couple of pairs of handcuffs wouldn't have come amiss either,' she thought grimly – awarding the motor cab driver a perfunctory smile. "Harpur Street off Theobald's Road, my good man – Number 19 if you please. And let's see how many horses this contraption thinks it's good for on the way, shall we?"

They'd sawn off the black-painted iron railings from either side of Simmie's front door, to be melted down for munitions. The paint was flaking off the door itself, and someone had replaced two of the dining room window panes with ragged squares of cardboard.

"Heavens, look at this place – it's a regular disgrace! The sooner you're out of it the better, Simmie Sims – that's clear!" They were her first words, even before she kissed her friend. She had a great deal more to say too, while the hat came off and Gladys organized the coffee. Just as she thought, Simmie had been dithering around doing practically nothing since they'd spoken on the telephone. She hadn't any timber, she hadn't spoken to the Gas Company, she hadn't sheeted so much as a footstool – and even now all she seemed to want to do was stand around smiling helplessly, producing half-baked objections to any kind of constructive progress.

In the end it had taken seven hours of concentrated effort to separate Simmie from her home. They'd had to lever up floorboards in one of the attic rooms to board the shutterless downstairs windows, and push wardrobes against the rest. A charge of verbal dynamite had been required to get the gas man out at short notice. Someone of a more practical turn of mind had been forced to wrest a host of worthless articles from

264

Simmie's hands, to prevent her from packing the entire upstairs parlour into her two battered cabin trunks, and at the last minute George had disappeared – to be discovered at the end of a forty minute search inadvertently shut in the understairs cupboard.

But Meriel emerged in the end, as she knew she would, to the satisfaction of frogmarching Simmie across the sooty concourse of Victoria to the Lewes train – with trunks and porters following on, and Gladys bringing up the rear stiffernecked and bootier-faced than ever.

'All she needs now is a big, fat Havana cigar from the tobacconist's,' Meriel thought, 'and she'd be my faithful old San Lorenzo Maria to the life!'

Another raid on the East End soon after their arrival back in Sellington, confirmed Meriel in the wisdom of her action, if any further confirmation was needed after the boys' enthusiastic reception. Simmie had always been popular with the children on their trips up to London; and when she insisted on going up to see them in bed that first night, they both popped up from under the covers with ear-to-ear grins, like two jolly little jack-in-the-boxes. They both kissed her too, without prompting; and Robbie reached up to stroke her fluffy, thistledown hair.

"Yes of course, my lambkins, I'll be right here when you wake in the morning, and won't that be fun?" Simmie's voice was so nice, so soft and clear when she spoke to the children. No wonder they adored her, Meriel thought.

"If you like I'll come and help you get dressed for school, shall I? Then you can show me how it's all done and where everything lives. And when you get home we'll have a grand exhibition of all the treasures I've brought down from Harpur Street, shall we, to see if we can find nice homes for them all in your house?"

For the first time since Ned had left for his wretched training camp, they began to feel like a proper family again. Dear old Simmie was too much a part of them all now to bother with dredging up old worries and petty jealousies – too loving and negligent and utterly inoffensive.

From Simmie's own point of view there was still a great deal left to worry about. She worried terribly about the home she'd abandoned and the household she'd entered – about old Mrs Ashby in her silent bereavement, and Ned so close to his leave, and those two little ducks of his who'd lost their nurse. But most of all she worried about Meriel. For someone like Simmie who'd always struggled to hold her own emotions in check, there was an unnatural intensity about Meriel's anticipation of her husband's return. Even allowing for that inexhaustible energy of hers, there was something altogether too bright in her eye, too strident in her voice. You could never be sure from one minute to the next whether she'd scream with laughter, or fly off the handle, and days before the wire came through with the time of that long-awaited train, she had worked herself into a frenzy of over-excitement.

"You've got to come with me to keep me company, Simmie, you must! I've got to have someone to talk to all the way. I'll just blow up and burst with impatience otherwise, I know I will! Then we can go on to collect the boys from school after we've picked up Ned, and all come home together! Perfect! So go on then, get your hat."

"But, Meriel, there'll hardly be room for all of us in the trap. And, my dear, this really is a family occasion, Ned won't want . . ."

"Oh good God, we're not going through all *that* again are we?! When are you going to learn, woman, that you *are* family – you have been for donkey's years! So do me a favour, will you, just stop drivelling and *put on your hat!*"

It was a mellow, early autumn day, the day they went to fetch Ned home from Seaford, with flocks of well-fed wood pigeons picking over the corn stubble and blue sloes in the hedges. The hills were pale now, bereft of sap and energy, and the new telephone line that looped down between them was crowded with swallows and martins, congregating for their migration south. But Meriel was in no mood for endings of any kind. Ned was coming home – and for her the year was just beginning, whatever the swallows cared to make of it! She'd got herself up in emerald green plaid for the occasion, with button-down pockets, a tasselled beret at a rakish angle and the latest thing in glass drop-earrings – a black diamond patch on one sleeve her only concession to mourning. Her hands were gloveless, Simmie noticed, clenched white on the ribbons as she belaboured Archie into a reluctant trot. The green glass earrings swung wildly with every lurch of the vehicle, and her voice kept time, rising and falling in a continuous hymn of jubilation.

"I wonder if he's changed, Simmie? Do you think he will have lost weight? I expect he has. Might not be a bad thing, mind you, he was getting just a bit too tubby round the middle. I only hope they haven't cut his hair too short, that's all. I do so *hate* to see the back of a man's neck, don't you? And Ned's hair's so nice, isn't it, if only he'd look after it properly."

Nothing was required of Simmie but to be there, and to listen, to provide Meriel with the excuse for proclaiming her love for Ned quite literally from the hilltops.

"Do you believe in destiny, Simmie? Because I do – and I'll tell you why if you like. You see, when I was a girl in Queensland I positively *knew* that I'd marry Ned one day, even though I'd never set eyes on him. Can you believe that?"

She turned to her friend with great, shining brown eyes, sucking in her lower lip like a child. Like a child at Christmastide, Simmie thought, confidently reaching out for the gift that she'd asked for. "I knew what he'd look like, how he'd be, everything. It all came true, you see, just as I'd imagined it! And if that isn't the hand of fate, then I don't know what is!"

Beyond the chimneys and gables of Seaford town, Ned's train revealed itself as a long ribbon of white smoke streaming out across the salt flats.

"That's it! There's the engine! Come on you measly old leg-lapper, *move!*" For all Meriel's shouting and cursing and rein-slapping agitation, they barely reached the station entrance in time to see the train pull in on the other side.

"Whoa! Stand still, damn you!" Meriel abandoned the trap slewed across the station forecourt, tossing the reins into Simmie's lap and rushing off to force her way through the ticket gate.

Simmie had never had any talent with horses, and was finally obliged to get out in order to persuade Archie to move in a little closer to the kerb. In her mind's eye she could see Meriel racing down the platform, knocking people flying to right and left in the urgency of her search for Ned. As she climbed back into the car to take the reins again and rearrange the rug over her knees, she pictured Ned stepping down from the train, gladly bracing himself for the impact of that small, violent body.

"All change! All change!" someone was shouting amidst the noise of banging doors. Then a porter with suitcases emerged from the station, and behind him a broad, upright figure in khaki uniform, with Meriel strolling alongside nonchalantly swinging her reticule.

'He has changed,' Simmie thought. 'What is it – not just the cap and the moustache? Something's gone – something in his face.'

"Hello, Simmie." It wasn't the smile at least. That was as sweet as ever, thank heaven.

"Ned! Welcome home, my dear! Come over here this minute, and let me kiss you!"

"Scratches like the very devil, doesn't it?" Behind him Meriel's voice was drawling with anti-climax. "He's not kissing me again, I can tell you, not until that damn thing comes off! And it's no use looking at me like that, Ned Ashby. You should have thought before you grew it, shouldn't you? No one likes pallid, wishy-washy soup strainers like that, for heaven's sake. They look like fungus, don't they, Simmie – everyone says so."

Chapter Twenty-Five

"Ned, are you listening to me?"

"Yes darling, of course I am."

"Then what was the last thing I said?"

"You said that you'd agreed with the Committee Inspector and the estate trustees that fifteen acres of the old Rough should go down to ryegrass instead of barley."

"Right, and what I was about to say – oh Noggin, for pity's sake stop pawing me about and *pay attention!* What I was about to say was that with three half-reasonable Land Girls in the sheds and Irish cows at only twelve pounds a head, we'd be mad not to double-up the herd right away. Fifteen shillings a week, that's all we'd have to pay the girls, and they could billet up in the village, there's masses of room. Frank Longhurst's using them over at Great Dean. There's even talk of him putting in a steam-milker – although I personally doubt that he'd go that far, knowing what a miserable old skinflint that man is. But he is expanding his dairy enterprise to meet the demand, that's the point – and so should we, Ned! Everyone says the bottom's going to drop out of the cereal market as soon as the war's over, and we've just got to be ready for it when it does. Well then, what do you think?"

"I think Frank Longhurst would willingly give his six best cows for a head cowman like mine – who'd sit on his knee for him and let him do this to her . . . and this!"

"Ye Gods, Ned! Someone might come in!"

He was sitting in his father's swivel desk chair at the time, and the force with which Meriel wrenched herself free revolved her husband through a full three hundred and sixty degree spin – to leave him facing out into the library again as she reached for the door handle.

"Anyone would think you'd had enough of that kind of thing in the past few days to last you a lifetime," she said severely. "But I can see you're still unfit for any kind of serious discussion, so I'll just have to leave you to that lot and hope they bring you down to earth at least." She indicated the ledger and cash book, and the paper tower of spiked invoices that littered his father's desk. "You're home for good now, Ned, and it's high time you stopped behaving like an over-sexed Jack donkey and woke up to your real responsibilities again. The farm won't run itself, you know, and I for one am a great deal too busy to canoodle about acting the trollop for you, when there are hungry mouths to feed and a confounded Agricultural Committee to keep at bay."

She was right, of course. He admitted it to himself quite frankly as the door closed behind her. But he couldn't help it. The war had made a sensualist of him, if nothing else. After the deprivations of the trenches he found it hard even to look at his wife without desiring her. When she spoke to him – when her eyes held his and her mouth opened to speak – he wanted to kiss her, to cover her parted lips with his, parted wider. And when she moved, her clothing was no barrier to him. He knew her, every part of her – wanted to caress her where the fabric caressed her, to feel her warmth. And when she yielded to him at last in the darkness of their bedroom in the Flat, the intensity of the pleasure he took in her, the shuddering violence of his climaxes were a revelation to both of them.

Simmie had been right too, he had changed in France. In six months of almost continuous action in the battle of Arras and the defence of Monchy le Preux, Ned had been forced to re-evaluate those old ideals of permanence and continuity that he'd once tried to explain to Meriel at Bodiam all those years ago. He had come to realize that as far as Nature was concerned, their lives had already run their useful courses, his and Meri's. They'd paired and reproduced – and were now dispensable. From henceforth each day of living was a bonus, to be taken as it came, hour by hour. He'd learned to live now for the present, to expect no more from life than the momentary pleasures of a dandelion flower on the parados, or a rat that subsisted on human flesh, threading its way between the shell holes with the daintiness of a ballerina. And paradoxically, the war had opened his eyes to a new kind of love – to a sense of male fraternity that he'd never experienced at school or university, a fellowship with men like him who lived one day at a time.

They were such a splendid crew, those gallant little Tommies of Arras and Monchy le Preux. Men elevated in some inexplicable way by the degradation that had been forced on them. Men who could think of the enemy as 'good old Jerry' even as he strafed them, and strive to find affectionate nicknames for every weapon and missile that he sent to destroy them – Flying Pigs and Plum Puddings for trench mortars, Coal Boxes for 5.9 shells and Whizz-Bangs for 77s. There was no substitute in Sellington for that kind of desperate levity. Nor for the stimulant of fear that bound him to those men in the trenches. Nothing but the reality of his wife's body and his own when they made love in the lotus bed. For it was stimulation and immediacy that Ned needed now, not peace and permanence. And that was something that none of them here at home seemed to understand, Meriel least of all.

Ned thought of her again – of how she felt on his lap, how she'd look now striding down to the dairy, swinging that firm little rump of hers with the marvellous unconscious provocativeness that she'd always had. And wanting her all over again, he drew an obscene little caricature of his own priapic state on the blotting pad – before tearing off the top sheet and hastily opening his father's account book.

There were the figures for the year-ending April 1917 to relate to Meri's idea for expanding the milking herd before his next meeting with the estate trustees; and after that at least two months of receipts and payments to enter up for the current year. The last entry for July was for a bill from Jack Henty, the Jevington blacksmith:

> *To twelve tines, 17 in.*
> *To drawing and mending 58 ditto*
> *To plating a scythe*

neatly recorded in Father's best copperplate. Father would have understood. He, above all people, would have known what it was like to feel excluded and superfluous while others faced the enemy.

It was strange when there'd seemed so little to Father during his life, how one missed him now that he'd gone. It had come to Ned the moment he walked in through the door of the library, and smelt the old books and saw Father's big oak desk open and waiting just as he'd left it. Father, who'd given his life in effect to keep Ned out there in France.

Ned shut the ledger with a thud that brought old Puck to life again on the hearthrug, and got up to walk over to the window. It none of it seemed important any more – blacksmith's bills and trading figures, whether or not they should double-up the milking herd, whether '17/'18 would be a better year for The Bury. By April 1918 the war in France could be won – or lost. That was what mattered.

"Did you kill any Germans, Daddy? Did you see anyone get blown to bits? Were you scared of the enemy? Did you get any rides in tanks?"

His children, his little boys – they were the only ones here at home who really wanted to hear about the war. But how could he look into those tender, innocent faces and describe the horrors that still came to him so vividly in his dreams? How could he tell them about rags of grey flesh rotting beneath the duckboards? Or the things that carrion birds, crows and magpies squabbled over in no-man's-land? Or the lice that left a man's body as soon as it was cold? Or the sheer, profound nobility of men who could take it all and still remember how to laugh? He had told Simmie instead. He knew she hadn't wanted him to, but he told her anyway, because he had to tell someone.

"I want to tell you what it's like out there, Simmie. I want you to *know,* all right?"

He caught her by the gate of the stable yard, on her way up to the village post office. And however she hated hearing it, she listened to him with such sympathy and concern in her face, that for the moment he felt all constraint fall away.

"I want you to imagine how it feels, Simmie, to be trained behind the lines for a coming offensive. To be carefully rehearsed in neat canvas replicas of the trenches you're to attack – then chucked into a system that's nothing like them, because your own bombardment has pulverized the originals out of recognition. And can you imagine what it's like to have to lead a platoon of men over the top – can you? Passing down the rum-rations and seeing them rest their elbows on their knees to stop their hands shaking? Seeing them clearing their throats and licking their lips and rocking to and fro on the firestep – watching you, never taking their eyes off you, as if you're their only hope?"

He'd been speaking too fast, he heard himself doing it, the words treading on each other's heels. But he couldn't stop them coming, the relief had been too great; he couldn't let her go.

"And when you have to go over, to climb the ladder and call them up after you – 'Good luck mates!' – and your mind's turned to ice, and your heart's thumping so hard that you think it's going to jump right out of your throat – and suddenly the world opens up around you. You run with your head down, as if that could make any difference, and you sweat, and your flesh cringes, waiting to be torn from its bones . . . " He was sweating then too, just telling her, trembling like a spooked horse.

"But you keep on, Simmie, you have to keep on because the

men are behind you. You shout – 'Close up there! Mind the wire!' – but no one can hear your voice. The noise of the shells is like a hurricane – roaring, whining for blood, beating the thoughts out of your brains. The ground quivers and heaves under your feet. But you keep on, stumbling, falling into shell holes, with briars of steel clutching and tearing at your clothing. You keep on because the men are still at your back, trusting you to lead them through.

But when you reach the Jerry front line, when you finally reach it, Simmie, there's nothing there but piles of earth and chalk, and heaps of mangled bundles of blood and uniform. Nothing worth having, nowhere to hide, nowhere to go but back – back through hell to the trenches you came out of in the first place . . . "

"Ned, dear, you're overwrought. It's been such a terrible experience for you, a dreadful memory to live with. But it's over now, isn't it? You've done your bit, and now you've got to look forward, my dear, to plan for the future when the war's over."

". . . and by the time you get back to your own trenches, Simmie, half your men have gone – sprawling, dangling in the wire, lying in no-man's-land waiting for the rats and the magpies. It's obvious that the whole thing's been a waste, *a total bloody waste!* But nobody says so – they can't, can they? Later on they'll march you back to the Caves, what's left of you, for a bath and a brush-up, and a whole futile series of fatigue duties behind the lines while the Brass decides where to deploy you next.

You can't imagine then that you could ever go through it again, but you don't have any choice. Because they send you back quite soon to another part of the Front, always somewhere different, so you can never really know what you've gained or lost. Wound up like machines and pointed at the enemy. You keep on because the men expect you to, because they're the best, the very best, because the only honour in this bloody war is the honour between fighting men; and because you feel closer to them, somehow, than you've ever felt to anyone – even in bed, Simmie."

She coloured a little at that. "Meriel needs you too, Ned, and the boys," she put in quickly. "If you'd seen her, dear, as I saw her on the way over to Seaford to fetch you, I think even you might have been surprised. She throws up such a smokescreen, doesn't she? I think it's sometimes hard to guess what she's feeling, difficult to realize that she needs love and support as much as any of us do. Perhaps more, Ned?"

She had missed it, of course, even Simmie; totally missed the point. When he looked at her over the gate in her ludicrous hat and unsuitable London coat, with her hair in its usual state and her sweet uncomprehending face doing its utmost to frown, Ned realized the impossibility of making her understand, or any of them – ever.

"The war will be over soon, dear, I'm certain it will. Then you'll be able to settle down again and forget." She leant over impulsively to lay a gentle palm against his cheek. The wraith of a gesture that he'd once made in her parlour at Harpur Street a million years ago, and they smiled bleakly at each other in recognition of the memory.

"Four black Very lights," he told her. "Had you heard, Simmie? That's meant to be the signal for the end of the war, you know."

From behind the tall window of the Bury library, Ned followed the leisurely progress of a great Jack heron slowly rising into the upper air. The hills across the combe still glowed pale, as if the chalk within them had some luminous quality of its own, but the lower ponds and pools from which the heron had risen had long since surrendered to shadow. The flocks would be returning soon, with old Bat plodding in behind them.

As he turned back from the window, Ned saw the affirmation of his own thought in the wagging stump of Puck's tail.

"All right then, old fellow, let's go up and give him a hand. The books can wait one more day, and I daresay we could both do with the exercise, eh?"

Outside at the edge of the drive a couple of blackbirds were sparring noisily amongst the fallen leaves, too preoccupied with their own territorial battle to notice the man and the dog pass by. There were still scarlet rosehips and grey beards of clematis on the briars and vines of the lower slopes. But the early frosts had robbed the hills themselves of their wildflowers – and of their merry little blue butterflies, dormant now in their chrysalids beneath the grass stems.

With the harvest safely in, Shad had already begun to plough up the old Rough with Ab'ram, Shem, Caesar and Flook, the only working team that still remained to them. The new furrows showed white across the valley, packled with flint and chalk, and Ned privately doubted that Meriel's ryegrass ley could ever be persuaded to take there successfully. If the land had been worth salvaging, Grandfather Ashby would never have allowed it to tumble-down to couch in the first place. By now, years of flintpicking, sheep-folding and dung-clatting would surely have converted it into something worthwhile? But Meri would find that out soon enough for herself, with her first crop of thistles in the spring!

The ewes and tegs were still grazing, sharing the turf with flocks of starlings and migrating shore birds, dotterels and sand-pipers busily working over the insects and chrysalids that the sheep exposed. Arable encroachments and trends towards a larger type of sheep had reduced the number of flocks on the hills quite alarmingly since the beginning of the war, but not here in Sellington, where Bat and his Southdowns still ruled supreme.

The old shepherd never waved or moved in any way to acknowledge your approach when you climbed to him in his downland kingdom. He simply waited. Seeing him standing there so patiently in his grand old cavalry cloak, the toes of his ancient boots curling up to the sky, Ned knew suddenly why he had come and what it was that he wanted to hear.

"Bat."

"Mus Ned." A brief, jerking Sussex nod and a briefer glance from the deepset grey eyes, while beside him his old bobtail silently exposed her fangs at the inoffensive Puck.

"Thought you might like a hand to bring 'em down, now that you and Lass are on your own?" They both recognized the fatuousness of the statement. Bat had lost his teg boy, his grandson Jemmy, on the first day of the Somme. But he'd coped on his own and without apparent difficulty, before and since. So he simply nodded again at Ned, still waiting.

"I wanted to talk to you, Bat. I wanted you to understand why, why I've got to go back to France. Because I'm damn sure nobody else will."

The sagacious grey eyes looked out steadfastly across the valley – waiting still.

"I feel an obligation to the men who're still out there." Ned indicated the Gap and the Channel, and the distinctive sausage-shape of a patrolling Sea Scout airship from the Royal Naval Air Station at Willingdon. "The best chance most of them have of seeing Blighty now is to get wounded. Perhaps if they really got lucky and lost an arm or a leg, they might even be allowed to stay at home like me. That's what they all want, you know, a nice 'Blighty one' to send them home. They dream about places like Sellington, talk about them all the time, but they have to stay and fight. There's no choice for them, do you see?"

"Yus, Mus Ned, I rackon I do."

"When they sent me home, Bat, none of them begrudged it me. They all said they were sorry about my father, as if death wasn't all around them, and slapped me on the back, and told me to give their love to Blighty." Ned swallowed hard, stooping to collect a pebble of chalk from the bostal path, to juggle it rapidly from one hand to the other.

"There's another big show brewing out there, Bat, that's what they're all saying. Perhaps even the biggest show of all, the final push. And I just don't think I could bear for them to finish it now without me. I've got to be there. Does that sound daft?"

Waiting for the shepherd to answer was like waiting for the chalk hills themselves to speak. The pebble was already sticky with sweat, and Ned hurled it from him far out into the valley. They both watched it fall.

"Nope." Bat spoke at last as the chalk dropped out of the sunlight and into the anonymous shadows, following it with an eloquent flash of his own spittle. "No dafter, anyways, than settin' still in Sel'ton when y'er itchin' ter bannick they Germin varmunts from 'ere ter Sally'onicker. Now than, I niver did 'old wiv anybuddy jackin' in a job afore it were 'arf finished. Doan' matter whad et is – t'ent the way ter do et an' niver wus."

The old man's far-sighted gaze contracted from the flight of the chalk pebble to somewhere within himself, as he reached down into his own arsenal of maxims and proverbs for something appropriate.

"Ef I 'ad store, by shi'p an' fold I'd give yer gold, Mus Ned. But since I'm poor, by crook an' bell I'll wish yer well! You be right 'nough, boy."

Bat had always been a great one for proverbs. But he very rarely smiled. As he did so now, to reveal a crooked collection of tombstone teeth interspersed with expanses of pink gum, a sudden gust of wind ruffled the fleeces of the sheep on the slope above them and sent the shore birds flapping into the air.

Chapter Twenty-Six

As he'd anticipated, Ned had to fight every step of the way back to his old battalion in France. The family hadn't scrupled to enlist the official support of the War Agricultural Committee once again in their efforts to keep him in England; and in the end it had taken a directive from the War Office itself to release him. At the Base in Étaples they'd insisted on taking the time to retrain him to operate with the improved Mark IV tanks that had proved so successful at Cambrai the previous autumn. And what with one thing and another it was March of 1918 before the powers-that-be were finally persuaded to return him to his regiment.

At first Meriel blankly refused to believe that he could even contemplate abandoning her and the children a second time. He'd clearly discharged his duty to the wretched country already, nobody could say he hadn't, or even think it. Then, when she saw that he could be neither shamed nor bullied out of his preposterous notion, she'd marshalled her own opposing forces – Gran and the boys, Simmie, Helly, the Agricultural Committee, even the estate trustees – anyone with any kind of interest in keeping him home. And finally, when all else failed, she herself totally refused to speak, even to look at him for the whole of the last miserable day they'd spent together in England.

It had been childish, unworthy of Meriel to send him away

like that, but the fact that he understood the fear and the wounded pride that made her act that way, hadn't prevented Ned from feeling the weight of her rejection like a great crushing burden across his shoulders. A burden that grew heavier with every mile that he put between them.

He wrote to her from Étaples, a gentle, loving treatise defending himself as best he could and recording for all time the depth and breadth and constancy of his love for her. But in her reply she refused to acknowledge much more than the material facts, setting the tone for all her future letters with a brisk head-in-the-sand domestic bulletin that made him smile ruefully, even as it twisted the dagger in the wound.

> The Bury, Sellington
> March 7th 1918

My dear old Pook-noodle,

Well here we are again then, in spite of everything, with you gallivanting off round France on this fool's errand of yours, and me staying home to do what *really* needs doing – and the Base censors utterly baffled as usual by the lack of any definite information of any kind in your letters!

Your effort of the 3rd arrived this morning well up to time, and of course clean as a whistle as far as the purple pencil was concerned (although I must say I don't feel very happy about perfect strangers reading all that rather personal stuff you go in for). You may not be exactly enjoying yourself over there at the Base, Noggin, and whose fault is *that,* may I ask?! But be thankful at least that you're out of harm's way. I'm sure I am.

The answer to your (one sensible) question is yes we're still finding the rations quite adequate, thank you, or would do if I had charge of them! Some things remain in short supply, of course, but it was *absurd* of G.M. to say that I couldn't have sugar on that pudding! We've been using golden syrup on most things recently, and should certainly have saved *pounds* of the stuff by now. It's a great mistake, I think, to give Cook control of the supplies, because I'm convinced that it's she and Gertrude who use them up. Even so, we're still a great deal better off than most. The only 'meat' that some people can afford now is offal or macaroni flavoured with Bovril (can you imagine?)! And when you think what everyone else has to fork out on dairy products and that filthy margarine, you can see how *dead right* I was, Ned, to insist on those extra milking cows. It's all milk, nowadays, the United Dairies will take everything we can produce now, and more.

If only your blessed old army would hurry up and put an end to this beastly war, then perhaps we could have our men home where they belong and get things back onto some kind of an even keel again over here. Don't take this the wrong way, Noggin, but you know it does so *spoil* a man to get involved with all this military tomfoolery. I've always said it. It seems to me that after a time all soldiers begin to think of themselves as little tin gods (and everyone knows that army officers are always perfectly *ghastly* when they're old!), and I shouldn't at all like that to happen to you . . .

Saddening as Ned found it, Meriel's written style was hardly a surprise. In his more philosophical moments at Étaples he was even able to draw some comfort from the typical matter-of-factness of her letters. And he wasn't to know, because nobody told him, that she herself carried his letters around the farm with her – reading and re-reading them until they parted at the folds.

The pain involved in his eventual reunion with his unit was something else that Ned had not anticipated. He guessed from his Movement Order that the battalion must now be somewhere in the line well to the north of Arras and Monchy le Preux. In the event he found them entrenched between Armentières and the old 1915 battlefield of Neuve-Chapelle, enduring a fierce bombardment from superior enemy positions on Aubers Ridge. It was a familiar enough situation, with the usual routine of trench reliefs and working parties behind the lines, the usual gloomy labyrinths of mud and wire and rotting sandbags. But for Ned the whole atmosphere of the battalion had changed. In the protracted battle of Cambrai that followed Monchy, more than a third of their number had been killed or wounded – so many friendly faces gone. Now he felt estranged in some way from those old comrades-in-arms who still remained – by the signs of strain he could detect in them, by the things they'd had to endure while he walked free on the Sellington hills or lay clean beside Meriel in the big lotus bed. Time seemed to have accelerated in his absence. He felt like Rip Van Winkle returning to strangers where once there'd been friends – closer now to death than he'd ever felt before, even going over the top.

On March 21st, long before Ned could personally feel that he'd earned it, the battalion was marched back from the Front. Only to be informed on arrival at their rest area, that the long awaited German counter-offensive had begun with a terrific bombardment that morning on a forty-mile front south from Vimy Ridge. Jerry had transferred hordes of troops from the Russian Front, it was said, in a final attempt to smash Allied resistance before the Americans could arrive in force.

Two days later, amidst blasphemous rumours of British defeat, Ned's battalion received its orders to dump all surplus stores and kit and to prepare for an immediate move south.

"They've 'ad a bloody cave-in down there," a lance corporal in Ned's platoon commented gloomily. "So now I s'pose they'll be wantin' us for effin' pit-props!"

A battered column of London motor buses awaited them on the Lillers-St Pol highway, at the end of a fifteen-mile night march past growing munition dumps and hastily constructed stretches of fresh back-up rail. The moon was sufficiently bright to make the larger Brigade convoy they were joining an obvious target for enemy aircraft, and as they approached they saw bombs exploding in the fields on both sides, with furious retaliation from their own Archies. They watched and noted, but they didn't stop marching, or singing, as they moved up to climb aboard the buses. 'Sussex by the Sea' they sang, and 'Mademoiselle from Armentières', and 'Tipperary' the best of all the marching songs, in defiance of Jerry and Brigade H.Q. and the worst that anyone could do to them.

Singing with his own unit at the very top of his voice, Ned experienced at last the relief of coming home. It was a strange thing, but at that moment his love for Meri and the children, even the probability of death or injury in the coming show, seemed less important than the old reassurance of feeling at one with the splendid men he'd come back to lead.

At the village of Pernes, no more than three or four miles down the road, the entire convoy halted to take cover from hostile aircraft. From the window of a half-ruined cowshed, Ned and his platoon sergeant watched helplessly as an unlucky bomb reduced the bus in which they'd been travelling to an inferno of blazing paintwork. Crammed with the best part of their platoon into a repair lorry barely large enough to hold half the number, they chugged along behind at the end of the column to St Pol, where once again they were forced to take cover from enemy planes. This time their overheated vehicle refused to co-operate altogether when they returned to it, delaying them for over an hour while the mechanics cursed and scalded themselves and attempted to bandage a fractured radiator hose with someone's webbing straps. Meanwhile, the Brigade column lumbered on and away into the night, and it was only when the repair lorry was finally cool enough to proceed, that it was discovered nobody on board actually knew where the Divisional rendezvous was supposed to take place.

"Bound to be Albert, Sir," the driver said, automatically addressing himself to Ned as the senior officer. "Everythin' always ends up in Albert sooner or later, an' if you take my advice, Sir, that's where you'll 'ead us now."

Ned took his advice, for want of any better. It was common knowledge that in the past few days Jerry had regained most of the ground he'd lost in his retreat to the Hindenburg Line the previous spring, and had now reached the line of the old 1916 battlefields. If Albert had been the centre of Allied operations for the first Somme show, it was a fair bet then that it would be performing the same function now.

From St Pol they crawled south against a never-ending stream of oncoming traffic – foot soldiers with French civilians among them, motor ambulances, draft horses, mules and every kind of limber and transport vehicle the army possessed – tangled into mammoth traffic jams in Frévent and Doullens, where westbound streams from Vimy and Arras intersected. An army in retreat, creeping on through the grey turn-of-the-world time between dark and dawn – bloodstained limbs protruding from the backs of ambulances, draft animals flayed and spattered with congealed blood, senior officers in staff cars slumped glassy-eyed, Lords of Creation no longer. Behind them motor lorries were stacked with the luxurious furnishings of Corps Headquarters, while the walking-wounded slipped and stumbled along on foot as best they could. The appalling seriousness of the situation was apparent more than anywhere else in the condition of the Tommies themselves – many of them without rifles or steel helmets, all of them haggard, bleary, demoralized even beyond the reserves of humour that had sustained them for so long.

"Are we downhearted?"

"Yes – yes we are."

The retreating army called out to Ned and his men as they passed – news of Péronne and Bapaume falling to the enemy, rumours of a long-range gun already shelling Paris, half-expressed fears of numberless hosts of grey uniforms advancing up the *pavée* behind them. "'Fousands an' 'fousands of 'em, mate! Can't 'ardly 'ope to 'old 'em back now!" And unstated in the drained hopelessness of their faces was the unthinkable thought that, despite the Americans, the war might already be lost.

They entered Albert through a crazy tangle of splintered wood where once there'd been a poplar avenue. Here and there, where an individual tree had escaped destruction Ned recognized the untidy shapes of magpies' nests in the upper branches. And sidling slyly into his mind came the hideous thought that this season, this spring of 1918, it could well be his flesh and the flesh of those who rode with him to the Somme that would go to nourish the fledgeling brood.

The centre of the town was frantic with hurrying figures and wheeled traffic, converging with dire results from a knot of seven or more approach roads. Spirals of dark smoke rose from the ruined villas and factories to the east, where howitzer shells were still falling. The air was thick with brickdust, the streets strewn with the débris of a major bombardment – rubble, horses dead and dying in the shafts of stranded transport waggons – and human bodies, boneless rag dolls in khaki and black, abandoned wherever they had fallen on the pavements and in the gutters. In the Place d'Armes the red-tabbed Staff Officer they were hoping to find actually charged up to them of his own volition, brandishing a brass Very pistol and panting like a blown heifer.

"Never mind the 12th Division! The Boche have broken through, they're up the road in Beaumont-Hamel! That's the score, boys!" he shouted wildly. "So now it's up to us to stop 'em! Halt the advance, boys! We've got to halt the advance!"

"Take it easy, old man, we'll stop them all right." Ned was as anxious to reassure his own men as to calm down this poor fellow. "Just tell us where we can find the 36th Infantry Brigade H.Q., if you've heard, and leave the Hun to us." He injected as much firmness and confidence into his voice as he could, and something of it must have communicated itself, because the Staff Officer stopped waving his arms about and peered at him through the windshield, as if he'd just recognized him as a face he knew.

"Henencourt, Warloy," he muttered jerkily, ". . . first right turn off the Amiens road, to Lavieville." The next moment, to everyone's embarrassment, he began to whimper like a child.

Above them, high on the spire of the basilica of Notre Dame de Brébières, the famous Leaning Virgin of Albert seemed ready at last to plunge down into the ruins of the Place. Since the town's first bombardment in early 1915, and for more than three years of war on the Somme, she had remained poised head-down in a diving position with her gilded babe held out before her. A story had gone round amongst the soldiers who'd marched out beneath her to the Front, a legend that her final descent would bring with it the end of the war. And in the shambles of the British retreat, with the enemy shells still crashing in on the town, another tiny sly voice in the depths of Ned's consciousness was telling him now that it could be true.

It was raining at The Bury, a fine drizzle dripping from the trees and damping Meriel's hair. She didn't care about rain, she never had. As a child in Queensland she'd learned to think of the Wet as the benevolent sponsor of growth and new life; and even if English rain never did quite know when to stop, it had to be good for the land after such a dry, mild March. It had brought the primroses on, in any case, and the cowslips, to join the daffodils on the drive and the glossy little celandines – all the early yellow heralds of springtime. The anemones in the wood had done well too this year, a veritable galaxy of white blossoms, anticipating the greater glory of the bluebells that were budding beneath. As she hurried up the path to the Bury-house, the little flowers clutched at Meriel's boots and at the hem of her twill overalls, smothering them in white petals.

She didn't ask herself why she was climbing all this way in the rain. She could have read Ned's letter uninterrupted in the library, or up in the Flat, or in any number of places about the farm. God knows the staff weren't that numerous, nowadays! She'd done it on the spur of the moment, intercepting the postwoman on her way up from the yards, and continuing on through the wood almost without thinking.

She would read the letter aloud to G.M. and the family later – omitting the hot bits of course – but not yet. Not until she'd kept it to herself for a little while, to suck out every last drop of love and comfort that it held for her personally. And somehow today in the rain the Bury-house was just the place for it.

There was a little Field Service postcard with the letter, postmarked for April 2nd, only four days ago. And because everyone in England knew of the desperate counter-offensive that was now being fought in France, she stopped to read the card right away with the rain dripping down her collar. On the back there was the usual exhortation in printed officialese:

> NOTHING is to be written on this side except the date and the signature of the sender. Sentences not required may be erased. *If anything else is added the postcard will be destroyed.*

Ned, gloriously, had crossed out all the options for being sick or wounded! All he'd left for her was 'I am quite well' (with the 'quite' illegally underlined), and 'Letter follows at first opportunity'. And he'd signed it Nogginissimo, the idiot, with the date April 1st '18 'All Fools' day.

Meriel bent over it for a time, ignoring the rain, studying every dear stroke of his pencil for some clue as to the way he'd looked, the way he felt when he sent it. Then she slipped it into her pocket with the unopened letter and continued on through the wood.

'I am *quite* well.' That meant 'quite safe', didn't it? 'And thank God for that,' she thought as she reached the Bury-house steps. 'Thank God he's safe! I don't care if they do break through to the Channel ports – I don't even care if they beat us in the end – just so long as my Ned's safe and unhurt!'

The Bury-house was derelict and dismal in the wet. Part of the ceiling had come down that winter, littering the bench and table with plaster and bits of old birds' nests. Ivy crept out across the floor, and a vigorous growth of elder had already half obscured the famous view of the valley. But Meriel didn't notice. Sweeping a clear space for herself to sit down, and lighting a Gold Flake with trembling fingers, she fished out the letter and ripped it open. It had been written on Monday March 25th, a full week before the Field Service card.

My darling, darling girl,

No letter from you to answer, unfortunately, and it will probably be some little time, I fear, before you get another from me. It really isn't my fault, darling. Please understand. We are quite cut off from the mails on the move, you see.

Tonight as I write this, we are in billets behind the lines and ready to move again in the morning. We have been told to get rid of practically all our personal belongings (including that good camp bed of mine), and I'm afraid the next few days are likely to prove a fair sort of Hades for our Div. As you will have read in your newspapers, the old Boche is in a pretty desperate mood now – so it's no good expecting any real respite for a while. We have had one or two shells down here near our billets this afternoon, but none have burst really close. In fact it's almost quiet, considering.

The men are all very scattered, most of them in the fields under canvas. But my servant, Rogers, and I are going to be sleeping in the attic of an old French farmhouse tonight, with the Padré and one or two other officers as neighbours – in real beds, with clean sheets! I can hardly believe it! The village here has been knocked about a bit and is now deserted, but this little farm has hardly been touched. From the window where I am sitting I can see three speckle-faced cows tethered to pasture on some rough grass beyond the yard wall (three old friends!), and on my side of the wall a group of bantams scratching around the maxon. There's a big walnut tree, too, and a fine old flint dovecot like a miniature oast house all complete with birds (although how they've survived an army of hungry Tommies, I can't think!). I can hear them now, just like English pigeons, such a peaceful sound.

The family who farm here are rather splendid, I think, like so many others I've met in this area. Madame and Marthe, who still work in the fields in their kilted-up skirts and ploughman's boots, and Marie with her hair still in ties, and little Jean-Baptiste, the man of the family now, asleep in his cradle in the kitchen. The farmer, who was Madame's son and Marie's husband and the father of the two children, was killed two years ago at Verdun, but the women mean to keep on exactly as they had before. As if the war around them were no more than a severe freak of the weather that had taken to sowing their land with jags of iron. They work on in the fields as if the din of cannonading and the drone of aeroplanes was as normal as a squabble of rooks or a flight of pesky starlings. And they treat us soldiers so well too, darling, as if it were we and not they who were suffering the most. I only wish I could make up to them just a little of what the Boche and our own politicians and generals have between them managed to destroy . . .

"Oh God, how typical! As if . . . as if . . . !" Meriel flicked the page over in exasperation. How typical of Ned to waste his sympathy on a bunch of ignorant peasants, when he should be thinking of his own safety, and his own family, for heaven's sake, worrying themselves half to death over him back at home.

Where was the wretched farmhouse, anyway? She ran her eye swiftly down the close-written pencil lines to find the place-name code that Ned had concocted with his grandmother – to be commenced with the name of a fictitious farm labourer and completed with the phrase 'I would advise'. And there it was halfway down the fourth page, plain as a day too, to all it seemed but the obtuse army censor:

As regards instructions for old Jim, sow all our barley on leys, I would advise. It's by far the best plan . . .

'Last letter of word following name,' Meriel repeated the cipher to herself while she scrabbled around on the floor for her own used matchstick to mark the letters with. 'Then first, third and fourth letters of the words following, and first, third and fourth again to the end of the message'.

Let's see: . . . so<u>w</u> <u>a</u>ll ou<u>r</u> bar<u>l</u>ey <u>o</u>n le<u>y</u>s . . . w – a – r – l – o – y . . . Warloy! So that's where he was. She'd look it up on the big map on the library wall as soon as she got back to the house.

Ned left his farmhouse billet near Warloy on the morning of March 26th. By the morning of April 6th, as Meriel climbed up through the wood to the Bury-house, he was crouching in the scrape of discoloured chalk that called itself the front line trench, on a ridge to the west of Albert. It was ten days now since Jerry had crossed the River Ancre, but the war wasn't over. The Leaning Virgin of Albert still clung to her steeple above the Place d'Armes, while the British stubbornly held the line of chalk hills that rose above the river to the west.

In the defences of Aveluy Wood and Bouzincourt village, Ned's battalion had been stretched like a piece of tired elastic, looped in, cobbled up wherever they were most needed along the Front, wherever the bombardment was most intense – until eventually their fighting strength had been reduced to little more than that of a single company. In a week Ned had seen more men die than in any other month of the war, including the battle of Arras. Friends, comrades, men with the same physical aspirations and fears as he, crumpling beside him in the trenches – falling face-down in the mud, silent or tensed in one last long scream for life, bloody or outwardly unmarked – dying all around him. In all probability, today or tomorrow, sometime soon his turn would come too. He accepted that now as everyone did, because it was the only way to face what they had to face and remain sane. And if he had to die, it was only fitting, Ned thought, that it should be here on the Somme, where he'd first heard the sound of the guns from Sellington Gap.

"*But what happened to his babies when he died?* . . . "
Patrick's little humming bird, Patrick's anxious little face. Ned
closed his eyes, unwilling, unable to think it out. The bombardment would begin again at any minute. As he opened his eyes
he quite expected to see the first flash down at the foot of the
scarp, to hear a split second later the sound of the first explosion.
You could see clear to Albert from the lip of the trench, despite
the drifting rain in the valley and the sunlight that pierced it.
There really ought to be a rainbow somewhere.

Meriel stubbed her cigarette out on the stone bench and
crammed Ned's letter back into its envelope. If only he could
see her as she was now, looking out over his beloved valley
from the top of the Bury-house steps, with the wind in her face
and the collar of her overalls turned up against the rain.

"Don't die, Noggin!" Her thought was spoken aloud like a
prayer, and feeling the tears swimming in her eyes she blinked
deliberately to make them fall. She wished he could see that
too, Meriel crying for him just like any other idiotic war wife!

'I've never told him how frightened and alone I'd be without
him,' she thought. 'I've never really told him anything in my
letters. But I will! I'll write to him this afternoon, and tell him,
all of it, every damn thing.'

The clamour of the bombardment quickened to a drumming in
Ned's ears, too loud, one would have thought, too continuous,
to distinguish the individual signature tunes of Flying-Pigs and
Weary-Willies. Yet he heard the leisurely rustle of the 5.9 quite
clearly. He looked up to see the sunlight on its polished surface
as it came in to find him, And something passive at the centre
of his fear accepted his own death.

"Christ!" It was the last word he was ever to utter.

Meriel, pacing slowly down the Bury-house steps in the rain,
was chanting to herself the little rhyme that he'd once taught
her there:
    "Hey diddle derry, dance round the Bury . . . "

Ned actually heard the sound of the shell thudding into the

chalk beside him and had time to thank God it was a dud after all. Then a roaring, blinding inferno of heat and light and searing pain consumed him. He was conscious of being flung upwards and backwards, the muscles of his arms and legs convulsed and rigid, before something heavy and silent blotted out his memory of the event – then and forever.

A few minutes later a young soldier of the 5th Royal Berks slithered down into the crater. As he stumbled onto Ned's body, he registered with revulsion that the lower part of his face had been partially blown away. In the bloody pulp of Ned's remaining features one eye was scorched and blackened. The other stared back at him in sightless astonishment, a clear unclouded blue.

"Poor beggar!" The man hesitated, distractedly casting around for cover. Before he could find it a second shell fell, to tear him as Ned had been torn, and to toss him lifeless into the mud.

Chapter Twenty-Seven

The bluebells were out early that spring, and the whole wood was filled with their fragrance. Such an exquisitely limpid blue, Simmie thought, like pools of water, so lovely and yet so sad. They always reminded her of the days when she and Kit had first begun their solitary rambles in Richmond Park. She'd never forget that first spring, the year she met Robert Llewellen. She'd picked a great armful of bluebells in the woods around the Pembroke Lodge. How that perfume brought it all back! Burying her face in a mass of rustling bell flowers, hurrying down the hill, so eager to get home with them and to give them to Isobel. And how strange that they should still have the power to sadden her. All because Isobel had laughed at her gift of wild flowers and left them on the doorstep to wilt.

"Come on up here with us, Simmie! Come on, Gladdie's almost made it!" Robbie's gleeful voice soon put paid to any nostalgic nonsense of that kind; and Simmie looked up gratefully to where he stood, on the very top of the lopsided structure they'd just completed. Poor Gladys was clinging desperately to the last shreds of her professional dignity, and to an old rick-ladder propped against its side.

The Hut in the Bury wood was a well-established tradition dating back to Walter Ashby's childhood, when he and his cousins had first built themselves a bivvy-house there out of dead branches and sycamore saplings, and roofed it with turfs from the bank. And when Margaret Ashby consented to make an opening ceremony speech from the roof of an improved version a few years later at bluebell time, the Hut's future as an institution had been assured.

"Come on, hurry *up*, Simmie! Great-Grannie'll be along any minute, and we've jolly well got to make sure the roof's strong enough for her, haven't we, Pat? 'Cos she's beastly heavy, and I think she might fall through!"

Patrick at the foot of the ladder squealed with delight at the idea of his revered great-grandparent slowly subsiding through the roof of the 1918 Hut. The two little Belgian boys, who imitated everything he did, both began to giggle too as a matter of course. Gladys, meanwhile, seized the opportunity of making good her escape.

"Gawd a'mighty, I'll swear it's like tryin' ter ride a bloomin' fruit jelly up there!" she declared. "You kin test it fer the young article, Mum, an' welcome. 'Cos I'll tell yer straight, I ain't got no 'ead fer it!"

Simmie laughed. "No I'm sorry, Robbie," she said firmly, "wild horses wouldn't get me up there. I've seen what's holding that thing up, don't forget! And I'm afraid you boys will just have to face the fact that Mrs Ashby won't be coming up either this year. I really don't think it would be safe on that roof for any grown-up, let alone a lady as old as your Great-Grannie."

"Stuff'n nonsense!" Margaret Ashby's bass voice a foot or so from her ear nearly frightened poor Simmie out of her wits.

"The day that an Ashby child fails to build a Hut strong enough to support my weight, Miss Sims, will be a sad day for The Bury, I can tell you! And thank you very much, but I'm not altogether ready for the scrap heap just yet. Come along down now, Robert, and make way for the old lady!" Only waiting for her great-grandson to slither to the ground, she thrust her blackthorn stick into Simmie's hands and began her slow ascent of the rick-ladder.

From below, Mrs Ashby senior made a fearfully imposing spectacle in her long black silk and gold chains and best tricorn hat, climbing like some latter-day martyr to a certain and terrible doom. As the supporting branches groaned and crackled beneath her, the small boys at the foot of the ladder confronted each other with round eyes and madly flickering grins.

"She *is* going to fall through, Pat, I know she is!" Robbie whispered excitedly. But miraculously she didn't. In an impressive act of faith she stepped straight off the top of the ladder and onto the sagging turf – staggering, but regaining equilibrium superbly as she launched herself straight into her customary bazaar-opening speech.

"Ladies and gentlemen," she bellowed through the bluebell wood, "we are foregathered this afternoon for a *most important event* in the Sellington calendar." She paused dramatically to survey her audience – four small boys on Easter holiday, an elderly spaniel, a middle-aged spinster and her maid, the bemused and bespectacled Belgian couple who'd escorted her up from the house, and Meriel, striding up behind them in her working overalls, impatiently knotting and ravelling the cotton bandana she'd just removed from her hair. Only Helen, absorbed with her Supply Dêpot and canteen work, was absent – and Ned of course, somewhere in the turmoil of the German counter-offensive across the Channel.

"Now I've seen a good many Huts built in this wood in my time," Margaret Ashby continued with thunderous emphasis, "and with a few regrettable exceptions, they've all of 'em been well up to the mark, I consider. However, I'm sure you will agree with me, ladies and gentlemen, that this year's effort is somethin' in the nature of an engineerin' triumph!" She paused again, swaying ever so slightly as she bent her steel blue gaze on Simmie. "A round of applause would be in order I think for our intrepid builders – Masters Patrick and Robert Ashby . . . "

The little boys flushed and squirmed with pleasure at such public recognition, while their mother gave her bandana head-scarf another violent twist.

". . . with able assistance, I must add, from Messieurs Gaston and Bruno Waedemon, and from Miss Beatrice Sims . . . "

"Oh Lord!" Meriel rolled her eyes skywards and wrenched the bandana into a knot that Simmie could see would take positively ages to undo. "Look, be a brick and send Gladys down to buck Gertie up with the tea things would you, Simmie? God only knows what those girls will have got up to in the dairy by the time I get back to them, and at the rate G.M.'s going we'll be here half the afternoon!"

This was a little inconsiderate of Meriel, knowing as she did of the friction that still existed between Gladys and the Bury indoor staff. But Gladys had gone anyway, marching as to war through the bluebells, to reappear stern-first a few minutes later, backing up the path on the forward end of Gertrude's tea hamper. What a pity it was, Simmie thought, that servants invariably found it so much harder to adjust to each other than to their employers.

Yet as she watched the two maids struggling up through the wood with that absurd great hamper, Simmie sensed a new phase in the conflict that had been simmering below-stairs for the past few months. How extraordinary! Only this morning these two had been daggers-drawn, manufacturing grievances out of silver polish and boot-blacking; and now here they were, not only co-operating with their awkward burden, but actually talking as they came – discussing some serious topic like two old cronies!

The explanation arrived with the final blast of Mrs Ashby's invective, when Gertrude carefully set down her end of the hamper and edged across to Meriel, the rictus of a nervous smile twitching at the corners of her mouth.

". . . And so it is with great pleasure, ladies and gentlemen, that I declare this year's Hut – *well and truly open!*"

The birdsong in the wood suddenly ceased. The Waedemons' solid backs hid the yellow telegram from the old lady as it passed from Gertrude's hand to Meriel's. But Simmie saw it; to re-live the moment of numbing fear that she'd experienced in September with the arrival at Harpur Street of Meriel's black-bordered letter. This time she knew there could be little hope of a reprieve.

Meriel opened the telegram immediately, without a moment's hesitation, and the next instant she turned on her friend with such vehemence that Simmie actually let out a little squeak of apprehension.

"Well you can wipe that barmy, suffering-angel expression off your face for a start, Simmie!" she said, throwing up her head defiantly. "It says he's missing, have you got that, *missing!* So just don't start trailing round behind me telling me he's dead. Because, whatever the War Office likes to presume, I know that he *isn't!*"

For Simmie, the weeks that followed the building of the Hut in the bluebell wood were one long nightmare of worry. From the day they received the telegram that declared Ned MISSING PRESUMED DEAD, she watched Meriel intently – determined to take her cue from her. But in the end all she had been able to do was worry, because she wasn't constitutionally capable of Meriel's kind of optimism.

"Tommyrot, he is *not* dead!" Meriel repeated it after milking that first evening in a voice that left no room for argument, and at the same time she scooped up a Lafayette studio portrait of Ned in his second lieutenant's uniform, to thrust it beneath Simmie's inoffensive nose. "Look at that if you don't believe me! Go and look at the clothes in his wardrobe! Go and look at Puck – go on, look! And if you still think he's dead, Simmie, then I don't want to hear it!"

Simmie looked sadly at the calm and the lovingkindness in Ned's posed photograph, and lied to her friend as convincingly as she could. 'After all,' she told herself, 'there's nothing really to say that she couldn't be right.'

It was true, certainly, that the news from France had been more confused and contradictory than ever, since the beginning of the German counter-offensive. In many places along the Front communications had entirely broken down; and in the absence of definite information, the War Office was always prepared to encourage hope. In recent weeks receiving hospitals on both sides of the Channel had been fairly flooded with casualties, they said, many of them still to be identified. As in any retreat numbers of prisoners, wounded or otherwise, had been taken by the enemy. In other words, there were thousands, tens of thousands of men still to be accounted for. One of them could be Ned, it wasn't impossible. If only Meriel wasn't so totally unprepared for the alternative. If only she'd make some allowance for how the others felt; for the two little boys who so desperately needed her love and reassurance, now more than ever.

But Meriel made no allowances. So certain was she of her husband's survival that she left the daily scanning of *The Times'* casualty lists to his grandmother, grim-faced in her upstairs sitting room; to Helen any tears to be shed over premature letters of sympathy from well-meaning friends and relatives. She even scorned to pray for Ned's deliverance, as the rest of her family and the Bury servants did regularly at Prayers in the breakfast room each morning.

Every minute she could spare from the farm she spent in the library at her father-in-law's old desk composing appeals for the personal columns of the daily newspapers, and firing off written demands for information in all directions: to the War Office, to a cousin of Reggie Baxter's in the Foreign Office, to Ned's Colonel in France, even to the enemy via the Geneva Red Cross.

"Someone, somewhere knows where he is," she insisted. "And sooner or later I'm going to find them!"

In July the tide began to turn for the Allies. The German advance had been halted, then pushed back. In August Albert was reoccupied, with the gilded figure of its famous Virgin lying shattered in the ruins of the basilica; and through it all the Red Cross continued to pursue its enquires for missing persons. The name of Lieut. E. C. Ashby had been near the top of the long lists its Searchers carried from bed to bed through hospitals in France, England and Germany, from man to man on parade grounds and on troop trains and in prisoner-of-war camps from Westphalia to West Sussex. And there it remained, without annotations of any kind.

In September, at the end of a difficult harvest, The Bury foreman Shad Caldwell succumbed to the influenza epidemic that was sweeping across Europe, to die of pneumonia a fortnight later in a crowded annexe of the Victoria Hospital in Lewes. Shortly afterwards the official Bury estate trustees were granted legal control of the farm, *pro tempore*, on the presumption of Edwin Ashby's death.

Meriel, meanwhile, remained stubbornly unshaken in her belief. "You think what you like," she said, busy with the milk cooler. "I'm not creeping round like some snivelling war widow, not for you or anyone, Simmie. And if you aren't going to make yourself useful, I'd be grateful if you'd kindly clear out of the way before you make me go and knock something over."

Or down on the Rough, compressing her mouth to a thin line as she thrust and jabbed with her dodging-stick – felling a creeping thistle with every utterance: "Why can't you people *understand*? Why is it so damn *difficult*? He's got to come back, can't you *see*? There'd be no point *otherwise!*" She flourished the thistle-dodger in the general direction of The Bury and its farm buildings. "What good would this place be to any of us without him, answer me that!"

On the second Monday in November, with news of the Kaiser's flight to Holland still dominating conversation on the Seaford station platform, Simmie and Gladys took the first available train to London. It was a pilgrimage that they'd made at regular intervals over the past year, to air the house and collect any stray mail, and catch up on local gossip via Gladys' niece in Percy Street. A journey, Simmie felt, that even the War Office must recognize as 'essential'.

For Gladys, who'd left town under protest in the first place, these brief returns to the smoke were the very breath of life, something to sustain her through weeks of heathen Sussex. Each time their train pulled into Victoria, she sprang up to be the first to open the carriage door and breathe the sooty soul of the place into her lungs. But for Simmie, the sight of her home under dust sheets was invariably a depressing experience. She came to dread the sound of the lock turning over to her latchkey, the sight of stairs bare of carpets and rods, a front hall as dark and fusty as the entrance to some forgotten tomb.

Gladys was hopelessly circumscribed at The Bury and never allowed to do enough, and the house in Harpur Street represented a permanent challenge – a justification in a way for her whole existence. She happily blundered about, flinging windows open and rattling buckets, filling the silent rooms with the sound of her own voice.

"Will you look at the state o'this soap, Mum! Did you ever, 'arf et-up by mice, fer gracious sake! Artful little beggars! Well, I may as well finish it up on the kitchen, wouldn' you think? 'Start wiv the kitchen floor,' that's wot my ol' sister Eliza always said, 'once that's clean y'er 'arf way there, gel!'"

But for Simmie, alone on the first landing that grey November morning, her old home had become little more than a shell, a relic inhabited by the phantoms of another time. So many ghosts. Cécile Llewellen, emerging from the bathroom in a cloud of scented steam. So many young men – young soldiers in the making, pounding the stairs, shaking the house with their energy. Fat little Gussie. And George pestering her for his afternoon milk. Poor George, who'd gone missing again the day after arriving in Sellington – to be discovered at threshing time halfway through the wheat stack, so very dead, poor dear.

Simmie paused on the landing as she always paused. The parlour held the strongest memories, of course, and it was never easy to go in. It smelled of camphor mothballs now, no longer of potpourri. The old Kidderminster rug had been rolled and tied, and all the ornaments and photographs packed up and locked away. The light from her oil lamp showed distinct square patches of unfaded wallpaper where her favourite pictures had once hung, the Raphael Madonna and the view from Richmond Hill, and the lovely mauvey watercolour of Dartmoor by Widgery. The light fell on the empty fireplace where Ned had burnt Robert Llewellen's letter, and on the bare unpolished boards of the hearth where she'd first seen Ned himself, kneeling crimson-faced in the ruins of her mantelshelf.

Simmie had already left the parlour, hurrying back to the landing and the present, when a sudden explosion of air raid maroons pulled her up – echoed and re-echoed by others booming across the city.

'A daylight raid!' she thought, 'but it can't be!' Then she heard a commotion outside the front door, someone cheering, and Gladys came running up the stairs from the hall with a scrubbing brush in her hand and a look on her face that could only mean one thing.

"The war's over!" They both said it at once, just as everyone else was saying it in every other house, and down in the street, and in every other street – shopkeepers to their customers, cabbies to their fares, perfect strangers turning to each other on the pavements of Theobald's Road and Bloomsbury Square. "It's over – the war's over! Germany signed the Armistice at five o'clock this morning!" Nobody thought of saying "We've won the war!" because for the millions whose sons and husbands and brothers had died in that tragically mismanaged conflict, there was no victory.

Simmie was already crying. She'd been crying when she left the parlour. But as she waited to be crushed to her maid's bony bosom, she felt no sense of pleasure, no relief, nothing but a great weariness. All she could think of was a quotation she'd once heard, goodness knows where, flashing up into her mind like a cinema title: 'Nought's had, all's spent, when our desire is got without content.' Ned's four black Very lights – that was how she felt.

Outside, the crowds had already begun to gather, blowing whistles, beating tin trays, commandeering omnibuses and taxis, flocking back to Trafalgar Square and Buckingham Palace to hear the Guards' band playing 'Tipperary', just as they had in 1914.

'But how different they are today!' Simmie thought. There were no familiar muffin-men or organ-grinders in their ranks now. They'd all abandonded their occupations long since, or died, and precious few straw hats or butterfly collars either. Most of the men were in khaki or hospital blue, so many of them with crutches. Many of the women were in uniform too, of one kind or another, as WAACs and nurses, or as overalled munitions workers and office girls. They had their vote now, those that were over thirty. They could even sit in Parliament if they chose; and so many other barriers had fallen for the rest, for the younger girls amongst them, in their coloured overalls and abbreviated skirts. In November 1918 at the end of the war to end all wars, the kind of girl whose life and prospects could be ruined by a brief, reckless liaison with a married man was already a thing of the past.

Chapter Twenty-Eight

"I'm going to France then." Meriel tossed the statement across the bubble-and-squeak at the Bury dinner table the Sunday following the signing of the Armistice. "The Red Cross people are totally clueless, that's obvious. Why, they can't even trace their own Searchers half the time! And now the war's over, there's nothing I can see to stop me going over to find Ned myself."

"Nothin' but Lloyd George and the Military and the French Consulate and the Transport Officer at Folkestone," Margaret Ashby said sharply. "Don't be such a little muff, Meri. You know as well as I do that there isn't anythin' useful you could do over there. If the authorities are still turnin' back people like the Waedemons with homes to go to, they aren't likely to let you loose on the Continent, are they now?"

"I don't see why not." Meriel's chin was up. "It's no use making objections, G.M., because I'm going and that's it!"

"Might as well look for a thatchin' needle in a haystack," the old lady continued as if she hadn't heard her. "And in any case we're going to need you here on the farm, my girl, at least until I can get Goodworth demobbed. Frank Longhurst's finally agreed to send over a man to plough up the Brooks for us next week, and if it's that squab Swales you can be sure he'll want watchin' for depth every second turn."

"Then she'll just have to watch him herself, won't she?" Meriel remarked to Simmie as they boarded the early train for London the following morning. "She's perfectly capable, and it's high time G.M. realized that she can't go on relying on me to organize every damn thing around here – not when I've more important fish to fry."

It was almost the last thing on earth that Simmie herself would have chosen, to accompany Meriel on her one woman assault of the War Office. She'd always hated scenes and was scared to death of men in any kind of official capacity, but Meriel had decided she was to come, and of course it was useless to argue. So she simply sat quietly beside her in the railway carriage, like a woman on a tumbril, humming a thin little tune to herself to steady her nerves.

"Firmness, that's the great thing," Meriel was saying. "No good *asking,* for God's sake, or writing them letters for some idiot clerk to lose in the files. I've tried that and it doesn't work, Simmie. No, the only way's to face them man to man, and stick it on a bit if necessary, and be ready to kick up a shindy and smash up the furniture if all else fails!"

At the central War Office block in Whitehall they were required to complete a pink admission form, then sent on to an even more forbidding looking building in Northumberland Avenue where Meriel harangued everyone indiscriminately, until a junior officer finally escorted them up to a green-painted office on the second floor. The man behind the desk was a major, moustached and sandy, and punctilious in the courtesy with which he'd come forward to receive them and settle them into their chairs.

"Mrs Ashby, isn't it and Miss Sims? Won't you please sit down? I must apologise for keeping you waiting, but the truth is we're very short-staffed – this wretched Spanish 'flu, you know. Mind if I smoke? You won't, I take it? Well now, let's see, your husband was Lieutenant Edwin Charles Ashby of the 7th Royal Sussex?"

"*Is,*" Meriel corrected. "He *is* Edwin Charles Ashby. Still alive – I know that for a fact."

"Ah – quite so." The Major considered her for a moment over his glasses before returning to the file in front of him. "Reported missing, I see, on or about the sixth of April of this year . . . "

"Almost eight months ago," Meriel interrupted, scraping her chair on the oilcloth as she jerked it in closer to his desk, "and no news whatsoever since."

"Nothing at all?"

"Not a sausage." She stared at him accusingly with her obstinate chin in the air and the brim of her hat visibly trembling.

The Major cleared his throat. "Well, Mrs Ashby, you're entirely right, of course, to keep hoping. At this moment there are some thirty thousand British soldiers still officially designated as missing. And I have no doubt at all that many of them are still alive, in camps or hospitals, or even in transit . . . "

"Look, let's skip all this, shall we?" Meriel jumped up again impatiently to lean over him, palms flat on the leather surface of his desk. "I *know* that my husband's still alive, all right? And since no one else seems remotely capable of doing it, I intend to go out to France to find him myself. So I suggest you save us both a great deal of time and tell me how best to go about it."

The Major took off his reading glasses and began to massage the bridge of his nose slowly between forefinger and thumb. He was being most awfully tolerant, Simmie thought. "My dear Madam," he said wearily, "I am afraid that you have quite failed to grasp the situation we're having to cope with out there at present. It's an armistice that Germany's signed, not a peace treaty. So far as our Army's concerned we are still technically at war. Special cases aside, there's no intention as yet to demobilize our troops. So you see, private civilian travel is entirely out of the question. In fact the Secretary of the War Office has made a categorical announcement to the effect that civilian visits to war graves will be impossible for some months to come."

"Ye gods!" Meriel thumped the man's desk with such force that Simmie distinctly saw his silver inkstand jump several inches to the right. "Do you take me for a fool? If it was only a *grave* I was after, I wouldn't be here, would I? Can't you get it through your thick, military skull that my husband's out there somewhere, sick or incapacitated, waiting for us to *do* something; while you sit there on your fat khaki back-end and spout categorical-bloody-announcements at me!"

Simmie thought she might close her eyes for a little moment; it was the only means of escape open to her. By the time she felt ready to open them again, the Major had replaced his glasses and braced himself up in his chair to face the barrage – a trained soldier.

"You're naturally upset, Madam," he observed stiffly, "but please try to understand my position. Believe me I'd like to help you, but I really have no authority to issue you with a Special Passport for France. Any serious application would have to be made in writing, and in fact the final responsibility would lie with the Secretary of State for Foreign Affairs at the Foreign Office. However, I would advocate most earnestly . . . "

But Meriel was no longer listening. "The Foreign Office," she exploded, "now we're *getting* somewhere! For heaven's sake, why didn't you say so in the first place? I know someone there who'll sort this ridiculous business out for us in two shakes! Come along, Simmie." She wrenched the door open and was already halfway down the corridor before the punctilious Major could find his feet; and the next thing Simmie knew, she was hurrying back down Whitehall again, panting in her efforts to keep up.

"I'll give them 'categorical announcements'," Meriel threw over her shoulder as she strode on ahead. "Just you wait until I get my hands on that cousin of Reggie's in the Treaty Department, Simmie, then we'll hear some announcements all right!" And she wheeled in through the main entrance of the Foreign Office swinging her arms like bludgeons.

Harpur Street had been too depressing under dust sheets, so the two women put up that night at Meriel's Aunt Alice's in Pimlico; to return to the Foreign Office Treaty Department at three o'clock the following afternoon, to collect and sign for one special viséd passport for France.

"There you are, Simmie, what did I tell you?" Meriel said triumphantly as she forced the bulky document into her reticule. "Got to be firm with them you see, it's the only way."

From her terrorization of her brother-in-law's luckless cousin at the Foreign Office, Meriel had gone on to bully the Red Cross people at Carlton House Terrace into providing her with a letter of introduction to their French headquarters, at the Hôtel Christol in Boulogne. "Because that's where I'm starting, Simmie," she announced. "There's bound to be a matron or someone over there with lists of unidentified patients. So all I'll have to do, you see, is to work my way through them. And if Ned's there I'll find him all right, you can certainly depend on *that!*"

The loud, positive sound of her own voice had always been vastly reassuring to Meriel. "Action is what's needed." She repeated it aloud to herself from the deck of the Folkestone Packet. G.M. could call it a wild goose chase if she liked – *action*, that was the important thing! But then, from behind her mental image of Margaret Ashby's impassive face had appeared that of her own ten-year-old son, staring up at her anxiously from his pillow. And Patrick's voice: "You are going to find him – you are going to find Daddy, aren't you?"

Hastily Meriel swept the memory from her mind and stepped forward to grip the rail, peering through the rain for her first sight of France. "I'll find him all right," she muttered. "Of course I will." And it wasn't until the facts were actually staring her in the face that she permitted herself to grasp the true magnitude of the task before her.

"My dear, I really must make you understand that you have absolutely no hope of gaining access to all our 'unknowns'." The caped and striped Sister who received her at the Christol and gave her tea in the small common room there broke the truth as gently as she could. "We have thirty-five base hospitals over here now, and goodness only knows how many provisional evacuation units and field hospitals besides. If your husband was seriously wounded, I'll grant you that he could still be in one of them. We've two or three neurological cases in this unit who've been with us easily that long. But however could you hope to find him? I mean, just think, you'd have to visit each hospital individually, and almost every patient too – thousands, tens of thousands of them – because no one keeps central records of who's been identified and who hasn't. Why, it would take you months, dear; and by the time you'd got around, half the patients would have moved on, anyway."

"Well, do you have any here that I could look at – any 'unknown' patients I mean?" She wouldn't be put off by the logistics of the thing. She'd look wherever she could, that's all. And she could be lucky – she damn well *would* be lucky!

"Yes indeed we have, Mrs Ashby." The Sister was clearly

relieved to be moving from the general to the specific. "Uniforms and identity discs are all too easily mislaid in transit, I fear, we even get cases without medical labels. But of course you'll have to wear a mask. We're over-run with *grippe* – influenza you know – far worse killer than the Boche this season."

It was the same down the coast at Camiers and Étaples. Beds in the corridors, stretchers end-to-end in the aisles of the Nissens and tents and the rows of wooden hutments that served as wards; surgical units converted to medical wards, men wounded in action displaced from their cots to make way for more recent cases of influenza and bronchial pneumonia – and to create a human obstacle course for Meriel, threading her way between them.

In all the years of the war she'd invariably succeeded in thinking of 'the wounded' as the press depicted them, or as she herself had seen them sallying forth from their convalescent homes – cheerful, cheeky, making light of their crutches and empty pinned-up sleeves – too happy to be out of it and alive to reckon the cost. But for the patients in these French hospital wards life could be nothing more than a goal in view – something to be fought for through irrigation tubes and wads of blood-stained gauze, and an atmosphere already tainted with sepsis. She moved quickly from man to man, scanning the personal details at the foot of each cot or stretcher – looking for blond hair, for blue eyes – and after a little while, just looking.

"That one actually had a fragment of someone else's skull driven right through his spinal cord – hard to believe isn't it? And this man was alive with maggots when they found him." The professional detachment of the Charge-Sisters was almost harder to bear than the injuries themselves.

"Don't worry, dear, they can't possibly hear us, deaf as posts both of them. That's shell-shock – mustn't drop anything or make any kind of row around these chaps. Go through the roof at the slightest sound, poor things."

Meriel saw a number of men like that, jerking and convulsing as if an electric current was passing through them. She saw men with hacked-off stumps for limbs, men with blistered, suppurating skin and repulsively disfigured faces, men stripped of all human dignity. And by the time she emerged from the last foetid hutment of the 24th General at Étaples, she'd entirely convinced herself that Ned wasn't, could never have been, amongst the pathetic remnants of men that lay in these wards.

'It's not me. I can take it all right, I'm not afraid!' she told herself stoutly. 'Good heavens, if those little mice of nurses can cope with it, then I most certainly can!' But still she leant back against that last hut for a moment to breathe in the cold clean air, unconsciously brushing at her coat, as if the smell of pus and Jeyes Fluid was something physical that clung to the fabric.

A handsome, white-barred magpie rose up from the area between the huts where the nurses kept their disposal bins, and then another. Meriel watched them whirring up to their perches in the poplars; and she watched the leaves they dislodged, gold as guineas, fluttering and spinning to the ground.

'Oh yes, I can take it all right. Why, I could go through every stinking hospital ward in France if I had to! But what would be the point?' She asked herself the question in all seriousness. 'When I know damn well Ned's not going to be there.' She wasn't going to ask herself how she knew, or what she could possibly expect to find in his old trenches at Bouzincourt or his billet at Warloy after all these months. It was just that she had to see them for herself. She had to *do* something, something outside in the fresh air. And when she'd done it, when she stood where Ned had stood and looked down from that farmhouse window in Warloy – well then, then perhaps she'd know. Because that's how it had always been with Meriel; she'd travel any distance, go to almost any length to avoid the shortest excursion through the unexplored areas of her own mind.

The following afternoon, in an hour and a half of deadly boredom on Abbéville station, she shared a bench and a conversation with two young Graves Registration Officers returning to their unit at Corbie. By the time their train reached Amiens, she'd extracted promises of practical assistance from both of them. And true to their word they'd drawn up outside her hotel the next morning in a splendid great Ford ambulance, with a red cross and '4 *assis*, 3 *couchés*' painted on the side.

They could take her to Warloy, they said, *en route* to some necessary survey work at the village cemeteries there; and if she didn't object to a bit of practical fieldwork along the way, they might even manage the trench system at Bouzincourt as well.

The pair had been employed on graves registration work since the reorganization of the Imperial War Graves Commission back in 1917. Inured as they were to the business, neither man could have any conception of the effect the Somme battlefield might have on someone like Meriel Ashby, whose solution to anything unacceptable had invariably been to look the other way. They planned a circular route around Albert, through Fricourt and Contalmaison, up into the battered chalk hills between the Somme and Ancre rivers, where two of the most violent convulsions of the war had combined to produce a new kind of landscape.

Sitting between them in the open cab of the ambulance, with the rain wetting her face and the speed-lever constantly bumping her knees, Meriel looked out on a country unlike any that she'd ever seen. She thought of that first thrilling glimpse of the snowcapped cordilleras of Chile from the poop of the *Catriona*, of Cartagena from a one-horse *coché*, bursting with new sights and sounds and smells. Of the pastel, salty brilliance of the Sussex downs from the seat of a free-wheel bike. Even of the rainswept quay at Boulogne from the deck of the Folkestone Packet, swarming with soldiers and smothered in red, white and blue. Novelty, colour, stimulation – the challenge of a new land to assimilate and to conquer. But here there was no colour – nothing but desolation, grey under a drizzling grey sky. No challenge – nothing but a brooding sense of doom and destruction. No trace of natural order or human achievement. No unbroken line, no complete tree. No hips and haws or seeding wildflowers, no drifts of fallen leaves. Nothing but a vast upheaval of mud and chalk, with black spikes for trees and snaggled fences of picket stakes and rusty wire, between canals of slime where men had once lived. Here and there and everywhere wooden crosses sprouted, scattered along the roadways and the wavering lines of the trenches, sticking up at odd angles from mounds and ridges and pools of stagnant water.

As Meriel sat staring out at those lines of wooden crosses,

her companions talked loudly across her of actions and movements and army regiments, importantly flexing their grid-maps, jumping down every few hundred yards to chart the details of an unrecorded grave, insensitive to her silence.

From the window of the Abbeville train the previous afternoon she had watched farmers with oxen teams ploughing for their spring corn. Where roads and waterways crossed beneath the rail she'd seen Frenchwomen with bundles of faggots on their backs and men pollarding poplars, and children hunched over fishing rods. But in this godforsaken chalkland the only moving figures were members of the Labour Corps, most of them Chinese, drearily working to restore roads and ditches, searching the craters for unexploded missiles and old graves, and for fragments of human beings. Their eternally exhausted faces peered out from cowl-like hoods at the passing ambulance, inscrutable, colourless, strangely in keeping with the desolation around them, like beings from another planet.

The Picardy villages that Meriel had seen from the train were prosperous, gold and russet, with encircling apple orchards and tall brick churches. But here there was little more than a pulpy reddish stain in the mud to show where the houses had been; a fang of scorched masonry at Fricourt, an island of compacted brick at Contalmaison. At Aveluy, on the far side of the valley that divided the battlefield, they came upon some villagers picking their way through the rubble of their old homes. But there too the faces that turned towards them through the rain were expressionless and devoid of hope.

The appearance of an unattached woman on the Somme battlefield had inevitably acted as a stimulant on the two young subalterns who escorted her. Without any conscious wish to intrude on so fresh a widow, they found themselves automatically competing for her attention – with the detail of their knowledge or the skill of their driving, or the old-fashioned gallantry with which they'd offered first an umbrella and then an arm for the slippery climb up through the mud to the trenches at Bouzincourt. The chivalrous arm belonged to Lieutenant Ripley, the elder of the two by eighteen months. The military umbrella and the voice that expounded on the valour of the British battalions who'd held the ridge was Lieutenant Scott's.

And in the heat of the contest, the lady's silent indifference to either young man had fortunately passed unnoticed.

As for Meriel – at Bouzincourt she found herself not merely on the lip of some squalid trench that might briefly have been Ned's, but on the edge of the abyss that threatened to swallow everything she'd clung to so tenaciously for so long. On the slopes below the shattered village the surface of the downs was eaten away, wormed and pitted, strewn with human debris. Chaotically, breached sandbags disgorged their contents of chalk and flint into a tumbled *mélange* of splintered trench boarding and iron weaponry, rags of khaki serge and sodden scraps of letters and snapshot photographs pathetically protruding. A single boot lay in the ruins of one sandbag close to where Meriel was standing, in the abandoned way that empty boots have of lying around all the world over, in ponds and ditches and along the tidelines of even the most respectable beaches. Only this boot wasn't empty. Meriel discovered that as she turned it over and the stink of putrefaction assailed her nostrils. Dear God, there was a man's foot inside! As she stared in horrified fascination at the discoloured shinbone that projected from it, her thoughts went back sickeningly to the bonfires and the dancing and the mad spate of bellringing that had followed the news of the Armistice back home in England. She thought of the ease with which sophisticated people had discussed armaments before the war, and later of the glib detachment of the newspapers as they reported advances and retreats and human casualties. Yet all the time this had been the reality – death, destruction as deliberate and brutal as anything in man's uncivilized past, and infinitely more thorough.

There was only one farm with a dovecot and a walnut tree that anyone knew of near Warloy. For two sous a morose old Frenchman consented to show them the way, perched on a running board and clinging to the iron roof support of the ambulance to direct them by a muddy track through the fields. It had stopped raining. The clouds had paled to the west, with the sun flickering behind them like a candle in a horn lantern. Someone had been busy ploughing here, too. The air was filled with the strong earthy scent of freshly turned clods, and the fields closest to the track were the colour of weathered stone – scattered with flints and streaked with the characteristic light and dark gradations of a chalky topsoil, just like the upper laines of Sellington. Next year, Meriel thought, this land would be green with growing corn right to the very margins of the old battlefield. The thought was comforting.

As the ambulance lurched and skidded on through the mud, a pheasant suddenly shot out from beneath its wheels in a commotion of tartan feathers, to tear away across the furrows and flap noisily into the air. "*Faisan!*" the Frenchman cried joyously, "Bang – bang!" And seeing how easily the sad creases of his face lifted at the sight of the gamebird, Meriel felt a little more of her own confidence returning. In a moment they'd come on the farm, nestling in a fold of the downs just as Ned had left it, with its soft-throated pigeons and protecting walnut tree. There'd be peace and stability there after the horrors of the Somme villages. She could feel it already in the familiar maternal swell of the ploughlands. Very soon she'd be standing in the window where Ned had stood, talking to the kindly women who'd fed and sheltered him – discovering some relic or memory of him, something new and hopeful to hang onto in the weeks and months to come.

At last they saw the conical slate roof of the dovecot exactly as she'd pictured it, except that it stood alone, the only complete building in the ruins of the old farm. The long range shells, the Weary-Willies, had made a thorough job of it. They had to abandon the ambulance at the obstruction of brick and timber that had once been the farm gate.

While the Registration Officers floundered about pointlessly in the mire and rubble, Meriel made straight for the dovecot. It was like climbing to the top of a steep hill. She'd decided at the first glance to regard its survival as a miracle, and her mind refused to think of anything now but the goal of reaching it.

'It's still here, his dovecot's still here,' she told herself, forcing her way through to the doorway and ignoring the litter of broken walnut twigs that crackled beneath her boots. Inside it smelt like a cave, dank and dimly lit from the two little flight hatches high in its roof.

'*I can hear them now, just like English pigeons, such a peaceful sound . . .*'

But the nesting ledges and crossbeams, and the ladder of wooden perches that descended from them were as deserted as the farm ruins. No obvious signs of destruction, no corpses here, nothing but feathers and droppings, and total silence.

'Oh Noggin – oh darling where are you?!' Meriel leant back against the door frame and remained there, staring dry-eyed at the feathers.

Chapter Twenty-Nine

After waving Meriel off from Victoria, Simmie ferreted in her bag for her own return ticket and hurried off across the station in search of the Lewes train. For once she'd had the forethought to wire Mrs Ashby to send Cheal with the trap for her, and it was more than her life was worth to miss the Seaford connection.

By now the rail journey down through Sussex was almost as familiar to Simmie as Sellington itself. Yet she'd never been able to complete it, not once, without recalling that distant pre-war summer with the bicycles, Meriel in her absurd motoring cap, and Ned's beloved chalk hills shimmering up out of the hayfields to meet them. She wiped the grimy carriage window with the back of her glove to watch the drab November landscape racketing by. MISSING-PRESUMED-DEAD . . . MISSING-PRESUMED-DEAD . . . wheels and rails and gusts of sooty steam . . . MISSING-PRESUMED-DEAD . . . PRESUMED-DEAD . . . PRESUMED-DEAD. . . . Yes, poor Ned had gone – his day was done. She found she could face that now, because she had to. Because however she might long to yield to Gladys' promptings to return to London, she knew that there was still work for her to do in Sussex. She must be there to help Meriel face it too, when she returned empty-handed from France – and for those two little boys who so desperately needed her support, with their mother abroad and no one to 'Betty them', poor lambs.

So it was that Simmie found herself in her usual place between the stolid Belgian couple at the foot of the Bury dinner table that night, after the usual struggle to settle the boys, the usual last minute scramble into evening dress. For whatever else she might sacrifice to the war, Margaret Ashby made no concessions when it came to dressing for dinner. There were empty places at her table now where her son and grandson had once sat. It had been more than two years since she herself had employed a lady's maid. Unaided it now took her almost an hour to do her hair and get herself up in her decent black brocade. But still she insisted on doing so each night without fail, and in forcing her family and guests to do likewise. She was like the taciturn old shepherd who moved his Southdown flocks each day from the farm to the hills and back again – part of a generation who never had lowered their standards, and never willingly would.

After a full year of residence at The Bury, Simmie was still almost as much in awe of Ned's grandmother as she had been on the day that sonorous voice first echoed through her own front hall at Harpur Street. And at dinner that evening she found herself flinching just as she had that first time when the old lady's penetrating blue eye lighted on her.

"I see you've decided to come back to us after all, then." Mrs Ashby bellowed down the length of the dining table, "when we all quite thought you'd be press-ganged into carryin' Meri's suitcase for her halfway to Paris. Not that you'll find me complainin'," she continued before Simmie could think of a suitable reply. "Quite right too, Miss Sims, the gel's no business to go chargin' off like a breachy bullock when she's needed back here at home. Now if she only had the sense to stay put a little longer. . . ."

"Well, I don't blame her, Gran!" Helen's voice – taut and harsh, and quite unlike her – took even her grandmother by surprise. "At least she hasn't given up on Ned yet, has she? At least she's still thinking about her husband – when all anyone else ever thinks about round here are cows and sheep and rotten crop rotations, and useless war memorials for men who'll never ever come back, whatever we do!"

Poor, busy little Helen, who'd tied herself up so thoroughly in bandages and balaclavas at the War Hospital Supply Depôt that she'd missed her one real chance of breaking free – an old maid already at thirty-two. "I hate it, I hate the war!" she said recklessly. "It's just about killed everything worthwhile – well it has, hasn't it? Not just Ned, but every man I ever danced with – dead now, or crippled. None of us are ever going to dance again are we – not me or Meri, or anyone?"

"As I recall it, Miss, you weren't exactly celebrated for your twinklin' toes before the war," Mrs Ashby remarked, but not altogether unkindly. "Listen to me, Helen, there *is* a future for Meriel Ashby in this valley – a fair one too if she's the courage to face it. And the same applies to you, my girl, if only you'll make the effort."

The old lady pulled herself up in her chair, with more authority and conviction than Simmie had seen in her face since the day she'd stepped out so splendidly onto the flimsy roof of the children's hut in the bluebell wood. "*Effort,* that's what we're all goin' to need," she said resolutely. "And good strong boots, Helen – no time for dancin' pumps now! Miss Sims knows what I mean."

If Simmie had no more than the vaguest idea just then of what the old lady meant, she wasn't to remain in ignorance for long. In the past Margaret Ashby had been more or less content to leave the daily administration of the Bury estate to Walter and Ned and to their foreman, Shad Caldwell – discounting the personal interest she'd always shown in her own pedigree Sussex cattle. But gradually the war had changed all that. With Ned's return to the Front in February, his grandmother first found it necessary to transfer the farm ledgers and cash books to her own writing desk, observing that no one else in her household had the head for them. Then, on the afternoon of poor Caldwell's interment in Sellington churchyard eight months later, she had seen the need to summon Meriel to her upstairs sitting room for a review of work-in-progress on the farm itself. And now finally, with her grand-daughter-in-law in France and the younger Bury employees still to be demobbed, the old lady had telephoned the legal trustees in Lewes to inform them that she would be overseeing the estate personally until further notice. Never mind that she had only old men, women and children to call on, or that she herself was now in her eighty-fourth year; it was simply a case of marshalling available resources, she said, all hands to the pump.

The old gardener, Zachariah Cheal, had long since been prised from his cabbage rows to drive the milk float and to carry the two little Ashby boys and the Belgian children in to school in Seaford. Now the indoor staff were compelled to help him out in the kitchen garden – an indignity the urban Gladys deeply resented. Helen was pressed into service in the stables and cowstalls, with equally unenthusiastic assistance from the Waedemons. At weekends Patrick and Robbie and the Belgian boys fed the calves and the fowls and collected the eggs. To her own astonishment, Simmie found that from the day of her return from London she was expected to perform identical weekday tasks, fair weather or foul. And as an example to them all, old Mrs Ashby herself now rose before dawn each morning, to dress with her usual painstaking deliberation in a dreadful old mackintosh of Ned's tied around the waist with a length of binder twine. It had already been agreed with the Agricultural Committee that the Land Army girls should stay on in the milking sheds into the new year of 1919, but they needed supervision Mrs Ashby said; and at six every morning she sallied forth into the darkened yards with a lantern in one hand and her trusty stick in the other, to see the milk churns filled and loaded satisfactorily for their journey to the station.

To say that Margaret Ashby took her responsibilities as farm overseer seriously would have been an understatement. It seemed to Simmie as she watched her that the old lady somehow contrived to be always where she was most needed – waving her stick, shouting out encouragements and criticisms, driving them all as she drove herself. Within three days of the Belgian family's eventual departure for Antwerp she had convinced the military authorities of the necessity for releasing Dan Goodworth to the work in the valley that awaited him. And in amongst it all she'd still found the time and energy for an unexpected trip to London, her first in five years, to go over the farm books, she said, with her personal accountant in Chancery Lane.

"But if you're thinkin' of offerin' to go with me Helen, you can think again," she stated baldly. "For one thing I'll need you here, girl, on the farm, and for another I'm not so ancient yet I hope that I can't be trusted to doddle out of a train and into a taxi without breakin' me damn neck!" And although she returned from her expedition that evening grey with exhaustion, it hadn't prevented her from rising at her accustomed hour the following morning, to plod off into the frosty dawn with her stick and her lantern to see the churns loaded up as usual.

For all her admiration of the old lady's stamina, Simmie found it difficult to share her enthusiasm for the work itself. Nobody had instructed her in the complicated mysteries of agriculture, beyond the rudimentary demonstrations that she needed to complete her tasks. In contrast to the neatly overalled Land Army girls she felt constantly out of place in the slosh and bustle of the yards. However carefully she hoisted her skirts or picked her way through the puddles, she invariably returned to the house spattered with mud and shamingly reeking of cows; and everywhere around the farm she felt the lingering sadness of Ned's death. Not even Dan Goodworth's return to the valley could dispel it. Over the years Simmie had retained a clear impression of the man from her first visit to Sellington, as a brawny young giant with an impudent twinkle in his eye. But the war had left its mark there too, it seemed. Something of the erect, intimidating authority of an army captain still clung to Dan, even in the cattle yards. Four years in France had been more than sufficient to extinguish the twinkle from his eye. And Simmie found herself fumbling and stumbling about her chores out of sheer nervousness before the grave assurance of the man's stare.

It was not on the farm but in the nurseries that Simmie earned her keep that autumn of 1918. Ned's little boys were her joy – the games she played with them, the comforting routines she established. And the knowledge that the love she gave them helped to keep the cruel world at bay – in the end that was all the reward she needed.

The wire bearing the news of Meriel's return to Sellington arrived soon after breakfast on the first Monday of the boys' Christmas holidays. The boys themselves were both out in the hall with Simmie at the time, waiting to see Mrs Ashby off on another of her precipitate accounting trips to London; and they all of them watched anxiously as she tore open the ominous yellow envelope.

"Eleven-forty train this mornin' – you'll have your mother back in time for lunch!" The old lady flourished the telegram at her great-grandsons. "Not before time, either," she added on a suddenly gruffer note, as she caught the expression on the older boy's face and turned away abruptly to thrust another hatpin through the crown of her black highwayman's tricorn.

"No sense in Cheal hangin' about gettin' into mischief between trains," she boomed down at Simmie from the waiting trap a few minutes later, without a glance at the wooden little man on the seat beside her. "I'll be sendin' him back for the old governess-cart, so you and the boys can drive down to meet her. And when you do, Miss Sims, would you do me the kindness of tellin' Meri that I'll want to see her this afternoon the moment I get back from town. She's not to go gallivantin' off around the farm 'til she's spoken to me – is that clear?"

Meriel stepped down from the Seaford train pale, red-nosed, bunged up with cold – but unsubdued. "Don't be ridiculous, Simmie, I never get colds," she snapped, automatically chivvying the boys out through the ticket gate to the waiting conveyance. "Up you go then, Patrick and you, Robbie – jump in, chop-chop! Thank you, Cheal, but I'll be driving back. And in the name of goodness stop *fussing*, can't you, woman? I tell you I've never felt better in my life!"

To prove it she filled the journey down through Cuckmere and up the long hill to Sellington with complaints on the state of the railways, with an inquisition of the luckless Cheal on the subjects of ploughing and threshing and daily milk yields; talking nineteen to the dozen, plugging every gap in the conversation with cries of encouragement and exasperation at the plodding horse, and successfully avoiding the silent query in Patrick's dark eyes.

It was the same through luncheon – she never drew breath, leaving her baked pudding half-eaten and jumping up immediately afterwards to march the boys off for a brisk walk on the downs.

"But darling, do you think that's wise?" Simmie followed them out into the porch, to find Meriel forcing Patrick into a pair of boots that were clearly sizes too small. "You know Mrs Ashby particularly wants to see you when she gets in, she's quite set on it – and if you leave now, dear, well I really can't think that you'll be back before her."

"You bet your sweet life we won't! Here Puck, here boy – now where the hell's that old mutt got to? Go and find him will you, Robbie?" Meriel wrenched the belt of her mackintosh a notch tighter and turned to deal with her friend. "Now look, Simmie, when G.M. gets a bee in her bonnet, I tell you the best thing to do is to take to the hills – isn't that right, Patrick? Don't think you're getting out of it that easily yourself, either. Helly can do the hens for once in her life – and anyone can see that you could do with a good blow, Simmie Sims, we all could. So go on then. Don't just stand there like a fool, woman, go and get your coat!"

The wind had got up during luncheon, and as it turned out Meriel's idea of a good blow was something little short of a gale – tearing up the combe to howl through the branches of the Bury wood, scattering leaves and sending the rooks tumbling and flapping into the air like pieces of burnt rag. Simmie had always loathed high winds. There was something malignant, she felt, in the way they buffeted and tugged at your clothing, and clawed out your hair from beneath hats and scarves to send you home looking like a scarecrow. But she set her teeth and endured the windswept barrenness of the hills that afternoon, because Meriel asked her to, and because for all her bustle and bombast, there was a desperate tension in her manner that scared Simmie rigid. 'Keep back,' it seemed to say. 'Don't crowd me, don't expect me to talk about it. Just do as I ask, Simmie, because I'm telling you – I've had just about as much as I can take!'

Patrick sensed it too. You could tell from the way he walked close in beside his mother half-enveloped in the flapping skirts of her mac – looking up into her face, watching her intently as she spoke, bravely holding back the questions he so needed to ask about his father. But not Robbie. For that little imp there'd been nothing to feel but the sheer joy of his mother's return, all wrapped up in the blustering excitement of the gale.

"Look at me, Mummy, look, Simmie – I'm leaning on the wind, it's holding me up! Look, it's holding me up all by itself!" They looked and laughed, and Meriel responded to the self-centred charms of her younger boy with an obvious relief. "If you lean back any further you'll fall flat," she shouted back. "And serve you right if you do, you ragamuffin! No nearer the cliffs though, do you hear me, Robbie? The wind won't hold you up in mid-air, you know!"

Simmie acknowledged the inevitability of their destination with the first audible rhythms the wind carried up to them from the Gap. They could hear the sea long before they saw it – hissing and growling, lying in wait for them at the end of the valley like some great, spume-flecked monster.

"Let's go down to the beach, shall we, to see the white horses?" They were already well on their way down the path to the coastguards' cottages before Meriel troubled to frame her intention in words. "Look, Robbie, look, boys, did you ever *see* such a high tide? Why it's already up to the old bathing machine!" Her voice was loud and animated like Robbie's, ignoring all but the immediate prospect. Yet she was drawn to the violence of the ocean because it matched something inside her, you could see it in her eyes.

All the urban comfort-lover in Simmie shrank from the turmoil of sky and water that faced them at the entrance of the Gap. Cravenly she longed for the warmth and security of the Bury day nursery, with the children safe inside by the fire and the gale shut out, reduced to a sigh in the chimney or the tapping of a blind cord against the window. But if it helped Meriel to have her there beside her on that hostile shore, why then of course that's where she must be. So rather than begging her to turn back as she'd liked to have done, she forced herself instead to scramble up after the boys into the creaking old bathing machine – to witness the destructive force of the waves, curling and smashing and raking back around it – and to leave them there, whooping and laughing at the spray, to walk on down the beach with their mother.

Stumbling along beside her, Simmie strained to catch the

flippant offhand remarks Meriel tossed at her through the wind – watching her restless hands twisting and tearing at a piece of sticky brown seaweed she'd snatched up from the waterline. 'And now it's up to you, Simmie,' she told herself. 'Up to you to make her stop this dangerous pretence and to begin to face the truth as it really is, for the children's sake as well as her own.'

"Meriel," she said aloud, "darling – could you bear to tell me about France?" But she hadn't said it loudly enough. The wind snatched the words from her lips, and Meriel crunched on heedlessly across the shingle, absorbed in the violent destruction of her seaweed. "Meriel, darling . . . " She tried again.

"Well then, what *is* it, Simmie?"

Confronted with the frowning belligerence of Meriel's reaction, Simmie faltered. But before she could collect herself, the sound of a barking dog, a sudden change in the tone of the children's voices behind them broke in on her, jerking her attention back to the old bathing machine, and to the sea. And the next moment she was clutching at Meriel's arm, dragging her round – running, both of them running, tearing frenziedly back down the beach. Oh no – oh God no! Those precious children – in the water, out in that dreadful sea! Two heads – two white, terrified little faces desperately lifted above the waves, fighting for their lives out there in the swell beyond the capsized bathing machine.

'God of heaven, help them – *help them!*' Simmie couldn't swim, she'd never learned. She could only stand with the waves drenching her, buffeting her body, to stretch out her arms helplessly across the water – while above her a gull soared and sideslipped, mocking her with its laughter.

"Coastguard – for God's sake, Simmie, fetch a coastguard!" She glimpsed Meriel briefly, stripped to her petticoat, as she shot past into the surf. Then Simmie found herself running again – panting, sobbing in her anguish. "Don't let them drown, please – oh *please* God, don't let those little boys drown!" But as she floundered up the beach towards the cottages, the wet shingle slipped and shifted beneath her feet, tripping her, delaying her, wasting precious time . . .

*

They put Patrick to bed with a hot-water bottle as soon as they could get him dry; and Simmie sat beside him on a hard nursery chair, talking to him, stroking the dark hair back from his forehead, waiting for the sedative to work. But Meriel had refused even to see the doctor. All evening she paced to and fro before the dining room windows, watching for lanterns, for the first sign of the returning search parties.

"They haven't found him you see, G.M., nobody's found him yet. And shall I tell you why? Because he's still alive – that's why! He's out there sheltering under the cliffs somewhere. I know I'm right, you'll see, they'll find him when the tide goes down."

But when they found him the next morning, it wasn't beneath the cliffs. They found him floating face-down between the anchored vessels along the coast in Newhaven harbour.

Margaret Ashby insisted on going in place of her grand-daughter-in-law to identify Robbie's pitiful, battered little body. When she returned at dusk – smaller, frailer, more subdued than anyone had ever known her – it was to find Meriel back at her old post at the dining room window, standing with her arms straight at her sides, staring out into the December twilight. The old lady set her face and went in to speak to her alone, closing the door behind her. Later she sent out for the doctor. But they still had to administer the bromide to Meriel by subterfuge, disguised in a mug of cocoa.

Meriel resisted sleep for as long as she could. Sleep was like death – and she wouldn't have it. She lay listening to a clock chiming the quarters, to the stealthy whisper of Simmie's knitting needles outside in the hall. She pressed her two thumbs to her temples, deliberately tightening the band of conscious tension behind her eyes. But in the end it was the tension itself that overwhelmed her, insidiously, by changing its form to become a great weight dragging her down, down into the dark whirlpool of her own subconscious.

Then she was sliding, stumbling down a scree of shifting shingle – black sea-worn flints wet with moisture, moving beneath her feet, carrying her downwards. And there before

318

her, running before her, a hooded figure – someone she feared yet had to follow. A sloping tunnel green with slime closed in around them as they ran, she and the hooded figure. Then suddenly he turned in her path to fling something at her. It struck her on the cheek, something small and hard; and the next instant she passed through a door into a vast subterranean chamber where men sat eating and drinking, their backs towards her. Then on, alone now, through more doors – deeper, damper, further from the surface – until at last she came to a small lamplit room where children perched on benches between hooded gaolers – swaying, back and forth, from side to side. And Robbie was there amongst them as she'd known he must be, pale and thin with great dark rings beneath his eyes – Ned's eyes . . .

Meriel leant forward to touch him. He was real, she could feel the bones of his arms. Then before anyone could stop her she'd scooped him into her own arms to run with him back up the steep passageway – back through door after door – back through the cavern where the men sat eating, up the long slope to the surface. In the distance she could see a dim circle of daylight reflected on the walls of the entrance – and silhouetted against it the thing she feared, the malevolent hooded figure who'd led her down. She had to pass him. She had to get Robbie past him – there was no other way. And all the time the child was growing heavier in her arms – growing, a man now, Ned now – and the slope was getting steeper . . . Now the entrance, at last, and the daylight beyond. But the figure was there too, blocking her path, moving slowly towards her, lifting his face for her to see. His face beneath the hood expressionless, Chinese, the colour of parchment – the face of the Somme! And the finger – that terrifying, pointing finger . . . !

"Warloy, I am Warloy," he cried. "Warloy needs him – his Country needs him – give the child to me!"

"No – no! I need him more, a damn sight . . . damn sight . . . damn sight more!" Meriel pushed at him, struggling to get past. But the shingle was moving again, moving beneath her. The man's fingers were reaching for Robbie, fastening around him, dragging him – dragging Ned from her arms . . .

"No, no – *no!*" She was sweating, weeping, struggling with all her strength to hold them, not to wake – not to wake, for God's sake, and find her arms empty . . .

After she'd woken, Meriel lay quite still, listening to the sound of the wind in the beeches and the chiming clock, and the gurglings of the water pipes behind her bed – and the sweat dried cold on her skin.

Chapter Thirty

By morning the wind had dropped. There was even sunshine, slanting palely through the breakfast room window and onto the carefully brushed crown of Patrick's head. He sat straight at the table as his mother and Betty had taught him, with his hands and forearms well clear of the cloth. He ate his cereal automatically without looking up. His hair was so like his grandfather's in the sun, Simmie thought, shot through with bronze like Robert Llewellen's. She wanted to touch it quite desperately, to stroke the little boy's hair again and share with him the burden of his grief. It was all she could think of now, all she dared think of.

"Patrick, would you believe me if I told you that I think I understand a little of how you feel?" she said gently. "I really do, darling – you see, when I was younger I lost everyone in the world that I cared for, all at once. And I felt miserable and lonely then too . . . "

He was looking at her now – such a pathetic, swollen, mumpy little face! Simmie's heart ached with pity. It took a real effort to prevent herself from jumping up and throwing her arms round him there and then. But at the age of ten, Patrick Ashby was already too defensive, too private a person to be forced. If he came to her, he must come of his own accord.

"But someone was very kind to me then, Patrick," she went on, "when I was so unhappy – an old lady, your Mummy's Grannie – and oh it did make such a difference . . . "

He was pushing his chair back, sniffing and fumbling with his table napkin. In a minute he'd be within arm's reach, hovering, waiting for her to stretch out and pull him to her . . .

"Morning all!" Meriel's voice – younger and gayer than Simmie had heard it for years.

Meriel herself stood poised in the doorway, eccentrically dressed in a striped summer blouse and ankle-length skirt, her hair untidily piled up and padded out in crude imitation of the style she'd affected in the old days before the war. "Morning, I *said*," she repeated impatiently. "Well come on then, Simmie, when are you going to get around to introducing me to this handsome young man, I should like to know?"

"Meriel, for God's sake!"

"Don't be such a humbug, Simmie. Anyone can see he's simply dying to meet me!"

The sight of Patrick's tearstained face struggling to replicate his mother's arch smile was altogether more than Simmie could bear. "Stop it, Meriel, stop it!" She found herself almost shouting it – on her feet between them, pushing at Meriel, at the unaccustomed rigidity of steel-boned stays, as she propelled her backwards through the doorway and out into the hall.

"What the devil . . . ? Have you taken leave of your senses?!" It was Meriel's turn to be angry, and she did so with every evidence of justification. "Being his brother's landlady doesn't give you the concession for the whole damn family, you know," she hissed, giving back shove for shove. "Look, I wouldn't be in Sellington, would I, if the old lady hadn't invited us both to stop over for the night? And now that I am here, I should jolly well suppose I've as much right as you to hob-nob with the natives!"

"But darling – I don't understand – what are you saying?" Simmie stared at her aghast, fumbling for words as she felt the whole perspective of their tragedy shifting and changing around her.

"Well, I would have thought that was obvious to anyone but an idiot." Meriel's eyes were challenging, dilated, darker than Simmie had ever seen them. "What I'm trying to tell you, old bean, is that you've been playing the giddy-goat ever since we put our bikes on the train at Victoria. And I for one am getting pretty damn sick of it! Now for heaven's sake pull yourself together, woman, and introduce me properly to that nice little boy in there, before he decides that we've both of us gone off our rockers."

Four days later the Ashby family doctor called in a private consulting physician from Eastbourne to examine Meriel, and afterwards to report his findings to Mrs Ashby and Simmie over tea in the drawing room.

"Wilful dissociation is a strange and wonderful thing. 'Out of sight out of mind', how often have you heard that said, Mrs Ashby?" the Eastbourne man enquired, "and in the unfortunate case of your grand-daughter-in-law, I fear that has proved quite literally to be true."

With an obvious effort the old lady braced herself up on her cushions to put the man in his place. "Under the circumstances, Doctor, there's nothin' to be gained by talkin' to us like a couple of your half-wit lunatics," she said wearily. "Miss Sims and I have been through a very great deal durin' the last few days, but we have retained our sanity, thank God, and we do both of us have a rudimentary grasp of the King's English. So perhaps you'd oblige us by dispensin' with the penny-proverbs, young man, and gettin' on with the prognosis?"

"Well then, I can confirm that the young woman is suffering from a form of amnesia or loss of memory that is almost certainly attributable to purposive hysteria," the physician said in a noticeably brisker tone of voice. "The purpose, you understand, being that of saving herself from a reality she finds unacceptable."

"Mad as a hatter, in other words."

"No I wouldn't say that, Mrs Ashby, I wouldn't say that at all."

"What then?" The melancholy, pale blue eyes considered him unwinkingly from behind the silver barricade of her tea things.

"Well, in my experience the capacity for dissociation varies considerably from one person to another, but in certain predis-posed cases – and I believe your grand-daughter-in-law to be one of them – severe emotional shock can produce hysterical reactions of this type, which may or may not prove temporary in their effect. Unhappily, the war has provided us with innumer-

322

able instances of this kind of thing, our institutions are full of them. We had a fellow at the East Sussex Asylum at Hellingly, for example – found wandering between the lines at Lens with no memory whatsoever beyond the Bank Holiday weekend of 1914. That is until he heard the news of the Armistice, at which point I can assure you that he achieved a total reversal of his amnesia – recalled everything up to his discovery between the lines."

"But surely Meriel isn't . . . ? I mean, you wouldn't consider it necessary to – to certify her, would you, Doctor?" Simmie had to interrupt him. She just couldn't bear to hear them talking so calmly about lunatics and insane asylums without asking, without knowing the worst for Meriel – and for poor little Patrick.

"No indeed, Miss Sims." The physician was commendably positive. "I can see no grounds in this case for writing out a certificate. On the contrary, the important thing now is for the subject to remain with people she knows and trusts. Although in this instance an immediate change of environment might also be advisable, I think."

"But where could she go, Doctor?" Simmie's voice was weak with relief. Whatever happened though, she mustn't break down – she mustn't cry now, with the valiant old lady sitting like a rock on the sofa beside her. She could cry later. "And what about her little boy?" she added quickly. "He's only ten, Doctor. He's lost his father, and now his only brother. It would be too cruel if he lost his mother as well – now when he needs her most."

"But you see, to all intents and purposes he has lost her, Miss Sims. Subconsciously he's bound to be a constant reminder of her own loss. And so long as she refuses to acknowledge that, then she'll be genuinely unable to recognize him as her son. No, far better for both of them, I consider, if you can get her right away from here for the inquest. She has a married sister, I believe?"

"Yes she has, in Bedfordshire. But I really don't think Meriel could go to her, they never got on, you see. She does have an aunt she likes though, up in London. She stayed with her only last week, as a matter of fact, on her way back from France." (Only last week – and already it seemed an age away.)

"Capital." The consulting physician brushed a crumb from his knee with a brisk dismissive gesture and rose to his feet. "Well then, if Mrs Ashby is agreeable, I'd suggest you arrange for her to stay with this aunt for a week or two – perhaps even longer if the change of scene proves beneficial. And at all costs avoid over-exciting the young woman or increasing the stress on her in any way. There's a possibility, you understand, that she could still be adversely affected. She may regain her memory quite suddenly, like our man from Lens. But there again, she could equally withdraw from reality altogether if she felt sufficiently pressured. Give her time, plenty of time, and try to keep things on an even keel, that's my advice. And don't expect too much of her too soon, Miss Sims," he concluded in the hallway as Gladys produced his overcoat and Simmie herself held the door for him. "I may be wrong, indeed I sincerely hope that I am; but I fear it's likely to prove a long business."

Chapter Thirty-One

He wasn't wrong. On her return to Sellington early in the new year, Meriel remarked on the changes war had brought to town and country with the listless indifference of a convalescent. She was surprised to see so few horses, so few young men in the streets. She remarked on the sudden proliferation of motor cars and of women drivers – women bus conductresses, women road sweepers – women everywhere in ugly, functional clothing. Yet none of it seemed to touch her or to affect her personally. She accepted the death of her mother, the defection of her father to the United States and the loss of thirteen years of her own life with an unnatural calm. References to her husband and children she ignored. Patrick she ignored. And it was heartbreaking to see him waiting, watching his mother day after day for some gesture of recognition or affection that never came his way – a relief to them all when Mrs Ashby returned the child to school in Seaford as a weekly boarder.

Meriel reminded Simmie of nothing so much as a bored

adolescent, that January of 1919. Less that her mind was unhinged than as if she'd simply lost interest in life – mooching about smoking, staring out of windows, starting books, starting solitaire and patience, but never finishing anything. Meriel, of all people, morose and uncommunicative, her lovely hair dragged back into a lank horsetail, all the bounce gone from her step as she drifted aimlessly from room to room. The very food she ate seemed distasteful to her. She grew thin, hollow-eyed – the pallid little ghost of a lost generation.

"Na'ven, Missus Edwin, you've gotta build yerself up, so you 'ave. Cook's sent this in special for yer, an' I'm sure I 'ope yer won't let good vittals go ter waste." At mealtimes Simmie's old Gladys took to tempting her with extra little titbits from the kitchen – a sherry gruel or a mug of savoury beef-tea – coaxing Meriel into tasting them, watching her make faces and push them aside unfinished, but reluctant ever to take no for an answer. "Cryin' shame ter leave that good gruel, Missus Edwin, *wicked* – what wiv you so skinny an' all. Come along, dearie, try a little more do."

'Keep things on an even keel.' That's what the doctor had advised. 'Don't force her, but try to encourage her to remember things from those lost years if you can – little things, minor details of life unconnected with her husband or son. If you can once demonstrate to her that she hasn't forgotten everything, you see, then it may be possible to extend her memory gradually over time.'

Simmie and Helen, even old Mrs Ashby, had certainly done everything they could think of to engage her interest – in the milking herd and the dairy, in corresponding with her brother Gareth in South America, and in any number of minor projects around the farm. But Meriel was proof to them all. She'd thrown up a wall around her reactions and emotions that nothing it seemed could penetrate.

A long business, the doctor had predicted. But for someone as hopelessly prone to nostalgia as Simmie, it was hard to be patient. She saw the old, vital Meriel everywhere she looked – whenever the trap drove out, when one of the Land Army girls walked up with the butter for the house, or when a horse and rider crossed a distant flank of the downs. And one morning in

February, as she made her own way down through the overgrown stable yard to the calf pens, she had a sudden vivid image of Meriel at the gate in her ridiculous motoring cap . . .

. . . *"Don't be silly, it can't possibly be trespassing when we know Ned – not when you're his landlady, Simmie, for Lord's sake!"*

. . . her bright little face alive with excitement as she shot the bolts back and ran from stall to stall to count the horses, standing on tiptoe to peer through the bars. . . .

. . . *"Aren't they fine, Simmie, aren't they lovely! When I marry Ned you can have that soft old bay cob – and I'll have this handsome black devil here. Look, Simmie, his name's Balthazar. I bet Ned rides him!"*

The image had remained with her for the rest of the morning. "Helen and I thought we might start clearing out the old stables this afternoon, Mrs Ashby," she heard herself suggesting over lunch. "Meriel could help us too if she'd like to – we could certainly do with the extra pair of hands."

While her grandmother-in-law endorsed the idea with her customary vigour, Meriel herself remained silent – staring at the plate before her, forking the food from one side to the other like a finicky child. Later in the stables she handled the broom they'd given her in exactly the same way, dragging it purposelessly back and forth through the litter.

"When you think what this place used to be like before the war, when you and I first saw it, Meriel – with all those gorgeous great horses. Fifteen, weren't there? You counted them, remember?" Simmie rattled on bravely, doing her best, willing Meriel to remember. She could recall it all so perfectly herself – with golden barley straw in the stalls and fresh hay in the racks, mingling their summer fragrance with the coarser scents of horse-sweat and ammonia and the harness oil in the tackroom. Why, when she thought about it she could almost smell it herself, the efficient working hub of the farm – its horsepower.

But Meriel simply went on swishing her broom mechanically from side to side, backwards and forwards across the bricks.

And the old stables continued to smell of dust and decay just as the empty house in Harpur Street had done. Limewash that had once been renewed each spring was peeling, flaking from the walls. Keys rusted in locks that would no longer turn, a barrier of brittle nettle stalks fringed the doorway. The horses themselves had gone – the last complete working team – all but Achie and old Caesar, transferred long since to more convenient quarters alongside the fatstock pens. For two years or more time had stood still. The place remained empty, accumulating cobwebs and every kind of farm refuse; the physical manifestation of all that the war had done to Sellington, and to the Ashbys.

Not that anything in life could ever really stand still – Simmie knew that only too well. Life itself went burgeoning on regardless, regenerating, putting out new growth, even in the bleakest of ruins. Although paradoxically the fresh evidence of its healing power that she'd hoped to discover in the old stables that afternoon had come not from Meriel Ashby, but from her sister-in-law, Helen.

While they worked together to restore some semblance of order to the place, Simmie became aware of something different about Helen – something she'd sensed before but never bothered to analyze. For all the frustration and disappointment the war had brought her, Helly had worked hard on the farm in the past weeks, even her grandmother acknowledged it. And clearly the work was agreeing with her. There was something animated, even eager, in the movements of her stocky little figure, Simmie thought, as she watched Helen emerge from the stalls with another barrow-load of ancient bedding straw. The bitter twist had gone from her mouth. There was colour in her face now, where before there'd been so little. And when she trundled on down the alley to where Meriel stood leaning on her broom, the contrast between the two young women was striking – as if the will to survive had passed out of one and into the other.

"I say buck-up, Meri, you'll never get clear at that rate." Helen smiled good-naturedly at her sister-in-law as she bustled past. But Meriel wasn't looking. She was peering instead at the tarnished brass plate on the stall nearest to her, spelling out the name to herself in a toneless faraway voice: "Bal-thaz-ar . . . Balthazar – whatever happened, I wonder, to that handsome Balthazar?"

"Remount boys took 'im, Missus Edwin." Goodworth's voice from the doorway, just as before and right on cue. "'E died tho', did poor ol' Balfy – bought-it in a rail smash-up at St Omer so they say, afore 'e even reached the Front."

Meriel didn't look up at him or react in any way. But someone else did. Watching Helen carefully setting down the handles of her barrow – pulling in her spine and bracing back her shoulders to emphasize her breasts as she turned to catch Dan's eye – Simmie at last understood. Poor Meri had already returned blankly to her ritual sweeping of the stable floor. But for Dan and Helen life went on – yes indeed.

In April at bluebell time Vicky Baxter swept down to Sussex in her new bottle-green Bentley tourer, with the declared intention of spiriting her sister away back to Bedfordshire for a nice long rest. But Meriel had stubbornly refused to recognize the tall, matronly figure who hurried forward to enfold her in fox fur and velveteen, let alone return with the woman to the fleshpots of Biggleswade.

Nor had their father fared better when he arrived in Sellington during haymaking the following summer. The respectable Mrs Baxter had advisedly lost contact with her disreputable parent back in 1917, when the Ministry of Munitions effectively put him out of business by taking over his American purchasing function. But Simmie finally succeeded in securing his address in Philadelphia through Gareth Llewellen in Colombia. She'd written out of duty to inform him of Robbie's death and of Meriel's desperate reaction – adding as a postscript the news of her own decision to put his mother's old house in Harpur Street on the property market, and to make over the major portion of its selling price to his surviving grandson, Patrick.

It was July of 1920, however, and long after she'd given up any hope of an acknowledgement, when the youngest Caldwell boy panted down from the village with Robert Llewellen's response:

ARRIVED YESTERDAY TRANSATLANTIC STOP

PLEASE MEET ELEVEN FORTY TRAIN AT SEAFORD
STOP RL

'But he isn't coming to see you is he, you old goose?' Simmie
reminded herself sternly at that first little flutter of excitement.
'He's coming to see his daughter.' So after they'd sent Cheal
off to Seaford in the trap, she'd spent the waiting time on
Meriel's hair and appearance, not her own.

"She didn't recognize me, Simmie." Llewellen had eventually
found her alone in the Flat, in her own little sitting room with
the familiar clutter of her things around her, darning a grey
worsted stocking of Patrick's.

"Oh but that's nonsense, surely? She started talking of you
the moment your telegram arrived. Only this morning she was
telling me all about the time you swam the Brisbane river with
your breeches on. Why, she could hardly wait for you to get
here."

But in all honesty Simmie wasn't surprised, not after Meriel's
treatment of the over-effusive Mrs Baxter. The thing that
surprised, that fascinated her, was her own reaction to this man
– the curious detachment she felt, like a third person, watching
these two old lovers meeting again so calmly . . .

She released his hand quickly and re-seated herself in her
dear old button-back, indicating the chair opposite – watching
him move towards it to settle himself, heavily for the man she
remembered. No trace now of that confident, carefree stride.

"Perhaps she'll come round to you in a little while," she
suggested kindly. "Perhaps if you reminded her of her adventures in Colombia – and that tremendous journey through the
mountains? The consulting physician says it would help a great
deal if she could be made to recall anything from that period of
her life, however minor . . . "

"She didn't recognize me," Llewellen repeated dully, "said I
was too old to be her father." He was crouched forward in his
seat staring at the carpet, shoulders rounded, belly between his
thighs. He'd been forty-three when Simmie last met him to
receive the deeds of his mother's house, a man in his prime still.
Now he was sixty-one, and the excesses of his life had left their
marks. Now his hair was grey, the skin of his face coarsened

and lined, pouched beneath the eyes and chin. "You think that health and energy and all the good things of life will last forever, Simmie," he said, as if he could read her mind. "But they don't, do they?"

And Simmie saw then that she'd been wrong in thinking his daughter so like him. For the walled-up grief that made of Meriel what she was, had been generated out of love for the people most dear to her – love for her husband and her little boy. This man mourned only for himself.

"We all of us have to grow old, Robert," she said. "Look at me, a dull old spinster with nothing to show for my life but laundry receipts and memories."

"And regrets?" He raised his brows at her in an attempt at his old irony, and she remembered how black and oblique they'd once been, like the wings of a bird in flight. Now they were untidy, tangled with white hairs. Even the splendid darkness of his eyes had faded to a muddy brown – bloodshot, lifeless as bottle glass. "Are you sorry, Beatrice, that you never came out to me in Anaime after all?" he asked.

No one had called her Beatrice, not for years, not since she'd last seen her own father in Richmond the year she'd lost this man's baby. And now here he was telling her that he'd known all along how near she'd come to joining him. He'd known all this time and never spoken!

He smiled at her surprise, a painful, lopsided smile. "Did you think I hadn't heard? Young fellow had the decency to tell me that at least before he stole my little Meriellie away." The smile wavered, then faded as he returned to his scrutiny of the carpet. His hands trembled on the arms of the chair. (That would be the drink, Simmie thought.)

"But it isn't too late – not too late even now, Simmie," he mumbled without meeting her eyes. "I still have some investments in the States – enough to set up a decent home, and to make an honest woman of you at last."

For a moment Simmie didn't know whether to laugh or to hit him – to whack her darning mushroom into his pathetic, debauched old face. But then she'd never been one to kick a man when he was down; and in the end she settled for feeling sorry for him. She'd always thought him so confident, so strong;

and now she was stronger – perhaps she'd always been in the sense that mattered. In any case there was no choice for her to make, any more than there had been that day in Richmond Park when he'd subjugated her with a chain of dog daisies.

She rose again and crossed to the old Harpur Street bureau where she kept her papers and writing things. The 1890 journal was still there exactly where she thought, in the bottom drawer:

T. J. & J. Smith's Large Quarto Manuscript Diary with almanack. Interleaved blotting.

The front cover was coming adrift. The ink of her own neat entries had faded to sepia, and the whole thing smelt of musty old paper. She found the June entry easily enough. The daisy that he'd tucked into her hat-brim was still there too, where she'd pressed it – colourless, desiccated, thin as a wafer.

"Do you remember the daisy chain that you made for me, Robert?" she asked. "It bound me to you in a way, you know, all those years you were travelling abroad. And this little daisy? The one you put in my hat?" She lifted it out for him to see, and as she did so Simmie was conscious not only of the withered flower, but of the age, the veins and wrinkles of her own hand. Then, when she was quite sure that he understood, that he remembered how it had been all those years ago in the park, she crumbled the brittle flower between her fingers and let it fall to the carpet at his feet.

"Memories and dust – all that's left, you see, of our grand passion," she said, smiling a little at the melodrama of her own gesture. "Whatever we might have had once, believe me we have nothing to offer each other now, my dear, nothing in the world . . . "

After he left her, Simmie carefully repaired the cover of the old journal with a strip of gummed calico, then replaced it in its drawer. 'And that's that,' she thought. He was a shallow, selfish man, she faced the truth of it as she'd always faced it in her heart. 'He's feckless – you never really had any doubt of that, did you, Simmie? He used you like a whore, abandoned you when you needed him. Only came back to you in the end because he was afraid – because he needed someone for himself, to warm and comfort him in his grey hairs?'

It was true, all of it. Yet as she lay in bed that night Simmie couldn't help wondering if Robert Llewellen hadn't loved her just a little all those years ago, when she had loved him so much. Not that it mattered, she assured herself, or that it could make any great difference to anything now. One simply wondered.

Chapter Thirty-Two

Simmie was never sure in her own mind what it was about Helen that first seriously attracted Dan Goodworth. For someone of his background her pedigree breeding as a Sellington-born Ashby might have had something to do with it, and of course men were notoriously susceptible to the flattery of a woman's admiration. Although in fairness there had always been something in poor Helly's clumsy vulnerability that virtually begged one to love and protect her, just as there'd been in Ned once. And Simmie knew Dan to be a kindly man.

But whatever his motives might have been, the effect of the Bury cowman's gentle barndoor courtship of Helen Ashby through the summer and autumn of 1920 was eventually to face her grandmother with the choice of dismissing the man or of sanctioning his elevation to the status of a relative. And the old lady who'd fought so hard to maintain her standards through all the years of the war, accepted the inevitable with her usual pragmatism.

"Can't say I like the idea," she said bluntly, "not one little bit. But there you are, Miss Sims, he's too good a man to lose. No, we'll just have to get the trustees to make him up to Manager, won't we, seein' he's doing the job anyway. And then look sharp about gettin' Helly to the church, eh? Before that young ram beats us to it and cuckolds the parson!"

So in the spring of 1921, shortly after lambing and three days before her own thirty-fifth birthday, Helen became Mrs Daniel Goodworth. And Warry Hurst, a one-time Bury stable boy who now worked as a motor mechanic in Eastbourne, drove them down from the church in the shiny Ford motor car Mrs Ashby hired for the occasion. It seemed appropriate somehow, that wedding car, the symbol of a new era in the valley and of the changing circumstances that the twenties had brought to Sussex.

Elsewhere, from Seaford and Brighton, ranks of hideous little brick boxes were advancing steadily up and over the bare slopes of the downs. 'Homes fit for heroes' they called them – even as they sold them to successful war profiteers, or to retired hearth-rug strategists to whom the Western Front had never been much more than a line on a map – while the 'heroes' themselves, so many of them, were forced to stand in dole queues.

In Sellington things were better. As Meriel once predicted, the cereal market had slumped after the war with the abolition of guaranteed prices. But with a rapidly expanding dairy herd and more land down to grass, the Bury farm had suffered less than most. Little Stumpy Pyecroft and Cook's nephew, Shaver Tinsley, both returned gratefully to their work in the valley. In 1920, Caesar, the last old plough-horse, had been replaced by a new Titan motor tractor. A petrol engine now drove the threshing tackle in the aisled barn; and by the autumn of 1922 a steady rise in milk receipts emboldened Dan Goodworth and the estate trustees to invest in a modern vacuum-milking unit for the cowsheds. So far as the Bury farm was concerned one might even say that the years following the Great War were good years – a time of reconstruction and of growth.

Inside the old farmhouse, though, antique clocks still chimed out the quarters. Antique plumbing still gurgled, sparrows still chavished in the eaves much as they always had. Electricity had been laid-on to the cowsheds and outbuildings as a matter of necessity. But Mrs Ashby still refused to contemplate its harsh lighting for the house. Old Cook still clung stubbornly to her open fire range. In many respects domestic routine had returned to the old, slow pace of Edwardian days, before Meriel Llewellen breezed in from South America to set the household by the ears.

Meriel's own condition had improved very little over the years. She rode now, endlessly, on a lively little Welsh pony that Dan had found for her at the Heathfield Fair – up over the downs to Crowlink and Birling Gap and the ruins of the old lighthouse on the cliffs at Belle Tout – riding astride, drawing energy, borrowing excitement from the movements of the horse beneath her, and returning breathless with some of the old sparkle restored to her eyes. But it never lasted for long. Within the confines of the house she remained as bored, as uncommunicative as ever, sitting for long periods in total silence – refusing to participate in the activities of home or farm, refusing to remember anything but the distant past. She accepted Patrick as she accepted the others, simply as part of the furniture – seldom speaking to him, never seeking his company, never even looking at him as a mother might look at a son.

From the age of thirteen Patrick himself had boarded at his father's old school at Lancing – tall and gangling now, with hands and feet too big for his body and a shy, uncertain smile that reminded Simmie so much of Ned, for all the boy's Llewellen colouring. He seemed to accept the burden of his mother's indifference as children accept what they must from their parents. But in his holidays he spent every moment that he could out on the farm, in the easy company of Dan and the men, or up on the chalk hills with old Vine and his Southdown sheep.

Margaret Ashby too, had withdrawn to a great extent from the day to day routine of the Bury household. She was feeling her age at last, often declining to join the family for luncheon or tea, and only attending dinner for the sake of good form. In recent years her visits to London and her accountant had become steadily more exhausting and less frequent, until finally they'd lapsed altogether. Helen kept the farm books now. The old lady had even turned her back on her beloved Red Sussex cattle – devoting her time to copious letter writing in her upstairs sitting room, and to concentrated daily assaults on *The Times* newspaper.

But despite everything, despite all that had happened, it suited Simmie, the feeling of calm and of permanence that had returned to the old house. The housemaid Gertrude had left long since, snapped up after the war by a wealthy neighbour. But Gladys was still with them, as much a part of the Bury staff now as old Cook at her range or Zachy Cheal bent over his hoe in the kitchen garden. And now it was to Simmie that they all came with their menus and laundry lists and their orders for the day. On the rare occasions when Meriel wanted to talk – when she felt like reminiscing on Australia or Chile or her exciting voyage between the two on the coal clipper *Catriona* – it was to Simmie's crowded little den in the Flat that she came. When Patrick tore his good school suit, it was Simmie's invisible mending that concealed the damage from his great-grand-mother. When the faded rose brocades in the drawing room needed replacing, it was Simmie who chose the fabric and made the new curtains up. It was to Simmie that Helen whispered the thrilling news of her first pregnancy, even before she'd told Dan.

All her life Simmie had yearned to be needed as the Ashbys of Sellington needed her now. And the peace that she'd found at last in Sussex was shared and reflected in the atmosphere of The Bury itself throughout those post-war years.

Even death when it returned to the old house seemed ready to come quietly now, and without fuss. In the summer of 1925, Margaret Ashby celebrated her ninetieth birthday by failing to dress for dinner for the first time in her adult life. And the next day, exhausted by processions of visitors, she'd firmly declined to get up.

"Doctors – what do they know?" she muttered in response to Simmie's urgings to sit up on her pillows at least. "If I choose to run the risk of pneumonia, well then that's my business, isn't it?" And in bed she remained, no longer daunting. A flattened little figure in men's striped pyjamas and an absurd boudoir cap that Helen had once made for her – demanding *The Times* still and Simmie's clear voice to read it, but withholding her customary verdicts and criticisms of the news, as if the world had at last placed itself beyond the reach of her advice.

The course of the pneumonia when it came was predictably swift. The old lady lay still, breathing with difficulty but making little apparent effort to resist. Sitting beside her, reading at random of hatless ladies in Parliament and the coming of the automatic telephone, Simmie experienced the same feeling of strength, of enhanced capability that she'd drawn from Cécile Llewellen in the days of her final illness. As if she had already taken the old lady's mantle of responsibility onto her own shoulders.

Margaret Ashby seemed to recognize it too. "Up to . . . up to you now . . . ," she rasped out at the end of that last long afternoon, just when Simmie felt sure that the power of speech had finally left her. "Listen . . . listen . . . Simmie . . . " It was the first time she'd ever used that name in all the years they'd known each other – she saved a breath for it – and as she spoke a frail little hand reached out, fluttering feebly above the counterpane. Simmie caught it and held it fast between her own, leaning over to catch each word as it gusted up to her.

"Yes, Mrs Ashby, I'm here – I'm listening," she reassured her. "Is there something you want to tell me?"

There were sticky deposits of mucous at the corners of the old lady's mouth. Her breath smelt sweet and a little bad, like a neglected apple store. Her eyes when she opened them were misted and drowsy. Yet there was strength in her still – just a little, something she had been holding back for this last . . .

The social observances of death – the old-fashioned, draped farm waggon that was to carry Margaret Ashby's coffin up the hill to Sellington church, the genteel barbarity of a wake in the Bury dining room – these things were for others to organize, for Dan and for Helly. Simmie's business now was with life – and it was business that couldn't wait.

'We have so few years, so very few,' she thought as the train pulled into Richmond station. 'They must be used – they *mustn't* be allowed to go to waste.'

It was a new experience to drive up Richmond Hill in a motor cab – to see slouch-hatted men, slouch-figured women with powdered faces, all but exposing their knees where Simmie herself had once swept the pavements with her skirts. Impossible to believe all that had been more than thirty-five years ago! That before the end of next year she herself would be sixty! And did the fast and the wealthy still meet in the park, she wondered, chauffeur-driven now in their glossy black limousines? Or had the war finished all that too?

The view from the hill was the same at least – just exactly as she remembered it, with the silver curve of the river through the trees and the little pleasure boats and all the coloured parasols, as gay and as carefree as if nothing of any great consequence had happened in the years between. And now within a few minutes, just a few minutes, she'd be meeting him again – here of all places. How life turned in circles!

As she alighted from the cab and paid the driver, Simmie remembered so well how she'd felt that other time, waiting by the railings with her heart beating like a sledgehammer. Now she felt numb, empty, searching for some response within herself and failing to find it. The railings where she'd left the daisy chain had gone, gone to the war and munitions. The old hotel façade had gone too, replaced with a modern opulence of red brick and Portland stone. The new door she must enter was grander, even more imposing than the original – overshadowed by a sculpted shield and vast Corinthian pillars, giving onto a marble vestibule of equally epic proportions. Inside there was a porter's desk, looking a little lost amongst the grandeur, and from somewhere beyond it the sound of music. Simmie cleared her throat. Robert had spoken that other time, she'd merely had to walk. But this time it was she who must ask. Mrs Ashby had said it, it was up to her now. She must ask for him by name.

"Good afternoon," the sound of her own voice echoing through the vestibule, infinitely calm and remote, steadier even than she'd hoped. The porter looked up.

"Yes?"

"I was told to ask for . . . that is, I've come to see . . . "

"Yes?" The casual friendliness of the man's smile seemed strangely inappropriate to Simmie. Then all of a sudden the words leapt out of her in a single spasm.

"I've come to see Mr Edwin Ashby."

Before she died, Margaret Ashby had managed to convey the facts of her grandson's survival and of his whereabouts, but very little more. Now, in a small office off the main reception hall, the Matron of the Star and Garter Home for Disabled Servicemen enlarged on that information. "An unusual case, Miss Sims." She prefaced the remark with a look of professional disapproval. "And not at all the kind of thing we'd expect to have to cope with here at the Star, I do assure you."

But for Simmie, normally cowed in the presence of officialdom, this unbending woman in her starched bonnet and ridiculously goffered collar was certainly no harder to face than the hall porter. She was here now and she had to go through with it, that was all. She'd arrived at the Home and declared her mission. Now the only thing that really mattered was her meeting with Ned himself. So she simply nodded, and waited politely for the woman to get to the point.

"We don't have access to his entire medical history, you understand," the Matron continued, leafing through a pile of typewritten notes on the desk before her. "He first came to us at our convalescent home at Sandgate via the Brook Street Hospital for Facial Injuries in London – and came on here when we finished rebuilding the old Star and Garter Hotel last year. According to his records he was also at the Third London General in Wandsworth, Queen Mary's at Sidcup and the Fourth Stationary Hospital at St Omer. But very likely he'd have been through at least half a dozen field hospitals and evacuation units in France before that. You see, there was nothing to identify him by the time he reached St Omer – no uniform or identification discs, or papers of any kind. And naturally he wasn't able to tell anyone who he was or where he'd come from until he was fit enough to use a pen."

The Matron glanced up then, followed the direction of Simmie's gaze to the corner of a full plate photograph that was projecting from her notes, and hastily tucked it away again out of sight. "I'm not sure how much you know of his current condition, Miss Sims?" she enquired.

"Really very little, I'm afraid. His grandmother was only able to tell me that he was badly disfigured and unwilling to leave the Home, or to see anyone from outside it."

"An over-simplification, I fear." The Matron closed the file and faced Simmie squarely across the desk. "Disfigurement certainly – and other severe injuries: loss of all nasal cartilage, lips, lower mandible and of course speech, impaired hearing, the loss of one eye . . . "

"Oh-ooh . . . " Simmie's hand flying to her mouth stifled the rest. All the way up from Sellington, on trains and railway platforms and in the backs of taxis, she'd been nerving herself – preparing to face the worst, however bad, preparing not to flinch. Yet in the end all it had taken to pierce her armour was a single sentence, the briefest catalogue of words. That and the memory of a sixpenny wax doll that her mother had once given her. She'd put it to bed with the sun full on its face, such a sweet little face – but when she'd come back its mouth and chin had fallen in, quite melted away.

"Oh dear, I'm so sorry, how silly of me." She found her handkerchief and mopped up quickly, grateful to the Matron for staying where she was, for failing to touch her or to say anything nice. "Just a bit of a shock, that's all. I didn't realize you see – I had no idea his injuries were so extensive."

"Yes, they are extensive." The Matron's voice had lost a little of its asperity. "But believe me, my dear, there are many other men right here in this building in a considerably worse condition. The majority of our cases here are paraplegics, you know, amputations and spinal injuries. Very few of them can walk as Mr Ashby can. Or could hope to survive on their own outside the Home, as he could tomorrow if he chose."

"But I thought you said – his jaw . . . ?"

"Prosthetics, Miss Sims, modern prosthetics." The Matron gave her the briefest little smile of reassurance. "Why, with his dental and facial prostheses in place, you might say that Mr Ashby's almost as good as new!"

"But I don't understand. Do you mean some kind of cosmetic surgery?"

"No, no not surgery – although naturally they've done all they possibly can at Sidcup and Brook Street. No, prosthetics are external contrivances of one sort or another – mechanical dentures for example, operated on springs and hinges. It's remarkable what they've been able to achieve in that field since the war – really quite excellent results. In many ways you might say that your Mr Ashby is a very fortunate fellow," she added, ignoring the expression on Simmie's face. "He could well have died a dozen times, you know, during his early treatment – from shock or haemorrhage, or during anaesthesia. But he's unusually strong, you see, and basically very healthy. Not at all a Star type, in fact. To all intents and purposes what we have here is a home for 'incurables', Miss Sims, and that he most certainly is not."

"Do you mean that you actually want him to leave the Star and Garter?"

"But of *course,* isn't that what we're discussing? Isn't that why you've come – to help us persuade him to go home?"

"Well no I . . . that is to say, I didn't know . . . I simply wanted to see him. To see how he was – and to beg him to send some message to his wife. Or at very least to let me tell her that he's still alive after all. I think it could do her so much good, you see . . . "

"Just a minute, Miss Sims," the Matron's apron crackled audibly as she leant forward over the desk. "Are you trying to tell me that his wife doesn't *know* that he's alive? Because if so, I have to tell you that she must certainly have been informed by the War Office when the people at the Third London General discovered who he was. She'd have to know!"

"No, I'm afraid it's true, she really doesn't know. I'm still not certain how it happened in the first place, but I think they must actually have contacted his grandmother while Meriel – while his wife was still out in France. She went out to look for him, you know, just after the Armistice."

"But he had visitors at Wandsworth and at Sidcup, even at Brook Street – it says so in his files. And he's always had letters. Naturally we assumed his entire family knew."

"No, just one visitor and one letter writer, you see. His grandmother used to imply that she was going up to see her accountant in Chancery Lane, and of course we had no reason to disbelieve her. When she first heard the news I suppose she must have decided to see him herself before breaking it to the rest of us. And I do remember her telling Mr Ashby's sister that Meriel shouldn't have gone abroad, that she should have waited a little longer – that there was still a future here for her. But I gather that when she did see him, Mr Ashby made her promise not to tell any of us. I believe that he can't bear anyone to see his face, Matron, even now?"

"Few of them in that condition can without some sort of prosthetic camouflage." In her agitation the Matron had quite forgotten to be reassuring. "But let me get this perfectly clear, Miss Sims, are you saying that Mr Ashby's grandmother never even attempted to inform his own wife of his survival?"

And then of course Simmie told her the rest – of the old lady's intention to speak to her grand-daughter-in-law the moment she returned from London, on the day Meriel herself arrived back in Sellington – of Meriel's subsequent escape to the beach, of all the horrors that followed – and finally of the doctor's caution to avoid confronting her with facts or increasing the stress on her in any way. But even when she'd said it all, she somehow felt the need to go on talking – to make the antiseptic woman across the desk from her understand and sympathize.

"I've thought about this a great deal in the last twenty-four hours, Matron, and I believe I can understand how Ned must have felt with this terrible injury. His wife was so proud of his looks, you see – in love with them right from the start. And without them – worse than that – he'd be so afraid, wouldn't he, that she'd be unable to love, even to pretend to love him? That she'd be physically repelled. And how could a sensitive man ever face that prospect?"

"In the same way that other men in his condition have faced it – as we who nurse them have to face it daily – by developing an immunity to pity and to self-pity, Miss Sims," the Matron said crisply. "No I'm sorry, but it's not our function here to help people to hide from their responsibilities." To emphasize the point she gathered up Ned's file and tidied it away into a drawer of her desk. "If I'd had the slightest inkling of his domestic situation I'd never have accepted him from Sandgate in the first place. He's fit now – as fit as he'll ever be. And he clearly has family obligations to fulfil that must over-ride any personal reservations he may have about his appearance. You say that he still has a little boy?"

"Well, Patrick's seventeen now."

"Just so – and very much the age that a lad needs a father, wouldn't you say?" In command of the situation once more, the Matron pressed an electric bell on her desk, and rationed out another of her bracing little smiles. "I think we understand each other, don't we, Miss Sims? So I'll leave it to you, to make Mr Ashby see reason. Ah, Staff Nurse, take Miss Sims here down to see our Mr Ashby in the Quiet Room, will you? He's already expecting her, I believe? And do pop in again when you're

through, won't you, Miss Sims? I'd very much like to hear how
you got on."

Chapter Thirty-Three

'It won't be so bad,' Simmie told herself as the Staff Nurse led
her down an elegant circular staircase to a lower floor. She'd
weathered worse than this, they all had. It couldn't possibly be
as bad as it would have been for the old lady that first time. Or
when she had to tell him about Robbie. And Simmie remembered with shame how callous she'd thought Mrs Ashby then,
arranging to see her London accountant so soon after the little
boy's funeral.

At the bottom of the stairs there were full length windows
looking out onto a garden with a fountain and a little goldfish
pool, and men in wheelchairs enjoying the sun – men without
arms and legs. Beyond the garden there was a parapet, and
beyond that the view – the same view. The past and present
meeting at last in this place, where on a summer's day such as
this Simmie had first discovered the power of love.

"Lovely garden isn't it?" the Staff Nurse said. "Mr Ashby's
out there in all weathers – loves it he does."

They crossed a long common room with American leather
armchairs, and men smoking, and the gramophone that Simmie
had heard from the vestibule. It was blaring out 'Sitting on Top
of the World' – such a silly, frivolous little tune.

"You do realize that he'll be wearing his prosthetic mask?"
The Staff Nurse gave Simmie a quick sidelong glance. "He
generally does with someone new, with anyone from outside –
hospital visitors, student doctors, anyone like that."

"A mask?"

"Didn't Matron tell you? Well don't you worry, it's really
most awfully good – a regular work of art, you might say.
There's this marvellous sculptor at Wandsworth who makes
them up from photographs and plaster casts and the like. 'Tin
noses shop' the patients call it!" The nurse smiled apologetically.

"Not that they are tin, really, actually silver-plate I believe, light as a feather. And then of course in cases like Mr Ashby's there's room inside for pads, to take up the excess moisture, you know, saves the poor chaps such a lot of embarrassment."

"But silver? You can't mean that he'll be wearing a silver mask?" Suddenly Simmie felt a desperate urge to run: not from him, not from poor Ned – but from the things that they'd done to him.

"Oh it doesn't *look* like silver," the Staff Nurse assured her, "hardly at all. It's all most beautifully painted – really artistic. You'll see in a minute. Only don't go overboard and admire it too much now," she added with a wink. "We're a bit touchy about it still, if you know what I mean." And the next moment she flung open a door at the further end of the common room and ushered Simmie through. "Here we are then, Mr Ashby!" she shouted. "Here's your visitor come to see you!"

He was standing in a small, oak-panelled room with the sunlight streaming in. Standing with his back to them, in flannels and a clean white shirt – with his arms folded, wrapped tightly around him. And surely taller than Simmie remembered him? Taller and thinner? He moved at the sound of the Staff Nurse's raised voice, but he hadn't turned, and she was quick to take the hint.

"Well, I'll be leaving you two alone then," she sang out. "Show the lady back up to the desk when she's ready will you, Mr Ashby? I know Matron wants another little word with her before she goes." She shut the door noisily behind her.

The garden side of the room gave onto a long, tiled colonnade, where more patients in more wheelchairs were enjoying the sun. Simmie could hear the sound of their voices, their laughter, through the glass door that shut them out.

"Ned." Her throat was parched, she discovered. She'd croaked his name hoarsely, and had to repeat it, much louder. "Ned – my dear!" The blond hair was the same, curling softly into the muscles of his neck; and as he turned she smiled at him sweetly, lovingly – the smile she'd practised in the train.

Two masks confronting one another.

The Staff Nurse was right, it was a work of art – that certainly – a face scrubbed pink like a young boy's, with red parted lips and a moustache of real hair, and Ned's fine nose faithfully rendered. And how beautifully neat the way it hooked back over the ears like spectacles, the way it fitted so snug to the neck and cheek and forehead, and tucked up under the hairline. How clever the way they'd matched the eye – the other eye . . .

'Ned – I know it's you, my dear.' She willed him to understand her without speech. 'I know you're there behind that thing . . . Look at me, Ned – see, I'm smiling . . . See my smile, Ned, don't hear the screaming, the weeping inside me . . . It's nothing, my dear, just my weakness – you know what a coward I've always been . . . Just see my smile . . .'

A museum god, a graven image looked back at her, itself unable to smile – classical, perfect, terrifying – all but the desperate living blue eye that blinked.

Meriel was galloping flat out, savagely kicking her pony faster and faster down the long slope to the cliff edge – conscious only of the sky, of the great force of the wind that beat up against her, into her open mouth, down into her lungs, lifting her out of herself free as a swallow, swooping down and out and away into space . . .

"Whad the nation!" Watching her from the ridge above, the shepherd's bent old figure straightened on his crook, tense against the skyline – only to relax and settle back into its customary stoop, as Meriel pulled the pony up on its haunches within a yard or two of the sheer cliff.

"Damme Lass, ef I ent gettin' reg'lar soft," Bat Vine remarked to his dog. "Bin nursemaid ter too many lambs I shouldn' wonder. But thad young 'ooman'll tarrify this ol' bugger ter death one o'these fine days, an' I doan' deceive ye!"

Meriel was sitting quite still now on the cliff edge, blank-faced, watching a shoal of whitebait curving, flashing silver beneath the water – thinking of the *Catriona,* of a young girl in a borrowed cape standing in the bows. The chalk headland was like a ship too, in its way, she thought – a great white ship, ancient, timeless, sailing forward into the future with The Bury and the Sellington Valley as its cargo. And old Vine with his precious Southdown ewes, and the dairy shorthorns, and the hay in the barns, and the barley ready for harvest . . . *continuity, the only kind of permanence there is* . . . Who said that – whose voice? And why were the words so familiar?

She turned the pony's head back up the slope through the grazing sheep, with something fretting and chafing inside her like a piece of rusted machinery grating into movement. The old man was still watching her from above, damn him, waiting for her to climb back up the hill towards him. So she left the ridgeway instead, to keep him waiting, to explore the hollows, to feel the long dead haulms of the grass brushing the pony's flanks and belly – and rising only by degrees to the patient figure on the hill. She wasn't bound to speak to him. He didn't *own* the chalk hills, for heaven's sake! They were just as much hers, for that matter, as ever they belonged to Bartholomew Vine or his smelly old sheep!

In the places where the grass was longest and coarsest, in the lew of gorse banks and in the deeper depressions, there were scores of little butterflies clinging to the stems. Scores of pointed grey winglets patterned like old lace, opening to nutbrown or azure blue as they fluttered up from the movements of the horse.

Butterflies – and the thudding vibrations of hooves on chalk – and the echo of guns...

"Wunnerful cunnin', them blues," Bat commented as she drew level. "Tucked up afore six iv'ry evenin' reg'lar as clockwork – like kiddies, ye might say. Jes' folds the'r lit'le wings an' 'ides theirselves away." He shifted his gaze from the valley to the pale face of the woman on the pony. "'Eads down in the shadows where the bents is thickest, Missus, thad's 'ow they protec' theirselves, them lit'le blues."

Butterflies . . . butterflies and guns and something stirring – something hurtful, irresistibly painful waking into life . . .

"Meriel!"
She turned her head with a sense of relief. Her mother's voice, the Mater calling her in to change . . .
"Meriel! Me-ri-el!"
No, not Mother, you duffer – dunderhead! How could it be? It's Simmie, of course it is – Simmie come back from London.

345

And, God in heaven, she's running up to meet us – Simmie actually *running!* How terribly funny!

The recovery for which Simmie had been hoping and praying for for so long, came with a suddenness that left her gasping. Ned's name had meant so little to Meriel these past years – it was too much to hope that she'd understand about him and about the Star and Garter. But she did, immediately. It was as if Simmie had tentatively opened the door of a cage to coax out some poor little captive – only to find herself trampled, ground underfoot in Meriel's mad stampede for freedom.

"*Of course! Of course he's bloody alive!*" She shouted it across the hills, sending Bat's sheep hummocking panic-stricken away into the combe. "I've always said so, haven't I? Well *haven't* I? But you people don't listen do you? *You never, never listen!*"

What was more, within minutes of the news Meriel had come to her first concrete decision in years. And poor Simmie, already drooping with emotional exhaustion, was in no fit state to restrain her.

"He'll be coming back for G.M's funeral, that's the first thing, of course." Meriel announced it even before they'd left the bostal path. "Oh come on, Simmie, don't be so damned *feeble!* He's got to, hasn't he? The whole village will expect it."

"But darling, that's so public! And Meriel, you really must give yourself more time. We all need time to decide what to do for the best . . . "

It had all been too quick for her, she couldn't seem to take it in. But Meriel was getting it wrong, that much was obvious – seeing it all too simply.

"You don't understand, Meriel. He's so unsure of himself. He can't talk to you, darling – he can't eat, not normally. He's so terribly damaged . . . " She was trying so hard to explain it to her. "And he's going to need time too, such a lot of time and patience – and all the love in the world, darling, before he'd ever be able to face all those people."

"Rot! Ned needs pushing, he needs organizing – always has. Do you think I've been married all these years without knowing what my own husband needs, for God's sake? He's too slow, Simmie, too damn sensitive to get anything done under his own steam. Why, you know as well as I do that he'd never have married me in the first place if I hadn't practically forced him into it."

"He did go through the war though, didn't he, dear?" Simmie reminded her gently. "And that was very much his own decision, I think?"

"I'll say it was – and look where it got him, look where he is now! And what's he doing at this moment to help himself or me or Patrick, I should like to know? Answer me that! No, Simmie, you're just going to have to leave this to me – and *stop fussing,* all right?"

Half an hour later Meriel was on the telephone to the Star and Garter Home, shouting into the mouthpiece with all her old impatience. Within thirty-six hours she was all ready for Richmond – after a lightning dash into Eastbourne for the latest thing in jersey suits and a proper grown up three-piece for Patrick – and for a modern shingled haircut that did nothing at all for the gaunt planes of her face.

On the morning she was due to leave, Simmie went up to help her dress – miserably, dreading what she'd find. "There you are, Simmie," Meriel cried as soon as she caught sight of her, "I thought you were never coming! Look, are my seams straight, can you see? They're a perfect swine to get right – and you have to, don't you, with these skimpy little frocks? Honestly, the things we women have to go through to look our best!"

Simmie could never quite get used to the sight of middle-aged women baring their legs like young girls. Worse, the stockings were of shiny pink rayon and clashed horrendously with the knitted orange chevrons of Meriel's costume. But what could she do – what was the use now?

"Yes, they're fine, perfectly straight," she said. "But surely you're not planning to wear mascara in the daytime are you, Meriel? I must say, dear, I really don't think that's quite the thing . . . " But Meriel was already at the mirror, enlarging her coppery-brown eyes with a hand that made up in generosity what it lacked in finesse.

"Oh, you have to with these modern styles, it's part of the effect," she said airily, "everyone says so. No earthly use spending a fortune on the togs and then going round looking like a damn peg doll!" The lipstick was too dark as well, far too dark. It made her mouth look enormous. But of course Meriel didn't see it – it wasn't what she wanted to see. She simply blew a kiss at her own smiling reflection, moving her head to catch the light on her gold Tutankhamen earrings, before jamming on a preposterous cloche hat and springing to her feet again.

"No use looking like that either, Simmie Sims," she said. "Oh yes, I know you, I know what you're thinking. You're thinking that I've been ill for a long time, aren't you? That I'm not going to be strong enough to cope? You think that I won't be able to do all the things for Ned that he's going to need, that I won't be able to love him enough – as much as you would in my place, Simmie?"

There was a bright, hard edge on her voice, but before Simmie could speak or respond to her in any way, Meriel clattered off on her high heels, out of the room and across the landing to the top of the stairs. "Come on then you dreadful old stick-in-the-mud and just watch me do it!" she called back. And with a desperate sinking feeling Simmie followed her down into the main hall.

From the garden of the Star and Garter Ned could see the Staff Nurse hurrying through the common room, peering at the patients in the leather armchairs – looking for him, he had no doubt. In a moment she'd come to the window and discover him out here beside the goldfish pool.

"*There* you are, Mr Ashby – why, whatever can you be thinking of? Matron's been expecting you for ages, surely you must remember? Your wife and boy will be here for you after lunch, and there's still a great deal she wants to talk to you about."

She'd spotted him already – frowning at the window, rapping on the glass, trying to catch his attention . . . Matron upstairs in her office, ready with her lecture and her goodbye handshake . . . and Meriel – gripping him by the arms, shaking him, glaring at him fiercely . . . "*My kind of man wouldn't want a wife who pitied him, do you hear me, Ned? And he wouldn't come home maimed or crippled either, unable to eat without dribbling or to function properly as a husband and a father...*" Oh Meri . . . !

*

348

Dan had offered to drive them to the station, to go with them to Richmond, but Meriel turned him down. "Nonsense," she said briskly, "my son will drive me – won't you, Patrick – his father will be expecting to see him, in any event. But you can come with us to Seaford if you like, Goodworth, to bring the cart back." And the look in young Patrick's face as his mother turned to him for confirmation brought a lump to Simmie's throat.

They all crowded out onto the front steps to see them off – Helly holding her new baby, with old Nanny Jefferies behind her, and Gladys, and three-year-old Maggie Goodworth toddling through to the fore with her father's slow deliberation. Others too, less obvious: Zachy Cheal nibbling unnecessarily at the lawn edges with his long-handled shears, Pyecroft loitering on the path from the old brew-house. And the old shepherd up above them on the chalk hills – he'd be there, Simmie felt sure, somewhere with a good, clear view of the Sellington road.

Then at the last minute, Cook hurried breathlessly up from the kitchen, a little lame now and more comfortably upholstered than ever – to hand up a covered maund-basket to Dan. "Somethin' ter eat on the train, Missus Edwin," she explained. And on an impulse that cut through a lifetime's observance of etiquette, she reached up to squeeze Meriel's hand. "Bring 'im 'ome safe to us, darlin'," she said, stepping back hastily as Patrick slapped the reins and chirruped to the pony, and the old governess-cart crunched forward over the gravel.

"Upsy-daisy, Maggie, that's the girl." Simmie hoisted the child to wave with her, to reinforce her own artificially bright smile. "Let's wave bye-bye to Daddy then, shall we? And to Auntie Meri, and to Patrick . . . "

Dear Patrick, so proud and protective in his new dark suit – with Dan facing him, hands on knees, exuding calm and kindness. And Meriel laughing and waving to them all, her eyes sparkling, all her brightest flags flying – so thoroughly, so terrifyingly ill-equipped, Simmie thought, for the ordeal that lay ahead of her. But then Simmie herself had never been very brave.

"Look, Sim, look!" The old governess-cart was gathering speed, bowling down the drive towards the gate. And all the time Maggie's fat little hand was tugging insistently at Simmie's soft hair, dragging it out from its pins.

Simmie waited for the last glimpse of Meriel's hat above the shrubberies, and then looked. On the old mounting block at the side of the steps a tiny pale blue butterfly was sunning itself, opening and closing its wings. It looked too pretty, too perfect somehow to be real. But as they watched it rose effortlessly in a series of circling upward spirals, up past the window of Ned's old bedroom and the great timbered gable of the house, and on upwards until they lost sight of it against the blue canopy of the sky.

Fiction

☐ **The Chains of Fate**	Pamela Belle	£2.95p
☐ **Options**	Freda Bright	£1.50p
☐ **The Thirty-nine Steps**	John Buchan	£1.50p
☐ **Secret of Blackoaks**	Ashley Carter	£1.50p
☐ **Hercule Poirot's Christmas**	Agatha Christie	£1.50p
☐ **Dupe**	Liza Cody	£1.25p
☐ **Lovers and Gamblers**	Jackie Collins	£2.50p
☐ **Sphinx**	Robin Cook	£1.25p
☐ **My Cousin Rachel**	Daphne du Maurier	£1.95p
☐ **Flashman and the Redskins**	George Macdonald Fraser	£1.95p
☐ **The Moneychangers**	Arthur Hailey	£2.50p
☐ **Secrets**	Unity Hall	£1.75p
☐ **Black Sheep**	Georgette Heyer	£1.75p
☐ **The Eagle Has Landed**	Jack Higgins	£1.95p
☐ **Sins of the Fathers**	Susan Howatch	£3.50p
☐ **Smiley's People**	John le Carré	£1.95p
☐ **To Kill a Mockingbird**	Harper Lee	£1.95p
☐ **Ghosts**	Ed McBain	£1.75p
☐ **The Silent People**	Walter Macken	£1.95p
☐ **Gone with the Wind**	Margaret Mitchell	£3.50p
☐ **Blood Oath**	David Morrell	£1.75p
☐ **The Night of Morningstar**	Peter O'Donnell	£1.75p
☐ **Wilt**	Tom Sharpe	£1.75p
☐ **Rage of Angels**	Sidney Sheldon	£1.95p
☐ **The Unborn**	David Shobin	£1.50p
☐ **A Town Like Alice**	Nevile Shute	£1.75p
☐ **Gorky Park**	Martin Cruz Smith	£1.95p
☐ **A Falcon Flies**	Wilbur Smith	£2.50p
☐ **The Grapes of Wrath**	John Steinbeck	£2.50p
☐ **The Deep Well at Noon**	Jessica Stirling	£2.50p
☐ **The Ironmaster**	Jean Stubbs	£1.75p
☐ **The Music Makers**	E. V. Thompson	£1.95p

Non-fiction

☐ **The First Christian**	Karen Armstrong	£2.50p
☐ **Pregnancy**	Gordon Bourne	£3.50p
☐ **The Law is an Ass**	Gyles Brandreth	£1.75p
☐ **The 35mm Photographer's Handbook**	Julian Calder and John Garrett	£5.95p
☐ **London at its Best**	Hunter Davies	£2.95p
☐ **Back from the Brink**	Michael Edwardes	£2.95p

☐	**Travellers' Britain**	} Arthur Eperon	£2.95p
☐	**Travellers' Italy**		£2.95p
☐	**The Complete Calorie Counter**	Eileen Fowler	80p
☐	**The Diary of Anne Frank**	Anne Frank	£1.75p
☐	**And the Walls Came Tumbling Down**	Jack Fishman	£1.95p
☐	**Linda Goodman's Sun Signs**	Linda Goodman	£2.50p
☐	**Scott and Amundsen**	Roland Huntford	£3.95p
☐	**Victoria RI**	Elizabeth Longford	£4.95p
☐	**Symptoms**	Sigmund Stephen Miller	£2.50p
☐	**Book of Worries**	Robert Morley	£1.50p
☐	**Airport International**	Brian Moynahan	£1.75p
☐	**Pan Book of Card Games**	Hubert Phillips	£1.95p
☐	**Keep Taking the Tabloids**	Fritz Spiegl	£1.75p
☐	**An Unfinished History of the World**	Hugh Thomas	£3.95p
☐	**The Baby and Child Book**	Penny and Andrew Stanway	£4.95p
☐	**The Third Wave**	Alvin Toffler	£2.95p
☐	**Pauper's Paris**	Miles Turner	£2.50p
☐	**The Psychic Detectives**	Colin Wilson	£2.50p
☐	**The Flier's Handbook**		£5.95p

All these books are available at your local bookshop or newsagent, or
can be ordered direct from the publisher. Indicate the number of copies
required and fill in the form below

11

....

Name..
(Block letters please)

Address..

_____ _____

Send to CS Department, Pan Books Ltd, PO Box 40, Basingstoke, Hants
Please enclose remittance to the value of the cover price plus:
35p for the first book plus 15p per copy for each additional book ordered
to a maximum charge of £1.25 to cover postage and packing
Applicable only in the UK

While every effort is made to keep prices low, it is sometimes
necessary to increase prices at short notice. Pan Books reserve
the right to show on covers and charge new retail prices which
may differ from those advertised in the text or elsewhere